MW00464185

HEAT WAVE

KARINA HALLE

Also by Karina Halle

First edition published by
Metal Blonde Books November 2016

ISBN-13: 978-1537606781

Cover design by Hang Le Designs
Edited by Laura Helseth
Proofed by Roxane LeBlanc
Formatted by Champagne Formats

Metal Blonde Books
P.O. Box 845
Point Roberts, WA
98281 USA

Manufactured in the USA

For more information about the series and author visit:
www.authorkarinahalle.com

For Kauai – you regenerate our souls

And for LOVE – may you always win

PROLOGUE

I SAW HIM FIRST.

It shamed me to think it then, it shames me to think it now.

But that's what the truth does to you sometimes. It shames you because it's only in the truth that you realize how human you really are. What a raw, devastating thing that is, to embrace your humanity and learn to live with all your sharp points, the hollow places, the cracks and the crevices. To be utterly real. To be terribly flawed.

Those cracks had always been forming inside me, slowly making their way to the surface over the years. In my family, there wasn't much you could do but try and hold yourself together, to stick glue on your wounds, to paste over the imperfections. But the cracks still grew, until all of us were held together by crumbling cement, just statues waiting to collapse.

That was years and years ago. I was just twenty-two at the time. A baby. I'm still a baby in the grand scheme of things, but there's something precious about your early twenties, where you think you're so much older, bigger, than you are, where life is just about to deliver the crushing blows that will knock you off your feet for the rest of your days. The small things become the big things and the big things become the small things and you aren't quite sure when they made the switch.

But in the end, I saw him first. He was mine, even before he knew it. He was mine in some strange way that I still don't understand. The only way I can think of to explain it is…

You just know.

There are moments in your life, people in your life, that when they cross your path and meet your eye, you know. Maybe it's all in the chemistry, certain pheromones that react when they mix together, maybe it's a smell that triggers a memory, maybe it's a glimpse at a future you don't recognize or a hint at the past, a life you've lived and forgotten. Whatever it is, you know that moment, that person, is going to shape you for the rest of your life.

That's what it was like when I saw him. Standing over by the windows and staring out at Lake Michigan, like he was wishing he could be anywhere but there.

I wished the same. My mother's the deputy mayor of Chicago and this was another one of her fundraisers I felt obliged to attend. It was tradition in my family, for my father, for me, for my sister, to show up and wave the flag of support. It didn't seem to matter that the stuffy politicians that surrounded these events never paid me any attention. And if they did, it was the wrong kind of attention, always the sixty-year-old man leering after the young thing with the nice smile.

Luckily I didn't smile all that often. My resting bitch face took over whenever I was deep in thought, which was pretty much all the time.

But this guy…I felt a kinship with him. I felt like I knew exactly what he was thinking, feeling, and that it was completely wrapped up in and connected to everything that was going through me.

I don't know where I found the nerve to go over and talk to him. He seemed so much older, not quite the sixty-year-old politicians I was used to seeing, but maybe in his early-thirties. More than that, there was some kind of aura around him. Sounds stupid, I know. Whatever it was, it was like he belonged in some whole other universe than here, a star on earth, permanently grounded and yearning to be in the sky.

It was usually Juliet's job to go around and make everyone feel warm and comfortable at these events—hell, in every event—but she wasn't here yet. And though I could have easily stayed in the shadows, I was pulled to him, like he had a wave of gravity whirling around him.

I remember what I was wearing. Strappy flats because I hated wearing heels, a knee-length cocktail dress in emerald green, sleeveless, high-neck. It made me look older and I wore it because my mother always wanted me to look like a lady.

With a glass of champagne in hand, I made my way over to the windows, my heart racing the closer I got to him. He looked taller up close, well over six feet. His shoulders were broad, like a swimmer's, and suddenly I had a vision of him diving into the lake. The navy blue suit he was wearing looked well-tailored but he seemed uncomfortable in it, like he couldn't wait to get rid of it.

I stood beside him for a moment, following his gaze out the window. He seemed lost in his thoughts but out of my peripheral his head tilted slightly and he brought his eyes over to me while I kept staring at that wide expanse of water, stretching out to the horizon.

"Can't wait to get out of here?" I asked, but though my tone was mild, my delivery was bold. It was as if someone else had taken a hold of my body, forcing me to speak. I slowly turned my head to meet his eyes.

I was taken aback for a second. He was staring at me like he knew me, even though I'd never seen him before. Then again, I was sure I'd been staring at him in the same way. That feeling of knowing. He knew me, I knew him, and who the hell knows how that was possible.

His eyes were brown—are brown—dark with currents of gold and amber, giving them beautiful clarity. Slightly almond shaped. His brows were also dark, arched, adding to the intensity of his gaze. He's the type of guy whose eyes latch onto you, dig deep, trying to sift through the files of your life, see who you really are.

"How did you know?" he asked, a full-on Australian accent rumbling through his gruff voice. It made my stomach flip, my core smolder. *How deed you now*, is what it sounded like. Funny how I stopped hearing the accent after time.

I gave a half shrug and looked back to the party. More people had flooded the room, mingling around the appetizers. My mother was in the corner, a crowd of politicians around her. She didn't see me. She never did.

"Because I think I'd rather be in the middle of Lake Michigan too," I told him, "than be stuck here with all these people."

"These people," he repeated. My focus was drawn to his

lips, full, wide, tilting up into a smirk. Beneath them was a strong chin and even sharper jaw, dusted with a five o'clock shadow that seemed permanent, like the man couldn't get a clean shave even if he tried. "How do you know I'm not one of these people?"

"Because you're over here and not over there. How come you keep answering my questions with more questions?"

He studied me for a moment. My blood pounded in my head and I felt a giddy kind of thrill at how this was progressing. If anything, I was proud for holding my own with this handsome stranger. He was the first man I ever really felt at ease with.

He cleared his throat, offered me a quick smile before he nodded at the lake, his hands sliding into his pockets. "She almost looks like the ocean, doesn't she?"

"Not quite the same as Australia, I would imagine."

"No hiding this accent, is there?" He glanced at me and stuck out his hand, which I shook for a moment, warm palm to warm palm. "I'm Logan Shephard. Australian. And the reason I'm here is because I was invited by a friend of mine. I'm only in town for a few days and he didn't want to go alone. He's over there." He nodded at a tall man in the corner, listening intently to another man.

"Warren Jones," he said, as if I should know him. Perhaps I should. He probably thought I was *one of them.* "He's local and the key piece to my investment."

I wasn't one for business talk—I never had anything to contribute other than lamenting student loans—but I wanted him to keep talking. "What's your investment?"

"Starting my own hotel," he said. "In Hawaii. Have you ever been there?"

"Once. When I was eight. I think we were in Honolulu. I remember a city, anyway. Waikiki Beach."

"This hotel is in Kauai. The Garden Isle. Went there once after college and couldn't get it out of my mind."

I didn't know the right things to say. I wanted to ask more about the hotel, what it means when you have an investor, but I didn't want to appear dumb. I kept my mouth shut.

"You haven't introduced yourself," he said. "Protecting a secret identity?"

I smiled, close-lipped. "Not really. I'm Veronica Locke. American. And unfortunately I don't have much else to add to that."

"Locke?" he repeated, eyes darting to my mother. "Are you the daughter of the deputy mayor, Rose Locke?"

"One of them," I told him.

He nodded quickly. "I see. No wonder you'd rather be in the middle of the bloody lake. I bet you have to do this stuff all the time."

"It's not so bad." I took a sip of my drink so I didn't have to say anything more and looked away at the crowd. The bubbles teased my nose, making my eyes water.

I could feel his gaze on me as he spoke. "I'm sure you have plenty more to say about yourself though. Where do you work? Student?"

"Culinary arts," I told him. "I'm one of those crazy people who dream of being a chef one day."

He frowned. "Why is that crazy?"

I gave him a look, forgetting that most people have no idea how hard it is. "Because it's a long road, long hours, and nothing is guaranteed. People think being a chef is easy. They see Gordon Ramsey or Nigella Lawson and think it's all fame and food and money and they have no idea what it's really like. I'm not even out of school and already I feel half-beaten."

He was still frowning. He did that a lot, I would soon learn. "Sounds like life to me." His eyes dropped to my lips and something intensely carnal came over them, like suddenly I was the food, not the wannabe chef. "Did you want to get a drink somewhere? After this? When you've done your daughterly duties?"

I swallowed hard. I didn't know what a drink meant. Just a drink? A date? Was it sex? I started going through my head, trying to think of reasons why it was a bad idea. My legs were shaved, did my bra and underwear match? Did I have a condom? I had taken the pill this morning, even though my last boyfriend and I had broken up months ago. I hadn't been with a guy, let alone a man, in a long time.

Don't flatter yourself, I quickly thought. *What makes you think he'd be interested in you that way?*

"Yes," I said when I finally found my voice. "Yes, I would like that."

A spark flashed in his eyes, lighting them up in such a way that made my toes literally curl. Damn. I was in trouble with this man. "Any way you can get out of your duties sooner?" he asked.

I couldn't help but smile, raising my brow at his presumptuousness, while simultaneously trying to hide the fact that I was freaking out. I looked around the room and tried to judge how likely it was that someone would notice if I was gone. My mom was still surrounded by a wall of people and no one was paying any attention to us, standing by the windows, already removed.

A sad thought hit me, sliding past before I could really dwell on it: *no one even notices when I'm here.*

"If we're quick and sneaky," I told him.

"Being quick isn't in my repertoire," he said, "but I could give it a shot."

Again. Damn. I wasn't one to blush but I could feel my cheeks heating up and hoped my skin supressed the flush. He was so much older than me in so many ways, the last thing I wanted was to appear the naïve schoolgirl.

And I didn't know what to say to that. He was staring at me with those dark eyes, a look so intense yet sparkling with charm and something…wicked.

I'd never find out how wicked they could be.

"Ronnie!" A melodic, ultra-feminine voice sliced through the moment like an unwieldy machete, causing me to flinch, my fingers tightening around the stem of the glass.

Oh no, I thought. *Not now.*

Logan's head swiveled toward the sound of the voice, like a hound picking up a scent. I didn't bother looking over, I kept my focus on him, watching his expression intently. It changed, as I knew it would.

She had walked into the room.

He saw her.

And like it was for so many men, that look of lust I had thought was for me, was now for her.

That's when I knew it was over. Whatever thing I had felt for him, it didn't matter anymore, not when she was in the room. Nothing ever mattered as long as she was around.

I might have saw him first.

But he was all hers after that.

CHAPTER ONE

Seven Years Later

"**M**ISS, ARE YOU DONE WITH THAT?"

I can feel the man in the seat next to mine subtly elbowing me until I turn my head and glance up at the flight attendant. She's nodding at the nearly finished glass of Mai Tai on my tray table, the very reason why my response time is epically slow.

"Uh, almost," I tell her with a smile that I hope looks sober and pick up the thin plastic cup so she won't snatch it away.

Not that it really matters—I've had four syrupy cocktails in the last six hours. From the moment I boarded the Alaska Airlines flight heading out of Seattle for Lihue, I've been drinking my nerves away. It doesn't help that the Mai Tais on this flight have been free the last two hours, even

1

for us poor people in coach. It seems the airline wants everyone to get excited about the impending paradise, and drinks are on the house.

I finish the rest of the cocktail while she patiently waits, the sticky sweetness of rum and fruit-juice puckering my tongue, and hand her the empty glass. I immediately bring my attention back to the window, not wanting to miss a thing.

We've already passed over Maui as we started our descent, a brilliant color show of red and green, ochre and sienna, and now we're over the ocean between the islands, the water a shimmering aqua that seems so alive and hypnotic I can barely tear my eyes away.

I can't believe I'm doing this.

Those words won't stop ringing in my head. They started when I began packing a week ago and haven't stopped since. I've always been so organized, so planned, so careful with my life, and now I'm heading to Hawaii of all places based on nothing more than a promise and hope for the future.

I never thought my future would have me way out in the middle of the Pacific Ocean, on one of the most isolated places in the world. Beyond the eight islands lies 1,860 miles of empty ocean before the nearest continent. To know I'll be staying here is a sobering, terrifying thought.

Yes, I know, it's not the typical outlook of someone going to Hawaii on a job prospect. I should be as happy and excited as the rest of the passengers on the plane, chatting and laughing merrily through their Mai Tai buzz, flipping through the in-flight magazine and pointing out the different places to go. But while they're most likely going on vacation, I'm going there to live.

And once again...

I can't believe I'm doing this.

In an ideal world, I would have found a job right away after my last one. As the *chef de partie* at one of Chicago's biggest Italian chains, Picolo, I thought finding another job would be easy, even in such a highly competitive business. But it didn't matter that I'd worked at the place steadily since I got out of culinary school, starting as a line cook and working my way up. The pickings were slim, (for a reason I might add) and without a job I couldn't afford my apartment, which meant moving back home with my parents for one-hellish month. Sure, they live in a multi-million-dollar house in Lincoln Park, but if you knew my parents at all you'd understand why I had to get the hell out of there.

And get out of there I did. I'm pretty sure my parents felt the same way about me because it was them, my mother specifically, who told me about the cook position at Moonwater Inn. Of course, it meant leaving my friends and life behind and moving to the island of Kauai, but even so it was an opportunity I couldn't afford to pass up.

At least, I keep telling myself that. In reality, I don't have a choice in the matter.

It's not long before the plane gets lower and lower and then the wings dip slightly to the left and the blue blue ocean comes crashing against dramatic green cliffs, the island of Kauai, my future home, rising dramatically from the depths.

A thrill runs through me, the kind that tickles your heart, makes your stomach dance. My hands grip the arm rest as the plane goes through some mild bumps.

"Afraid of flying?" the man beside me asks. He's in his late fifties, a round face, skin that's so tanned it's almost red, and wearing a rumpled white shirt. He hasn't said two words to me the entire flight.

"Afraid of crashing," I tell him and turn my attention back to the window just in time to see the runway rushing up beneath us, red dirt bordering the asphalt. But instead of feeling relief as the wheels make contact with the ground and the plane does its overdramatic braking, another wave of nerves goes through me.

This is it.

If this doesn't work out, there's no way off this island except for a six-hour flight over open water. If this doesn't work out, I'm back at square one with my tail between my legs. If this doesn't work out, I'm once again a disappointment in the Locke family.

Kauai's airport is in Lihue and it's small. Like, way smaller than I had imagined, and dated. It looks like it was built in the 70's and hasn't had a single upgrade. I always assumed that a city's airport was indicative of the city itself, which makes me think that Kauai is a little more backwoods than I thought.

And it's muggy too, I realize as I step out into baggage claim to find my two suitcases. It's open to the outside and a hot blanket of air settles over the carousels, nearly choking me with the humidity. On the screens above the baggage are safety videos droning on and on, warning visitors of the millions of dangers that wait on the island.

There's also a damn chicken hanging out near the entrance.

I'm definitely not in Chicago anymore.

Eventually I find my two giant suitcases—there was no chance of me packing light for this—and I'm already sweating by the time I haul them out to the road, hoping to spot a taxi.

"Veronica?" a voice asks.

I look over to see a guy with a big smile and a goatee,

holding a piece of lined paper that's obviously been torn out of a notebook with *Veronica* scrawled across it in blue ink.

"Yes?" I say, frowning at him. "Are you from the hotel?"

He nods, offering me his hand. "Yup. Charlie," he says. "Sorry the boss couldn't make it, he's tied up in some emergency with the pool. You know how it is."

Actually I don't, but I shake his hand and give him a tight smile. Truth is, part of the reason my nerves are going all crazy was because I thought Logan was picking me up and I'd have to endure an awkward car ride with him. Yes, Logan's my new boss and I'm sure there will be plenty of awkward times to come, but for the moment I'm relieved I don't have to face him.

Yet.

"Nice to meet you," I say. Charlie's easy on the eyes, I have to admit. The goatee, the spiky light brown hair, the tanned limbs and tattoos. Then I notice he's not even wearing shoes.

His eyes follow mine and he grins broadly. "Welcome to Kauai," he says. "No shoes, no shirt, no problem." He tugs at his neon green Billabong tank top. "Though I wore the shirt just for you. Come on, let me help you."

He takes one of my bags and I follow him along the road and across to the short-term parking lot. A rooster struts past the chain-link fence and I stop, quickly pulling out my phone to take a picture. Paolo and Claire are going to go nuts when I show them there's a chicken at the airport.

I look up, still smiling at the sight, to see Charlie watching me with amusement. "You're going to get real bored of the chickens, real fast. The rest of the world has pigeons. We have chickens." He starts pulling the suitcase along and says over his shoulder, "At least pigeons don't wake you up at 4 AM."

"Why are there so many chickens?" I ask as he leads me toward a beat-up green Toyota Tacoma from the 80's, a surfboard in the back.

"Hurricane Iniki swept through here in ninety-two, let them all loose. Here." He grabs my other suitcase from me and swings it in the back with a grunt, shoving them under the board. He wipes his hands on his surf shorts and gestures to the passenger seat. "Hop on in."

"Were you here for the hurricane?" I ask him as I settle in the seat, the raw leather hot against my hands as I adjust myself, stuffing coming out of the torn seams.

He starts the car, a beefy rumble from the engine. "Nah, I've only lived here for six years. Before that I was in Boulder, Colorado, dreaming the dream. You know?"

"And now you're living the dream."

"Yeah," he says with a laugh. "This island will shake-up your soul, I'll tell you that much." He glances at me as he pays the parking fee to the attendant with dimes he scrounges out of a compartment on the dash. "Aren't you here to live the dream?"

"What did Logan tell you?" I ask him,

"Shephard?" he says and the name jolts through me like a bullet. "Nothing. Our cook Hugo left a few weeks ago and it's been a scramble to find a new one. Me and Johnny been working overtime. Not that that's anything new."

"You're a cook?" I ask, surprised. I'm not sure what I thought Charlie was, maybe a surf instructor.

"Cook, errand boy, Jack of All Trades," he says, rolling down the window as we pull onto the highway, my gaze stolen by the contrast of colors around me. The rich rusty earth juxtaposed with the startlingly bright greens of the lush land, the ocean in the distance. "At the compound, everyone has more than one job. I wonder what yours will be."

"The compound?"

"That's what we call it. Once you start working at Moonwater Inn, you don't leave. We're like a big family."

Family. Another word that cuts like a knife.

"Or a cult," he adds with a chuckle. "Depending how you look at it. I'll tell you, finding a good permanent job on the island isn't easy. Shephard treats us well. It's a small hotel but it's got a good reputation, and even if we're all stretched thin sometimes doing side jobs, he makes sure we're still living life. Ya know? That's why people live here. To live the life. To take that away…might as well go off-island." He glances at me over his shades. "So how do you know him, anyway? It's not every day that someone comes all the way from the mainland. You from Seattle?"

"Chicago," I tell him. "Changed planes in Seattle."

"Bears, Cubs, Blackhawks?"

I grin. "Cubs."

"This is your year."

"Hope so. 2016 has been a shit-show."

"Well you came to the right place to escape all that. I know how it is. Why live and work where there's winter and cold and gloom and shitty people, busy, busy, busy, when you can live and work here?"

The thing is, I liked the winter and the cold and the gloom and the shitty people. Maybe I didn't like it all the time, but it's what I knew. Better the devil you know, they say, and I've lived in the Chicago area my whole life. I knew many devils and I knew them very well.

I turn my attention to the scenery whizzing past. I shouldn't say whizzing since we aren't moving very fast—the highway is two lanes for the most part and traffic has been steady—but it gives me a better chance to soak it all in.

Not that it helps.

To be honest, it feels like *none* of this is real. To the right of me, golf courses and resorts stretch out among palm-strewn grounds, to the left, verdant hills lead sharply to jagged peaks, the razorback cliffs lined with thick vegetation. When we cross a bridge going over a river, I get my first true glance at the ocean, azure waves pounding a golden shore, a few surfers bobbing out on the swells.

"How do you know Shephard anyway?" Charlie asks. "He a friend of yours?"

"Through family," I tell him, my voice firm.

"Ah," he says. "Then you know what you're getting into."

I give him a sharp look. "What do you mean?"

He raises his brows. "Oh, well, you know there are… *were*…two Logan Shephards, right?"

I swallow hard, having a feeling I know where this is going. Sometimes I think there are two Veronica Lockes, even if the differences between them are slight, they're enough. "What do you mean?"

"Well, there was the Shephard I started working for. The *Shephards,* I should say. It was Logan and his wife that started the hotel. I was one of their first hires. Then she died, drunk driving accident just around the corner from the hotel. Wasn't her fault but her car went over the edge and…well, he hasn't been the same since."

My fingernails are digging deep into my palms and I'm trying to breathe normally. "I haven't seen him in a long time…not since the funeral."

He looks at me with a guilty expression. "Ah, shit. I had no idea you were that close. I'm sorry for your loss. I knew they sent her...well, that the funeral was out east, but we had a little vigil for her on the beach anyway. She was a great girl, lady, you know, really nice. Always had the right thing to say. Just...perfect, I guess."

The thought of a vigil on the beach makes my heart feel like it's imploding in my chest. "So Logan's different now," I say, switching the subject slightly.

"Still has his sense of humor, but yeah. I don't blame him. Angrier. Moodier. We call him the grump. *Habut.*" He pronounces the last word like ha-boo-t. "That's local speak for all that stuff. But I mean, he still has his sense of humor, right, so he doesn't mind the nickname. It's only fair since he has nicknames for all of us."

I want to ask more about him, but I'm getting more anxious than I already am. Why oh why did Logan even agree to hire me? My mother says it was his idea, but he's never been known to be all that charitable. In fact, our relationship has been strained for a long time (if you can even call it a relationship), which is why this whole arrangement has been a shock. It's either he's that hard-up for cooks here, or this was my mother's idea. My parents have shares in Moonwater Inn, so for all I know they could have threatened him.

Great, I think to myself. *I'm probably being forced upon him. A charity case. Logan doesn't want me here as much as I don't want to be here.*

To get my mind off of things, I make myself pay attention to the scenery of the cute town we're passing through called Kapaʻa, with its old-west style storefronts, the people milling about on the streets, the coconut palms as they sway lightly with the breeze.

And chickens. More and more chickens, strutting their stuff down the sidewalk with the tourists.

Charlie pulls over on the side of the busy road. "Want a coffee?" he asks me, nodding to the quirky-looking coffee shop called Java Kai.

"Sure," I say and the minute I do I'm hit with a wave of jetlag, as if the distance has finally caught up with me across the Pacific.

The coffee shop is absolutely adorable, with a turquoise exterior and a few tables and chairs that seem to meander over to the equally charming Mermaid Café. But inside it's chaos, completely full of people, with a long-line snaking toward the counter.

It takes at least five minutes before we finally get to the front of the line, and I take the opportunity to soak up the local atmosphere. There are some couples peering over their laptops, others that are deeply tanned and chatting to each other, adhering to the same barefoot policy that Charlie seems so fond of. I'm guessing they're locals.

When we finally reach the counter, I order an iced banana mocha from the red-headed barista. She's nice to me, as she's been with all the customers ahead of me, but when she starts talking to Charlie, it's like the sun has just broken through the clouds.

Charlie is a flirt, I can tell this much already, and this girl seems head over heels for him. I make a note to ask him later on about her but she's already addressing me.

"Are you the *haole*?" she asks.

I give her a look, wondering if she just called me some Hawaiian version of asshole.

"*Haole*?" I repeat. "I don't get it."

Charlie nudges me with his shoulder. "It means outsider. Not from here."

Well that doesn't sound very nice. *Haole* to you too.

"I guess," I tell her, my smile feeling forced now. "I'm

the new cook at Moonwater Inn." I wonder if she even knows where that is.

"Oh, I know," she says, smiling again at Charlie as she hands me my iced coffee. "Charlie fills me in on everything. The restaurant is one of my favs."

I think she means to say that Charlie is one of her favs.

He gives her a wink goodbye to which she nearly melts, and we head out of the crowded shop. Despite all the fans that were whirring in there, I'm covered in sweat.

"Is she a friend of yours?" I ask, stepping around a clucking chicken before I get in the truck.

He shrugs as he pulls out into the road. Someone honks at us from behind since we apparently just cut them off, but Charlie just sticks his hand out the window and gives the hang loose sign with a twist of his wrist. "She's harmless. Went on a few dates but that was over a year ago."

When the driver of the Jeep behind us gives an accepting wave, I turn back to Charlie. "Seems she's still hung up on you."

He gives me a grin. "Can you blame her?"

I roll my eyes. "So what is this *haole* business? Do the locals hate outsiders here?"

"Not at all," he says. "But it's a term and it sticks. I'm still *haole*."

"Really? But you've been here a few years now. Six, right?"

"Doesn't matter. I wasn't born here, so I'm not local."

"And is that girl local?"

"Ana?" he asks. "Yeah. Born and raised."

I want to make a remark on how she doesn't particularly look Hawaiian because of her red-hair, but I'm starting to think that the whole island is one big melting pot of cultures.

"And in case you're wondering," he says to me as the road dips closer to the coast again, the brilliant blue of the waves dazzling my eyes, "you don't have to be of Hawaiian origin to be considered Hawaiian."

As I mull that over, my eyes are constantly drawn to the lush vegetation as it swoops past us on one side, fields of dry grass and red dirt on the other. Ahead of us the sharp spears of a low mountain range rise up, looking positively Jurassic, dark clouds hovering behind it.

"That's King Kong," Charlie says. "Once we get to the side you'll be able to see the profile better."

And as the road turns around the mass of jungled peaks and past the town of Anahola, I can actually see what looks like the profile of a gorilla peering across the land.

The sight doesn't last for long though because now those dark, distant clouds are right upon us, unleashing rain with one swift movement, like King Kong himself just turned on a shower head.

I twist in my seat to look at my suitcases in the back, glad that Charlie had tucked them under the surfboard.

"Are they getting wet?" Charlie asks, frowning in the rear-view mirror.

"So far so good," I tell him. "Did you know it was going to rain? It was so nice before."

"It rains all the time here," he says. "That's why it's called the Garden Isle. But don't worry, it never lasts all day and there's always some sunny spot on the island at any given time. Sometimes that means you're heading all the way to the southwest, to Waimea or Polihale Beach to get the rays, but I actually like the rain. And once you're in the water, it doesn't really matter." He shoots me a sly look. "Do you surf?"

I shake my head. "No. I've never tried but I don't think it's my thing."

"That's fine. I'm going to teach you how."

I laugh. "Oh you are? You think you can teach me-of-little-balance?"

He nods. "It's all in your head, not your body," he says, tapping his temple. "And I'm a master of it. I teach surf lessons in the winter to make some extra cash, the swells up at Hanalei can get pretty good. I'll totes teach you for free."

I frown at him and his use of the word *totes*. "I don't know…I feel there's a catch here."

He wiggles his brows. "You'll find out sooner or later."

I'm not sure if that's innuendo or not, but from his interactions with Ana, Charlie already seems to have a bit of a reputation and I've learned my lesson when it comes to sleeping with the staff. I learned it big time.

Charlie turns the radio up for the rest of the drive, playing some ukulele music that makes me feel like I'm in the movie *The Descendants*, as the land becomes more tropical and green as we head north. The rain isn't letting up and Charlie tells me how as we get into winter, the north takes the brunt of the bad weather.

Along the way he starts pointing out more sights— the open plains where they filmed scenes of Jurassic Park (my inner nerd girl freaks out over this one since I can tell you exactly what scenes those were), the turn-off to some lighthouse, the resorts of Princeville, until the road curves along a cliff and the bay opens up below us.

Even with the clouds and the rain, I can still see the green expanse of what Charlie tells me are taro fields, backed by the stunningly rugged peaks of the mountains, half-hidden by cloud. It's absolutely gorgeous and I snap a few pictures in vain, trying to capture it.

"Wow," I say softly, craning my neck behind me as the view disappears. We're heading down the side of the cliff now, back toward the water.

"Next time it's sunny, we'll stop there, make sure you get some good pictures. Nothing beats Hanalei on a gorgeous day. Make the people jealous back home." He pauses. "You have a boyfriend?"

I give him a wary look. "No."

"I guess if you did, he would have come with you," he notes.

I make a dismissive noise as we come to a one-lane bridge, the traffic backed up by a few cars as we wait for the other vehicles to come across. A sign indicates that you should let five to seven cars pass or go ahead of you when you're crossing, as a common courtesy. After our turn, we wind past a swollen river and wet fields that resemble rice paddies. With the lush, ragged mountains rising dramatically behind it all, it reminds me of pictures I'd seen of Vietnam, or some place in South East Asia.

The town of Hanalei passes by us quickly, which is supposed to be the closest town to the resort. Even in the shitty weather, people are strolling down the road without umbrellas, laughing at the rain with surfboards tucked under their arms or sucking back iced drinks. Cute storefronts, bars, and restaurants abound on either side of the road.

After we pass Hanalei, the road becomes this twisty, winding vein as it skirts the rough ocean, the surf pounding up against the lava rocks, palm trees waving in the wind. We pass one one-lane bridge after another, the scenery causing me whiplash as I try and take it all in.

Charlie continues to name certain beaches and places but I'm not really listening. I'm nervous all over again. Maybe it's the iced coffee I just drank down, but even without him saying anything, I can tell we're getting closer to our destination. We're close to the scene of the accident. We're close to the end of so many truths, so much heartache.

I close my eyes for the rest of the journey.

CHAPTER TWO

"AND HERE SHE IS," CHARLIE SAYS.

I take in a deep breath and slowly open my eyes as we slow down in front of a large tiki-style sign saying Moonwater Inn, the scene of a moon rising over surf carved into the wood. He pulls the truck to the right and into the parking lot of the hotel.

Oh my god.

This is it.

This is my new home.

Fortunately, it's gorgeous.

"That's the restaurant just up there," Charlie says, jerking his chin toward the large building near the water, done up in a tiki theme, similar to the hotel's signage. "Home sweet home." He parks the truck in a spot labeled "staff" and we get out.

The rain has let up slightly, a light drizzle, but the wind

is driving it sideways. It's still warm though, and to be honest the feeling of it on my skin is refreshing. It makes me realize how badly I need a shower. I resist the urge to smell myself and hope that Charlie didn't think I needed extra deodorant.

Aside from the restaurant, there's a tennis court to the left and a small lawn area bordered with torches. To the right, skirting along the beach and the ocean is the hotel, spread out into small, two-story buildings. It's nothing fancy, a bit on the dated side, which is a relief. I'm not sure I could work at a high-class establishment.

Charlie brings my suitcases out of the back of the truck and gives me a triumphant grin. "Dry as anything."

He wheels them over to me while I go back to staring at everything, aware that the longer I stand in the parking lot, the more wet I'll become. My hair is already sticking to my face.

"How many buildings are there?" I ask, reluctantly following him toward a single-story building named Reception. "How many rooms?"

"Two buildings right on the beach, three with ocean views, set a bit further back, and two that have mountain views, facing that way." He points to the razor-ridged mountains that rise sharply from the other side of the road, their tops shrouded by cloud. "Thirty rooms in total."

It's almost heavenly, this place: the clouds, the rain, the steady, rhythmic pounding of the waves, the rich and clear birdsong that sounds from the trees. But the closer we walk to the reception area, the worse I feel. Because this is no longer me in Chicago, wondering about the journey. This is no longer me on 'the airplane, imagining how things are going to be. This is no longer me in Charlie's truck, getting a quick tour of the island as we make our way north.

This is me at the start of my new life.

I think I'm going to be sick.

"Here we are," Charlie says as he pauses by the open doors of reception. Is it just me or was there a flicker of uncertainty passing over his eyes? Considering how calm and easy-going he's been, that definitely doesn't help the situation.

"Shephard?" Charlie says, knocking on the side of the door. He pokes his head in and looks around the corner. "Where is Shephard?"

Knowing he's not in there, I poke my head into the office and see an Asian girl sitting on the other side of the reception desk, two empty chairs across from her. She's super pretty and about my age, with dark hair cascading over her shoulders, and staring at Charlie, completely unimpressed.

"This her?" she asks, not getting up, not smiling at me either.

"It is," Charlie says. "Veronica, this Kate."

"Hi," I say as brightly as I can. "You can call me Ronnie."

"Right, Ronnie," Charlie corrects himself.

Kate studies me for a little too long, her expression hard to read.

She looks back at Charlie. "Shephard is still at the pool. He told me he'd give her the tour though, so don't think you don't have to get back to work."

Charlie checks the clock on the wall. "Damn, time is a bitch." He looks at me with a shrug. "Wish I could continue being your tour guide, sweet thing," he says. He looks at Kate, who is in the process of rolling her eyes. "I'll leave her bags here, for now. Do you know where she's staying?"

Kate's dark eyes fly to mine. "She's staying with me."

I blink at her, surprised. "Uh, I was under the impression I would get my own place."

She laughs dryly, tossing her hair over her shoulder. "Right. Because that would be fair. Look, if you had a place to yourself, you'd be docked a lot more pay. Rent in Kauai isn't cheap. You're more than welcome to go find a beach house up the street or down in Hanalei, if you want to share with six other people, most of whom will leave empty beer cans lying around the place and piss on your head in the middle of the night, thinking you're a toilet. Not that I'd know. But if you want to stay at the resort, you're staying with yours truly. Believe me, I don't like it either." She sighs. "I just had a wonderful month with the unit to myself after Charlotte started shacking up with her boyfriend. But it is what it is."

"Dude, Kate, lighten up," Charlie says, taking me by the elbow and giving her a dirty look. "I'll come by and get the suitcases later." He leads me out of the office. "I should also mention that I'm also the bellhop sometimes. So is Johnny. Or really any staff member who happens to be walking past guests with luggage. Be prepared to add that to your job description as well."

I nod absently. "She seems ... nice," I whisper to him as we walk down the path and away from the office, skirting alongside one of the buildings.

"Kate? She's actually great once you get to know her. She's just one of those people who you can never tell is joking or not. Deadpan, you know? But she's good people. Hey that's your unit there. Corner one, great view."

I look up to where he's gesturing, the second floor of the building, an outdoor staircase leading up to it.

"The units are nice," he says. "I share one with Johnny over there by the pool. You guys get a view so there's that."

"How many other workers stay here? Does Logan?"

He shakes his head. "Nah. Shephard has a house up the

street, just across from the beach."

"The same one as before?" For some reason I thought that maybe the house would have been empty after the accident.

"Same one," he says. "And Nikki and Shannon share the unit next to us. We get docked a bit in pay for it but it's not as much as if we were to live elsewhere, so no one complains. Only drawback is that you live where you work, you know? So in a way you're always working. Just try and have a nice evening off without someone knocking on your door, asking you for something."

We pause outside a gate with a sign displaying the pool hours, lush foliage with bright hibiscus flowers on either side.

"Well this is the—" Charlie begins but is interrupted by a loud, "FUCK!" coming from the other side of the fence.

Charlie winces. "And that would be Shephard. Sorry you have to meet him on a day that he's losing his shit." He pauses. "Then again, you know him. Try to think of the happier times."

The happier times? My brain chugs back to the past, where all the happier times reside. It pauses on the sight of him, seven years ago, looking out over Lake Michigan in that uncomfortable suit, the way his eyes looked as they first glanced at me. Like I was someone he knew. Like I was someone he wanted to know.

I'm prepared not to know him anymore.

Charlie swipes his key card at the gate and it swings open.

To get to the pool you have to walk through a small, open-air structure that has the change rooms, washrooms, and a small outdoor kitchen. There are a few barbeques scattered about and an eating area, as well as some loungers, couches, and a fire pit, all surrounded by lush potted plants and palms, adding to the tropical feel.

Beyond that is the tiled patio leading to the pool where a tiny balding Korean man is hunched over the filter, concentrating as he sticks his hands inside.

"Anything yet, Jin?" A brash Australian accented voice yells from the right of us. We look over to see the door to a maintenance shed open, a tall hulking figure half-hidden inside.

"No, nothing," Jin says. "It's not the filter."

Charlie swallows, looking nervous again, which in turn makes me feel like I'm about to throw up.

Get it together, I tell myself. *You'll be fine.*

"Still working on it?" Charlie comments.

"Oh hey Charlie," Jin says, glancing up at us. "Seems like an element has gone out, I think."

But I'm not looking at Jin. I'm looking at Logan as he sticks his head around the door and steps back a foot.

I feel the air being sucked out of me. I never knew how hard it would be to see him again, and somehow it's harder than I imagined. It's like a sticky, sharp feeling that settles in your bones, the result of having far too many emotions about one particular person. Hate, fear, disappointment, distrust, shame, sadness.

Affection.

Lust.

No, I tell myself. *Don't even think about that one.*

"Veronica," Logan says and my name sounds darker when he says it, like I'm the name of a hurricane that's about to slam into the island. Maybe let another generation of chickens loose.

I nod at him because I can't think of anything to say. I haven't seen him since the funeral, and it feels like I did nothing more than glance in his direction as the coffin was lowered into the ground.

"I got her here safe and sound," Charlie says rather awkwardly, looking between the two of us.

"You look just like her," Jin says. Startled, I whirl toward him as he slowly walks over. He has kind eyes and smooth skin, even though he must be in his seventies, but his words are still jarring.

"Excuse me?" I repeat.

"Like who?" Charlie asks.

"Like his wife," Jin says, nodding at Logan.

I try not to look at him.

"Juliet? Shephard's wife?" Charlie asks and he takes a step back, eyeing me up and down. "I guess ... I ..."

"Well, doesn't she?" Jin says to Logan, adamant.

Now I dare to look at him. Logan is staring at me, his eyes dark and pensive under those arched brows, though I know inside he must be reeling at the comparison.

"Juliet smiled more," Logan finally says. And the moment her name comes out of his lips, I realize how much of a mistake this was and how hard it's going to be.

I can't do this.

"Can someone fill me in?" Charlie says, exasperated, pressing his palms together.

"You didn't know?" Jin asked, brows raised. "This is Juliet's sister. Logan is Veronica's brother-in-law."

Was my brother-in-law, till death did them part, I want to say but I don't dare. For all that I know about Logan, the horrible things he's done, the way everyone in my family feels about him, I can't pretend that losing Juliet wasn't hard on him. Even though I want to.

"You're Shephard's sister-in-law?" Charlie asks incredulously. "Dude, why didn't you tell me that?"

I don't say anything but Logan does. "Probably because she didn't want any special treatment. Isn't that right, *Veronica*?"

I hate the way he says my name. The last seven years have been all about trying to get him to call me Ronnie, like everyone else does. He calls me Veronica on purpose, only because it pisses me off.

"Pretty much," I tell him, giving him a tight smile.

He holds my eyes for a moment, as if he's already trying to wear me down. I won't give him the satisfaction. I stare right back. Silence stretches between us, broken only by a calling bird.

"Uh, so Kate said you'd give her the tour?" Charlie asks warily.

Logan tears his eyes off me and I shudder inside with relief.

"I'll finish up here. Bloody pump isn't working. Might have to get a professional in here and go without heat for the rest of the week, fuck knows how fast I can get a guy."

"It's hot as balls. I don't think anyone will care aside from that couple from Boston. They've been complaining about everything," Charlie adds lightly.

Logan's eyes narrow. "And we can't afford to have a single complaint, got that N-Sync?"

"Yeah, yeah," Charlie says. He looks to me. "Come on, I'll take you to your new home, you can get settled while the *habut* stops grumbling."

"Okay," I say quietly. I look to Jin. "Nice to meet you."

"Nice to meet you too," he says with a wide grin. "We'll be spending a lot of time together."

I don't even have time to wonder what work I'll be doing with Jin the pool-man. I look at Logan to nod farewell, but he's already turned his back to me and is busying himself with the pool problems.

It isn't until the pool gate closes behind us that I finally let out a deep breath.

"So Shephard is your brother-in-law?" Charlie asks. "Or I guess, *was* your brother-in-law. Either way. Wow. Dude. This has got to be all kinds of…weird for you."

You have no idea.

"I mean, Juliet," he goes on, running a hand through his spiky hair. "Shit. I'm so sorry. I know I already told you how amazing she was but in case you need to know it again, there you go. She really had the hotel running at its best. To be honest Shephard has kind of been struggling with it ever since. I'm sure some of us stay here because we feel sorry for him."

I don't like the idea of feeling sorry for him. I want to feel *nothing* for him.

As we head back to reception to grab my suitcases, he says, "I guess coming here is kind of like … another way to say goodbye. Communicate with the ghost."

I know Charlie is speaking metaphorically but even so, a shiver runs through me. Juliet's ghost is here, all over the hotel and the grounds, in the memories of the people who worked here, the man who runs the place, in the trees and the birds that saw her. I'd always thought that moving here would be another way to connect with her, to get a glimpse at the place that occupied her heart and mind for four years of her life.

But already it seems like it will be more than that. Her ghost might become something I can't escape.

We grab my bags at reception, Kate on the phone with someone as we do so, and head back to my unit. Even though I try and stay fit by jogging every morning, I'm out of breath and sweating again by the time I bring my bag up to the second level. Charlie keeps insisting he can handle both, but since he warned me that we all have to act as bell-boys at one point or another, I figure I can use the practice.

He swipes the key card at the pad on the side of the door and it beeps open.

I step inside my new home.

CHAPTER THREE

THE UNIT IS EXACTLY WHAT I PICTURED. WELL, ASIDE from the whole having to share it with someone aspect, though I tell myself I'll get over it soon.

There are tiles on the floor and thatched walls that look like they're made from palm leaves. The whole place is open air except for the bathroom to the right and a bedroom to the left.

"So Kate is in there," Charlie says, hauling the suitcases across the floor and nodding to the door. "And let me tell you, she's one lucky bitch. I think Shephard has a soft spot for her because that's the only room any of us have."

"What do you mean?" I ask, following him into the apartment. There's a kitchen on one side, small and a little dated but totally functional, and a large living area with rattan and bamboo furniture with palm-printed cushions. In front of that is an expansive balcony with chairs and a table, the view stretching across a wide lawn and finally to the ocean. Many of the condos face inward to the grassy area, like a courtyard, giving us all a partial ocean view at the very least, palm trees swaying in the wind. Even though the screen door is closed, I can hear the ocean clear as day, the chatter of a couple as they walk across the lawn in their bare feet, towels draped over their shoulders.

"This is your room," he says nodding to a sectioned off corner of the living room, tucked behind the kitchen. It's only half-walled in, so there's no real door, just some partitions you can slide across.

"Uh, this is a room?" I ask.

"Yeah," he says, running his hand over his jaw and nodding like he's contemplating it for the first time. "In the hotel units, this is where the kids sleep, I guess. It's where I sleep in mine. The bed is really comfortable, by the way. And Johnny doesn't get his own room like Kate does, it's kind of done up the same way as this. No privacy for anyone." He runs his hands along the edge of the partition. "Except Kate. Like I said, she's one lucky bitch. She can have all the dudes over and you probably won't hear a thing." His eyes seem to darken momentarily at that before he snaps out of it and gives me a cheeky grin. "You, on the other hand…"

I roll my eyes. "I don't think that will be a problem," I tell him. I'd pretty much sworn off men since I left Piccolo.

"Even so," he says. "You're better off staying the night elsewhere if you want to get laid. Though since Kate actually has a door, it shouldn't be a problem."

"Doesn't it bother you to live like you're in a dorm?" I ask him, folding my arms. "I mean, how old are you anyway?"

"Twenty-six," he says, raising his chin in defense. "And, this isn't living in a dorm room. This is just an affordable way to live in paradise. Not everyone can be rich here. The rich get the private condos and houses. We ain't rich and it ain't about that anyway. This is about really living life and finding out what's important. What's important to you, Ronnie?"

I'm half-pleased that he's called me by my nickname and half-ashamed that I sounded so snooty. I swallow hard. "I don't know what's important anymore," I admit, my voice dropping a register. "I just know that whatever it is, it's not back at home."

He purses his lips, eyes studying me. "Hmmm. Honest. I like that. Well, maybe that's why you're here. To find out what's important. What makes your soul sing. I told you this place would shake you up, didn't I?"

"You did."

He jerks his head into the room. "Anyway, you do have your own private bathroom, so if you must get busy, you can get busy in there. I can't tell you how many dates have ended up with a blow-job in the loo."

"All right, Charlie, that's enough," I tell him. "Or is it N' Sync?"

He scoffs. "I guess you heard Shephard dole out that one."

"Is that one of your nicknames?"

"One of them," he says. "Take care, I'll see you in a bit."

And with that Charlie leaves, while I ponder if the N' Sync comment is over his spiky hair or something else. He looks more like a surfing god than a boy-band member but I guess the best nicknames are the ones we don't suit. Or want.

With Charlie gone, for the first time in twenty-four hours, I am well and truly alone.

I'm not even sure what to do. Logan had said he was

coming to get me for a tour but I don't know if I have enough time to shower or not. So I stand here for a few moments, moments that stretch into minutes, while I try and absorb everything that's just happened.

Here I am in Kauai, in my new home, and not only do I have no idea what to expect, I have no idea if I'm ready to start working with Logan. I mean, he is, was, my brother-in-law, and even though Juliet died two years ago, he's somehow still family, whether I want him to be or not.

And I don't.

I just wish I felt something toward him other than … well, everything I feel toward him. The biggest one of all is resentment. I can't help but feel a hot fist of anger in my chest every time I think about the way he wronged Juliet. Even though I'd never confronted him about it, we all knew the truth, and that horrible dilemma that Juliet was living with in the months leading up to her death.

Even though she was hit by a drunk driver and her car plunged over the side of the cliff and onto the rocks below, I can't help but feel it's Logan's fault. Maybe if Juliet hadn't been so distraught by everything that was happening in her life, she would have been more aware, more on the ball. Maybe she would have survived. Corrected the car before it went over. I mean, it was Juliet Locke for crying out loud, my sister, the girl that could never do wrong, the girl who never made mistakes, the girl I spent my entire life living in the shadow of, trying to become someone half as good as her.

And Logan was her husband, the bastard who cheated on her.

We all knew. We could sense things were off before, about a year or two into the marriage, when Juliet would give a forced smile every time Logan's name was mentioned. My mother pulled me aside once when they celebrated Christmas with us and asked me, "Do you think Juliet's happy with Logan?"

At the time I thought it was my mother being a snob, because she always insisted her daughters do the best, marry the best, and Logan, for all his entrepreneurial spirit, wasn't considered to be one of the best. My mother would rather have the politician's sons for either of us, but especially for Juliet, her shining light, the daughter she was the proudest of.

But instead Juliet settled for a rugged Australian with little money, who had dreams of opening a hotel in Hawaii (a pipe dream, as my father had initially called it) and when Moonwater Inn finally did open six years ago, it was done with the backing of his friend, Warren Jones, and almost all of my parent's money. In fact, they're still part owners of this place, yet another reason why I think I was shipped off here.

Looking back now, I'm sure that's not what my mother meant, though. She must have sensed Juliet's unhappiness. Knew that Logan was having an affair behind her back. She's a politician and they're the first to sniff out the shady shit. Takes one to know one and all that.

When Juliet came to visit alone that one year, staying at my place, that's when the truth came out. Logan was a cheater. Had numerous affairs. Was an asshole of the highest regard.

I was livid on her behalf, knowing that I should have never trusted him, and I hated myself for initially being so attracted to the man. All before Juliet swept him off his feet, of course—and vice versa. Especially since my family had helped to fund his dream. This was how he repaid them?

But I never got to talk to Juliet about it again. She

became more and more distant as the months went on and wouldn't talk about it. My emails, my texts, my phone calls—it was like it had never happened, that she had never admitted anything. Which, when I think about it, is totally a Juliet maneuver. It hurt her to admit that anything wasn't perfect.

She wouldn't leave him either, which I never really understood. Was it that she had become so accustomed to the lifestyle that she was afraid to break it off? Was it that she still loved him somehow, despite all that he'd done? Either way, the Juliet I grew up with, my beautiful big sister, she never would have put up with anyone's shit. Her ego was strong, her pride was unbreakable. And yet she stayed married to Logan for reasons I'll never know.

But even still, I can't help but hold him partially responsible for her death. If anything, if she didn't fall in love with him, she would still be in Chicago. Maybe she'd show up at my restaurant and finally glimpse the career I was building for myself, see that I too was becoming something. Maybe we would have grown closer as we became adults. Instead I lost the last years of our relationship to long-distance. Kauai had become her new home and new life, and I was just the shadow left behind.

I was always the shadow left behind.

I sigh, trying to shake it all from my nerves. I refuse to be negative on my first day here. What I need is a shower.

I pry my phone out of my jeans pocket, the interior damp from my sweat in this tropical climate, and give it a glance. It's four p.m., October 2nd, and I think—I hope—I have just enough time to have a shower and wash the plane germs off me before Logan shows up. If he shows up.

I step into the bathroom, grateful that I have a private one, and get in the shower. The moment the hot water hits my skin, I sigh in relief. I literally stand there for five minutes, just letting it all soak into me, like I'm trying to wash every worry and fear away. I swear it works. By the time I lather up with shower oil, shampoo, and conditioner, I feel like a brand-new woman.

I step out and wrap the towel around me and lean over, wiping the steam away from the mirror. My reflection is a bit fuzzy, like I have the heaviest Snapchat filter on, which is probably why I look half decent. When Jin said I looked like Juliet, he wasn't exaggerating. We're not carbon copies of each other, but even so you can see the resemblance if you look for it, which is probably why Jin saw it (because he knew we were related) and Charlie didn't (because he didn't).

Juliet was tall and thin, with a giant rack which so wasn't fair, and light brown hair that was shiny like a Pantene commercial. In the summer she had Jennifer Aniston highlights from the sun, and that all came naturally. She was pale, but her skin was smooth and wrinkle-free, to the point that I started to suspect that our mother had given her the "treat" of Botox on more than one occasion. Her eyes were blue, just like our father's, and her lashes were long, looking positively fake when she loaded on the mascara.

As for me, my hair is medium brown and I have to pay for my highlights. I'm not very tall, about five-five, and while I'm somewhat thin, it's because I work hard at it. When you think of a chef or a cook, you think of a rather "rotund" person, and I do my best to buck the stereotype, and though I have a full ass and thighs that won't go away no matter how little I eat or many miles I walk, my upper body is tiny (which unfortunately means my boobs don't runneth over). My eyes are more narrow and dark brown, like my mother's (we give good resting bitch face) and my skin tans easily, which, for the first time ever, might be a good thing when it comes to living in Hawaii.

Overall I know I'm pretty. Not gorgeous like Juliet was, I mean, you couldn't find a person alive that would turn that woman down. She had everyone in the palm of her delicate hand. She was Blake Lively on beauty steroids. But I'm okay with myself, even if Veronica Locke is a person you usually end up forgetting in the end.

With that in mind, I slather moisturizer over my face, hoping to combat the dryness from the plane, and take in a deep breath.

I open the door and step out into my room.

Logan is standing there.

I yelp, clutching my towel to my chest.

"Sorry," he says quickly, taking a little too long to avert his eyes away from my legs and chest. "I didn't know you were in the shower."

I glare at him. "But that still gives you the right to waltz on in here?" I ask incredulously. Talk about no boundaries!

His eyes narrow in response, the kind of look that can nail you to the floor.

I don't let it.

"The door was ajar, I knocked. Again, sorry." When he finishes that sentence, his eyes trail down to my chest again, my boobs squished together by my hands at the towel. He clears his throat and looks away, staring out at the expanse of lawn and the ocean beyond it.

I hate, hate, hate the tiny thrill that runs through me from his gaze. This is so not what I want for my first day here. Even though it pains me to do so, I have to just push past all this and try my best to be the bigger person. Hell, Logan is almost forty but that doesn't seem to mean anything when it comes to being less stubborn.

"Well, give me a moment to get changed," I tell him.

He nods and steps out of my zero-privacy bedroom.

I sigh and quickly close the partitions, then bring down the blinds on the window. I can hear him as he walks along the tile floor, to the kitchen and back to the living area, pacing.

I wonder if he's nervous. Of me, of all people.

It's because he knows what you think of him.

Even though it's raining, I grab a tank top and slide on a pair of black board-shorts I picked up at Neiman's just before I left. I pull my wet hair back into a loose bun and clean up the bits of mascara underneath my eyes that smudged from the shower. I would have liked to have had more time to actually dote on my appearance for my first day and all—I know how important first impressions are in a business like this—but this will have to do.

I slide on my flip-flops and step out into the unit.

Logan is standing at the balcony, hands folded behind his back, staring at the ocean through the screen door.

I allow myself a quick moment to take him all in. Seeing him earlier at the pool was so jarring, I was barely in the moment.

He looks good. Really good. It physically pains me to admit it but it's the truth and my body often reacts to the sight of him before my conscience can. If anything, he's gotten better with age, like a very fine wine, the kind you can't wait to get drunk on.

His body is still built like he surfs and swims all day, and I have to wonder if that's true and if so, how he finds the time. His hair is dark, longer on the top, shorter on the sides, with just a peppering of grey in his sideburns and along his scruffy beard.

He might have a few more lines around his eyes, and

a definite crevice between his brows, no doubt a result of frowning all the time, but his skin looks taut—tanned and smooth.

And unlike the times I saw him in Chicago, where he was trapped in layers to fight the cold—hell, he even looked uncomfortable at his wedding, having to wear a tux—here he seems more at ease. He's wearing olive green cargo shorts that come to his knees and a plain white tee shirt. Unlike Charlie and so many of the guys I've seen so far, he is wearing shoes, simple sandals.

I know I'm staring for too long but to his credit, he lets me do this and doesn't call me out on it. I know he'd love to. Before Juliet told me the truth about him, we had more of a, well let's say, jovial relationship. He'd tease me all the time. "Little sis," he'd call me, before letting loose a one-liner about this and that. Luckily I was pretty good at the comebacks. "Big brother" or "old man," were my favorites.

I swallow hard and step forward.

"Okay, all ready," I tell him, my voice sounding terribly weak. I need to stop letting the past sneak into the present.

I also need to stop checking him out.

He finally looks my way and nods. I can't read a thing in his expression, other than the fact that he's frowning, and that could mean anything really.

"Are you happy with the accommodations?" he asks, sounding so formal.

I shrug. "I haven't had a roommate in a long time, but sure."

He squints at me. "You do realize that the two of you in here means I can't rent this unit out to guests. And we could use that money."

"So in other words, shut up, right?"

His frown deepens as he eyes me. "I wouldn't think

of being so rude, but yes, shut up. If you're going to work here, you're going to have to act like everyone else. This isn't Chicago anymore. This isn't the big bloody city. This is Hawaii, and if you're going to survive you need to leave your preconceived notions at the door. Got it? What I mean is, there will be no special favors from me to you. You'll be treated like everyone else and that means showing up to your shifts on time, working hard, helping out when we need you to, and learning to live with a roommate again. Are we clear?"

My heart is pounding louder, filling my ears. He doesn't have to be so condescending, I mean I just fucking got off the plane, give me a break.

"Are you a bossy asshole with all of your employees?" I ask him. "Because you just said I'm not getting special treatment and if this is the same way you treat them, then I think you might have a problem."

He raises his brow in shock. Damn, he gives good eyebrow.

"I'm not being a…" He stops and clears his throat. "Sorry." The apology sounds painful. "I'm just…finding this weird, that's all. I haven't seen you…"

"Since the funeral. I remember."

He swallows and looks away. "So where do I need to start? Did anyone show you around?"

I sigh loudly and shrug. "I'm not really sure. We met Kate at reception, and for your information, she didn't look too thrilled to be having a roommate either. And that's pretty much it. He mentioned a bunch of names that I can't remember and the fact that everyone has side jobs aside from their main ones." I pause, wondering for a moment if I should say more. "And he said he liked working here, that you're a good boss."

Logan grunts dismissively and looks away. "Doesn't sound like he filled you in on anything. Serves me right to send a monkey to do a man's job."

"Hey, he's been nice," I say, feeling particularly defensive of Charlie at this moment. "Much better than you're being."

He eyes me sharply and I know I've pissed him off.

Good.

"Look, Veronica," he says gruffly, crossing his thick arms across his chest, "I know we have our differences and this situation is less than ideal for both of us. But for the sake of the employees and this hotel, the very same one that was run so lovingly by your own flesh and blood, we'll both have to put it past us. I can be nice if you'll be nice."

He really doesn't sound like he wants to be nice. Frankly, neither do I. And the fact that he mentioned Juliet, that we have to be nice for her sake, reminds me that the ghost of her really is large and in charge.

It's also a bit of a sucker punch.

"Hey, I'm nice everywhere except in the kitchen," I tell him, standing up a bit straighter.

"Good," he says. "That's the kind of thing I want to hear. Johnny, the head cook, he's a good guy, talented, sweet as sugar. Without him, the restaurant would have floundered. He made it what it is. But he's good friends with Charlie and has a hard time keeping him in check. It will be good to have someone on the team that doesn't mind being a hard-ass. And I know you can be a hard-ass."

I smirk at that, feeling some strange sense of pride at that compliment.

"Well let's get going," he says quickly, starting off toward the front door, as if he regrets saying anything remotely complimentary about me. "The grand tour awaits."

We walk out the door, the rain having eased off. The air smells fresh, like cut-flowers and something earthy, with the ever-present tang of salt in the air. The breeze is warmer now, like a thick cloak as it blankets me, rustling my wet hair.

He points out the buildings, the units where the rest of the staff lives, the pool area, past perfectly groomed lawns, landscaped with palm trees and flowering bushes. There are some families out on the balconies, drinking beer or playing with their kids.

He leads me toward the water, through a short sand path lined with dark-leaved bushes and blooming white flowers. "So, this is the east beach. Perfect for sunrises, or so the brochure says."

It's beautiful. I mean, I kept seeing glances of it earlier but from this angle I can really get a feel for the entire place.

Moonwater Inn appears to be built on a curve of land that pushes out into the ocean like the slope of someone's hip, the beach swooping along the sides. If you look east, where we are now, you can see the land across the bay jutting out, the waves crashing against the shore while the green mountains rise inland. If you turn your head to the left and look north, there's nothing but open water, the swells so high that the horizon line is a wavering blur.

"Can you swim here?" I ask, my sandals sinking into the sand. I reach down and take them off one by one, my toes happy to feel the damp sand beneath them. When I glance back up, Logan quickly looks away. Was he checking out my chest? I look down at my B-cups, wondering what it is about them today that has them so damn captivating.

It's all in your head, I tell myself. *You're seeing what you want to see.*

And that's a problem too.

"Sometimes you can swim," he says, his face to the east. He's got an incredible profile, the wind swooping the dark hair off his brow. "In the summer. And even then, I wouldn't if I were you." He looks to me, his expression stern. "And when I say that, I mean, don't you dare unless someone is with you, preferably me or Charlie or even Kate."

"I doubt that would be a problem," I tell him, looking back to the rough seas. You'd have to be crazy to go in there now, especially as the waves are breaking twice, once at the shore and once at a shallow reef further back.

"I don't mean now," he says gruffly. "I mean ever. Even when this water looks crystal clear, calm as anything, don't go in alone. I can't tell you the number of times people have drowned in Kauai's waters. Every year, at nearly every beach."

Now this surprises me. "Have people drowned here, at Moonwater?"

His grim expression tells me all I need to know. "Yes," he says. "And those days haunt you for the rest of your life. We take the ocean seriously here. It can be your friend, but also your biggest foe. It demands your respect and if you don't give it, there are rips, and waves and sharks that would love to put you in your place."

Okay then. He sounds like that damn video that was playing at baggage claim. Suddenly the ocean doesn't look so appealing anymore. And to think that Charlie wanted to teach me to surf. No thank you.

We continue along the beach as it curves around the beachfront buildings. Despite the dangers, it really is beautiful, especially as it opens up to the dramatic cliffs to the west. It looks positively tropical, like the quintessential South Pacific scene, and I half expect Polynesians in a dugout canoe to wash up on the shore. There are even fucking coconuts littering the sand.

"And there's the restaurant," he says, gesturing to it. From the front entrance, I knew it was oceanfront but from here you can see it's literally right on the beach, to the point where it looks like the waves could crash against the windows if the storm was big enough. "Unfortunately the kitchen itself doesn't have ocean views."

"Probably better that way," I tell him. "Less distracting."

He gives me a look that borders on impressed. "I've forgotten what it's like to get workers from the mainland. Try and keep the ethic up."

Again, I'm not sure how to feel about the compliment.

I ignore it as we step inside the restaurant, my new job. With my new boss by my side.

I can only pray things get a little bit easier.

CHAPTER FOUR

"THE RESTAURANT IS ACTUALLY CALLED OHANA Lounge," Logan explains as he opens the heavy doors and we step inside. "*Ohana* means family in Hawaiian, by the way. But most locals call it the last stop."

The area inside is actually a lot more spacious than it looked from the outside. Skylights adorn the ceiling, and the entire back wall of the restaurant has the amazing ocean views I had noted earlier. Even though the lights are all off, the place looks bright.

There's an empty hostess stand at the podium with a sign that says *please seat yourself*. To the left of us are the washrooms, just off the small waiting area. To the right it looks like the door to the kitchen.

I follow Logan further inside, the decorating similar to my new room, perhaps with more of a Mediterranean or middle-eastern feel. There's a bar to the left of us, small and rounded, with five bamboo barstools along it, and to the right is the kitchen, open slightly to the restaurant.

Charlie is already in there, smiling at me through the open section before he quickly turns away and busies himself once Logan catches his eye.

I turn back to the room and take quick stock of my new workplace, my eyes immediately taking in everything that needs to be improved. I can't help it.

"How many of these tables are used on a given night?" I ask Logan. "How often are you full?"

He leans back on his heels, strokes his hand along the beard on his jaw. My god, he has perfect hands. Wide, powerful—I'd forgotten about that. It was one of the first things I noticed about him, though when the wedding band went on his left hand, I stopped noticing all together.

At least, I should have.

"Not every night. There's never really a wait for a table until we get into the busy seasons … Christmas, the winter holidays, summer holidays. Autumn is the shoulder season, which is why Charlie and Johnny have been able to manage with just the two of them. But the closer we get to December, the busier it's going to get."

"Well, my first thought is that the place is too cramped," I tell him.

He frowns at me. "Too cramped?" He looks personally insulted. "Look at all this space."

I shake my head. "It's spacious but the set-up is all wrong. You're crowding too many tables by the window."

"But people want the view."

"Then people will have to get here early or make reservations if they want the view," I tell him. I jerk my chin to two four-seaters by the window. "Get rid of those completely. Stack them in storage for now, put them somewhere more accessible when the busy season comes, but for now they're an eyesore. People might want the view of the windows but they don't want to share it so closely with others. Since you say not many families come here, the four-seaters aren't needed, not there anyway. Kids don't give a shit about the view. I say, push the four-seaters up there in that alcove, and that can become the family area. Couples don't want children causing a fuss over dinner, believe me. And if this means that more people will have to wait to get a table, let them wait. People stay at the hotel, they want to eat here because they're too lazy to go into town or they want to have a few drinks at dinner and don't want to drink and drive. So then you add a couple of more stools to the bar, there's room, and they can wait there. Maybe even serve drinks in the waiting area, or set up some tables outside. There's a whole beach out there with an even better view; they can relax while they wait."

I realize I've been totally rambling on and from the glower that Logan is given, I can tell my suggestions aren't exactly appreciated.

"Let me get this straight," Logan says slowly, not looking away. "I have this restaurant up and running for years, never had more than a few complaints, have a bloody brilliant rating on Yelp, and then you show up, fresh off the boat, and immediately have something to say about it. You haven't worked here even for a minute, Veronica. Why the hell should I suddenly rearrange what's working just because you've said so?"

Right. See the other thing I remember about Logan is that he's a stubborn son of a bitch and you better not tell him his way is the wrong way. Unfortunately, I'm also a stubborn son of a bitch, but at least in this situation I know I'm right. He may own this restaurant and the hotel, but he doesn't know the first thing about cooking food, about serving, about running a place like this.

"She's right, aye," a booming voice comes from behind me.

I whirl around to see a round, jovial-looking face staring at me from the kitchen. He smiles broadly, his teeth blindingly white, albeit slightly crooked, against his dark skin. "Hey, I'm Johnny by the way. You can call me Big J. Least that's what the *habut* calls me."

"Johnny is just fine," I tell him, feeling eternally grateful for this friendly face in the presence of the ha-boo-t.

"What do you mean she's right?" Logan asks, his voice on edge.

Johnny shrugs. "I mean she's right. Just because you have a good Yelp rating, doesn't mean people don't talk. Especially locals, aye? They won't write reviews but the word still spreads. And I'm the head cook, which means I have to hear about it. Not you."

I look back to Logan. He seems like he's ready to blow, his jaw is set in a tense line, his fingers are tapping against his arm, agitated. "What are they saying?" he asks carefully.

"Nothing you should worry about," Johnny says. "But I can tell you that people don't come here to eat for the ocean view. It's too crowded. Like she said. And having a wait isn't a bad thing. Most diners are our guests. If there is a wait, they can go back to their room. Or the beach. And adding some extra seats at the bar doesn't hurt at all."

I watch Logan, my breath in my throat. I'm afraid he's going to lose it on me or Johnny, not that Johnny seems to care, which makes me like him even more.

Finally, Logan's eyes meet mine and I see nothing but animosity in them. Something tells me that I made a big mistake speaking out like that.

I expect him to say something else that would shoot down my idea but eventually he lets out a ragged breath and says sternly to Johnny, "I have to check on the pool. I trust you'll get Veronica up to speed?" He glances at me. "Your first shift starts tomorrow. Come to the office later, I have papers for you to sign."

Then he turns on his heel and leaves, his hulking body pushing open the doors and disappearing into the bright world outside.

"So Charlie tells me Shephard's your brother-in-law," Johnny says, making me turn my attention back to him. "I thought he'd for sure treat you a little easier but I guess it's fair across the board here." He gives me a quick wave. "Come on back here, let's introduce you to your new home, little *wahine*."

I take in a deep breath, trying to shake off Logan's attitude, and head into the kitchen.

My first thought is that it's small. Barely big enough for three cooks and a dishwasher, assuming they have a dishwasher. I've heard a lot of the smaller places don't.

"She ain't much, but she makes good food," Johnny says. He comes over to me holding out his hand. "Now it's official. Johnny."

"Ronnie," I tell him as he takes my hand in his, his palm damp. He's a huge guy, tall and round, and yet despite the big jiggling stomach, he somehow exudes strength, like he could bench press you at any given time. "You can call me Ron if you wish. Or even hey you."

He grins at me and it lights up his face like a child on Christmas Day. "Nah, I don't think we'll call you hey you. Ronnie is just fine. Or little *wahine*. That's Hawaiian for pretty lady, you know." He lets go of my hand and twists around him to look at Charlie who is at the back of the kitchen, chopping up bok choy. "You didn't tell me she was cute."

"I don't have to tell you everything, Johnny Cakes," Charlie says without looking up. "And *wahine* means woman, Ron, so he's just trying to butter you up."

"I'm a cook, of course I'm trying to butter her up, I put butter on everything," Johnny says with a wink. "So now that you've seen the place, I guess you're figuring out where everything is. I'm pretty organized so you'll get the hang of things really quick and soon it won't feel like work at all." Charlie snorts at that but Johnny ignores him. "The only thing that will test you is trying to work with this *haole* over here."

"Yeah, yeah," Charlie says, heading over to the fridge and rummaging for something. He looks totally different now that he's in his white uniform. I always found that the uniform gives an air of respectability to anyone, even someone known for not wearing shoes. And to be safe, I look down and notice the skate shoes he's got on. Not exactly good protection if he drops something on it but good enough for Hawaii.

"Any questions?" Johnny asks me.

I raise a brow. "Um. I have a ton of questions."

"Let's hear it. I've got a few minutes before I have to get back to work. I keep myself on a tight shift."

I wonder if that's true after the comment that Logan made about him being all relaxed but I realize that I can't exactly take Logan's word for a lot of things.

"Well, for one … what's the menu? Who are the suppliers and how often do we get stuff in? Who handles that? Do we have a bartender? Who are the wait staff? Dishwasher? Is the menu always set or does it change from day to day? Do we do special events and if so, how do we handle those on top of the restaurant, considering there are only three of us."

Johnny is staring at me so blankly that I'm afraid he hasn't heard me.

Finally, he nods. "Okay. I think I may need a beer after that one."

"Yes, beer please," Charlie says, not looking up.

I want to ask if drinking on the job is a regular thing but I don't dare. I've already shaken things up enough with my suggestions, I won't be asking them to change how they work today.

Johnny raises his hand and starts ticking off the answers on each finger. "The menu is posted on the wall behind, changes are seasonal. If we sell out of something, then we're out of it and it's crossed off the menu. We have a local fisherman supplier for all the fish, and we use another supplier for a lot of the local vegetables and meat. Yes, we have a bartender. Daniel. He's also a real estate agent so he's going to try and sell you a condo, just warning you. May also try and get in your pants." Johnny glances at the clock over my head. "He'll be here soon. On Sunday's we open at six, which is in an hour, in case you're still on Chicago time, rest of the week we open at five. We stop serving at ten, though we tend to prepare a few pupus ahead of time on the weekend, for people drinking at the bar."

"Pupus?" I repeat.

He grins. "Yes. It means, like, tapas. Appetizers. Pupus are our selling point here. Lot's of variety and easy to prepare. People love pupus."

"We even have a tee shirt that says 'People Love Our Pupus,'" Charlie says with a laugh. "Which reminds me, we need to order some more in. Honestly there isn't a pupu joke that doesn't make me laugh."

"Aye," Johnny says. "Get Kate to do that. Anyway, where was I? Oh yeah. Pupus and fresh fish is what we're known for, and a lot of our food has a Mediterranean slant to it. You know, meze platters and all that. Cheap to make, the health nuts love it. What else? Ah, Nikki. She's our waitress. She works every week night. Kate will run food if it's really busy, which usually means Logan takes over reception. I know he sounded like he's large and in charge with the kitchen but that's his ego talking. I'm the large one here," he says, poking his thumb into his chest, "and I'm in charge. Logan doesn't step in here all that much, except to drink sometimes with Daniel, and frankly it makes the kitchen one of the best places to work at Moonwater."

"Sounds like it. Who waitresses on weekends?"

"There are a few local girls, one in Hanalei, one in Haena. They're great for back-up too."

"Hey guys," a man's voice breaks in, the accent high and lilting. "And Ms. Locke."

I turn to see Jin coming in, grabbing an apron off a rack and tying it behind his back.

"And Jin," Johnny says. "He's the dishwasher."

"It's a fascinating job," Jin says dryly, giving me a kind smile to let me know he doesn't really mind at all.

"He's the backbone of our operation," Johnny says. "And when he's not washing dishes, he's the hotel maintenance man. And sometimes the shuttle bus driver."

I laugh lightly. "I'm starting to think that everyone here is a shuttle bus driver at some point."

"Except me," Charlie says.

"Because you took the bus to Hanalei beach and gave rides home to the surfer chicks," Johnny points out.

"That was one time," Charlie protests.

Johnny rolls his eyes. "Useless, I tell ya."

After that I stay in the kitchen until the customers start coming into the restaurant. Just enough to observe how things are going without feeling like I'm inspecting them or getting in the way.

They have the music going on the radio, something with a ukulele and a soft singing voice akin to Jack Johnson, and all three of them seem to really enjoy their job. I can see how seriously Johnny takes his food, which is a relief, but he's also all smiles and easy-going, which is also a relief. Your job is only as good as the company you keep in it.

When I've watched enough, I leave, the jetlag seeming to hit me again. Even though I swore I'd try and stay up late, it's only seven pm and I can barely stand on my own two feet. I wave goodbye to Johnny, Jin, and Charlie and take a quick peek out at the floor. Just as I thought, about half the restaurant is occupied. I spot Nikki, the waitress, with her long highlighted hair, bustling about and Daniel, the bartender, a guy in his early-thirties with hair pulled back in a ponytail and a loud Hawaiian shirt, but save my introductions for tomorrow.

By the time I step outside, I'm met with a wall of humidity, darkness, and the thick hum of crickets. I walk slowly across the parking lot, my eyes closing momentarily as I breathe in deep, the smell of the ocean, the flowers, the everything. In some ways I feel ready for this next adventure, in other ways I'm a total fish out of water.

It takes me a few moments to remember where my new home is and I head to reception, remembering that Logan had a few papers for me to sign.

The doors to the office are closed but the light is on. I carefully open them and peer inside. Kate is at the desk, shuffling through papers, her dark hair falling over her shoulders. She doesn't glance up as she says, "So how was your first day?" she asks, her voice monotone.

"A whirlwind," I tell her. "How long is your shift?"

"Too long," she says. She looks at me. "I normally do seven am to three pm but Logan wanted the afternoon and evening off and he's the boss so whatever. As long as I get my overtime, I'm cool with it."

I'm trying to think of something else to say—there's a lot to say, yet I feel like it's crucial I say the right thing. I want Kate to like me. If I'm going to be living with her, this is one relationship I need to start off on the right foot.

"So how late do you have to work tonight?" I ask. "Because don't worry about me when you come in, I'm jet-lagged like hell. I'll sleep through anything."

"Until eleven, and then Shannon, our night shift, takes over," she says and I swear she smiles. "I'll try to keep it down. By the way, Logan has these for you." She grabs a stack of papers from the corner of the teak desk and holds them out for me. A keycard is kept under her thumb. "The keycard is yours. Opens, your room, the pool, maintenance areas, and housekeeping, as well as reception. You'll get separate restaurant keys tomorrow."

"I thought he was going to go over these with me?" I ask, coming over to take them from her. "This is my contract right?" I flip through the pages.

She shrugs. "Just read it. He went to Hanalei so he'll probably be coming back late."

"What does he do in Hanalei?" I ask. I have a sudden flash that he's there because of a girlfriend, maybe the same one he cheated on my sister with. The rage that boils through me gets caught in my throat.

"He drinks," she says. "Goes to Tahiti Nui. It's his bar. Well, aside from here, it's everyone's bar. I'll be sure to take you on a Logan-free day." She pauses. "The two of you aren't very close, are you?"

I shake my head. "He was with my sister in Chicago for a year before they got married. The minute they did though, and the hotel took off, they were pretty much living here. I've only seen him on a handful of occasions since then."

She seems to think that over with an air of disbelief. Finally she nods. "Well I suppose in-laws are complicated. I can't stand my sister-in-law. Thank god she lives back home. In San Francisco."

Ah, another *haole*, like me and Charlie.

I want to keep talking to Kate, shoot the shit, maybe get more information on Logan. But my tongue feels fuzzy, my head is swimming.

"I'll see you tomorrow," I tell her, waving the papers at her. "Thanks."

The unit is only a few steps from the reception building, so it's a matter of seconds until I'm waving the keycard in front of the door and stepping inside.

The wood fans whir overhead, and it's only then that I notice there is no air-conditioning in here, and no television or phone either.

It doesn't matter. The minute I open the balcony doors, keeping the screen closed, and the ocean breeze comes wafting in, I hit the bed.

I fall asleep with my clothes on.

CHAPTER FIVE

'M DREAMING.

I have to be.

I'm hiking through a jungle in the dark. Only a sliver of moonlight is breaking through the tops of the canopies, illuminating the leaf-strewn floor in cuts of silver and white.

I'm barefoot, in shorts and a tank top. The air is rich, as warm as an embrace.

I'm alone.

At least I think I am. I keep hearing a soft breath at my back, but I can't turn around. My dream holds me captive, makes my limbs feel like lead. I can only move forward on the dark and twisting trail, while the presence behind me gets closer and closer.

I can feel the heat of the person, the man, at my back. As I walk, the mud squishing between my toes, branches reach out and caress my skin, as tender as a lover's hands.

The path rises until the trees drop away and I am on the top of a razor-backed ridge. The world seems to fall away, leaving no distance between me and the stars, the ocean a blanket at my feet.

The back of my neck tingles as the heat intensifies.

I suck in my breath with a startled gasp as hot breath skirts over my skin.

The man is behind me. I can't see him but I can feel him.

I can feel all of him.

He presses himself against me, slowly, deliberately, as his hands wrap around my elbows, holding me back. His erection is hard against the top of my ass, and even though I'm dreaming, I'm calculating how tall he must be. His grip is strong, everything about him radiates strength.

He doesn't talk—he doesn't need to.

This is a man I know, a man who belongs to me. He can do whatever he wants and I want him to do whatever he can.

I close my eyes as one of his hands lets go of my elbow and roughly moves up to my hair. He makes a tight fist, yanking my head to the side, exposing my neck. His lips are both hard and soft as they press against my skin, his teeth nipping gently.

I want him harder and the response is automatic. He bites my neck, hard enough for pain to wash over me, the hand in my hair yanking me back, pulling at the strands. It's a sharp ache and I want more of it. He pushes further against me and his breath is hot and ragged at my ear, like some kind of primal beast.

I'm going to give it to you hard, so fucking hard, his voice says, sliding inside my brain, a voice I feel more than hear.

Starting now.

Suddenly I'm on my knees, sinking into the mud. My shorts are slipped down over my ass, my head is pushed forward until I have to put my hands out to brace myself.

He lowers himself behind me. The heat of his body is unbearable. I know he's naked, that he's just inches from my ass. I want to twist around and see him in all his glory, stare at his cock, take it all in, but I can't turn. I can't do anything but wriggle in anticipation. The moon starts to glow purple, pulsing like the heat between my legs.

How long have you wanted me? He asks gruffly, the accent fading in and out. *How long have you dreamed of this?*

How long have you? I want to ask but my mouth doesn't move, and I'm not sure if my thoughts reach him as his reach me. Every inch of me is coiled in waiting and it's then I know that as I sleep, my body in my bed is just as tensed up.

A rough hand glides over my ass before smacking it. One cheek. The other.

Crack.

CRACK.

His fingers glide down over the raw skin, down to where I'm wet and open.

They slide in with ease and I let out a moan, arching my back, wanting more.

So much more.

You may want to be quiet, he says as he reaches over and covers my mouth with his hand. *No one can know but us. It will only ever be between us.*

I don't want to listen to what he's saying. He's speaking truth and truth has no place in a dream.

In fact, I can feel it start to pull me out. Awareness trickles in at the corners of the frame.

I fight against it. Keep my eyes closed, willing myself to succumb back into the moment.

"Please," I manage to mutter against his hot palm.

How long have you wanted me? His voice is nearly a growl, rumbling inside my brain.

"Since the moment I met you."

Will you stay quiet?

I nod but his hand tightens over my mouth.

He leans forward until his lips are at my ear. His teeth graze my lobe.

It should have been you, Veronica.

I feel the hard tip of his cock sliding over my wetness.

Logan pulls back slightly and I brace myself for him to slam inside me.

But the dream fades away, the sensation falling off like rain.

I'm barely awake but I'm turned on as hell, my hand between my legs, that half-conscious state where you're aching to return to something your conscious mind would disown you over.

I drift off to sleep.

But I don't dream again.

"Hawaii lesson number one," a voice says, breaking into the inky darkness. For a moment I think I'm back in Chicago at my parent's house, snoozing in the guest bedroom and maybe I fell asleep with the radio on.

But then it all comes back to me. Hawaii.

The dream.

Logan.

I lick my lips and groan, my hands skimming over my body, everything damp. Dear lord, did I sweat my way through that sex dream?

"When you leave the door open all night, you'll wake up wet," the voice goes on.

I slowly open my eyes, blinking hard at the light.

"And that's not innuendo," the voice adds.

A shadow passes over me and Kate's face comes into focus.

Right. My new roommate.

Who looks like she wants to murder me.

"What?" I mumble and try to sit up, my head super swimmy. The light streaming in through the shades has this soft, airy quality to it, making me think it's early in the morning.

Kate puts her hands on her slender hips and jerks her head to the screen door. "You left the door open all night."

Did I? I barely remember doing anything. I mean I'm still wearing my clothes from yesterday. Thankfully. Because I half expected to wake up with my shorts half-off, my hand in my underwear.

"It was hot," I tell her, my throat parched.

"You'll get used to it," she says, strutting out of the room. She's wearing the tiniest boy shorts and I find myself both admiring her tiny, peach-shaped ass and envying it. No way I'm walking around like that. I have something called a booty and cellulite.

"But," she continues, her voice coming from the kitchen, "it's so hella humid here that everything will be soaked overnight. It will take days for our sheets to feel close to normal again."

I sit up and run my hands over them. She's right. They're almost sticky.

"Sorry," I tell her, feeling like a total boob. "Won't happen again."

"Oh I know. We always learn."

I sigh, swinging my feet over the edge of the bed.

"Coffee?" Kate asks, appearing back in front of me with a mug in hand. "Wasn't sure if you drank it or not but then I remember you're a chef. It's in your blood."

I manage a smile and tell her thanks as I take the mug, not bothering to correct her that I'm not quite a chef yet. I hope to god that whatever moaning I was doing in my dream I wasn't doing in real life. Jesus. What the hell was I doing having a sex dream about Logan anyway? I can practically still feel his breath at my back, the way he made me feel deep down in my soul, like I was finally submitting to something that had been denied to me for so long.

I shake my head.

"Jetlagged?" Kate asks. I look up to see her frowning at me.

"Oh. Well, yeah," I tell her, busying myself with a sip of my coffee. At least she knows how to make a decent pot. "What time is it?"

"Six thirty," she says. "Normally I wouldn't expect you to get up when I get up but I remember the first week I was here, dealing with the time change. My eyes were open like *bing!* Every morning at four am. It was great actually. Got in some morning surfs. There's nothing better."

"You surf?" I ask her, folding my legs under me into a cross-legged position, the damn sheets sticking to my skin.

She gives me a look of disbelief. "Yes. It's kind of what you do here."

"Is that why you moved here?"

She seems to think that over, tilting her head until her dark hair falls half across her face. "I thought it was. I honestly just wanted to live in paradise. I thought coming here would make my life a million times better."

"And did it?"

She gives me a look I can't read. "Maybe. A job is a job. A home is a home. Why not have both those things in a place like this?" She nods to the ocean.

"And love?"

She snorts, rolling her eyes. "You are far too deep for this time of day. No one comes to Hawaii looking for love, got it? Love of life, maybe. But men? Nah. I had better luck in San Francisco, believe it or not. It might not seem like it right now but an island is a small place. Just 60,000 people live on this island and there's no escape. Pretty sure I've dated everyone there is."

Now it's my turn to let out a snort. "Really?"

She manages a wry grin. "It feels like it, anyway."

"Anyone from here? Moonwater?"

She shrugs and turns away, walking back to the kitchen. "Maybe."

Maybe. Right. Well, I'm going to go ahead and assume that Charlie was one of them, just because the two of them are both very attractive young people with a similar approach to the opposite sex.

Then a terrible thought strikes me.

Logan.

Kate is so damn pretty, it would be extremely easy to imagine her and Logan together. Fuck. What if *she* was the other woman?

I try not to think about it. I have to tell myself that there would be no way that Kate would still be working here if that were the case. She seems to have some decency.

"Not that it's any of my business," Kate says from the kitchen. I can hear toast pop up in the toaster. "But what exactly brought you out here? I've seen your resume. I can't imagine that working at Moonwater is a step up for you."

I'm not sure how truthfully I want to answer. I give her my stock one, which is still the truth. "It's not easy finding a job in Chicago. The restaurant scene is highly competitive. I had to move back in with my parents and I was pretty much going crazy when this opportunity came up."

"Right," she says, coming back into view, munching on a piece of toast with avocado mashed on top. She leans casually against the wall. Still in her underwear. "So is Logan helping you out or are you helping Logan out?"

I swallow down the rest of the coffee. "Maybe a bit of both."

"Can I give you some advice?" she says. "You're helping Logan out. That's all you need to know. Never give him the upper hand."

I raise my brows, my grip tightening on the empty mug. "Personal experience?"

"We don't see eye to eye either. But I still like my job. I've learned to roll with it. And part of that reason is because I refuse to let him get under my skin. See…everyone liked working for Juliet. She was a lot more diplomatic than Logan. She was the one who dealt with the staff, not him. So when she…when she was gone, it was hard for all of us, and for Logan, to make that transition. It's still hard. But I don't put up with his shit. He's not doing me any favors; I'm doing him one. And that's really the only way to survive here."

Well I can pretty much rule out Logan and Kate ever getting together in that way. They seem just as incompatible as we do.

But slices of the dream cut into my vision. His lips at my neck, the feel of his fingers inside me, probing deep. The endless want that was seconds from being fulfilled.

Even though Kate can't see what I'm thinking, I look away, completely ashamed. I can't control my dreams but this is the absolute worst time to be thinking about it, when she's just mentioned Juliet.

"Hey," Kate says softly, bringing my attention back to her. "I know things are hella complicated for you. Just remember this isn't the be-all and end-all. If you don't like it here, you can quit. You hate the island, you can move. No one, not your family, not your resume, is holding you here. It's a big world and Kauai is a very tiny piece of the pie. You're in charge, you're in control and it's your life. No one else's. Right?"

I slowly nod. "Right," I say, managing a weak smile. Damn. It's this early in the morning and Kate already seems to know more than enough about me. I wonder if I'm that obvious or she's just that observant. Probably a little of both.

"Okay, I'm off to work," she says. "You know where to find me."

She gives a quick wave that reminds me of that monotone actress from *Parks and Rec*, and then disappears around the corner. The door shuts behind her.

I run her mini-pep talk through my head. She would be right if I were anyone else. I should be able to get a job back at home. I should be able to get a job anywhere.

But that's not the case at all. Moonwater Inn is the only place that I know didn't place a reference call, mainly because I never provided the information. And even if Logan did manage to scrounge up Erik's name and get a hold of him, it wouldn't matter the lies that Erik told him because, hey, I'm here aren't I?

To my parents, moving to Kauai and working at Moonwater seemed like the smart option. I'm not sure they realized that, short of starting my career all over again, it was the only option.

So as much as Kate says that I can do what I want, where I want, I really can't. Not when it comes to moving forward in my dreams.

It's Kauai or bust.

With that in mind, I get up and start getting ready for the day. If anything, one piece of her advice is ringing through my head.

Never give Logan the upper hand.

Even though I had gotten up early, I slowly ease into the day. I flip through my work contract, and though there's nothing strange about the way it reads, I still hesitate before I sign on the dotted line. When I do, I can't help but feel I made a deal with the devil. Overdramatic? Maybe. But if the devil came disguised as a handsome Australian man, I wouldn't be surprised.

I make myself more coffee and breakfast, stealing some of Kate's toast and a jar of pink guava spread, hoping she won't mind, and sit out on the balcony as the world outside slowly comes alive.

People are early risers here. I'm not sure if it's because everyone from North America has to be suffering some kind of jetlag, or they just want to get up early and seize the day, but it's not even eight a.m. and everyone seems to be heading to their cars, the beach, or the pool. I don't think Logan has fixed the heater yet, so I hope they know they're getting a rude awakening once they jump in.

As I watch the guests go to and fro, I can't help but

think about the contract, even though it's all signed and ready to be dropped off at reception for Logan. My mind, lulled by the rhythmic waves, then turns to Juliet, wondering what she'd think about this whole thing.

The funny thing is, if Juliet were still alive, I'm not sure she'd be all too enthused about me moving here to work at her hotel. After all, she spent four years running this place with Logan, and not once did she invite me to visit, let alone offer me a job. I mean, I knew she knew I was happy at Piccolo. But that was based on assumption. She never asked me if I was happy with my job or the way my career was going. I'm not sure if I'm good at faking happiness or what, but it's like the thought to check in with my well-being never crossed her mind.

Not that it surprises me. Juliet always had a lot on her plate with a million things to think about. Wondering about how her little sister was doing was always very low on her priority list.

Still, I'm thinking back to the time she came to Chicago alone and stayed with me. I always thought that was odd in its own way. Normally my parents were the default, not me. But she asked to stay at my tiny apartment and so she did. I was thrilled, naturally, since she never showed that kind of interest in me before, not really.

That was when she came clean about what Logan was doing to her—all the heartache brought on by his cheating and affairs. I felt strangely privileged that she was sharing all this with me, something that tainted her, something other than perfect. Even though she wasn't at fault, it meant that her marriage wasn't the happy one we all were led to believe.

I finish the rest of the toast, wiping the crumbs off of the contract. I bet if Juliet were still alive, I wouldn't be here.

I hate to think it, but if I hit a rough patch in my career and Moonwater was my only option and she knew that, I don't think she would have gone for it. It wouldn't have mattered what my mother told her or even Logan (there were a few rare occasions in the past where he stood up for me, but since he's such a dick now I tend not to think about them)—Juliet would have vetoed the whole situation.

Juliet always liked to keep me as separate from her life as possible. Even when growing up. She'd have secret clubs in her bedroom with her and her stuffed animals and dolls, meetings I wasn't allowed to attend. When she went out to play, she preferred to do it alone. Even when our mother would force us to play together on some days, she was always off in her own little world. Leaving me behind. Sometimes I chalked it up to the age difference between us, but even so there was always something a bit off about our relationship.

When we got older, the distance between us was magnified. She'd go out with her friends all the time. At the dinner table, she rarely spoke to me, let alone looked at me. The most I would get from her was a yearly Christmas and birthday gift, always something generic, nothing that ever hinted that she knew me at all.

And yet people thought the world of her. She was beautiful enough to be a model—and she did do some teenage modeling, something I was always deeply jealous of—yet smart enough to get scholarships. She was valedictorian and homecoming queen. She spent her Wednesday nights at a soup kitchen and she never got in trouble for anything, even though I knew she would go out drinking on the weekends. More than a few times I found pot or blotter paper in her bedroom when I was sneaking around to borrow one of her dirty books or find her secret diary (I was always empty-handed). I'm sure I found something that must have been cocaine once.

But I never brought it up with her—she would only deny it and my parents would never believe me. Besides, I didn't want to get her in trouble. As much as I envied her, I craved her attention. I wanted nothing more than for her to like me, to love me. The more distant and mysterious Juliet became to me, the more of her approval I craved.

And so here I am, sitting on a balcony in a tropical paradise, the sun breaking through the morning clouds and lighting up the ocean in dizzying rays of light, and I still need her approval. She's dead, gone forever, I'm not even sure I've started to properly grieve—and yet all I can think about is whether she would have wanted me to be here.

"Hey, sweet thing!"

Charlie's voice breaks through my thoughts. I get off my chair and peer over the edge. He's standing beneath the balcony, shirtless, his surfboard tucked under his arm.

I can't help but smile at him and his goofy charm, happy he's pulled me out of my thought spiral. "Hey!"

"I'm heading out to Hanalei. Fancy a morning surf?"

I shake my head, still horrified after what Logan told me about the ocean. "No way."

"You know I'm going to wear you down, right?"

"You know that ocean is waiting to kill me, right?"

He shrugs. "Whatever. It's what we have to tell newcomers so they don't go all crazy. You're safe with me. Come on, we have plenty of time before work."

"Maybe some other time," I say. "I'm just going to spend the day adjusting to everything. Take it easy."

"Suit yourself." He gives me a head nod and then walks toward the parking lot.

I sigh and head back inside, hoping that unpacking

my suitcases and putting things away will help me feel a bit more settled.

True to my word with Charlie, I take it easy for the rest of the morning. Once I'm unpacked, I head down to reception and drop off the forms for Logan. Kate's there but she says Logan isn't anywhere to be found. I'm relieved.

I decide to stroll around the grounds for a bit, taking in the surroundings and getting to know the area. I trace over the same route that Logan took me yesterday. It looks completely different this morning, maybe because the surf has died down a bit and the sun is coming through. The water sparkles a brilliant aquamarine and the breeze is soft, warm and fresh. I stand on the beach for a few minutes, letting the moment sink in, breathing that salty air deep into my lungs while the wind tosses my hair.

This is more like it. This is the paradise that everyone waxes on about. Yesterday with Logan, I didn't have a proper chance to enjoy it, let it soak in. I was too preoccupied with him, the way he was watching me, whether I was saying the right things or not. Everything had an ominous tone to it that seems to have been swept away overnight.

I round the curve of the beach, trying not to peer up at the guests on their oceanfront balconies, and stroll past the restaurant, glancing in the salt-sprayed windows as I go. It's dark inside, not open for lunch, and my stomach rumbles. Kate had mentioned that we could do a trip to the grocery store after her shift ended, but until then there's nothing much but a few pastries at the café and a juice and fruit truck down by Haena Beach. Apparently if I just follow the beach for another twenty minutes I'll come to it.

Of course twenty minutes to Kate is at least a half hour by my standards. She seems to be in incredible shape, while walking in sand has tired me out after no time. By the time

I reach the food truck in the Haena Beach parking lot, I'm dripping with sweat and winded.

That's not to say it wasn't the most stunning walk I've ever been on. The beach that leads away from Moonwater Inn eventually turns into Tunnels Beach, the island's best snorkeling spot, and then busy Haena. At the ocean's edge, beach houses stake their claim for best view. As you walk you head straight toward the lush green mountain peaks of the Na Pali Coast, made even more dramatic by the passing wisps of clouds. It's all so close you truly feel you're in the shadow of something otherworldly as your eyes pick up every wild detail of the sharp cliffs and valleys. Then there's the golden-white sand beneath your feet and the crystal-clear water as it slips past the outer reefs, lapping gently at the shore. Everything here is vying for your attention, daring you to look away.

There are people everywhere, for sure, but it's nowhere near as crowded as the beaches of Lake Michigan during the height of summer. There's just enough of a crowd so you don't feel so alone. The island feels so inherently wild, like it's a beast floating at the edge of infinity, that you almost crave the company around you.

After I get my fresh slices of mango and coconut, I eat them sitting on the beach, watching surfers play in the waves, until my phone rings.

Surprised I even get reception here, I fish it out. It's my friend Claire, wanting to Facetime.

I answer it. "Hey!"

"Hey Ronnie," Claire says. "I had to check in. How are things? You were supposed to text me, you loser."

Staring at my friend's cherubic face brings a pang of loneliness to my heart. I've never Facetimed her before. I never had a reason to—she always lived down the street from me. Now that I'm staring at her, in what looks like her apartment, probably having just finished work, I'm aware that this is the only way I'll be able to see her for the next while.

"I texted you when I landed," I protest. "And I sent you that picture of the chicken. Do you want more? I've got chickens all around me." And it's true. A group of hens are a few feet away, scratching at the sand and eyeing my fruit.

She giggles, brushing her brown hair out of her eyes. "Look, the next time you send me a picture of a cock, I hope it's not of the feathered variety." I roll my eyes. "Besides, telling me you've safely landed is not texting me. You were supposed to fill me in." Pause. "How's Logan?"

"Fine," I say dismissively. "Hey, look where I am." I bring the phone up and slowly bring it around me in a circle, aiming at the scenery.

"Seriously?" Claire's voice crackles until I bring the phone back to me. "And you said you didn't want to go."

"I didn't!" I tell her. "And I still don't want to be here."

Claire is the only person who knows the truth about everything. She knows how Logan and I met. She knows that he cheated on Juliet with God knows who. She knows why I was fired from my last job. She knows that I had no choice but to come out here. She knows everything. Yet another reason why I'm already missing her.

"Well I'm sure waking up to paradise every day will eventually start to wear your cynicism down."

"Cynicism?"

"You know what I mean, Ron. It could be worse. Everything can always be worse."

That's the other thing about Claire. She takes no crap. That might be why I like Kate, they're both similar in that way. There's only so much "boo hoo I'm moving to Hawaii"

Claire can handle, even if she knows the truth.

"Right," I say. "Well anyway, now you get to come with me on my walk back to the hotel. If the reception cuts out I'll try and call you back later. There's no TV or landlines at the hotel you know, but at least the internet somewhat works."

"I think that's charming. Makes you get out there and enjoy the outdoors. How is the hotel anyway?"

I explain to her the gist of it all, from the layout and the restaurant to the sleeping arrangements and the staff.

"So it wasn't weird when you saw Logan?"

I swallow, wishing she wasn't staring at my face and studying it. Fuck Facetime. "Um, well it was weird. Yeah."

"Did you talk about Juliet?" she asks softly. Claire always softens her voice when she mentions her name. I think it's because she's still not sure how I'm going to react.

"In passing," I say, then cringe at the poor choice of words. "I mean, she came up but indirectly."

"Did you see where … it happened? The crash site?"

That was one of the things I was trying not to look for. I knew it happened near the hotel but I wasn't sure where. "I closed my eyes for some of the ride over," I admit. "I don't know if I passed it or not. I'm not sure I want to see it, actually."

"Fair enough. God, sorry Ron. I can't imagine how hard it must be for you now that you're finally there."

Claire knows I was never close with my sister but she also knows how badly I wanted to be. How I lost that chance for good.

"Yeah well, I'm just going to take it day by day. Everyone here talks about Juliet like, well, like everyone else does at home. So I suppose that's a good thing. She wasn't just this amazing person in Chicago, she was the same amazing person here."

Claire falls silent, her brows furrowing as she thinks that over. "Are you going to talk to Logan about what you know?" she finally asks.

I sigh, looking up from the phone just as I round the bend and see the hotel creep into sight.

"I don't see the point," I tell her. "What's done is done."

"Well it might clue him into why you hate him so much."

"I'm sure he knows why. I don't have to say anything. He knows what he did. And he's probably always known that Juliet told me. That's why he's been a dick ever since then."

"Are you sure he hasn't been a dick because you've been a dick?"

I glare at her, hoping it comes through the screen. "Claire," I warn her before switching the subject. I start showing her the hotel as I get closer and eventually we end the phone call with me sitting out on the beach, right in front of the restaurant.

"I better go," she says. "Break a leg tonight."

I can't help but yawn, a wave of fatigue washing over me. Maybe such a strenuous walk wasn't the best idea when jetlagged and on minimal food. I'm used to eating a lot more than this.

"Break a leg," I scoff. "You know how many times that's nearly happened to me in the kitchen? Wet floors are no joke."

She laughs. "Then bring a mop. I love you. Talk to you later."

"Love you," I tell her, my words coming out almost in a whisper as the connection is severed.

Even though I know I'll get sand everywhere, I lay back

on the beach, my phone resting on my chest.

I'd met Claire back in culinary school. She had been just like me, a bright young thing with dreams of being the next cooking superstar. But Claire's talent for cooking only ran so deep and she was easily discouraged. She dropped out before it was over, even though it all worked out for the better. While I stayed with the program, she went on to combine the little experience she had with her love of wine. She's now a sommelier at one of the better wine stores in town and has her eyes on opening a vineyard in the future. As hard as it was to leave my best friend, I know she would eventually do the same to me one day. The woman belongs on a vineyard in Chile somewhere, living out her dream.

I close my eyes and take in a deep breath through my nose, willing the sweet, sultry air and steady crash of waves to calm my heart.

CHAPTER SIX

I'S NOT LONG BEFORE I'VE FALLEN ASLEEP, AND ONCE again I know I'm dreaming. My lucidness has been working overtime since I got here.

But my dream isn't a new scenario like the sex dream I had about Logan. It still features him, but it's set in the past, in a real event.

The Christmas we all spent together. The one the first year they were together, before they were married, before they moved to Kauai. The hotel was in the final stages of takeover and Logan was spending more and more time in Hawaii, but we were all together for the holidays.

In reality, Christmas was held at my parents' house. It always was. My mother always went way out—and by that, I mean she hired the same decorator every year to make our home look like a Christmas wonderland. Then the news channels and newspaper reporters would come by and do a yearly special on our place. Christmas in my family wasn't really about family—it was about showing off.

And Janice, our decorator, was a fixture around the holidays, popping in a few times a week between Thanksgiving and Christmas Day to add some touches. From the time my mom entered politics, when I was around seven years old, Christmas has always been the largest event of the year. But even as a kid, I could tell something was off. I was the envy of children at school and yet I envied after their tales of Christmas Eve when one of their parents dressed up as Santa, or the ritual of leaving out milk and cookies, or the next morning, ripping into their presents. I always got far more than them, sometimes as many as one hundred presents, which looking back now, was a disgusting waste of wealth. I would have rather gotten one or two gifts that had meaning and love behind them. Some parents underestimate how simple kids really are—love, unconditional and ongoing, is really all we need.

So with that in mind, Christmas was always a cold, joyless time.

In my dream, it was no different. Janice was there, as were my parents, Logan, Juliet, and myself. But instead of being in their house, it was held at my apartment. All of us were crammed in around my tiny kitchen table that Janice had decorated with fake snow. All of us were covered in it, white streaks down our faces. There was a Christmas tree in the corner but it was a palm tree, its fronds stretching out over the ceiling.

But even though the setting was different, everything else was the same.

My father, with his pinched nose and stern mouth, his grey suits and burgundy ties (always the same, my mother wouldn't let him try another color), barely said two words, my mother dominating most of the conversation. Her face was doing that weird thing where sometimes she looked like Juliet and sometimes she looked like herself, always interchanging, but the conversation was word for word.

I know because I've never forgotten it.

Juliet asked for my father to pass her the bottle of red wine, wanting to top off her glass.

"No, darling," my mother had said with that politician's smile. "One glass is your limit these days."

"Why?" I asked. Juliet loved wine.

Juliet and Logan exchanged a glance. My mother gave me a placating smile. "Because your sister is going to be married in the spring. As soon as it's official, I expect they'll be trying for a child. The last thing we want is a tainted child in this family. Juliet's diet will be very strict. Mothers have to start months in advance to rid their bodies of all impurities."

None of this was surprising to me. I had figured that they'd start having kids after getting married. Even so, there was something in my mother's tone, some kind of pride that hinted that the conversation wasn't over.

And it wasn't.

"Oh," I'd said and motioned for the bottle. If she wasn't drinking it, I was going to.

As my father passed it over, my mother eyed it with disdain. "You know, Veronica," my mother said, brushing back her blonde bangs from her face, "it would be nice if you followed in your sister's footsteps. Found a man. Started getting things lined up. Your future. You're not getting any younger. Your sister is already pressing her luck."

The whole table went silent. What she said was never news to me. There'd always been talk about me trying to measure up to Juliet, to become just like her. But this was the first she'd mentioned it on such a personal level and in front of everyone, including Logan.

I busied myself with the wine while I thought of what to say. Something light to throw the whole conversation away. "Well, we can't all be Juliet." I even gave my sister a wink, to let her know I didn't mean any harm by it.

And Juliet laughed. "No, you certainly can't," she said and she looked to my mother with a look of wry disbelief. "Mom, you know Veronica is going to end up one of those crazy cat ladies when she grows up. She has zero time for men."

That startled me. "Cat lady? I don't even like cats."

"Oh relax," Juliet said with a wicked laugh. "You're always overreacting to everything I say. You should learn to take a joke. Maybe you won't have a bunch of cats, but if you keep going at this rate, it's just going to be you surrounded by plates of food. I'm all for taking your career seriously, but after a while you should probably start exploring your options."

"See, that's what I mean," my mother said, jumping in. "You need to smile more. Become more diplomatic. More open. You won't ever attract a man, the right man, if you don't try and make yourself a little…nicer."

"We care about you," Juliet quickly added. "We don't want to see you unhappy and alone."

I was stunned in real life and I was as stunned in the dream. I still didn't have a good comeback. I just stared up at the ceiling which turned into clouds, snow falling into my eyes.

"I don't think Veronica has anything to worry about," Logan said, speaking up, wiping the falling snow from his arms. I looked at him in surprise. He rarely said anything in these situations, often letting my mother and Juliet dominate. He gave me a light, quick smile, even though his eyes were burning with something more grave. It was hidden just beneath the surface, like he was angered by all of this. "In a few years she'll have her own damn cooking show. I mean look at her. She'd be perfect for it. I know I'd tune in."

Then he scooped mashed potatoes into his mouth, averting his eyes away from mine.

Damn. Logan had just gone to bat for me.

Silence fell over the table again. Finally, my father spoke up, "That's not a bad idea, Logan. Ronnie, there's a new goal for you. You could be the next Nigella Lawson or, what's that woman's name? The skinnier version of her? Either way, it's better than working as an ordinary cook."

And just like that, the conversation was dropped. I know my mother wanted to point out that if anyone should be on TV, it should be Juliet, but she didn't. I'm also sure that was the first moment that really cemented in my mother's mind that Logan was the enemy.

And he was marrying her precious daughter.

Then the dream melded into other dreams. Colorful flying chickens swooping down mountainsides, plates of ahi tuna, swimming in a pool full of floating luggage. Everything drifting off into blissful nonsense.

Dreams upon dreams upon dreams.

"What the hell are you doing, beach bum?"

My eyes spring open at the sound of the Australian accent, my heart quick to start hammering away in my chest.

Logan is standing over me, arms crossed. The sun is at

his back, his face filled with shadows.

Shit.

I sit up and look around, my head foggy, like it's filled with water and sand. I'm still on the beach but the sun is in a lower position than it was earlier. "What time is it?" I manage to croak. Fragments of my dream come back to me, making me even more confused.

Logan just stares at me. I can feel his eyes burning into mine, even if they're barely visible in the shadows of his face. "What time is it? Time for you to start work, beach bum."

No way. Is it seriously four o' clock already? I blink and rub my eyes, trying to wake up.

"You know, I expected more from you," he says gruffly, "but something tells me you're all talk."

I can't help but glare at him as I quickly get to my feet, wiping off the sand angrily. "It was an accident. I fell asleep."

He moves to the left and I can see his face more clearly. His eyes are narrowed, the line deep between his furrowed brows. He's mad, and while I enjoy pissing him off, I don't like doing it when it comes to my job. "You know what we call people who fall asleep on the beach when they're supposed to be working?" he asks. It's then that I notice he has a damn apron scrunched up in his hand.

"Let me guess, a beach bum?"

He frowns. "You got it. Now hurry up. Don't bother changing, just get the apron on and get to work."

He throws it at me and stalks off down the beach and back to the hotel.

I throw up my middle finger at him, hoping he can feel it at his back, before I quickly hurry around to the restaurant and inside, tying my apron over my tank top as I go.

"There you are," Johnny says as I burst inside the

kitchen.

"Sorry, sorry," I say to him and Charlie, who is already chopping vegetables. "I fell asleep on the beach. Do you have a chef shirt I can borrow?"

"You can't cook like that?" Charlie asks.

I give him an odd look. "Not if I want potential burns all over my arms."

"Look, go back to your room and get changed, no big deal," Johnny says.

"And let Logan catch me? No way. I've already made him think I'm a shitty employee."

"Phhfff, that's how he thinks of all of us. You'll get used to it. Here." Charlie fishes something out of a cloth bag hanging on the wall and gives it to me. "This should be yours anyway."

I hold it up. It's rather large and says Moonwater Inn across it in the same tiki style as the hotel's sign. It's a cheap shirt but it will do.

"It ain't the pupu shirt," Charlie explains as I slip it on under the apron, "but it's something."

"Did Logan come in here looking for me?" I ask.

Johnny nods. "Aye. Said he wanted to see how you were starting out."

I eye the clock on the wall. Technically I'm only ten minutes late.

"Though we both know he was spying on you," Charlie adds. "Like he wants a reason to be mad."

I sigh. "Story of my life. It's too late now, I signed that damn contract. He's stuck with me. Anyway, enough about that." I clap my hands together, walking over to Johnny. "Get me up to speed. I need my first day to go well."

And, with the help of Johnny, Charlie, and Jin, it some-how does go well. Obviously there's a learning curve—the kitchen at Ohana Lounge is light years different from the one at Piccolo. Not saying one is better or worse, but the way I'm used to doing things doesn't necessarily work here. Everything is a lot more relaxed and laid back, to the point where it grates on my nerves a bit, and despite Johnny having the title of head cook, all the roles in the kitchen are shared equally.

That's probably my favorite thing about it all—the lack of ego. At Piccolo there was a hierarchy you could never stray from. Here, I really feel like we're working together as a team, an "us versus them" mentality. We want the restaurant as a whole to succeed, we want the hotel to succeed, we want the customers happy, we want ourselves to be happy.

Of course that doesn't mean I didn't screw up a few times. Some of the fish I'd never cooked before, let alone seen, so I overdid it on the Opah and Wahoo more than once (yes, those are the actual names) and I was so flustered when I made the papaya dressing for the salad that I forgot to put the lid on the blender. Suffice to say, all of us were were covered in yellow goo by the time the shift was over.

But I survived. The customers seemed happy and the food tasted great. I just wish that Logan had come by at least once to see me in action, to realize that I pulled through after all. Beach bum or not, I'm a damn good cook and he should be happy he hired me.

Instead, while Jin finished up with the pots and pans, the rest of us moseyed on over to the bar to have a drink with Daniel and Nikki. It was my first time officially meeting them.

Verdict is: Daniel the bartender, with his curly hair pulled back into a ponytail, his Hawaiian shirt, cheesy grin and the way he hands out his realtor business card like he's a quick draw in a Western, is the type to try and get in your pants. And Nikki, though frazzled from a busy night, is your quintessential waitress—sweet, talkative, and pretty, a combination that I'm sure leads to the perfect tips.

All in all, as the five of us sit at the bar and sip some beers, there's an easy sense of camaraderie. There's a bit of sexual tension between Nikki and Daniel…and Nikki and Charlie, for that matter, but that's to be expected. From what I've seen, seems like everyone gets along here like a big happy family.

"So the boys tell me you're Juliet's sister," Nikki says, her voice still bright, which I appreciate. Somehow it always makes things worse when people lower their voice, like they're ashamed or afraid to mention her name.

I nod, slowly twirling the beer around in my hand, studying the Hawaiian-style art on the bottle. "Yup."

"But this is your first time out here?" she asks.

I clear my throat. "I never really got around to visiting. You know how it is. Work kept me busy. And it seemed that Juliet and Logan were too busy running this place."

A silence falls over us, punctuated by the roar of the ocean. Daniel clears his throat. "How about we all do a shot in honor of your lovely sister." Before I can say anything, he's turning around and pulling out a bottle of Koloa Rum and several shot glasses.

He pours us each one, sliding them toward us. He picks up his and says, "Here's to Juliet. We miss her dearly."

"Here, here," we all say before shooting back the coconut rum. It burns pleasantly on the way down, immediately washing away the day's stress. I have another drink after that as the group starts chatting about the surf report and future hiking endeavors, but I'm starting to tune them out. Despite my long beach nap that afternoon, I'm beyond exhausted.

As I leave the bar and walk through the parking lot to the hotel, the crickets chirping, the waves breaking on the shore, I take in a deep breath of the soft, warm air, exhaling slowly. I did it. My first day here and I did it. I'm almost giddy with relief that I survived and it was nowhere near as bad as my worrisome heart made it out to be.

Then I see Logan disappearing into the reception, shutting the door behind him. If he saw me at all, he didn't show it.

Shit.

As well as the rest of my shift went, Logan missed all of it. He was only there to see me literally sleeping on the job.

What was one of the things Kate had told me that morning? Never give Logan the upper hand.

Moonwater Inn—Veronica 0, Logan 1.

I sigh and head up to the stairs to my unit. Better luck tomorrow.

CHAPTER SEVEN

"**N**ICE BUM, WHERE YOU FROM?"

I glare at Charlie over my shoulder and resist the urge to pull down my bikini bottoms. I knew I should have worn my board shorts, but they were still damp from yesterday. At least I've got a tank top on to protect me against board rash, which is no joke.

It's been two weeks since I first landed on Kauai, and this is surf lesson number two. The first one Charlie gave me was on the smooth waves of Hanalei Bay. He spent about an hour just going over the basics of the board, including form and posture, all while on the beach. The following hour was spent in the water, with me bailing on every single wave I attempted to ride.

That was a few days ago. Today we don't have as much time so we're hitting up the beach just to the side of the hotel. There's a narrow patch where the sand stretches out and the reef is set back far from the shore. Today the waves are coming in mild, rolling swells that can't be more than two feet high.

To anyone else they would be children's waves—and not even that. When we were at Hanalei, I was getting schooled by six-year-olds who could take the waves better than I could. But to me, they are just big enough. Even though I'd played it cautious with the ocean the last two weeks, it still makes me nervous.

I've got my own board now, tucked under my arm. It's a longboard, since they're easier to learn on and even though it's bruised and battered—Charlie says he reserves it for the timid learners—I've already formed a strange attachment to it. When we're out there, it's the only thing to keep me from sinking.

Charlie follows me into the water—I struggle a bit at the break—until my toes barely touch the bottom and he holds the board while I climb on.

"Okay," he says, letting go and moving away. I get myself into position, lying flat on it with my hands in the push up position, my toes pressed down against the board. "Don't look behind you, just look forward. You see that gnarly looking tree on the shore between the palms? That's an ironwood tree. Keep your focus there."

"When do I stand up?" I ask him nervously. I hate the feel of the ocean at my back, hate the fact that he lets go so soon. Even though the water is somewhat calm today, I still get the fear of an unseen rip coming underneath me and taking me and the board far out to where no one can reach me.

Not to mention sharks. They're real and I try my hardest not to think about them.

"You'll know," he says.

Right. Like the ocean is whispering its fucking secrets to me. I'm not Ariel!

"Not these waves," he says, "next ones."

I feel the board rise up, the sun filtering through the water and turning it a glowing aquamarine. It's not that deep here, and with the water so clear I can see the sandy bottom interspersed with the occasional rock that catches my eye. Is that a fish? Something worse?

"Focus on the tree!" Charlie says and out of the corner of my vision I see him treading water, being taken in closer to the shore with each pass of the waves.

I take in a deep breath and steady myself.

"Now!" Charlie yells. "Paddle, paddle, paddle!"

I stick my hands in the water and start moving them as fast as I can, which isn't very fast. I can beat an egg a mile a minute, but this is a total body workout, my shoulders and triceps working overtime as I try and keep up with the wave.

"Up, up up!" Charlie's now yelling.

I'm not sure I agree. I'm ahead of the wave now but it doesn't feel right. Still, what the hell do I know? Unsteadily, I push myself up onto my knees, trying to keep my balance and do that final, terrifying step to my feet.

"Focus on the tree!"

My head snaps up but instead of seeing the tree like I should, I see Logan, walking along the beach and staring at us with a disapproving expression.

Great.

That's all it takes for me to completely lose my balance.

I tilt to the left and hit the water just as the wave crashes on top of me. I'm swirling, the water rushing past my ears, the sand sweeping over my face. The board goes in another direction, still dragged by the surf, the band tugging hard at my ankle until I'm sure it's going to snap.

I swim for the surface and burst through as the bottom scrapes against my knees and I'm swept up on the shore.

I quickly wipe my eyes with one hand as I stagger to my knees, the next wave crashing behind me, and pull out the giant wedgie from my butt with my other.

"Ron!" Charlie is yelling from behind me and I can hear him splashing to shore. "Are you okay?"

But I don't turn around. My eyes are glued to Logan's. He's standing right in front of me, the ocean licking the tops of his bare feet as they sink into the sand, staring down at me with an expression I can't read.

Then he sticks his hand out. "Here," he says and I hesitantly put my hand in his. He hauls me up to my feet, his hand gripping my elbow. "You better free your ankle before the next wave yanks you back."

I nod, my head dizzy, my sinuses full of salt water, and he steadies me while I lift up my ankle and quickly undo the Velcro strap. I wrap it a few times around my hand and pull the board in to me.

His hand on my elbow still remains, his grip warm and firm against my wet skin. This is the closest I've been to Logan in the last two weeks. Even though I've been working steadily, he's only come into the restaurant three times to check on how things are going. And by "check on," I mean look around and make a grunting sound. I can't tell if he's been impressed with my performance so far or the exact opposite. My caveman deciphering skills only go so far.

Other than that, we've both managed to avoid each other. Sometimes I'll catch him at the bar after work, but that's when I just head straight back to my room. Once or twice I've run into him on the grounds and he'll usually nod me his greeting. While I've managed to slip into a nice, gentle routine with my days here, and have gotten to know the staff pretty well at this point thanks to Moonwater's camp-like vibes, Logan and I haven't grown any closer.

That's probably a good thing, I remind myself, eyeing his hand until it drops away.

"That was quite the wipeout," Charlie says with a laugh as he comes up toward me, dragging the rest of my board on the beach. "You need to work on your reflexes a bit more."

I open my mouth to say something but Logan is beating me to it.

"Don't blame all that on her reflexes," Logan says, raising his chin as he peers down at Charlie. "She's not the problem. You're the problem."

Charlie's scoffs, annoyed, and runs his hand through his hair. "Me? Dude, no offense, but you know I'm one of the best on the north shore."

"Sure you are, kid," Logan says. "Why don't you run along. I've got a shuttle bus full of people who want to head to Princeville in the next ten minutes. I'll take over from here."

Wait, what?

"What?" Charlie asks, obviously as taken aback as I am. "*You're* going to teach her?" Charlie glances uneasily at me and I give him a pleading look that says *help me, Jesus*.

"That's right," Logan says smoothly, folding his arms across his chest. "By the time you come back, she'll be a bloody Gidget."

I'm not even sure who—or what—a bloody Gidget is, but I have a feeling it involves me learning how to surf in a short amount of time.

"Seriously Shephard?" Charlie asks.

Logan jerks his head back to the hotel. "Bosses orders, mate. Get going."

I half expect Charlie to stand his ground, but he folds quickly, grumbling as he marches off to the hotel like a petulant child.

"You don't have to teach me," I quickly tell Logan, trying to gather up my board. "I think I've had enough."

"Oh, I'm teaching you," he says gruffly. "The kid doesn't know shit; he's from Colorado. You need an Aussie to show you how things are really done on the water."

Then he takes a step back from me and before I know what's happening, he's pulling his shirt over his head and throwing it on the beach behind him.

Oh.

My.

God.

And Christ on a cracker.

Logan Shephard has his shirt off.

And Logan Shephard is absolutely *ripped*, a beast of epic proportions.

I mean, I knew he was tall and burly and his chest and shoulders were always hard to overlook under the tee shirts he's been wearing, but I guess I was doing my best these last two weeks to ignore all that because now that he's bare-chested in front of me, I feel all words and thoughts drain out of my brain.

All that is left is acute amazement and a coil of heat building in my core. And maybe a bit of drool coming out of the corner of my mouth. From the sharp Vs of his torso and the thin treasure-trail of hair leading from his stomach and disappearing beneath the band of his board shorts, to the six-pack abs and wide, firm chest speckled with chest hair, he has the kind of upper body some mythical hero would have (or Jason Momoa). Logan is all man and then some.

And he's staring at me with the cockiest smirk on his lips, dark brows raised. "Never seen a real man before?" he asks.

I glare at him. "You think pretty highly of yourself if you're calling yourself a man."

"Oh yeah? And what would you call me?"

"Something that belongs in a museum, next to the woolly mammoth exhibit."

To my surprise he laughs. It sounds strange coming from him, and yet causes my stomach to flip. "Fair enough, Freckles."

"Freckles?"

He nods at my nose where I know my freckles have sprouted up after the weeks in the sun. "I can call you something else."

"How about Ronnie?"

"All right. Let's go, Freckles. Forget everything Charlie taught you."

"That shouldn't be that hard," I mumble under my breath as Logan effortlessly takes the board from me and props it up over his head, carrying it into the surf.

"Hurry up," he says. "I don't have all day."

I run into the water after him, rolling my eyes, which keeps them from staring at his ass as the waves crash around him. I mean, just look at his *back*…it's a giant wall of rippled muscle, something you'd see Tom Cruise hanging off of by his fingertips.

Keep it together, I scold myself. *Remember who this is.*

And I do remember. No matter how juvenile my hormones are acting, he's still the man who belonged to my sister before he threw it all away.

I'm not sure if it's because having Logan out here with me is throwing my world upside down, but it seems like the waves have somehow gotten bigger in the last five minutes. I dive under the break, my head bursting through the surface.

"You're learning," he notes as the water streams off my face, the salt water burning my skin. He brings the board around. "Here, get on."

Oh boy. This is going to be a lot more awkward with him than it was with Charlie. With Charlie, I didn't mind the fact that he was face to face with my ass when I was climbing on and getting into position. Charlie and I have been pretty flirty, but I know it's not going anywhere. If anything, he's like a brother to me and whatever innuendo he throws my way, I'm quick to crush it.

Logan's staring at me with a mix of amusement and impatience as he keeps the board steady, the muscles on his arms taut. It's hard to believe the man is pushing forty with the way his damn body looks.

"Freckles," he warns, jerking his chin at the board.

I make a noise of disgust under my breath and quickly get on the board as gracefully as I can.

I fail at it. I'm half on, trying to pull myself over and my fucking bikini bottoms are sliding half off my ass by the time I manage to hook my leg over the edge. I let out a string of grunts and expletives before I'm on and I know my cheeks are going red because I can feel his gaze on my half-covered ass, lingering there.

"Need some help there, Beach Bum?" He sounds way too amused.

I practically growl while I reach back and yank the bottoms up. I'm throwing this goddamn bikini away after this.

"All right, let's get you into the line here," he says, moving me and the board forward until he stops, scanning the horizon behind him.

"Aren't you going to let go?" I ask.

He looks back at me, frowning. His eyes look extra luminous with the water reflecting against them. "I'm not letting go until you're ready."

So far this is already wildly different than the way Charlie was teaching me. He was more trial by error. Logan seems to want to take his time, which surprises me. I thought I would be the first person he would willingly chuck into the deep end.

"Okay," I manage to say, completely aware of his arm across the back of my legs as he holds the board.

"What's your favorite song?"

I frown, the water rising beneath me as another wave passes. "What?"

"Tell me what your favorite song is."

"What's your favorite song?" I can't help but fire back.

"'Purple Rain,'" he says without hesitation.

"Prince?"

"Do you know anyone else with the song 'Purple Rain?'"

"No," I admit. I guess I never pegged him as a Prince fan. "Must have been a tough year for you."

"Well I'm a Bowie fan too, so yeah. Bloody awful." He pauses and I feel him adjust the board, his arm brushing higher against the back of my legs. "Was a fan of your sister too, so the last couple of years have been pretty shitty when it comes to people I love dying."

Holy fuck. That was pretty much the last thing I expected him to say.

"So what's your favorite song," he goes on, like nothing has happened.

I lick my lips, trying to think. They taste like salt. "Uh. Led Zeppelin's 'Kashmir.'"

It was the first thing that popped into my head. My brain is still trying to reel over what he said about Juliet. He *loved* her. How could I even take that as truth?

Logan eyes me with a hint of approval. "Really? All right. Fine. Good choice. Now, start singing it."

"Excuse me?" I have the worst singing voice in the world. I don't even sing in the shower, since all it does is just amplify my horribleness.

"Start singing 'Kashmir.' Not in your head. Out loud."

"You are so fucking with me," I say, glaring at him over my shoulder. His face gives me nothing. "It's an eight-minute song! How long is this wave?"

"I promise it will help you surf."

"How? I'll be trying to remember the lyrics."

"If it's your favorite song, it will come automatically. And when it comes automatically, your mind is free to latch onto something else. Surfing. You'll relax, you'll stop overthinking. Not to mention there's a natural rhythm to the ocean and I promise you it will match up with the song."

That all sounds like complete bullshit.

"Are you ready?"

"What? No." I look behind me again to see the swells approaching.

"You're catching this next one," he says calmly. "I'm going to push you forward to give you momentum. Start paddling and start singing. Now!"

"At the intro of the song or—?"

"*Oh let the sun beat down upon my face,*" Logan starts singing loudly and hell, can this man sing. His impression of Robert Plant is eerily accurate. "Your turn!" he yells and I feel him start to push me through the water.

"Um, um," I say, paddling before I find the strength in my chest and croak out, "*Stars will fill my dreams.*"

"Feel the song, keep singing," he yells and let's go of the board. "Get to your feet when you're keeping time with the wave."

"*I am a travel of both time and space*," I sing, horribly, and the board starts picking up more and more speed. "*Be where I have been*."

By the time I get to *elders of a gentle race*, I can feel it's time to ride. I'm not sure if it's the song or instinct but I can just tell. I push up off my hands and toes, get to my knees.

Here's the scary part. I'm slicing through the water, riding this fucking wave and feeling I'm on top of the world. I could just ride the whole wave to shore on my knees and it would be fun and thrilling all on its own.

It's that next step that scares me. It's the risk of standing up. Of giving up what's easy and trying something hard. It's where I've failed every time before.

"Don't be comfortable!" Logan's voice is small, disappearing behind me. "You're doing this!"

I've lost my place in the song. It doesn't matter. "*Ooooh, I've been flying, ain't no denying*," I sing, "*no denying*."

And I don't deny. I fly.

I get up onto my feet, inch by inch, but I make it.

My legs are shaking, I can feel the ocean rushing beneath my feet.

And just like that, I'm surfing. I really am a traveler of both time and space.

I'm powerful, unstoppable.

Free.

It's just me and the ocean, an ever-deepening connection to some part of nature, some part of me, that I've never felt before.

And then, it's over.

The wave gently places me on the shore, like I'm being

carried in the ocean's hand.

The board skids along the sand for a few feet and then stops. I hop off.

I did it!

A let out a little yelp, throwing my hands into the air and doing a little dance. My smile is so wide, it's hurting my cheeks and the pain is absolutely beautiful.

"Look at you," Logan calls out to me, as he walks out of the surf. I feel so high, my adrenaline firing through my veins, that it doesn't even bother me that I'm ogling his body once more. If you saw his hulking mass of muscles walk out of the ocean, dripping wet, his hair slicked back, you would do the same.

"I did it!" I cry out. "Yay me!"

He walks right over to me and stops a couple feet away. Close enough for me to see the tick of his pulse along his throat, the drops of water caught in his scruffy beard. Close enough for my already fired-up body to start overreacting, my heart picking up the pace even more.

"You did good," he says, peering down at me with an intensity I feel burning in my gut. His voice is rough and low, like he's telling me a secret. "I knew you would."

I smile up at him, my lips feeling stiff now. I'm happy, so happy, that I finally was able to catch a wave. But it was because of Logan. I owe him now and I'm not sure I like that.

And there's too much of his manly masculinity standing in close proximity to me.

"Well, I'm sorry you had to hear me sing," I say quietly, looking away.

"Are you kidding me?" he says. "That was the best part. I had no idea you were that horrible at it. Suspected, but never knew."

I snap my head back to him and playfully hit him across the chest. "Hey!" I admonish him, trying to ignore how hard his chest had felt under my hand. "Why don't you get on the damn board and sing me some 'Purple Rain?'"

"Maybe some other time, Freckles," he says. We stare at each other for a few moments. It's like he's actually trying to count the freckles on my nose. I'm not even sure I'm breathing, I'm kind of lost in the space between us.

Then he clears his throat. Loudly. "I'll see you," he says. His voice is stiff, as if he's been caught thinking about something he shouldn't.

"Okay," I manage to say as he walks away toward the hotel, clouds of sand kicking up behind him, beads of water still snaking their way down his back.

CHAPTER EIGHT

"AND THAT'S ALL YOU HAVE TO TELL ME?" MY mother's voice crackles over the phone.

"Pretty much," I tell her.

"What? I can't hear you."

I sigh and take my cell out onto the balcony hoping to get better reception, though to be honest I was done with this phone call ten minutes ago and a dropped call would be a great way to get out of it.

"I'm saying yes," I tell her, not even bothering to hide the exasperation in my voice. "That's all there is to report on."

The line goes silent for a moment and I think maybe I did lose her after all but she sighs. "I'm just checking up on you. If you don't want to tell me anything, that's fine. It's not like I've talked to you more than once over the last three weeks."

Here comes the passive aggressiveness. "Look, I like it here. People are nice. I like my job. I'm busy, and that's a good thing. There's nothing much else to talk about."

"And Logan?" she asks. "You've barely mentioned him."

"I have too," I tell her. "He's fine. He's been a fair boss. He's very busy too. It's not easy to run this place by himself."

She scoffs. "That's because poor Juliet was doing all of it for him. My poor baby." She sighs. "My biggest regret in life was letting her marry that, that…beast."

Beast? That's a new one. Caveman? Yes. I'm not sure what to say to that except, "You couldn't have stopped her mom, she fell in love."

"Bullshit," she says. "He tricked her."

"Tricked her?" I repeat.

"He came when she was most vulnerable. After she broke up with William, when she was getting tired of the politics. Your father and I knew we should have done more to get her back on her feet, back in the scene. And then this schmuck shows up with his irritating accent and promises of a hotel in the tropics. He duped her into thinking that was the life she wanted. He stole her from us, Veronica, don't you forget that."

"Uh huh," I say. "And so if that's how you feel, how come you have no problem with me being here?"

She sighs again, louder this time. "You couldn't live at home with us. The fact that you're my daughter and couldn't get another job was rather telling, don't you think?"

"Telling of what?"

"You're twenty-seven years old, Veronica. What does that say about me, about my role in Chicago, my role in the government, among the people, that my adult daughter is a complete failure?"

Stunned. I'm stunned. I'm used to low blows delivered

by my mother but this one takes the cake. And the fact that she's saying it in her politician voice, cold and factual, just adds to the injury.

"Mom," I say, trying to hide the hurt in my voice.

"Oh, toughen up honey," she goes on. "You know what I mean."

"You just called me a failure!"

"I'm not saying you're a failure, I'm saying that's what it looks like. People will think there's something wrong if you can't get a job, and I wasn't about to have you moping around at home and coasting your way through life. You're *my* daughter, Rose Locke's daughter, and you're the only one I have left. I don't have Juliet anymore and neither do you, so I'm sorry if you can't be the black sheep anymore. There's no room for it. You have a reputation to uphold here."

My heart is thudding in my brain so hard I can barely hear her. "I wasn't the black sheep," I say even though I know it's true. I was always lesser compared to Juliet, and now my mother hates me for it.

"All I wanted was for both my daughters to follow in my footsteps. Juliet would have made an excellent politician, she was caring, kind, beautiful, smart. She could charm anyone into doing anything. She could have carried on the legacy of strong women in male-dominated roles."

"I'm a fucking cook, mom!" I'm nearly yelling. The couple on the nearest balcony are looking at me curiously. I lower my voice, "I fought to be in the position I'm in right now, I've been fighting my whole life in a male-dominated work force."

"And see what good that did you."

"What?"

"I don't know what you did at your last job, but I know

you got fired, Veronica, and I know you screwed up."

My lips clamp shut. How could she know?

"And it doesn't matter," she goes on. "We all make mistakes and you're there fixing yours. Stay a year, get some new experience you can put on your resume, and then get out and come home."

Home? I know I haven't been here long, but this already starting to feel like home. And it's one place where I don't have to deal with the likes of my mother except for the occasional phone call. She may have wanted me to come out here in an effort to hide me but I'm not so eager to go back anytime soon.

"Maybe I'll stay here forever," I tell her. "It's not a bad life."

"Suit yourself," she says, "if you want to be on a sinking ship."

"What does that mean?"

"Don't forget that your father and I own that hotel as much as Logan does. The thing isn't making money, not like it was with Juliet. The moment it looks like it's going under, we're pulling out."

Good lord. My parents really do hate him that much.

As if she can hear my thoughts, she adds, "He made fools of us, a fool of Juliet. He's not family. He's nothing. Just an opportunity for the time being."

Then the phone crackles and like magic the call is mercifully dropped.

I'm left reeling. I quickly turn the power off my phone in case she calls back, and place it on the table, my hands braced on the edge. Even the sweet breeze coming off the ocean and the birdsong from the trees is doing nothing to shake some sense into me.

Normally I would have agreed with my mother on all

of that, would have been fueled by the same indignation against Logan. After all, I felt the exact same when I landed here.

But something has changed in me since I've become a part of Moonwater. I can't quite put my finger on it. It's not just the surfing lesson last week, it's the strange sense of ease I feel now being around him. We're interacting more and even though it's usually brief, there's some kind of unspoken understanding between us, a simmering connection that's getting harder to ignore.

And sometimes I wonder if it's a little more than that. I'll catch myself staring at him some days, my eyes lingering on the rugged lines of his face, the breadth of his shoulders. It's not a conscious decision, I'm not waxing on in my head about how gorgeous he can be. But I'm still drawn to him in ways that I really shouldn't be. There are a million valid reasons to never think of Logan that way, but the more I tell myself he's off-limits, the more I shame myself, the more I want to do it.

It *is* shameful. I've seen the crash site where Juliet's car went off the side of the road, I've felt the choking rage and regret every time the shuttle bus or Charlie's Tacoma takes us to Hanalei. I've had to stop looking at it, but even when I close my eyes, I can tell we're passing by it. It's on a sharp curve around the bay, just east of the resort. There's no shoulder, just a steep drop-off to the rocks and crashing waves. A cross and flowers marks the spot, and the few times I kept my eyes open to take it in, I've noticed the bouquets were fresh. Someone keeps putting them there and I'm too afraid to ask who. The idea of Logan being a still grieving husband doesn't jive with the idea I have of him in my head. It just complicates things and that's the last thing I want.

I should probably pull up my big girl panties and visit the site in person. Go by myself and let the scene sink in. It could remind me that I'm betraying my sister by even thinking about Logan in that way. It's just a case of wanting what was hers, some form of self-validation, of feeling that I finally measure up to her. That's all it is.

That's all it has to be.

"Ron?"

I hear the front door close and Kate appears standing by the sliding door, her long hair spilling over her tanned shoulders, a white plumeria tucked in her hair. She looks like a Hawaiian princess. "We've already started."

I frown, shaking my head slightly and trying to snap out of it. "Started what?"

"The staff meeting," she says slowly. "Let me guess, you forgot?"

It's Saturday morning, which is supposed to be a day off for most people here, including me, and though I know there's a monthly staff meeting for everyone, this is the first that I heard of it happening today.

Kate sighs, rolling her eyes. "Come on, it won't take long. It's in the restaurant."

I follow her out of the unit and over to the restaurant. It's another gorgeous day, even though the mountains are shrouded in cloud and mist. No matter the weather, it's always gorgeous and despite the looming clouds, it's actually been blissfully dry the last couple of days.

We enter the restaurant and see everyone sitting at a few tables in the middle. I'm immediately embarrassed. Everyone is here, even Shannon the rough and tumble night shift receptionist, and they're all looking at me expectantly.

"Sorry," I say quickly, taking a seat with Kate beside Johnny and Charlie. "This must have slipped my mind.

Who is watching reception?"

"No one," Logan says quickly, looking at the sheet of paper in his hand. "Which is why this meeting needed to start five minutes ago."

His tone is cutting even though he doesn't look at me. Sheesh, talk about mood swings.

He clears his throat and starts reading from the paper. "Okay, we're one week into November now, which means things are going to start getting more chaotic, especially after Thanksgiving. You all know the drill. You also know that if any of you were planning on flying home for Thanksgiving, you should have made those plans with me a long time ago. As it stands, Charlie you're off for a week and so is Nikki. That means the kitchen is going to be understaffed. Veronica, Big John, I trust you'll prepare for this."

I meet Johnny's eyes and he gives me an easy smile. We've already discussed what to do when Charlie is gone and all it means is a bit of extra prep. Thanksgiving happens to be one of the slowest times of the year here.

Logan goes on talking about the upcoming season and how things are going to get a bit more competitive because other hotels on the island are slashing their prices.

"I was thinking about bringing back Mai Tai hour on Fridays, and starting up the Wednesday night Luas, just like we did a few years ago. There are only three official luaus on the island and we know that when guests come to the island they're looking for the total Hawaiian experience. It'll take some extra work but we need to capitalize on that."

"Um, what's Mai Tai hour?" I ask.

Logan finally looks at me. "Every Friday from four to six, we serve free Mai Tais by the pool."

"Everyone loves free booze," Charlie adds.

"Then why did you stop doing it?" I ask. I look to

Daniel, our resident booze expert. "Too expensive?"

Daniel shakes his head. "Mai Tais are some of the cheapest drinks you can make. It's mainly fruit juice and a splash of a few cheap rums."

"We stopped," Logan says, eyeing me sternly, as if I'm stepping on his toes. Which I probably am. "Because there was no way to directly measure if it had any influence on whether guests stayed here or not. And if you can't measure it, then it's not worth the money."

"But what if you advertised it so that tourists in Hanalei came here for it? Or people on the way to Ke'e Beach or the Kalalau Trail? Or Tunnels? Put a sign on the side of the road, everyone welcome."

"No one is stopping just for free watered-down drinks," Logan says gruffly.

"Maybe not, but what if we offered free pupus as well?"

Like clockwork, Charlie snickers at "pupus."

"And who would be making them? You?" Logan asks. "You're willing to do extra work? Because you know I won't be paying you for that."

I purse my lips for a moment, narrowing my eyes at him. It feels like the whole room is watching us with bated breath. Lord knows how many of us do extra work on the side, from shuttle-bus driving to handling luggage to being a barista, without getting extra compensation. "I wouldn't dream of you paying me extra. I'd do it for the sake of the hotel and everyone who wants to keep their job here. Plus the fact that I enjoy cooking. I actually like my job."

"I'd be down for that," Johnny speaks up. "It will bring in new people. They'll take a look at the hotel, see the restaurant, the location. Our drop-dead gorgeous staff." Everyone laughs as Johnny pretends to preen himself.

"We'll see," Logan says, looking back to the paper.

"Hey, she was right about the seating in here, aye," Johnny goes on. God bless him. "The customers are happy and no one minds the wait for a table."

Damn. If looks could kill. I half expect flames to shoot out of Logan's head.

But he just clears his throat again and says, "The luau itself will attract people from all over the island. We'll deal with that first and see how it goes."

Johnny looks at me and shrugs to say that he tried. I could kiss my co-worker right now, just for that.

When the meeting is over and everyone starts scattering, Kate hurrying out the restaurant and back to reception, Logan walks over to Nikki and Daniel. "You guys ready?"

I know I should head back to my room and get a head start on my day off. Pick a book on my e-reader, bring it to the beach with some snacks and work on my tan, maybe Facetime Claire again since it's been a week since I last talked to her.

But I don't. I don't know why and I can't explain it, but I walk right over to them and I say, "What are you guys doing?"

"Nothing you'd be interested in," Logan says gruffly, obviously still miffed I spoke up earlier.

"We're hiking the Kalalua Trail," Daniel speaks up, ignoring the glare from Logan. "It's been dry the last few days so it's easier. Less mud."

"We're only taking it to Hanakapiai Beach and turning back," Nikki says with a bright smile. "You should come. You haven't done it yet, have you?"

I hadn't and it was one of the things Kate promised to take me on, except that our schedules keep having us miss each other.

"I'd love to," I say quickly before Logan says anything

else discouraging. He obviously doesn't want me along and that makes me want to come even more. "Give me five minutes—do I need to bring anything?"

"Backpack, water, snacks, a hat, sunscreen," Daniel lists off.

"And good shoes you don't mind getting dirty. Sneakers or hiking boots if you have them," Nikki adds.

I nod and flash Logan an overly sweet smile. "Be right back."

I swear I can hear him grumble as I hurry back to my room.

Five minutes later I've changed into running shoes (which have already turned red from Kauai's famous dirt), shorts and a tee shirt, have slathered on sunscreen, stuck on a baseball cap that says Java Kai, and crammed a few organic quinoa bars and some dried mango into my backpack along with bottles of water.

I stop by reception and tell Kate, "I'm doing the Kalalau Trail with Logan, Nikki, and Daniel. If we're not back in, well, however long it takes to get to that beach and back, send help."

"You're going with Logan?" she asks, brows raised. "Girl, you crazy."

I shrug, slipping my fingers underneath by backpack straps and biting back a smile. "You have no idea."

The four of us are riding in Logan's black Jeep, the first time I've been in his car. Like I expect, it smells like him, something like mint and coconut, and the seats are covered in sand. Daniel and Nikki are already in the back so I have no choice but to sit in the passenger seat. I don't look over at him as we take a right onto the road, heading toward the Na Pali Coast, though I can occasionally feel his eyes on me. Sometimes I think he's staring at my legs. Sometimes I think I'm losing the plot a little.

The start of the Kalalau Trail is located at Ke'e Beach and the Na Pali Coast State Wilderness Park, which is only a ten-minute drive down the road to where the highway literally ends. You can almost drive all the way around the island, but the jagged and iconic Na Pali Coast prevents it. The only way you can keep going is to get out of your car and hike in, which is what we're about to do. We're not doing the crazy version though. Daniel tells me that this one should only take three hours round trip—any further and we would have to pack in a tent and bring a permit. Apparently that hike gets pretty gnarly, and for someone like me who is sensitive to heights, it's not the best idea.

I've been to Ke'e Beach at the end of the road and gone snorkeling once with Charlie, so I'm not surprised to see the parking lot is absolutely packed. We have to park the Jeep on the side of the road a mile away and walk from there.

But in Kauai, even walking along the side of a road is a near magical experience. Yes, we're passing countless cars and more tourists and locals prepared for the hike, but we're also crossing fresh streams that spill across the road, thick, fragrant jungle peppering the sides with the occasional chicken scratching around in the bushes.

There's even a wet cave underneath a sheer overhanging wall. The water in the cave doesn't look too inviting—it's dark and disappears into blackness the more it goes under the rock—but I have to stand back and stare up at the vines as they tangle down the guano-stained walls, the lush vegetation that creeps over the side. Beyond that, the soaring peaks of the mountains reach up into the clouds. It nearly gives me vertigo.

"You and Juliet swam in here, didn't you?" Nikki asks

Logan.

He nods. "Not much to see. Cold as hell."

"Wait," I say, "Juliet swam in there?" I point to the dark water. The Juliet I knew never would have done something so…well, creepy-looking. Swimming in a dark, claustrophobic cave with a low ceiling? No thank you.

He nods. "She did. I may have coerced her into it, but she did it. To prove a point. She was bloody stubborn most days. Apple doesn't fall far from the tree," he mumbles that last bit under his breath.

I'm hit with the strangest feeling: jealousy. Juliet may have been stubborn, but even so I never knew her to do something as fun and adventurous as going swimming in a cave. And yet Logan, he got to witness that. To know her. Something I'd never have.

As if all my feelings so far weren't confusing enough.

CHAPTER NINE

WE CONTINUE WALKING ALONG THE ROAD UNTIL WE get to the trailhead. A bunch of walking sticks are stacked up against a rock as a steady stream of hikers head up and down the path that leads straight into the thick jungle. Even though it hasn't rained for a few days—least not at the hotel—the trail is slick and slippery in sections as we pass caution signs warning of hazardous cliffs, rock slides, and flash floods. I have to wonder how dangerous the hike really is.

I'm probably in the best shape I've been in a long time, thanks to all the fresh fruit and vegetables, the surfing and swimming and daily jogs on the beach I've been doing, but even so the start of the trail isn't easy. It snags and swerves, hugging the edges of the cliffs, the path of red dirt narrow in sections. Logan leads the party, followed by Daniel, then Nikki, then me. I'm slow, so every time Nikki looks over her shoulder at me, I have to give her a reassuring wave to keep going.

We reach the first view part of the trail, where a lot of people turn around. I'm breathing hard, sweat streaming off my face as I try and take a picture of Ke'e Beach from above. Here, you can see how clear the water is, the color is a brilliant blue, interspersed with dark reef. Waves lap the golden shore as the palm trees sway in the breeze. It's dizzyingly beautiful, and even though I know my company must have seen this all a million times, I take a moment to soak it all in. I'm also trying to catch my breath and not look like I'm having a fucking heart attack.

Honestly, if that was the whole hike, I'd be satisfied. I want to tag along with one of the groups heading back down the hill, go jump in the ocean to cool off, and pass out on the sand.

Alas, Logan clears his throat, a signal to keep going. And so we do.

And the trail starts to get a little more extreme. I would have thought that the parts where the trail follows the outermost near-vertical cliffs would have been the hardest for me. I mean, I get dizzy with great heights and there's nothing but sheer drops for hundreds of feet until it meets the ocean. The roar of the wild waves smashing against the rocks far far below is deafening even from all the way up here.

But actually, the worst parts of the trail are when they switchback and head away from the coast. Here the jungle is the thickest, there's a fine mist in the air, and everything is dripping with humidity. I don't think these nooks and crannies get any sun to dry them out, and the path turns into a rust-colored mud bath. I watch Nikki eat shit and slip right on her ass, then Daniel almost do the same. The hikers up ahead of us also bail as they round a corner where the path disappears and becomes slippery rocks you have to scale over. I try not to laugh because I know that's going to be me in a minute.

Everyone else is using the wooden poles to help them but I wouldn't trust anything other than my own body, even as we come to a stream that cuts across the path, more slippery rock to navigate on both sides.

The last thing I want to do is fall, so I'm going as slow as I can, and while everyone is stepping over the rocks and sliding around, I'm using my hands to balance, going across like a crab. I don't care if I look like a fool and my hands are covered in red mud, every part of me is a mess by now.

"Here," Logan says.

I cautiously look up from the rocks to see him holding out his hand for me. I've paused on the top of one slick rock and have spent the last few minutes trying to figure how to get down without killing myself. I mentioned early that I didn't have good balance, right? Well it's really being put to the test here.

"Take my hand," he says, more like an order than anything.

I want to push him away and insist I can do it myself. I think he knows that too, that's why when I look into his eyes I see a wariness in them. He expects me to reject him.

So I don't. I nod and give him my hand and put all my weight on him as I step down off the stone. When my feet hit the slick ground beneath, I slide but he's got me. He's as solid as a tree and he's got me.

I blow a wet strand of hair off my face and look up at him. "Thanks."

"No worries," he says as he gradually let's go of my hand. He then looks to Daniel and nods. "Keep moving. I have a feeling a system is moving in."

Daniel and Nikki start moving up the trail as it heads back alongside the cliff, and to my surprise, Logan stays with me, walking just a foot or two ahead. I'm staring at the wall of his sweaty back, his shirt clinging to it. It's a shame he's not taking it off. I mean, that can't be comfortable.

"How can you tell a system is coming in?" I ask. "Weather report said it was supposed to be partly cloudy. Least that's what my phone said."

"Never trust your phone here," he says. "I can just tell. You pick up on the changes." He breathes in deep and I watch his back rise, mesmerized. "Smell that? That's rain. Somewhere up in Waimea Canyon, but it's coming here and soon."

"Well I don't think this trail can get any more wet."

"You'd be surprised," he says just as my feet slip. I yelp as I reach out and grab onto his waist, my arms wrapping around him.

"Easy now," he says, sounding amused.

I swallow hard and take in a deep breath, carefully moving my feet so I'm back upright. "That was close."

"And if you fall, you fall," he says. "If anyone gets back up, it's you."

There's a strange tenderness to his voice but I'm not sure if I'm hearing things. My blood is whooshing in my ears pretty loud, my breath erratic. From the exercise, not because I just had a good feel of his abs, abs that felt as firm and hard as the rocks beneath my feet. Abs you wouldn't mind running your tongue over.

"You'll just have a permanent stain on your shorts," Nikki yells over her shoulder. I snap out of it and look around Logan to see Nikki wriggling her tiny butt at us.

I laugh. "Well by the time this is over I'm pretty sure

I'll be covered in mud head to toe. I'm going to look like Rambo or something."

"Rambo?" Logan asks. He stops suddenly which causes me to nearly run into his back, then he turns around. With a sly smirk on his lips, he reaches out for my face. I stay absolutely still, my breath in my throat, as he runs his cold, sticky thumbs under my eyes. "Now you're Rambo," he says rather proudly before turning back around.

I don't need a mirror to know that he's just rubbed red mud under my eyes like some tribal war paint. My skin tingles from his touch.

Fuck. That was an oddly intimate moment. I'm not even sure how to process that except give off a soft, albeit awkward laugh.

"Maybe I'll clean off at the beach, I packed a bathing suit," I say.

"*No*," Logan, Daniel, and Nikki say in emphatic unison. It's like I've just suggested we ride mountain goats on the way back home, clicking coconuts together with our hands.

"The number of people who have died at that beach is…well, you'll see. There's a marker," Logan says.

"Even the stream crossing can be dangerous," Daniel says from in front of us.

"We have to cross a stream?" I ask, feeling the panic swirl through me. "I nearly died back there on a bunch of wet rocks."

"I'll carry you across," Logan says.

"You fucking better."

He eyes me over his shoulder, frowning as always, though his eyes are twinkling.

The rest of the trail is a combination of the steep cliffs and stupendous views which I take a picture of every second, and those muddy, slippery switchbacks. It feels like we've been hiking forever and it's not getting any easier. I'm about to complain and ask how much longer we have to go when I see a family with two young children march past us, the kids in goddamn flip-flops!

"Oh my god," I say, breathless as we round yet another steep bend. "Flip-flops? Here? On the muddy death trail? Let me guess, they're locals?"

Logan shakes his head. "Locals would rather do this barefoot. Easiest to trust your own toes. Those are tourists and they're lucky they've gotten this far without incident. One wrong step, one slip at some parts, well, you've seen it. You're dead."

Sweet. I feel so lucky we get to do this whole thing over again on the way back.

"Almost there," Nikki shouts from up front.

We round yet another bend and finally there's a glimpse of a rocky beach way down below. In the valley below the mountains, clouds descending over the sharp peaks further inland.

"Are those clouds coming our way?" I ask Logan. Where we are, the sun is strong and hot as hell, turning the ocean a deep azure and making the red dirt glow.

He nods grimly. "They're moving slowly right now but the weather is unpredictable. I'm afraid we'll just have to look at the beach, have some water and turn back. Believe me, it's not a fun hike in the rain."

"It's not a fun hike in the sun either," I tell him.

"Here," he gestures to a wooden sign that reads:

Hanakapiai Beach Warning!
Do not go near the water
Unseen currents have killed:

And then beneath it there are a bunch of notches marking how many deaths there have been. I'm quick to count at least eighty.

Eighty!

"Holy shit, eighty people have died here!?" I exclaim, looking at Logan.

He shrugs with a sigh and wipes the sweat off his brow. "Not sure how accurate the count is, but it's a lot."

"So tell me, why are we going to this beach?"

He gives me a half-smile. "Because it's fun, Freckles."

"Fun?"

He turns and starts walking as the trail starts leading downward. "Admit it, you're having a fucking blast."

I roll my eyes and hurry after him. The ridge we're walking on is exposed to the sun, so at least there's no mud. "Yeah, walking for nearly two hours, covered in mud and sweat, with dangerous cliffs, rocks, and now killer beaches, is a lot of fun."

"At least you've been able to stare at my ass this whole time."

And just like that my eyes trail downward. Because, yes, I have been staring at his ass when I haven't been looking over the edge to my imminent doom.

"You wish," I tell him. "You're just mad that I had a good idea during the staff meeting."

He stiffens a bit at that. "You keep having your good ideas and I'll keep shooting them down."

"You didn't shoot the first one down about the seating by the window. And it's worked."

"I was just being polite with that one."

"Yeah right. You being polite for the sake of being polite. Now I've heard everything."

"Are you guys done bickering?" Nikki's voice comes from down around the bend.

"Have you ever known me to stop bickering?" Logan

yells back as we catch up to her and Daniel. "You guys call me the *habut* for a reason, I have to keep my reputation." He glances behind at me. "By the way, you can still ride me if you like."

My skin grows hot and it takes me a moment to realize what he's talking about. Further down the path, where it finally levels out, is the stream.

It's pretty wide but it doesn't look too deep. There are a bunch of people already crossing it, including the family we saw earlier with the kids in flip-flops. They at least have the sense to take off their shoes as they hop across the rocks, while the mother wades into the water, about thigh high. I think that's going to be my option. If I took either of the rocks, I'd slip and end up in the water anyway, and probably damage my phone.

"This is it," Logan says.

"I'll wade across," I tell him.

He looks across to the woman who has reached the middle of the stream and nods. "If the stream was any higher I'd say no. You'd be surprised at the current. Especially with this wind picking up. Things change fast."

I look at the water. It doesn't look anything but inviting and I can see the current with my own eyes—it's moving steadily but fairly slow, snaking past us until it meets a bunch of rocks at the end and drops down into a few more pools until it finally reaches the beach and spreads out for the ocean and pounding surf.

"I'll take my chances," I tell him, determined.

Nikki and Daniel hop across the rocks with ease, balancing only in the middle for a beat or two before arriving on the other side.

Logan is waiting for me.

"Go ahead," I tell him as I undo my sneakers, taking

them off along with my socks.

He grabs the sneakers and socks from me. "I'll hang onto these." Then he nods at the water. "I'll be right behind you."

I nearly roll my eyes. Nothing is going to happen. Even if I did slip on a rock under the water, I wouldn't fall down. And even if I fell down, I wouldn't be swept away in two feet of water.

Yet there's some sort of reverence in Logan's expression, so I take my time. And the rocks are slippery and hard against the soles of my feet.

But Logan is right behind me the whole way and I can feel him, tense and poised, as he follows me through the water, like he's prepared to catch me at any moment. I hate to admit it but I kind of like the feeling, like I'm being watched over. Like someone cares.

I make it. It's not as triumphant as when I finally got up on the surfboard, but it is a relief to know I didn't make a fool of myself.

Once Logan comes across, walking through the water with ease, we head down toward the beach, a small stretch of sand and rock between two sheer cliffs. I can see why it's so deadly. The waves are absolutely pounding the shore, scattering the rocks and boulders. The wind is picking up more, sending the sea spray flying.

We find a spot to sit down at the edge of the vegetation. I perch on an uncomfortable rock and bring my quinoa bars and fruit out of the backpack, letting my feet dry before I put my socks and shoes back on.

"Ten minutes, then we're heading back," Logan says before he downs a bunch of water. I watch his neck as he swallows until he catches me looking. I quickly avert my eyes back to the shoreline.

There's a lot of people on the beach and since half the beach is being swallowed up by waves, it feels strangely crowded. Quite a few are down by the shore and few of them are almost swept away from a rogue wave that reached in further than anyone expected. They shriek and run away from the surf playfully, like they have no idea how close they were to being sucked out to sea.

"Holy shit," I say. "Those people are crazy. Didn't they see the sign?"

"Ignorance heeds no signs," Daniel says, trying to retie his hair back into a ponytail, the wind making it difficult. "If they did, we wouldn't have people dying here all the time. Have you heard of Queen's Bath? Guide books won't even post about it because of all the people who die there. People just don't listen. They think the waves can't be that big, the current can't be that strong, that their swimming skills are better than the average person."

"The other year," Nikki says between handfuls of granola, "a family was here, just like this. Dad turned his back for a second to get out food and the kids got too close to the shore. The wave swept them out. Bless him, he swam right in the waves after them and got them."

"They made it out?" I ask.

"Eventually," Logan says. "They couldn't get back to shore. See the cliff right there? Around the corner is a small cave. He shoved his kids in there. Saved their lives. Hung onto the edge of the rock walls. The rescue boats came but it took a while—it's six miles to the nearest harbor. And there's no signal or reception out here so someone has to run back on the trail all the way to Ke'e Beach to get help. When the boats came, it was too rough and dangerous for them. Finally, two firefighters on one of the boats decided to swim for them. Took forty-five minutes for each person to be rescued. Fucking miracle. And that wasn't a case of being negligent. It just happened. But those folks over there," he says, pointing at the people by the water. "Are pushing their luck." He looks at his watch. "And we might be too. Five more minutes. I thought I heard thunder a few moments ago. Wind is picking up."

All of us look up to the mountain ranges behind us and the dark clouds that are swooping darker through the valleys. The wind is steadier now, colder and wet.

I finish my bar and dried mangos and slide my shoes on, hypnotized by the violent waves down by the shore, when I hear Logan mutter, "Shit."

"What?" Daniel asks.

I look over at Logan. He's staring off at the area where the stream runs across the beach before it's swallowed up by the ocean. "It's changed," he says. "The stream is running brown."

Just then, someone in the distance yells, "It's rising, it's rising, everyone out!" While someone else yells. "Flash flood!"

"Fuck," Nikki swears as we all quickly get to our feet.

"What's happening? Flash flood?" I ask with wide eyes.

Logan nods. "We have to hurry. Grab your stuff, we're running."

Oh my god. I pick up the backpack and hurry after them as we scamper over the rocks heading back to the stream.

There's a backlog of people there at the stream's edge on both sides. The stream is barely recognizable. It's no longer clear, but brown and growing and seems to be getting higher and wider right in front of my eyes. The rocks people were crossing over earlier are nearly submerged, and people are still trying to cross over them.

"What happens if we can't cross?" I ask Logan.

"We're stuck here overnight. Might have to be helicoptered out."

"Hey they have a rope," Daniel says pointing to a guy who has tied a long rope around one tree and now is crossing the rocks with it. "He'll tie it on the other side. You can cross by hanging on."

"I don't know," Logan says warily and just as he does so, the sky opens up and rain starts to fall. "We have to go now if we're going to go."

"I'm going," Daniel says. "Otherwise there's no bartender for tonight and I'm not giving up the tips." He makes his way to the swollen banks and grabs onto the rope after the guy has safely used it to cross the water. The rocks are now totally submerged and the water looks to be at least three feet high and moving faster and faster.

"Me too," Nikki says, going after Daniel.

Logan looks at me. "Get on my back. It will at least save your phone."

I look down at the stream. Everyone is steadily crossing using the rope. No one is getting a piggy-back ride.

"I'll keep it in my hat," I tell him and I quickly take out my phone and slide it in under my baseball cap.

He stares at me, the rain dripping down his face. A few beats pass and I can't figure out what he's deciding. Then he nods, once. "Okay. You're going first, I'll be behind you."

"Hurry up!" Daniel yells at us. He's made it to the other side and is helping Nikki out of the water.

And I'm trying to hurry. I get to the edge and then it's like I freeze. I can't see the bottom of the stream, it's just this swirling, brown, depthless water that's rushing past me, and even though there's another woman in front of me using the rope, the water is already at her waist.

You can do it, hold onto the rope, keep your eyes on Daniel, and go, I tell myself.

I grab the rope with shaky hands. It's thin and slippery and nowhere near as sturdy as I thought. If anything, it's loosened, creating a dangerous slack.

I look behind me at Logan. He picks up the rope, holding it taut, staring right into me. I can barely tear my eyes away from him to look at the rest of the people on our side of the shore. There's about a dozen of us and they're all waiting for me to hurry my fucking ass up and cross.

I take in a deep breath and start walking. The rocks are way more slippery, even though I'm crossing in my sneakers now and not my bare feet, and the current isn't helping. I can literally feel it pulling at my legs, trying to drag me downstream, and every step I take is a struggle to keep going.

I'm going slow. I know I am. I can't help it. I'm in the middle of the stream and now the water is at my chest and I'm starting to get that cold panic around my heart, the idea that I might not make it. The rope is starting to move away from my fingertips, my arms are tired.

Daniel and Nikki's faces, as well as the crowd behind them are out of focus, but I'm staring at them with all I have, afraid to look away. Nikki gestures with her hands for me to keep going.

And then someone behind me yells. "Hurry the fuck up, the rest of us have to make it!"

Fuck. That's all it takes to jar me. I try and hurry but my leg goes to the side, to a hole, and I start falling into the stream, no ground beneath my left foot.

"Veronica!" I hear Logan yell, and then my fingers can't hold on and I'm slipping.

It happens in a second.

I fall in with a splash. The water holds me, pulls me down, it's up to my neck, I'm swept away in a dizzying circle, the world around me swirling into a blur as I'm rushed downstream in a cold whirlpool.

I'm going to die.

My back slams against a rock and I try and turn around to grab onto it, but my hands slip and then I'm bounced around again, the water rising over my head. I forget about my phone, forget about looking like a fool, I forget about everything except the fact that I'm going to die, swept out to sea.

I go over the edge of the waterfall and slam into a pool below, my body slapping into the rocks at the bottom before I'm raised above it by the current and pulled away again. I try and keep my head above the water but all I hear is the current in my ears, the pounding of my heart, all I see is brown water and bubbles and blue sky, until I'm turned around again and I see the pounding waves. The ocean is another drop away, waiting for me. Once I go over the edge of this pool and I'm swept out there, I know I won't have it in me to fight. The waves will obliterate me.

But I have some strength left now.

As my side hits another rock, I reach out and grab it, using my legs to push off through the current until both arms are over the rock and I'm hugging it close to me, holding onto it for dear life as the current tries to rip me away.

"Help," I try to yell but my voice is so weak, buried by the roaring waves and white water.

But I think I can hear something else above it. A muffled voice. A panicked voice.

Logan's voice.

"Veronica!" he yells, and at that moment I realize how silly I've been to be mad at him for never calling me

Ronnie. How dumb and trivial that was, how dumb and trivial everything was, my whole feud with him over Juliet. What was their business was their business, not mine. I'm going to die now and nothing else really mattered all this time.

"Veronica!" he yells again, closer now, and I manage to raise my head and see him scrambling over the rocks near the edge. I want to yell at him, to tell him to stay where he is, that he'll be swept away too but I can't. I can barely hold on.

He's in the water now, the water rushing against his chest, but he's strong and he's solid and he's immovable. His eyes are laced with a fear I've never seen before on him, that I've never seen on anyone. I feel like we're both facing death head on.

"Hold on, just a few more seconds," he says, his voice deep and commanding, yet shaking all the same.

He comes closer. Just feet away. He can almost grab me.

I start to slip. I have no strength left to grip.

"No!" he yells. "I'm not losing you, too! Hold on."

I can't.

I can't.

I let go.

Just as he reaches out for me.

His hand wraps around my elbow, and with a roar of strength he pulls me toward him and out of the whirling pool and into the side stream.

"Hold onto me," he says as his arm slips around my waist in a vice-like grip. My own arms are weak and shaking but he's got me. He moves through the water, the stream rushing over my mouth at times until I'm spitting it out and then suddenly the water slackens. It's at my chest, at my waist, at my thighs, and now Logan is dragging me onto the rocks on the side of the stream where it meets the beach.

He's breathing hard, leaning over me. The rain falls into my eyes until I blink it away.

"Are you hurt?" he asks, running his hand over my head.

I close my eyes, not sure whether to say yes or no. I don't know. I just want to breath, want to find my breath again, get that assurance that I'm alive.

There's a rustling beside us and I'm aware of muffled, panicked voices.

"Someone's running to get help."

"Is she alive?"

"Anything broken?"

"Can the helicopters land in this wind?"

"That was a close call, that was such a close call."

"I'm so sorry I yelled."

I can't pick out the voices, I know they all belong to the dozen people stuck here on this side. I know that none of them dared to cross after what happened to me.

"Give us a minute, please," Logan says to them. I feel his hand on my forehead, touching it gently. "Veronica. Someone is going to get rescue. If the helicopters can make it, they'll come get you out. They'll take you the hospital."

I shake my head softly. "No," I croak. "I think I'm…I'm fine. Just bruised."

"Regardless," Logan says, "you need to be checked out. You could have a concussion." He pauses, his fingers trailing down my cheek. "Dammit. Dammit, I thought I fucking lost you. I am so sorry."

His voice sounds so broken, so unlike him, that I open my eyes and peer up at him.

"Don't be sorry," I tell him. "I'm the one who wanted to come on the hike. And I did it because I wanted to annoy you. Seems like it worked."

He's not smiling. "I shouldn't have let you cross. I saw the water levels, I saw the current, I should have stopped you."

"I would have gone anyway," I tell him. "You like the stubborn girls."

He frowns at me for a moment, his gaze intensifying. Then he nods, licking his lips. "I do. I do like the stubborn girls."

I was joking. It was a bad joke. But now he's answering me seriously.

"Anyway," I say, unsure how to go on. I'm shaking over what happened, my body torn by the thrill of being alive and the fright of almost dying.

"Anyway," Logan says. He lets out a soft breath of air. "If the rescue team can't get us, we'll be stuck here overnight. Believe it or not, it happens all the time."

I swallow hard at the thought. I just want to go back to the hotel. Even a hospital bed wouldn't be that bad. After all that just happened, the last place I want to be is here, overnight in the wet, soggy, and endlessly dangerous wilderness.

"If it comes to that, I'll make us a shelter. If someone here was doing the whole trail, they might be able to lend us a tent. There's a real sense of camaraderie here when this kind of thing happens. We'll be okay. I've got food in my backpack. It's a bit wet but it will dry out." He pauses. "The worst is over. I'll take care of you."

I'm not sure that the worst is over. But the fact that he said he'll take care of me, that's warming my chest, easing the shivers that have been rocking through my body ever since he pulled me ashore.

Eventually I find the strength to sit up, then stand up. With Logan's arm on me at all times, he leads me back over to the crowd. Everyone is super friendly and concerned and preparing for a night at the beach. The stream is still raging, even higher than it was earlier, which means that the rains won't let up for a while and there's no way we could cross it on our own until tomorrow.

The hikers on the other side of the water are almost all gone except for Nikki and Daniel. When they see me alive and on my own two feet, they literally jump up and down, hugging each other, before they turn and head back on the trail to go back to the hotel and tell everyone what happened.

It's not long after they leave that a couple of rescue workers and a lifeguard from Ke'e appear on the other side, but with the water still raging, they can't cross. There's a lot of yelling back and forth over the stream as they tell us that we have to stay put. The helicopters are having trouble in the weather and none of the zodiacs can brave the surf. Unless the wind and rain ease up before nightfall, we have to prepare for a long night.

Luckily there are a few hikers who had come back along the rest of the eleven-mile trail and have a few supplies. There are no tents for Logan and I, but they do have a small tarp for us to rig up somewhere to keep out of the rain, as well as an apple, trail mix, and packet of beef jerky. Not exactly dinner but at least we won't starve to death. Besides, I'm pretty sure if either of us felt adventurous after all that, we could probably hike into the bush and grab some wild mangoes or papaya. I make a note of asking Logan later if he can climb up some coconut palms.

"Keeping dry is the most important," Logan says as

he grabs my hand, wrapping his fingers around mine. His palm is warm, his grip strong. He holds my hand like he means to save me.

He leads me up a small path, away from the stream and the rest of the group. "Even though it's warm and humid, the constant rain here can make you nearly hypothermic. You're already cold from being in all that rainwater in the stream."

"So are you," I tell him quietly as we walk further into the jungle, my hand still in his.

"I have chest hair," he says. "I'm insulated."

He stops and gestures to an area where the cliff walls come into the path and a large, broad-leafed tree acts as an arch over it. "Here. There's dirt there that's somewhat dry. We can hang the tarp from the tree. With the overhang from the cliff, it'll create a bit of shelter. I'll start a fire, and we'll be dry in no time."

He turns to walk away. "Just stay here, the path up there leads out of the valley, it's wet and steep and dangerous."

Like I'd go anywhere, I think as I sit down on the narrow patch of dry red dirt by the cliff wall. My hand feels bare without his, my skin tingling.

He disappears from sight and it's only then that everything hits me. What happened, where we are, what's next.

But it's not even the ache in my muscles from the hike, the bruises that are popping up on my limbs from slamming into the rocks, the cold that's starting to seep into my bones, despite the fact that the temperature is at least in the late 70's.

It's not even that I'm going to be stuck in the wilderness overnight, waiting for rescue.

It's that for the next twenty hours or so, I'm going to be

alone with Logan. Sleeping with him, even.

And there's nothing scarier than that.

Because there's a small, terrifying chance that I actually might like it.

I can only hope he doesn't feel the same way.

CHAPTER TEN

WHEN LOGAN COMES BACK FROM THE OTHERS, HE'S carrying some matches, sticks, a few logs and a small white square.

"What's that," I ask, nodding at the square.

"Firestarter," he says, placing it on the dirt in front of my feet. "Light this up and almost anything will burn. Found some relatively dry kindling as well. It won't last all night but it will get us dried off. As long as the wind doesn't pick up, the tarp will hold and keep us dry."

I nod, biting my lip for a moment. "Have you ever been in a situation like this before? I mean, stranded in the wilderness kind of thing?"

"You think this is a regular occurrence for me?" he asks, cocking one brow as he eyes me.

I shrug. "Well you're Australian, didn't you hike into the outback and wrestle crocodiles on the regular? I've seen

Crocodile Dundee you know."

He watches me for a moment before getting all the kindling together. "You're taking the piss, aren't you?"

"When aren't I?" I tease.

He places the white square in the center of the sticks and strikes a match. The second the match meets the square, it goes up in bright flames.

"Whoa. That stuff works," I tell him.

He murmurs in agreement. "And to answer your question, yes I have been in situations like this before. In Australia. My brother is a tour guide out of Darwin. I may not be Croc Dundee—God forbid that bloody name is even mentioned in my country—but if anyone is like that, it's him. He's dragged me out on one too many adventures."

"You have a brother?" This is the first I'd heard of this.

"Kit," he says, adjusting the kindling so it will catch. "About five years younger. The same difference as you and Juliet."

"He wasn't at the wedding," I note. Come to think of it, I don't think any of his family was. It was just hard to notice since there were so many people there I didn't know, thanks to the reach of my mother. Talk about wedding of the century.

"No," he says. "He wanted to but finances were tough at that time for him and he wouldn't let me pay his way. As for my parents, I only have my mum and she's not doing so well. She's suffering from a whole whack of autoimmune disorders and flying does a number on her."

"Oh," I say quietly. "I'm sorry. I had no idea…"

"That I even had a family?" he asks, glancing at me quickly before putting a few logs on the fire. "No, I suppose you wouldn't. I reckon I know a hell of a lot more about you than you know of me."

I want to argue that, even though I know it's true. Still, I want to hear him talk. "Oh yeah? What could you know about me?"

He dusts off his hands and comes over, stooping under the blue tarp, the rain falling methodically on it. He settles down beside me, his long, strong legs to the side of the fire. His shoulder rubs against mine as he adjusts himself and my eyes are drawn to his neck, wondering what he would taste like. Probably mud.

"Well, let's see," he says, admiring the fire the way I'm sure Early Man did, proud that he has provided and ensured our survival. "I know that you hate being wrong."

"That's not true. I just hate it when you're right."

His face turns to me, the glow of the fire lighting up his profile. "So you admit I'm usually right."

"I didn't say that."

"Right," he says slowly, a small smile teasing his lips. "I know that you're a terrible singer."

"A new discovery," I concede, trying not to cringe over my rendition of "Kashmir."

"I know that you're not left-handed, but you put your fork in your left hand when you eat."

He noticed that? "A minor quirk," I explain. "Doesn't mean you know me."

"I know you would rather think the best of someone than the worst, and I know no matter how many times they disappoint you, it doesn't make you jaded in the least."

His eyes stay locked on mine, a thread of intimacy between us. How could he know that about me? I'd never thought of Logan as someone who watched me that closely. Sometimes it looked like he did, that intensity in his gaze, as if he was studying you, observing, taking you all in. Not quite like a lab subject, more as a mystery to be solved. But even so, I assumed his thoughts were always on anything else other than me.

He goes on. "And I know that you're damn good at your job. That's one of the reasons I hired you."

I frown, puzzled. "How would you know? Had I ever cooked for you before I came here?"

He nods. "Yes. You didn't know it. I went into your restaurant last time I was in Chicago. It was around noon. I saw you back there in the kitchen, and I saw you work on it. Spinach fettucine with shitake mushrooms and parm. Best I'd ever had."

I'm amazed. Floored, even.

"What…was Juliet with you?"

He shakes his head. "Just me."

"You came alone? Why?"

He stares into the fire, running his hand over his strong jawline, his beard sounding rough against his fingers. Above us the rain drips on the tarp, in the distance is the ever-present roar of the stream and the angry surf. The world doesn't seem to pause, but everything between us does.

"I wanted to prove everyone wrong," he eventually says.

"I don't…I don't understand."

He eyes me, his gaze resting momentarily on my lips. "Your sister. Your mother. Even your own father. None of them have any idea of what you do, what you're capable of. They just talk. They don't see. And I thought otherwise. So I went and checked it out for myself. And I was right."

I can't even believe it. My brain racks back, wishing I could have remembered that day.

"Do you remember Christmas?" he asks.

I nod.

You stood up for me.

"That was just an example...of their ignorance. Everyone is always so blinded by your sister."

"*Was* blinded," I correct him, my voice barely a whisper. I'm not sure we should even be talking about her in anyway other than complimentary.

"No," he says. "Still is. Present tense. When your sister died...she died as the person everyone loved. I know that she was what you were always measured against, and I knew after she died, that it wouldn't stop for you. If anything, it would be worse, because she'd forever be unflawed. And you...you're full of flaws."

I blink a few times. My heart is thumping louder, like it's trying to break out of my ribs. "Thanks." As if I needed a reminder of how imperfect I was. "You were blinded too, then."

"Yeah," he says softly. "I was." He sighs, then props his elbows up on his knees. "You know that's a compliment, right?"

"What is? That I'm terribly flawed?"

"Yeah."

I roll my eyes. "I shouldn't be surprised that you don't know what a compliment is."

"Yeah? But it is one. Because you wear your flaws, proudly. You are who you are. You aren't ashamed of it. You tell the world that you're real and you're trying. Why else would you be here?"

"Because I had no choice," I mutter. "We both know it. My mother made you hire me."

"You mother has never been able to make me do anything," he says, his voice gruff. "She's the most flawed of us all, and you know that. It's what makes her weaker than you'll ever be. Because you have strength in every dark crevice, you've had to fight and you have the scars. That's why you scare her, that's why you scared both of them."

"Both of them?"

He breathes out loudly through his nose. "You never realized that Juliet was afraid of you, did you?"

I balk at that. Literally flinch. "What the hell are you talking about?"

He twists to face me, his dark eyes glimmering from the fire. "You marched to the beat of your own drum. Juliet never got to do that. Her destiny was controlled from the moment she was born. Why do you think she married me? It was her only chance to rebel. To escape."

I swallow hard. All these truths coming out at once are a little hard to take, and what he's saying is exactly in line with what my mother was saying over the phone this morning. "I thought it was because you two were in love."

He doesn't say anything to that. Instead, he gets to his feet and walks out from underneath the tarp. "I'll be right back," he says. "I should get some more wood before it gets dark."

And then he's gone.

Fuck.

The idea that Juliet was afraid of me, when all this time I was afraid of measuring up to her has a hard time sinking in. I'm not even sure I believe it. Juliet *was* perfect. I'd never heard anyone say a bad thing about her, never saw her look or act less than anything beautiful. If she was suffering underneath it all because of the expectations my mother put on her, she never, *ever* showed it. If anything, those expectations were then handed down to me because my mother told the whole entire world how much she loved Juliet. Hell, she told her how much she loved her. I heard it, all the time, and I remembered it because it never sounded the same when it was directed to me.

I know I sound like the long-suffering youngest child, I know it's a part that's far too easy for me to sink into. But it's been a part of who I am since the moment I was born. That moment I was forever measured against what I could become. I was never taken as I am.

And yet here is Logan telling me everything I've always craved to hear and I'm not even sure he knows what he's saying. Juliet was his wife and in some ways, maybe every way, he's breaking her confidence by telling me these things.

Or maybe it's the kind of things I should have always known. Maybe the pedestal I put her on was always a little too high.

Logan is gone longer than I anticipated. With my phone completely destroyed by the water I have no way of knowing how much time has passed. The clouds are still coming from behind us, obscuring the sun, leaving a grey and shadow-less void over the jungle. I can hear the faint chatter of the other hikers far in the distance, a familiar sound that reminds me that I'm not completely alone out here. If things get weird between Logan and I, I can always head down to their camp and join them.

And aside from the sounds of the violent surf and the steady roar of the stream, I can hear birds singing, along with the occasional crow of a rooster. Even in the heart of the jungle, the damn chickens are everywhere.

I also hear what sounds like a *mew*. I turn my head to see a cat poke it's face out of a bush. It's grey and white, scrawny but not starving, with large dark eyes.

"Hey," I cry out softly, sticking out my hand and making the motion for him to come forward. "Come say hi."

The cat doesn't move, just eyes me curiously. Quickly and quietly, trying not to scare it, I lean over and pick up the packet of beef jerky and fish out a piece, holding it out.

The cat starts to approach then jumps and scurries back into the bushes.

Seconds later, Logan appears, branches in his arms. He eyes where the cat disappeared and looks at me, the lines in his forehead deepening. "And I thought you weren't a cat person."

Ah, the other thing discussed at Christmas.

"Ha ha," I tell him. "The poor thing is all the way out here by itself."

"I wouldn't worry too much about the cat," Logan says, stooping down to put the branches by the fire. "There are a bunch of feral ones out here. And they aren't suffering. A forest full of chickens like this? It's fucking KFC."

"Kauai Fried Chicken?"

He lets out a soft laugh. "Something like that. Here, we'll let the fire dry these branches out before we use them later." He sits down beside me and nudges me in the shoulder. "And since you were so eager to give the cat our rations, how about you share some with me? Or is it reserved for animals only?"

I look him over, pretending to inspect him. "That wouldn't be far off," I say warily. "You seem more like a bear than anything else."

"A bear?"

"Something large, dark, and hairy, anyway."

"Is that so?"

I shrug and hand him the packet. "But I can share all the same."

He takes it from me and for one beautiful, terrible second, our fingers brush against each other. It's like a lightning rod placed straight to my heart. But if the touch meant anything to him, he doesn't show it. Like usual, it's all in my head.

Forget your head, I remind myself, *it's your whole damn body.*

"Is that your nickname for me?" he asks, opening the packet and tearing into a piece. "The bear?"

"Nah," I tell him. "I actually don't have a nickname for you. Except *habut*, but every time I hear it, I think of booty."

"If it's my booty, I don't see the problem."

"This is the second time today you've referenced your ass."

"It's a good one, why ignore it?"

I pause, smiling to myself. "You're more like…Gruff."

"Gruff?"

"Mr. Gruff."

He laughs. "That's a name of a dog. Somewhere in the world, there is a dog called Mr. Gruff."

"How about Grumps?"

"Not sure if that's much better, Freckles."

"Sorry, you don't get to choose," I tell him, taking the beef jerky back. "Taste of your own medicine."

"I guess it's a good reminder that I have a reputation to uphold."

But Logan doesn't lapse back into the gruff grump I've known him as. Instead, our conversation continues to flow with a strange kind of ease. We talk about the island and how Logan's changed since moving here. We talk about his brother and mother back in Australia, how he'd love to go visit. We talk about his childhood, how he grew up father-less (his father was a deadbeat) and how I grew up essentially parentless, even though they were still there physically. My nannies raised me better than my parents did, even though there was always a revolving door of them and I never got to know one nanny longer than a year.

Soon night has fallen. The fire is still going, though it's

134

dwindling down into dark coals and glowing embers. The rain has stopped and we're both fully dry now, the heat and the shelter raising our body temperature back up to a normal level. Though the roar of the stream has died down, it's a steady reminder of why we are here. No matter what, there is no escape.

Our food is almost all eaten—the apple is saved for breakfast tomorrow—and it's time to worry about how we're going to sleep. Though the rain has stopped for now, odds are it will come back (it's Kauai after all) and there's barely enough room for one person to stretch out under the shelter.

Logan nods at me. "It's getting late. Why don't you lie down? There's enough room between the wall and the fire."

"What about you?"

"I'll sit here."

"And sleep?"

"If I can. Keep watch in case that cat comes back. I didn't trust his face."

I watch him for a few moments until he gestures at the earth again. Finally, I lie down, my back to the wall, my face to the fire, those last flames licking the logs. The ground is hard but it's warm, and even though I'm a finicky sleeper, my head already feels heavy. To be honest, lying down like this feels like bliss.

But it doesn't feel right. Logan should be lying down too, even though he has no choice but to lie with me. I wouldn't mind. In fact, as I start to drift off, I can't help but imagine that the warm, hard cliff at my back is him.

I wake up with what feels like a flashlight in my face. I blink, groggy, while everything comes back to me. My limbs are stiff and sore, and I feel exposed to the world.

I fully open my eyes to see the moon peeking out over a palm tree, full and bright and in my face, shadowed clouds passing beneath it. Crickets chirp over the sound of crashing waves.

Easing myself up, I look over for Logan. He's sitting up, his back against the wall of the cliff, his head slumped to the side. Sleeping.

I have to go to the bathroom and don't want to wake him up. I feel terrible that I've been lying down asleep and he's had to sit up like that most of the night, but I'm still too afraid to insist he lie down with me. He'd turn me down, I know this, and I'd be asking for all the wrong reasons.

Slowly I get up and step over the fire, keeping my head low so I don't hit the tarp. I don't go far, only a few feet and off to the side to pee. When I'm done, I step back onto the path and run right into Logan.

"Argh!" I let out a cry while he grabs my arms.

"It's just me," he says, voice low.

"I had to pee," I explain. My heart is beating a mile a minute. He scared me half to death and I've had enough scares to last me a lifetime.

"And I had to make sure you were coming back," he says. He turns and I follow him back to our site. "It's a gorgeous night," he says over his shoulder as he sits down where he was before. "The full moons here are something else. You really feel the pull. That feeling of being on a planet in outer space. So small. So insignificant."

I can't help but shiver at that as I sit down, which he notices.

"Want me to start up the fire again? I might be able to

get some kindling going."

"No, it's not that," I explain, wincing. Everything hurts. "It's that the last thing I want to be reminded of is how isolated and desolate we are."

"Right," he says. "Well, sometimes we need it. Helps put things in perspective."

"I think I've had enough put into perspective in my life, let alone the last twenty-four hours. So, earlier," I say, leaning against the wall beside him and hugging my knees, "when you said that you never listened to what my mother said…that you didn't hire me because of her. Was that true?"

"Of course it was."

"And you hired me then because you knew I was a good cook."

"That's right."

"You never called any of my references…"

"You never supplied any references," he says. "But I still called them all the same."

My chest goes hollow. "You did?" Oh shit. "Who did you talk to?"

"Erik," he says matter-of-factly. "He was your boss, wasn't he?"

Yes. He was my boss. He was also my lover. The man I fell in love with. The man that broke my heart. The man that got me fired.

"Look, shit happens," Logan says but I can't even meet his eyes. He knows, he knows! "I've…fallen for the wrong people myself and I've done some crazy shit. I might be almost forty, Freckles, but it doesn't mean I haven't forgotten my life before."

"And you still hired me," I say in disbelief.

He laughs. "Are you kidding me? It made me want you

even more." I glance at him wide-eyed and he just grins at me. "I told you earlier you march to the beat of your own drum. You fucking tried to burn the whole kitchen down because he pissed you off. That's crazy, and I'm sorry but I like it."

I sigh loudly, burying my head in my hands. "That's not exactly what happened," I mutter. "The kitchen fire was all his."

But here's what did happen.

Erik was the head chef at Piccolo, and the guy I'd been secretly, or not-so secretly, in love with since the moment he was hired, which was half-way through my career there. He was everything I thought I'd ever want in a man. Older, successful, cocky, handsome. A lot like Logan, which I try not to think about. But while Logan, for all his faults, has this sincerity underneath his gruff exterior, Erik was all show. He never had a heart, he never loved. He never cared about anything except himself.

And getting pussy. I knew he was a player but it didn't stop me from thinking I could be the one that changed all that in him. Like any romance novel fantasy, I saw Erik and thought that once he got to know me, once he fell in love with me, that he would realize he's finally found what he's looking for.

I changed for him. The minute we started seeing each other I did everything I could to keep him. I did everything in the bedroom. I dressed the way he liked. I did everything I could to be the best. I guess in some way I was trying to be Juliet to someone who didn't even know who Juliet was.

It worked for a short amount of time. I didn't know that though. I thought it worked for years. We kept our relationship pretty much secret (at least I thought we did) and like a fool I thought I was the only one in his eyes.

I wasn't.

He'd been cheating on me, and when I finally found out about the girls (yes, plural), he acted like it was no big deal. Just as easily as we'd started, he tossed me to the curb. To make matters worse, he told the staff what had been going on between us, and then he started up with one of the new waitresses, rubbing it in my face whenever he could. I even caught her giving him a blow-job in the deep freezer and before I shut the door he'd said, "Better luck next time."

Whatever respect I had tried to earn at Piccolo was gone in an instant. All those years of service, of starting from a line cook and making my way up to *chef di partie* was gone. I was the laughing stock. Everyone pitied me. I was the fool who'd been screwed over by Erik, I was the one who thought she could sleep to the top. That wasn't true, but that didn't stop people from twisting things around.

So I did whatever anyone else would do in my position.

I printed out a not so flattering picture of his dick and slipped it into everyone's menu with the headline "The Chef's Special—perfect if you lack self-respect. Order now and get a free side of garlic bread."

I thought it was hilarious—mainly because I'd absolutely lost my mind at that moment. And most of the staff had to agree.

But Erik was the boss. Obviously I was fired on the spot. Later that night he burned every one of those pics on the stove, causing a small fire in the kitchen, which he would later blame on me. I never lit shit on fire. The minute I handed out those dick pics, I was done. But he has to say he fired me for something, so that's what it is. He'd never admit that pictures of his flaccid penis were handed out along with the night's dishes.

So that's what happened. That's why even though I

spent most of my career at Piccolo, I can never use them on my resume. That's why working for Logan and Moonwater Inn is my chance to rebuild myself again.

"You know what?" I say to Logan. "I don't regret a fucking thing. If you fuck me over, I will fuck you over in return."

He watches me for a moment, the smile on his lips faltering. "I wouldn't doubt it."

I grow quiet for a moment, working up the nerve, working to open myself. The sounds of the jungle grow louder, the darkness seems thicker. "Thank you, by the way," I say, my voice low, as if I'm aware the jungle is listening.

"For what?"

"For saving my life. Earlier today."

He gives me a quick smile and shrugs. "You would have done the same for me." He pauses. "No wait, you wouldn't have. You would have watched me go downstream and waved goodbye."

Even though his tone is light, I can tell he's actually serious.

"I wouldn't have," I tell him.

"Oh, come on Veronica," he says with a dry laugh. "We both know I'm not your favorite person."

"That's not true," I say and I mean it. Because he's right but he's also so wrong. In some ways he is my favorite person, even though I still hate him.

I do still hate him, right?

"It's okay," he says. "I get it."

"Do you really?" I retort and I realize this is the closest that either of us have gotten to talking about the elephant in the room.

He shoots me a sharp look, his brows furrowed. "Yeah, I think I do."

"And that's all you have to say about it?"

He looks away, swallows thickly. A faint tic appears on his firmly-set jaw.

"You can't blame me," I go on. "How I feel about you. What you did."

"No, I can't," he says.

I growl in frustration, wanting to just address the damn thing and have it over with, be done with it. "Why did you do it?"

Silence. Eventually he says, "Do what?" His voice is hollow.

"Why did you do to my sister what Erik did to me?"

"It's hardly the same," he says.

"It hurt Juliet didn't it? Then it's the same."

More silence. He breathes in, breathes out. My nerves are prickling, head to toe, waiting, wanting, dying for a reason not to hate him anymore.

"The truth hurts, Freckles," he says with some finality.

"That's all you've got?"

He glances at me, his eyes shining in the dark. "You do know I loved your sister."

"How could I ever believe that?" I ask incredulously, feeling the need to get up and walk away.

"Because I'm telling you I did," he says.

"Actions speak louder than words!"

"I *know*," his tone is getting harder, an edge that could part hair. "And short of you being witness to our marriage, you're not going to understand. You won't allow yourself."

I shake my head, my cheeks turning hot. "You cheated on her. You had an affair. She told me this. She told everyone this. This is why everyone *hates* you."

"And why you hate me," he says simply. In the light of the moon, his eyes look dull.

"You want me to hate you!" I cry out, now getting to my feet.

"Maybe I do," he says, staring up at me with venom. "Would it make you feel better to know why?"

"Because you have a guilty fucking conscious!" I yell, throwing my arms out. One hits the tarp, spilling water onto the path. I don't know why I'm so angry, and I know this is the last place we should be having it out, but everything I've kept buried is boiling to the top and spilling out of my mouth.

"I do have a guilty conscious," he fires back. "But not for the reason you think."

We stare at each other for a few beats. The world is reduced to a dark, bittersweet syrup. It's him and me. Whatever desolation I felt moments before has been replaced with the acute feeling that there's nothing beyond this, beyond us. Like the world has moved chess pieces to get us to this moment. My blood hums.

"Then what is the reason?" I manage to ask, my voice sounding so small, so wrecked.

His gaze never wavers from mine. Whatever he's trying to say, he's saying it with his eyes. They burn, like fire, like a primal element, a basic need I'm just discovering in myself.

"I don't think you're ready to hear it," he says.

And then I snap out of it. Push through the syrup, find my clarity. The man is a joke. He may have saved my life, he may have told me things I wanted to hear, but the fact remains that he cheated on my sister and he's too much of a chicken-shit to even own up to it. He's just trying to get me to run around in circles instead of looking the truth in the eye. I did that with Erik. I'm not going to do that with him.

"Fuck you," I tell him and turn on my heel, stomping off into the forest, heading up, up, up the slippery path, branches and leaves slapping at my bare legs.

"Where the hell are you going?" I hear him yell from behind me, but the moon is lighting up the path clearly and soon I'm running, tears welling in my eyes, running away from everything I'm feeling.

I know I'm overtired, I know I've been through a lot, I know my body is hurting from the day and that I'm more than lucky to be alive. And I know that I owe Logan. But everything is coming to a head and I don't know how to deal with it. The way he was with Juliet, the way Juliet was with me, the humiliation with Erik.

The deep-seated need I have to believe that Logan is a good guy, to trust him, to put my faith in him. I think I want that more than anything, even though that scares me because I don't know what good could come of it. And then to have him be nothing more than another Erik at the most basic level.

Serves me right for even having feelings for him to begin with.

"Stop!" I hear Logan yell from behind me, and with my blurred vision I'm swerving, stumbling into trees and boulders, the ground slipping beneath my feet. I head toward the foliage to stop my fall.

Suddenly a strong hand is wrapped around my elbow, literally pulling me back mid-step.

"Don't. Move. Another. Fucking. Step."

Logan's hot breath is at my neck.

"Let go of me," I seethe, my teeth nearly grinding together.

My body stiffens.

His grip tightens.

"One step and you'd go right over the edge of the cliff. They'd be scraping your body off the rocks in the morning."

The gravity in his tone is leveling. And yet, some rebellious, stubborn part of me wants to test his theory.

I move.

He yanks me back.

"That's it," he growls.

Before I can even protest, he's picking me up like I weigh nothing more than a feather and carrying me back to the campsite. His arms are like fucking tree trunks wrapped across my chest.

Naturally, I fight against him. I'm angry. I don't want to go sailing off cliffs but I don't want to be in this makeshift campsite with him either, and I obviously don't want to be manhandled like he's an actual Neanderthal.

It doesn't do me much good. He sits back down where we were before, his back against the cliff, the dead fire at our feet.

But he doesn't let go of me. I'm held against him tight, my back against his hard chest, my ass pressed against his crotch. I can feel his breaths coming in and out, his heart pounding against my spine. He's breathing hard against my ear; my head is back against his collarbone.

"This is ridiculous," I tell him, my words caught in my throat.

"Agreed," he says gruffly, his voice causing the skin on my neck to prickle. "But I'm not going to let you march out into that jungle just because you're pissed at me."

"I won't go." I try and move again but he holds on tighter.

"Easy, Freckles," he murmurs, his lips dangerously close to my ear.

"Ronnie," I manage to blurt out. "It's not Freckles, it's not Veronica, it's Ronnie."

"I know," he says, his arms not loosening. "And I'll call

you what everyone else doesn't."

I exhale loudly, my voice shaking. My aggravation against him is fading—he's just too close to me in every single way. It's like I can feel the blood beneath his skin, the way his body is telling me everything I want to hear.

He relaxes slightly, his arms slipping down an inch. My skin is sweaty, hot, the friction of his skin on mine is making my nerves sizzle like an electrical fire. My breasts are nearly popping out of my tank top, the sides of them pressed against his arms. The moon's light makes them glow, their curves highlighted by a slick sheen of sweat.

Everything around us slows down again, that sticky reduction. My breath swirls in my chest, my heart beating unsteadily at first, then slowing as my body starts to turn on me.

I'm a radio, an antenna; I'm tuning into every feeling between us. My neck is exposed to his mouth; my legs are spread. I'm pulsing with a primitive kind of heat that I hadn't felt for a long time. The kind that makes you want to close your eyes and give into everything.

My mind is running away on me. No, it's galloping, a wild horse, desperate to reach a brand-new land. I'm imagining what it would be like if he let his hands slip a few inches lower. Beneath the waistband of my shorts. Under my panties. Down to where I know I'm slick and aching.

The thought makes me stiffen. Not from fear, but from want. A terrible kind of want.

What's wrong with me?

"You're very tense," he whispers to me, his breath tickling my cheek.

I can barely speak. "Because I'm being held against my will."

"Is that why?" he asks, his voice becoming rougher,

huskier. I feel it in my bones.

I try and nod. No sound escapes my mouth.

If I turn my head to look at him, my lips will be just inches from his.

Don't turn your head.

I turn my head. Meet his eyes.

If there's a crazy battle raging inside my own heart, battling my mind and hormones, there's something similar going on inside his. I see myself in his eyes, the confusion, the fight.

The lust.

But like always, it can't be anything more than what I want to see.

I close my eyes and move my head away.

He makes a sound that might be disappointment.

His arms loosen, then come off of me.

"Promise you won't go anywhere," he says. He sounds gravely, torn up. "No matter how much you hate me."

"I promise," I tell him. And against everything I'd felt in the last five minutes, I get up and move away from him, lying back down against the wall in the fetal position.

Neither of us say anything for a few minutes. The air is too heavy. Not with humidity but with things unsaid. After everything, I feel like we're back at square one with each other, back into the roles we knew each other in before. I'm no better to understanding him, if anything I'm even more confused.

And then his deep voice punctuates the darkness.

"Goodnight, *Ronnie*."

It's a small victory.

CHAPTER ELEVEN

I WAKE UP THE NEXT MORNING TO THE SOUND OF THE choppers. Logan is already up, gathering our stuff. If he's acting any different toward me because of last night, he doesn't show it. And why should he? Nothing happened. It was just a fight that never got resolved. In the end, he's still my boss, still my sister's widower.

In the light of day everything looks better. Your big problems of the night before are condensed until you see them for what they really are. In our case, it's nothing. Logan is my boss. I like my job. Everything that's going right in my life doesn't hinge on my relationship with him. We don't owe each other anything other than service and a paycheck.

With that new resolve, I'm more than happy to start heading back home. Of course, nothing comes easy, and the helicopter rescue proves to be just as scary as crossing the water the day before. The water is still high and roaring, so the helicopters take each stranded hiker one by one and physically deposits them on the other side of the stream. Which means everyone is getting in a tiny half-cage, kind of like one of those wicker swing-chairs from the 70's, and being flown across the stream.

Everyone except for me. I'm known as the girl who went down the river and nearly died. All the hikers are praising Logan as a hero, and when I hear them describe the event to some of the rescue crew, I feel deeply ashamed of even fighting with him last night. Apparently when I was swept downstream, Logan immediately went into the water after me. I was under the impression that he ran down the shore and then cut in, but thinking back, there's no way he would have been able to reach me so fast if he'd done that.

No, instead he jumped in the water and let it carry him down the same path. The only difference was when he hit the final pool, the water deposited him more to the side, which gave him just enough time and strength to reach in and get me.

Before I can even say anything to him though, I'm bundled into a helicopter by myself and flown all the way to the hospital in Lihue. The last thing I see is Logan's stern face as I rise into the sky.

Lucky for me, I don't have to stay that long in the hospital. I have some bruises and a large gash on my hip that I hadn't noticed that needed some stitches, but other than that I'm unscathed.

And incredibly lucky. The doctors and nurses go on to tell me how many hikers are killed by that stream alone each year, as if I haven't heard all the stories of fucking killer island already.

When I'm released from the hospital Kate is there to

pick me up, loitering in the waiting room. The minute she sees me, she runs forward and gives me a big hug then gasps, apologizing for possibly hurting me.

To be honest, I didn't feel a thing. This is the first I've seen Kate act like more than just a roommate and I have to admit, I'm pretty touched that I managed to make an impression on her so far.

She's got her new car that she bought a few weeks ago ("I don't want to be at the mercy of the shuttle or Charlie anymore"), a used but still slick Honda Civic hatchback that she can shove her short board in the back of.

We stop in Kapa'a to get some coffees from Java Kai. They didn't exactly serve the stuff in the hospital and I can barely remember the last time I had a cup. Everything seems like such a blur.

I've been to the coffee shop a few times since that day I arrived when I was with Charlie and the redhead behind the counter has been increasingly nice to me, though I still think she gives me a bit of the stink-eye.

But that's been nothing compared to what I see with Kate.

I'm first in line, ordering a shot of noni (which is a horrible tasting fruit elixir that does wonders for your insides) and my usual banana coconut mocha iced drink and the redhead gives me the head nod—no smile—while she takes my order.

When Kate steps up to place her order though, the redhead's eyes narrow into little blue slits, the line deepening between her penciled brows. I could feel Kate stiffening up a bit as we made our way through the line, moving her weight from one foot to the other, but I didn't think anything of it until now.

These two obviously know each other.

And the redhead seems to be the one with the grudge. She just stares at Kate, not saying a single word. Kate clears her throat. "Uh, I'd like an iced macadamia nut latte with coconut milk. Please."

The barista's eyes linger on her for another moment in that death stare until she starts punching in numbers on the register.

"Five dollars and twenty-five cents," she says in a clipped voice.

Kate can't pay her fast enough and quickly moves on down to where I am, picking up my noni shot from the end of the bar. Kate's eyes are wide, the first time I've probably seen her look anything more than blasé.

"What was that about?" I whisper before I down the noni shot, full-on shuddering at the taste. It's like bad, stinky cheese mixed with rancid fruit.

"I'll explain later," she says, looking furtively over her shoulder at the barista. "It's not a big deal." She frowns as I put the empty shot glass back on the counter. "Why do you torture yourself with that stuff?"

"Look, I've been living off beef jerky and granola bars for the last twenty-four hours, my body needs this." Thankfully my drink is ready next and gets the horrid taste out of my mouth.

Once Kate gets hers, we hurry back to her car, nearly tripping over a hen and her chicks as they dawdle down the sidewalk. Last month I would have been taking pictures of the sight, now the chickens are as natural as crows and pigeons back home.

"Okay spill the beans," I tell her when we're in the car, continuing on up the highway toward the north shore.

She rolls her eyes and turns down the volume on the radio that was blaring some new Rhianna song. "It's a long story."

"It better be a long story," I tell her, "because there has to be a reason why that girl hates you. I mean, she's always been kinda bitchy with me but not like that. She looked like she wanted to murder you."

Kate reaches into a compartment between the seats and slicks on some lip balm, rubbing her lips together. I'm not even sure if she's heard me or not.

Then she lowers her sunglasses down over her eyes and sighs. "This is a judgment free zone."

"Of course."

"I'm not asking, I'm telling you," she says. "All right. That girl, Ana, used to be one of the regulars at the restaurant and the bar. She lived somewhere in Hanalei and obviously had a giant crush on Charlie. She was there pretty much all the time. And Charlie being Charlie, well they start fucking around. Charlie never committed to her but that didn't seem to matter because she was head over heels and all that bullshit. Meanwhile, I started dating this guy call Honu. Honestly I don't even know what his real name is. He was a surfer and a good time and it wasn't anything serious. But it turns out Honu was her ex-boyfriend and even though she had a thing with Charlie, she wasn't too happy about that."

"Ah, I see," I say, sucking back on the drink and letting the sugary, caffeinated goodness pump some life back into my veins.

"Well that's not all," she goes on, quieter now. "See … before Charlie started up with Ana, well, he and I were kind of a—" she clears her throat, "an item."

"I knew it!" I exclaim, nearly jumping in my seat. "I could tell, I could so tell."

She cocks her head toward me and peers over her

sunglasses. "You don't have to act so smug about it."

I grin back at her and shrug. "Hey, I've worked in the hospitality business forever, you learn to pick up on those things." I'm tempted to start talking about what happened with me and Erik since we're in the mode of sharing with each other, but I decide to hold back for now. This is Kate's story and I've had a hell of a time getting her to open up about anything.

"Anyway," she says with a wave of her hand, "I'm not proud of it but it happened. What can I say … I had just started working here and I was lonely and Charlie, was … "

"Charlie."

"Exactly. Charlie was Charlie. And we broke it off because shit was getting complicated at work and yeah it kind of bugged me at the time but I try really hard to not let anything bother me. So we just moved on and stayed friends. Then he started seeing Ana and I started seeing Honu."

"And things got complicated."

"Well, yes." She clears her throat again. "Eventually Charlie stopped fucking around with Ana. And eventually I stopped sleeping with Honu. And then I guess we started up with each other again."

I nearly spit out my drink. "Again? You and Charlie."

"Judgment free zone," she reminds me gravely.

"I know but … okay, I didn't see that one coming. No wonder she doesn't like you."

"That girl doesn't like anyone that might be a threat to her Charlie, but yeah. That's the reason why. I can't really blame her but I'm also not going to stop getting one of my favorite coffee drinks either. If she wants it out with me, she can say it to my face. Though I'm sure that would probably end up with the cops getting called."

I stare at her openly.

She gives another shrug. "Girls on this island like to fight."

"That can't help Charlie's ego at all," I muse.

Kate giggles. "No, it doesn't."

"So are you guys still … "

She shakes her head emphatically. "No. No, the last time we were together was last Christmas. Almost a year. Charlie may have gone back to her, I don't know and I really don't care."

"So no residual feelings at all?"

"No." But somehow I don't believe her. She knows this too because she turns to look at me, her mouth pursed. "I mean it. Charlie and I are done. No hard feelings between us, we're better as friends."

"Sure, sure," I tease.

"Ron!" she warns. "Don't even. And don't tell anyone what I've told you."

I laugh. "Oh my god. First of all, I wouldn't. The only people I talk to are you and Johnny and Charlie. And second of all, I'm pretty sure everyone knows. You can't keep shit like that a secret. You might try but it's always obvious when two co-workers are banging each other."

She just grumbles something and puts her window down lower. The breeze coming off from the cattle fields to our left is sweet and tinged with the smell of sun-baked dirt and grass. "And Logan," she adds.

"Logan what?"

"You talk to me, Charlie, Johnny … and Logan."

I snort in disbelief. "I do not talk to Logan. You know this better than anyone."

"Mmmm," she says. "I don't know. You were just fucking stranded with him overnight. I'm sure you guys talked about something."

She's right. We did talk about a lot. But I'm not about to get into that with her. It's way too complicated.

"You know Logan and I are like oil and water," I remind her.

"Right. But you're the water who decided to go hiking with said oil on your day off."

"Because I wanted to annoy him," I explain. I know my tone is starting to sound a bit defensive.

"I know. You're always wanting to piss him off and get under his skin and he does the exact same with you."

"Yeah but you're describing everyone's relationship with Logan. He's the *habut*. The grump. Mr. Surly. Team Gruff."

"Team Gruff?"

"Whatever. You know what I mean. I'm no different."

"Uh huh." She puts her hand out the window and starts waving it up and down over the passing air. "You say you know people when you've been working in this business, and I can say the same. Me, the rest of us, we like to bug Logan. But we don't go out of our way. We don't think about it. He's just our boss and he honestly occupies a really tiny space of my brain. I'm sure it's no different for anyone else. Anyone except you."

"Oh, well," I trail off. "I mean, he was married to my sister. He's family. So of course I might think of him more."

"And vice versa. Because that man thinks a hell of a lot about you."

Something flutters in my stomach. I swallow. "What can I say, I'm like his annoying kid sister."

"Oh no," she says. "There's nothing sisterly about the way he looks at you."

More fluttering. A whole nest of birds is taking flight inside me.

"How does he look at me?"

She glances at me over her glasses. "And suddenly you want to know?" She lets out a dry laugh. "Next time, open your eyes a bit bigger and see the whole picture."

"I don't know what you mean."

"You will."

It has to be said. "Whatever it is that you're trying to get at, don't forget who he is. Juliet's husband. My brother-in-law. Death be damned. And that would be—"

"Completely and morally wrong," she finishes. "I know. And I know you both know it too. Which is why I'm not going to say anything else. No matter what happens, you're both well aware of the consequences."

The birds in my stomach have changed course, taking a nose dive. It feels like my heart is dropping with them.

Mercifully, Kate changes subjects, talking about our first luau of the year on Wednesday. It's last minute and just for the guests, but in time it will get more and more popular. I know Johnny and I will have to hunker down with Charlie, maybe even Dan, and start planning the menu. There's a lot to think about and when it comes to this traditional Hawaiian feast, I'm a noob.

Even so, the whole ride back to Moonwater I can't help think about what Kate was getting at. As much as I like to pretend that my feelings for Logan are mild and easily squashed, a crush more than anything, the fact that she's picking up on something says a lot. And it says even more that it's coming from his side. If he were anyone else to me, I would be grilling her on everything about him, wanting every last detail: how does he look at me? What do you think it means? Has he said anything?

But he's Logan. And that's that. Anything else would be morally wrong.

Anything else would have consequences.

So I bury it.

Forget it.

And try to move on.

The days leading up to the luau crawled by. I didn't see Logan much, which is both a good and a bad thing, other than him checking up on me as soon as I got back from the hospital. But even though he kept to himself, he passed down orders to Johnny and Charlie to not let me work. I protested, of course, and kept showing up at the start of my shift anyway. And they kept pushing me out of the kitchen—gently, I might add—telling me I needed to heal.

To be honest, I was kind of grateful for it. My body really did hurt from the accident and my mind was having a hard time slipping back into reality. But it wasn't the trauma of nearly being swept away that had my brain all up in knots, it was what happened with Logan.

What could have happened. Kate told me to open my eyes, and now I was looking back on everything, dissecting every word, every touch, every gaze. Could Logan have feelings for me in the ways I never let myself imagine? How different are our interactions now compared to that moment we first met?

And like clockwork I would remind myself that nothing good could come of this. And in turn it made me want to think about him even more.

Tonight, though, it's the luau. I finally got back to work yesterday and spent the whole day with Johnny and Charlie preparing the feast. We've got eleven guests signed up, way smaller than your average luau, but at least it's something we can handle. All the side dishes are ready to go with only some reheating at the time of the feast, and of course there's the whole kalua pig that we're going to cook underground.

That's all Johnny's job. I'm watching and learning but he's the pro here. My contribution was making traditional poi, which is basically mashed up taro root until it has a pudding consistency. I wanted so badly to sweeten the goop up, even with something like agave syrup, but Johnny chastised me for the thought. The purple white goop must be eaten as it is—bland and tasteless.

There's an electricity crackling in the air tonight, and it's not just the dark clouds that have gathered at the Na Pali Coast, burying the sunset and reducing it to streams of orange and red. All of us are helping out and a few of our on-call waitresses are on duty.

The grassy area beside the restaurant has been transformed into a tiki-styled paradise, with lit torches around the tables. There's even a small band and a hula dancer.

Johnny, Charlie and I dish out the food, Big J cutting into the roasted pig with a pride I'd never seen before, and Daniel's special Mai Tai punch starts making the rounds. The live music starts, giving us a moment to relax in the background, the three of us taking a seat at a small fold-out table behind the food as we watch.

It's pretty magical. Not just because it's my first luau, but because I finally feel at home. Daniel comes by and gives me a glass of the punch as the band plays a quiet number (oh who am I kidding, they're all quiet numbers) and the hula dancer sways to the music. One of the members reads out the interpretation of the dance and I'm lost in the girl's movement and grace.

"Do you know what the band is called?" Charlie

whispers in my ear. "Three men and a Ukulele." He pauses. "Wait, you're old enough to remember that Tom Selleck
film, right?"

I laugh. "Are you?"

"I thought it was Ted Danson," Johnny says as Daniel
hands him his glass. "Hey Danny Boy, you ever watch
Cheers? Did Sam Malone make you want to be a bartender?"

"Are you kidding me?" Daniel says, thumbing the col-
lar of his ever-present Hawaiian shirt, "I'm the tropical version of him."

"Pretty sure the tropical version of Sam Malone is Tom
Cruise in Cocktail," Charlie says, taking a sip of the drink.
He coughs, his face going red. "Jesus, Dan. What the hell
did you put in here?"

Dan shrugs. "Figured the drunker the guests got, the
more they'd think the night was a success. You know, in
case things went to shit." He looks over his shoulder at one
of the tables where Logan is standing, glass in hand, and
talking to the guests. "And I may have given Logan an extra
lethal dose or two. Figured the *habut* could loosen up a bit."

Charlie and Johnny burst out into gleeful laughter, like
wicked schoolchildren, while my eyes are still focused sole-
ly on Logan.

He looks nothing short of amazing, actually. I wish I
could say otherwise, but at this point I'm starting to realize
that he could wear a potato sack and look as hot as fuck.
And hell, I'm imagining that potato sack right now, the way
it would show off his muscular thighs, and I'm practically
squirming in my seat.

Fuck it. I'm owning this feeling. I have an even bigger
sip of my drink, enjoying the fruity burn as it goes down,
and commit myself to not giving a shit tonight. For once I
just want to feel everything but the shame.

Logan isn't wearing a potato sack of course, but a white short-sleeved shirt that's unbuttoned enough to show a hint of his chest, and knee-length black shorts. His hair is pushed off his forehead, his beard trimmed, his skin a golden tan. I should be looking anywhere else, but I can't tear my eyes off of him.

He looks up, his gaze meeting mine for the first time tonight. I can only stare right back as seconds pass between us, the connection a livewire, palpable. Even with the distance and the people between us, his eyes seem to crackle and flame like the torches in the background.

"*Aloha kaua,*" Johnny says, his voice making me jump.

I tear my eyes off of Logan and glance at Johnny. "Huh?" I quickly sneak a peek at Logan again but now his back is turned to me. I can still feel his gaze, like it's branded me on the inside.

"*Aloha kaua* is Hawaiian," Johnny says as he leans into me. His dark eyes are glossy, his cheeks pink. I think the punch is hitting him hard too. "It means how are we?"

"How are we?"

"Yes. Instead of checking up on just you, it means how are we, how is our relationship. It's about strengthening the connection from people."

"Oh." I raise my drink to him. "Well I think we, as you and I, are doing just fine tonight."

He raises his drink and clinks it against mine. "I have to agree. And how are you and everyone else?"

I shrug. "No complaints at the compound."

Johnny takes a gulp of his drink and coughs. "I just wanted to check in. Everyone really likes you, you know. We don't want you to leave. You are *ohana* now."

I look at him in surprise, my heart rattling in my chest. Why would he even ask this? The thought is unbearable.

"Why would I leave?"

"Because sometimes people move to Hawaii thinking it's all going to be one way and it turns out to be another. Island life isn't for everyone. Island fever is a real thing. You've been here a month, that's past the vacation period. Usually around this time, people decide if the spirit of aloha is really for them."

I laugh. "Well I'm not even at my probation period," I remind him. "I'm sure Logan would love it if I left before three months but I'm not giving him that satisfaction."

"Are you kidding me? The *habut* will never let you go."

That phrase alone feels like a warm bath.

"I don't know about that…"

"Little *wahine*," Johnny says with a big smile. "You're one of the best we've had. That dish you added to the menu, the kimchi calzone, is a hit. Logan knows your worth as much as the rest of us. And…"

"And what?" I ask, twisting around to face him better.

"I think you're good for him. Even if he might not know it himself."

I let out an awkward snort. "Yeah right."

"Nah, I mean it, aye." He nudges me with his elbow and nods his head at Logan who is drinking and talking to Daniel over by the pig. "I know he's a grump but he's better. He's been better ever since you showed up. You're a breath of fresh air."

"There's plenty of fresh air here," I mumble. "We live in fucking paradise." And the minute I say that, a warm breeze floats past, smelling of one of my favorite flowers, plumeria. I have the urge to go gather a bunch and put them all over my hair.

"And yet he hasn't been able to appreciate it. His heart is broken and it was making him sick. They have a saying in

Hawaiian you know..."

"Another one?"

"We have many. This one is *pono*. Which is making right your wrongs and practicing forgiveness. Once an apology has been made, it becomes your responsibility to forgive. If a grudge is held instead, it becomes *kaumaha*, a burden, and it will make you ill at heart."

I swallow hard, staring at Logan again. "I don't see what that has to with Logan."

"Sometimes you can wrong yourself. Sometimes you don't honor your own truth. Sometimes you forgive but the person isn't alive anymore to accept it."

I stare at Johnny for a few moments, weighing my words before I say them. "I don't think you really know the real Logan."

"Do you?" he counters. His eyes are glittering, trying to tell me something but I can't quite figure it out.

"No I suppose I don't," I concede, wanting to drop the subject now.

Johnny just nods. "It's a magical night. Breathe it in. Appreciate it. See people in a new light. The torches illuminate so much more than the surface. A luau is about thanks and celebration of family. Give thanks for being here. Celebrate your *ohana*. Your family." He pauses. "And remember Shephard is your family too. Not just because of Juliet." He finishes the rest of his drink. "More punch?"

"Yes please," I tell him, handing him my cup. As Johnny goes off, I look around for Charlie, wondering where he's gone. I spot him in the parking lot talking to Kate about something heated. Kate's throwing up her arms like he's said something that's gotten under her skin, which is a rarity, and Charlie is rolling his eyes.

I don't mean to spy, though I do mean to grill Kate

when we head back to the unit later.

Eventually Johnny comes back with more punch and we have a few more cups until it's time to serve dessert. Despite all of us feeling tipsy, and now Charlie and Kate having totally disappeared, we manage to get out the buffet of mango and rice pudding, lilikoi cheesecake, and coconut pie.

As the night wears on, everyone is drunk and happy, guests included. Dan was right about making that punch extra potent. Johnny, Dan, Jin, and Logan put everything away after the guests leave, so the girls can relax. I have a few more drinks with Nikki and our Saturday waitress, Lucia, sprawled out on the coarse, spongey grass, tiki torches wavering in the breeze. Above us the sky is dark and open, the stars a dusting of sparkling sugar.

"Where is Kate?" I ask, rattling the ice in my cup.

Nikki laughs, throwing her hair over her shoulder. "Do you even have to ask?"

"Do you see Charlie?" Lucia asks wryly. "No. Put two and two together."

"In other words, don't head back to your apartment so soon," Nikki says with a smirk.

"Figures," I mutter. Fighting leads to fucking. Well, for everyone but me.

"Hey, can I ask you guys a question," I ask after a few minutes, my voice low as Daniel takes in some of the chairs back to the restaurant.

"Sure, what?" Nikki asks.

"After my sister died…was there ever anyone else? I mean, with Logan?"

Nikki and Lucia exchange a furtive glance.

"What?" I ask because that glance sure as hell meant something. "One of you?"

"No, no," Nikki quickly exclaims. "Not us. Nothing like that anyway."

"What do you mean?"

There! Another sneaky glance.

"You guys! Come on. I need to know. I won't say anything."

Lucia sighs. "Well I don't live here, so I don't have much to lose. And anyway it isn't a big deal. A girl Charlotte used to work here. She and Logan went out a few times."

"Oh my god," I exclaim, feeling somehow both jealous and angry. "When?"

"Maybe six months ago?" Nikki muses.

"Did he cheat on Juliet with her?"

"What?" Nikki asks, scrunching up her nose. "Cheat on her? Logan would never do that."

How badly I want to tell her otherwise.

"No, it was short, maybe a few dates. Charlotte had a mad crush on him hey, and finally he gave in," Lucia says with a laugh. She gives me a quick shrug. "I don't know. I think he kind of needed it. It was really hard seeing him after she died."

"Like he was actually upset?"

Nikki frowns. "What kind of person do you think Logan is?"

What kind of person? Once again, I think I have no idea.

We stay there on the lawn for a while longer, talking about Lucia's newest boyfriend in Hanalei, a lifeguard, and some live music show playing at a lounge in Kapaa'a tomorrow. But all I can think about is Logan. Now this Charlotte woman. It's completely possible that this was the person he cheated on Juliet with, especially if she worked here. Nikki and Lucia might think they know Logan, but I'm pretty sure they aren't privy to anything important. Not like that. Juliet had a hard-enough time confiding in me, I'm sure she would go out of her way to make sure no one else here knew what was really going on.

The night is balmy and the clear sky is doing something to my head. Or maybe it's the copious amounts of punch. When Nikki and Lucia decide to leave, I wander past the restaurant and down to the beach, passing a plumeria tree. I shove my nose into the center of the white flowers and breathe in deep, then start plucking them off the tree. I know it's wrong and I should only pick up the ones that have fallen to the ground, but I'm drunk and the idea of making my own lei or decorating my body with them is extremely appealing.

Plus the smell is so intoxicating. It's just as sweet and heady as the air here, a smell that makes me really feel I'm in paradise and has an immediate relaxing effect.

"Duplicitous," Logan says from beside me, his voice low and rough.

I jump, the flowers flying up and out of my hands and twirling to the sand below. "Jesus, way to sneak up on me!" I cry out, hand at my chest.

He stares at me, the corner of his mouth lifting slightly. He looks different, his eyes less hard, his face more open. The half-moon illuminates his face just enough for him to look both mysterious and devastatingly handsome.

Damn him.

"Sorry," he says, quickly bending over to pick up a flower. He holds it out in front of me, then his hand goes over my right shoulder and he slides the flower behind my ear, his fingers rough as they graze the tip of my lobe. I can't help but close my eyes, my breath stilling inside me. Even the waves seem to slow down, the surf echoing in my ears.

"The right side means you're not taken."

"Well I'm not," I say, but my words come out in a whisper. I slowly open my eyes again and he is still there, this beautiful, troubled, strange man that no one seems to know and everyone thinks they've figured out.

"No, you aren't." His voice drops a register, sounding almost melancholy.

"What did you mean? You said duplicitous. Just now. When you scared the shit out of me."

"The flowers are not what they seem," he says, finally breaking our heated gaze. Thank god, because that was getting a bit intense. My heart is still pounding so hard I'm afraid he might hear it over the waves.

He runs his hand along the flowers and their dark, shiny leaves. "Plumeria, Tiare, Frangipani. No matter what name we give them, they remain a lie."

I peer at him closely. "Are you drunk?"

He cocks a brow. "What makes you say that?"

"Well I'm drunk and we've all been drinking Dan's potent punch. Plus you're talking about lying flowers, so there's that."

"I'll have you know I'm not drunk," Logan says but he kind of slurs it. And it's kind of adorable. "And I don't have to be drunk to be talking about lying flowers. Here, smell." He plucks one off the tree and steps even closer, the distance between us tightening up into intimate levels. He raises the center of the flower to my nose and I don't have to lean far to stick my nose in. I take a deep breath just as I had been earlier when I was hitting the blooms up like I was huffing paint.

"They bloom at night," he says, taking the flower away and smelling it himself, rather delicately. "To lure the sphinx moth. Only they don't have any nectar—it's all a rouse. So the bloody moth flies from flower to flower, in a fruitless search for nectar. And while it does that, the moth pollinates, ensuring the flower's survival." He flicks the flower to the sand and stares at it for a few moments.

"Is this a metaphor for something?" I ask after a few beats.

He glances at me quickly before turning his attention to the waves, the spray illuminated by the moon and the faint light of the hotel rooms. "If it is, you'll have to let me know who you'd be…the flower, or the moth."

"Neither," I say. "I'm just the girl who wants to put the flowers in her hair."

He chuckles at that and nods a few times, shoving his hands in his pockets. Silence is a line between us, weighted and heavy. I have this feeling that if I don't say a word, the silence will continue, thickening by the minute, like adding flour to water.

I look at him. "Can I ask you something?"

"No."

"It's about Juliet."

Finally, his eyes come back to meet mine, brows furrowed with worry. "What?" he says hesitantly.

"Did you cheat on her with that girl Charlotte? The one who worked here?"

For a second it seems like he hasn't heard me. Then his eyes widen and he physically recoils, shaking his head. "What the bloody hell, Veronica?"

"I just want to know. I need to know."

"Why?"

"Why?' My voice can't help but rising an octave. "Because she was my sister. I have a right to know."

"We've already been over this. You don't have a right to know. That was our marriage and our business."

"She confided in me!" I exclaim. "Don't you understand? That means that she saw me worthy of her secret, worthy of me knowing she was married to a liar and a cheater, that one aspect of her life wasn't perfect."

"You think that gives you the right?"

"Yes! I do! You don't understand, she never gave me anything. That's all I got from her and I need the whole truth."

"Fucking Jack Nicholson."

I twitch in confusion. "What?" I hiss.

He rubs his hand down his face and sighs. "I can't even respond to you without sounding like I'm borrowing from a movie cliché."

"What? That I can't handle the truth?"

"Much better when you say it."

"I can handle it!" I yell. "I just need to know."

"Why?"

"Stop asking me that!"

"But I want to know. Is it because if you knew how terrible I was, you would stop being attracted to me?"

Now it's my turn to recoil. "Oh my god." And fuck! Dammit! My cheeks are flaring up, betraying me right away. I turn away from him, shaking my head, wondering how on earth I can squash his idea. This is the last thing I want, the last thing his ego needs, the worst thing for my job.

"Is that why?" he keeps going, following right behind me as I walk aimlessly down the beach, sinking into the sand with each step. "Why you're walking away right now? Because it's your *own* truth that you can't handle?"

"Oh fuck off, you don't know me," I scowl. I keep going and I don't turn around. "Don't change the subject."

"This has nothing to do with me at all, Freckles, and you know it. That's why you're so fixated on it."

"I'm fixated because she was my sister."

"And because she was your sister, that means that whatever you feel for me, whether it's lust, whether it's more, you think it's wrong. Unforgiveable. You hate yourself for it."

This can't be happening; this can't be happening.

He grabs my arm, whirling me around. The sand goes flying.

"It's easier for you to hate me then to like me, isn't it?"

"You're an easy person to hate!" I fire back. "That's on you."

I try and get out of his grasp.

He doesn't let go.

He's staring at me so intently that I'm nearly pinned to the ground.

"Charlotte," he says slowly, "was a friend of mine. I knew she had a crush on me and she was a nice girl. It took a year and a half after Juliet died for me to finally agree to a date. We went on three. That was all. I went back to being alone. She went and found someone else. Eventually she quit her job and moved in with him. Everyone was fine." His grip on my arm tightens. "I did *not* cheat on Juliet with Charlotte."

How diplomatic, I think to myself, *not denying he didn't cheat on her, just denying he cheated on her with this Charlotte woman.*

"But," he goes on, "the more excuses you can find to hate me, to bury your attraction to me, the better."

God, I want to punch in his smug, handsome face so fucking bad!

"You're a dick," I say bitterly. "A dick with an unstoppable ego."

"Or maybe an ego with an unstoppable dick. But no, that thought won't help you, will it?"

"Fuck you."

"You've said that already and nothing's happened."

I try and wriggle out of his grasp again.

"I'm not letting you go," he says. "Until you tell me I'm right."

"About what? That I'm attracted to you?"

He hauls me closer to him, so our faces are just inches apart. My breath catches in my throat and stays there. I'm afraid to breathe. I'm afraid…of everything. My little world I've built for myself on this island is tipping and I'm moments from being lost to the waves.

Lost to him.

Like I've always wanted to be.

"Then kiss me," he says. It's both a command and a growl and it nearly knocks me off balance. "Prove me wrong."

I'm staring at his mouth of course, the way he's holding it, the way his lips almost snarl. It's an invitation, it's a trap. And I would never give him the satisfaction of being right, no matter how badly I want his lips on mine.

"No," I tell him, fixing my gaze on his eyes with as much strength and venom as I can handle. I'm a woman and my venom is as powerful as my heart. I have endless reserves. "That's what you want me to do."

"And if I say yes," he murmurs, his face coming closer, the top of his nose brushing against mine, "that I want it too—would that change anything?"

It would change everything.

Everything.

"It wouldn't matter," I tell him. I don't know where I find the strength.

"I think you're lying," he whispers. His hands let go of my arms and reach up, disappearing into my hair. "And I'll prove it."

Before I can protest, he swiftly leans in and kisses me. His lips are pressed, flush, wet to mine and in that moment a million waves could crash over my head and it wouldn't come close to this feeling. I'm sinking, drowning, swimming against his lips. His mouth works against mine in perfect rhythm, his tongue so warm and soft and fucking addicting. He tastes like rum punch and lies and the first rays of morning.

Your sister, that voice, that loud and important voice, speaks up. It's nearly buried by the lust that's building through me, the same lust that's making my knees weak, my limbs tremble and shake.

But it's there.

I put my hand at his chest and push him back. Not hard, just enough for our mouths to break apart. He's breathing heavily, his nostrils flaring, his eyes drenched in desire, and I already feel empty without his kiss. Every part of me aches.

"We can't," I tell him, wishing I didn't sound so weak.

"Because of Juliet? Your mother? Which person in your family is it?" His tone is borderline nasty.

"Because," I say feebly, but my fingers are already trailing to the button on his shirt, just beneath his collarbone. "It's wrong and you know it."

"We're adults," Logan says. "We can make our own decisions. We can decide what's right for us, not anyone else, not because of what anyone else thinks." He runs his hand through my hair, scratching along the scalp and I nearly melt right there. "Fuck, Veronica. Tell me this isn't what you want. Tell me it's not me and I'll walk away and we'll go back to what was."

But the truth is so confusing, so dicey.

"I'll tell you what," he says, running his thumb over my lips. "I've been wanting to kiss you for a long time. And I've been wanting to do a hell of a lot more. If you think it's been easy for me to deal with that…"

"You were married," I tell him.

"I'm aware of that," he says. "But the past tense is *was*."

I look at him sharply, like I've been kicked in the shins. "That's a terrible thing to say."

"It's the truth, isn't it?"

"She's dead," I cry out softly. "If she wasn't, you wouldn't be saying this." I pause, the reality kicking in. "But, wait, of course you would."

He flinches. "Easy now. This is about us."

"There is no us without her, don't you see that?"

His brows knit together as he stares at me, his jaw set hard. "All I know is how I feel. And I know how you feel too."

"I never admitted anything!" I say, about to push him away for good.

But his hand in my hair makes a tight fist, pulling on the strands and he brings my face right up to his. "If you think any of this is easy, you're wrong," he growls.

And then he's kissing me again and I'm a goner. His hand pulls at my hair and I moan into his mouth while his other hand grabs hold of my ass, yanking me into him. I feel everything all at once. I'm overloaded, like a million dreams have just been dumped on me from above. His hard-on pressing against my pelvis, my thighs clenching together, his tongue sliding against mine at a slow and languid pace, the hard and soft of his lips as he both soothes and devours me.

I'm not bashful either. I grab the back of his neck, feeling his hot skin, and I run my nails over his shoulders and the tight, hard muscle underneath. Johnny once told me the Hawaiians saw fire as a force that gave instead of took and here, as we stand on the beach, the waves crashing angrily at our feet, I understand what he means. We're positively volcanic and the fire between us is growing and giving life to something else entirely. Something new. Something unstoppable.

"Logan?"

Daniel's voice cuts between us like we've been doused with ice water. We both let go of each other and jump back, our chests heaving, fear in our eyes.

It's then that I realize how wrong this has been. Our reaction says it all.

Logan clears his throat and starts marching down the beach toward Daniel's shadow. "Over here. What's going on?"

Daniel stops and I think he's looking over at me. I'm not sure if I'm hidden by the bend of the plumeria bushes or not, I'm not sure if I have to hide. If we were just talking to each other, I wouldn't be thinking it. But since we weren't—since he was kissing me, and vice versa—now I have something to feel guilty about.

And do I ever feel guilty. As Logan talks to Daniel about what to do with some of the excess items from the luau, I slink back into the bushes and go the long way around the restaurant.

I know it's wrong, I know I shouldn't be running away like this, that I should stay and wait for Logan and talk about what just happened, set things straight, but I'm a coward. Right here and now, I'm a coward. I just want to forget that anything happened. I want to pretend that I don't know what Logan Shephard tastes like, what his erection feels like, what his voice sounds like when it's choked with lust for me. I need to forget it all.

I'm quiet when I get back into the unit, just in case Kate's asleep. In fact, I don't hear anything until I've washed up and I'm crawling under the covers. A set of murmurs and giggles comes from her room. I can pick out Charlie's voice.

Fuck. They sound cute and happy together. Once again, what the hell did Daniel put in that punch?

It doesn't matter because at least it makes me sleep. I put my earplugs in so I can drown out Kate and Charlie and then I'm dreaming.

CHAPTER TWELVE

"KILL ME NOW."

I blink a few times at the sound of Kate's voice. At least it sounds like Kate. It could also be a toad. I've seen a lot of them on the lawn between the buildings. It's croaking like one.

I roll over in bed because I can feel her hovering over me, and when I do it's like the pits of hell open and a million fiery jackhammers are released, heading straight for my brain.

"Ugggh," I moan, holding onto my temples.

"I know, right?" Kate says. "I think Danny boy was up to some real Bill Cosby shit with that punch last night. I feel like death."

I slowly sit up and Kate thrusts a glass in my hands. "It's coconut water," she says. "It should help. I already drank the carton and I toasted all the bread we had. And then I

174

ate it. Sorry."

I wave her away and try and down some of the drink. "It's fine. Wow. I've felt better." I finally open my eyes fully and get a good look at her. She still looks pretty, though she has a slight green tinge to her skin and her mouth looks a bit swollen. As in bruised. As in, I know exactly what went on between her and Charlie last night.

You also know what happened with you and Logan, I remind myself and of course all those memories decide to come flooding back. Did that *actually* happen?

But it's Kate who is looking at me with the extra-innocent expression which I know means she's extra-guilty. I wonder if I look the same.

"So," I say, biting my lip to keep from smiling. "You turned in early last night."

She stares at me and her features harden, giving me nothing. "Yeah. Like I said. The punch. Bill Cosby. Roofies. That whole analogy." She makes a dismissive gesture with her hand.

I match her innocent expression from earlier. "Charlie disappeared too."

She shrugs and plucks the empty glass from my hand. "Maybe, I don't know." She walks out of my bedroom and over to the kitchen where I can't see her.

"I saw you guys arguing in the parking lot," I say loudly so she can hear.

"What? Oh. You know Charlie."

"I also heard you talking and giggling last night when I was going to sleep. You know. From your bedroom."

Total silence. She could butter the silence, it's so thick.

"You don't want to talk about it, that's cool," I say, getting out of bed. "I ain't one to pry. But if you do want to talk about it, you'll know where I am. Right here. Or in the restaurant. That's pretty much it. And I'm all ears."

To Kate's credit she keeps mum about the whole thing, at least for the morning. I head out on the balcony with a large cup of coffee and watch the waves in the distance, listening to the soft coos of the tiny zebra doves that have perched along the railing.

And I ruin all that morning Zen and calmness by thinking about what the fuck happened last night.

Holy. Shit.

Logan kissed me. Logan basically told me he wanted me, was attracted to me, as much as I wanted him. And he wasn't just leading me on, not in that way. I felt his desire, I felt everything I'd always wanted.

And yet the minute that a light was shone upon us, we both balked. We both acted like nothing was happening because we both felt guilty. He can tell me how badly I want him and how I beat myself up over it and I'll admit he's right. I'm not sure how he knows that, if I'm that transparent, if it was wishful thinking, but he's right. And the guilt has been eating me alive.

But that same guilt plagues him. Maybe it's the cheating he did on Juliet, maybe it's because of the same reason as it is for me, but he can't pretend that his own desires and ego aren't slave to the same machine.

So where does that leave us? What has changed now? That kiss woke me up, made me realize not only how deep my own feelings went, how badly my body craved what it couldn't, shouldn't have, but it showed me it wasn't one-sided. Logan wants me too.

Logan wants me too.

I think that's the one I'm having the most trouble with. Why a man like him would be interested in a girl like me is beyond my comprehension. It's not a matter of false modesty and humility. I get why Charlie might want me (not that he does since he's currently boning—or reboning—Kate) or maybe even Dan. But Logan is older. Probably the most handsome, manliest, most fuckable man I've ever met. And he can—and has—attracted the most gorgeous women. I'm just the cook at his hotel.

And, fuck, that's another reason why all of this is a big mistake. You'd think I would fucking learn from last time, from throwing my future all away because I slept with my boss. I mean, what the hell am I thinking?

That question will get me through the rest of my day. It makes the hangover peel away and forces me to look at last night as a drunken, momentary lapse of judgment. Whatever feelings I have for Logan have to end now, because as we both proved last night, alcohol is a bad idea and being horny is never an excuse to do something you regret.

Because now I do regret what happened. I'm not going to dwell on it or beat myself up anymore but I am going to make sure that it will never, ever happen again.

When I head back into the unit, I'm full of new resolve. Meanwhile Kate is looking guilty, standing in the corner of the kitchen with a mousy expression and drinking coffee.

"Am I an idiot?" she asks me quietly.

"Are you kidding me?" I ask, putting my coffee cup in the sink. I fold my arms across my chest, grateful to worry about someone else's mistakes. "Why, because you slept with Charlie?"

She nods. "I didn't mean for it to happen."

I smile. "That's usually how these things start out. I wouldn't worry about it, honestly. I mean, it's Charlie. You told me about your relationship with him before. You work together, you got drunk, he's a nice guy. It's not a big deal."

Kate doesn't look convinced. She raises a brow. "Did

you rehearse all that stuff to say to me?"

"No!" I quickly tell her. "No, not at all. It's just…don't feel bad. You're not an idiot. Just…chalk it up to what it is and we'll all move on. I mean, you'll move on." Her brow remains raised, and I clear my throat. "I'm, uh, going to go take a shower."

Since I have the morning and afternoon free, I decide to Facetime with Claire for a bit (I purposely steer the conversation away from Logan), then I head to the Limahuli Gardens by myself. It's located between the hotel and Ke'e Beach, and one of the places I've always wanted to go. And today I don't want to be at the hotel at all and I don't want the company. I'd rather be alone with my blackened thoughts.

The gardens are lovely and set high on the hills, cutting back into the sharp mountains of the interior. There are a few tourists here but it's nice to actually be able to watch them. Some of them are families taking in the flora and fauna of the island, from macadamia nut bushes to coffee plants and taro. The kids shriek and run around while the parents either laugh or chastise them for disturbing people, but no matter the reaction, the fact that they're a family remains.

I never had that. And Johnny's words from last night come cutting into my brain. The crew at Moonwater Inn is my family now. Maybe not by blood, but by choice. And that has to count for a lot more. They've embraced me whole-heartedly, flaws and all, and they like me, not because they have to but because they want to.

And that's why Logan and I could never work out. Because the moment you start sleeping with the boss, that's the moment you put everything else at risk. Even if everyone could somehow get past the morally deplorable part of the arrangement, there's that cold fact again that I would be fucking the one in charge and if shit hit the fan? Well I'd be out of a job. It wouldn't matter our bonds, I wouldn't keep working here. I'd be on the next plane back to Chicago.

I don't want to do that. I don't want to give up everything I've worked so hard for here. I don't want to fuck up like I've fucked up before.

Even if it means shutting down the attraction I have for Logan, the feelings I've acquired, I have to do it for the sake of my new life.

Fuck, it's not fair. But I should be used to that, too.

When I'm done at the gardens, I head across to Haena Beach and then walk back to the hotel along the shore, ready to face my new decision.

And the first thing I have to do is find Logan.

Of course, now that I'm actually looking for him, I can't find him. He's nowhere to be found during the day, and no one seems to know where he went. Only Daniel thinks he might be in Hanalei at Tahiti Nui but I'm just about to start my shift, so there's no way I can verify it until afterward.

"Charlie," I say at closing, as the two of us are washing up over the sink and Johnny starts turning off the restaurant lights. "Can you do me a favor and drive me to Hanalei?"

He looks both relieved and surprised. I bet he thought I was going to ask him about Kate. "What, now? Sure." He pauses. "With me? You want to grab a drink?"

I think that over. Charlie wasn't part of my plan but maybe it would be a bit weird—and definitely out of character—for me to have him drop me off. "Yeah, at Tahiti Nui," I tell him. "I just feel like getting out of here." I pause. "You think Kate will mind?"

He narrows his eyes at me. "If this is all a rouse to get me to talk about Kate, you can forget about it, sweet thing."

"Not a rouse," I tell him. "Your business is your business."

"All right then," he says warily.

It's not long before we're finding a parking spot in Hanalei. It's late, so aside from Tahiti Nui and the bar beside it, everything has shut down for the evening. It's kind of nice, actually. I love Hanalei—it's the prettiest town on the island with the striking green mountains behind it and the smart-looking shops—but in the day it can get pretty busy.

Charlie and I head into Tahiti Nui, which has live music tonight in the form of a man and a guitar poised in the corner. It's pretty crowded, considering it's only open for another hour, but I manage to spot Logan sitting at the end of the bar, palming a beer.

"Hey it's the *habut*," Charlie says, looking over. "Should we say hi?"

I nudge the empty table beside us. "Sit here, I'll go get us drinks."

Charlie seems okay with that and takes a seat. "Are you paying?"

I sigh. "Yes. Just sit tight."

Tahiti Nui is one of the cooler bars I've been too. It's like a Tahitian dive bar, except it's not dirty or gross. The locals love it here and it has a really laid-back vibe and a lot of history within the thatched walls. Lots of celebrity's pictures are on the walls, including George Clooney's, since scenes of The Descendants were shot in here. Plus, their pizzas are to die for.

I'm practically in Logan's face before he even notices me, and when he does he barely moves. Just keeps his elbows on the table and side-eyes me.

"What are you doing here?" he asks flatly before taking

a sip of his beer.

"Looking for you," I tell him, trying to take the edge out of my voice and failing.

"Why?" He says this in such an "I don't give a shit" manner that I can feel my blood pressure rising. I'm going to need a drink, stat.

"Why? You know why." I lean in and lower my voice. "We need to talk about what happened last night."

"No we don't," he says, clearing his throat. He signals for the bartender to give him another and then glances at me. "Guess I should have been a gentleman and ordered one for you too."

"Gentleman?" I repeat. "That's a stretch." And when the bartender gives him his drink I put in an order with her for two Longboard beers, sliding a few rumpled bills on the counter.

"You're not here alone?" he asks, looking around the bar.

"No, I'm with Charlie," I tell him.

"I see," he says, staring me dead in the eyes. "And you needed him here so you could talk to me?"

The bartender gives me my beers. "I mean it," I tell him. "We need to talk. I'll be right back."

I quickly squeeze my way past the patrons and find Charlie at his table.

Talking to a girl, of course.

I give her a quick smile even though I have no idea who she is and give Charlie his beer. "I'm just going over there for a minute," I tell him and point in no particular direction.

I think Charlie thinks he's busted or something because he's all wide-eyed as he nods.

I head back over to where Logan is sitting, only to see

him heading out the back door of the restaurant. What a fucking sneak!

"Where are you going?" I ask as I burst out of the back door and into the parking lot. He keeps walking, so I run up to him and thump him with my fist, right on his back. It's like punching a wall.

But it gets him to stop. He whirls around and fastens his eyes on me. "What is your problem? Can't a man drink in peace?"

I hold my ground as he takes a step closer, refusing to back away. "You've had the whole day and night to drink. Is that why you've been here? You're hiding from me?"

"Don't flatter yourself," he says with the surliest expression I've seen on him yet.

I blink at him, wondering how it's possible to go from making out with him to being completely aggravated by him in such a short period of time. "So then let's talk."

"There is nothing to talk about," he says, looking away. Even nearing midnight, there's a rooster strutting along the edge of the parking lot. "It was a big mistake."

Ow. I feel like I've been kicked in the ribs. I know I came here wanting to tell him the same thing, I know it's what I'd been stewing over all day, but the fact is, it hurts to hear him say it.

"That's what I was going to say." The words come out in a hush, distracted by my wrenching heart.

"Good. Then we're on the same page," he says, running his hand along his jaw. He looks at me and sighs. "I shouldn't have kissed you."

"No, you shouldn't have."

"You did kiss me back, though."

It was impossible not to.

"Momentary lapse of judgment," I tell him. "I blame

Dan's punch."

"I'm your boss. It was reckless of me. I took advantage of you."

"Whoa, hey now," I tell him. "You didn't take advantage of me. I wasn't that drunk. I knew exactly what I was doing."

"And yet you still did it," he says, his tone softer, his eyes searching mine, shining in the streetlights.

"As I said…it was a momentary lapse of judgment." I avert my eyes, feeling that pull to him, like the waves to the moon. I can't put myself in that situation again.

I can see him cock his head out of the corner of my eye, studying me. "Do you regret it?"

I swallow. "Do you?"

"I just said it was a mistake."

I nod. "Yeah. Yeah and you're right. It was."

"People make mistakes all the time," he goes on, his words taking on a silken quality. I can't help but close my eyes as he comes forward. His fingers trail along my jaw, disappearing behind my ear and into my hair.

Oh, god, not again. This is a test. Stay strong.

I keep my eyes closed.

"Some people never learn from them," he adds softly.

I suck in my breath as my nerves dance from head to toe. "Why are you doing this?" I whisper.

He exhales slowly, his hand leaving my hair and drifting down my shoulder, my arm, leaving a wake of heightened skin. I supress the urge to shiver.

"Touching you?" he asks.

"Yes." My voice shakes.

"Because I want to."

"And you think you just can?"

"Because I know you want me to."

"You just said it was a mistake."

"Maybe I'm testing you." His hand comes off of me. "To see if you'd make the same mistake again."

Remember everything you decided.

Remember who he is.

Remember what's at stake.

He leans in, his mouth at my ear. My world smells like coconut and mint and whatever pheromones he has that drive me so goddamn crazy. "Last night was nothing. Not an appetizer or even an aperitif. You have no idea the things I want to do to you. No idea of the way I can make you feel."

I think I have some idea. I'm so fucking turned on it's not even funny. I'm not even breathing. I'm on an edge and I'm seconds from falling.

His hand slides up the side of my tank top and brushes over my breast, sending a shower of sparks down my spine, making me tingle from head to toe.

"And I know you want me to try."

It would be so easy to take the plunge. Throw my arms back, close my eyes, and go off the deep end. To just give in and see how that feels. To be free. To want for nothing but pleasure.

His lips tease beneath my ear before he gently takes my lobe between his teeth.

Sweet Jesus.

I can't take much more of this.

"The other side of desire is fear," he murmurs, his voice reaching through me like a hot knife. "The other side of fear is desire. What side controls you?"

"Fear." I pull away, staring at him with wide eyes. An ounce of strength and common sense is rising through me and if I don't use it now, I never will. "Because of what will happen to me if I give in to you."

"Give in to me?" he repeats, blinking at me.

"I'll ruin the one thing I have going for me. This job. This life here. You and I would never become anything, we never could, and so then what happens? I'll be forced to walk away. To quit and not look back."

He's staring at me like I spit in his face and takes a step back. "Why the hell would I force you to walk away?"

"I've been down this road before. You of all people know this."

"Veronica, you know that I'm not like that," he says imploringly. "I would never put your job here in jeopardy, ever. No matter what happens between us."

I'm half inclined to believe him. He sounds sincere. And yet…

He continues. "Are you serious? You think I'm that big of a wanker that I would do that?"

My mouth opens and shuts. I want to tell him I want to think the best of him. I want to tell him I don't trust him at all. I want to tell him that he's worth the risk and that he's not worth the risk. I don't know what I want. Maybe that's the problem.

"You're never going to forgive me, are you?" he says bitterly, shaking his head.

"For what you did to Juliet? No. And why should I? You never told me you were sorry for it. You never told me anything that would make me like you a bit better, if not understand you better. You act like nothing happened."

"Maybe because nothing did happen," he says this so quietly I barely hear him.

"That's bullshit and you know it!" I yell at him just as a couple of people walk past us to their car, giving us the hairy eyeball as they go. I lower my voice. "Juliet told me and you know she did, so don't deny it."

"I'm not denying anything," he says. "But I am leaving."

He stalks off down the parking lot, a car's headlights highlighting him from behind.

I ran away last night, tonight he's doing the same. I suppose it's only fair.

I contemplate going after him, but what would the point of another argument be? We've already been over it. It's getting redundant. He's never going to tell me he's sorry for what he did and I'm never going to stop hating him over it. Maybe it's not hatred, but it's one of those many valid reasons why all of this is a bad idea. I know the battle between fear and desire is raging inside me, and when it comes to Logan fear is going to win each time.

I finish my beer standing there in the parking lot, watching as Logan disappears around the corner, probably to the bar next door. When I'm done, I head back inside Tahiti Nui to find Charlie, totally defeated.

Charlie is now sitting at the bar, talking to the bartender, the other girl nowhere in sight.

"Where the hell did you go?" he asks, looking me up and down as I plunk the empty beer on the counter. "I was afraid you'd been swept off your feet by some strapping young lad."

I roll my eyes. "Not exactly. I was just talking to Logan."

"What about?"

"Family drama, really," I say just as the bartender informs us it's last call. I order two shots of dark rum.

"Shots?" Charlie asks. "You know I'm driving."

"They're both for me," I tell him.

"Well damn, dude. What kind of family drama is this?" he asks.

I shake my head, unsure if I should get into it or not. Honestly it isn't Charlie's business and it's not really my business either. I know Logan keeps saying that and I keep arguing, but I think he's right. I fucking hate it when he's right.

"Double shot drama," I tell him.

"I've been there," Charlie says. "In fact that's one reason I'm not looking forward to Thanksgiving next week. I haven't been back in a few years and I know that my family has just been hoarding all their craziness somewhere, waiting until I arrive to unleash it all."

"I'll tell you one thing, if I stay here long-term I don't see myself going back home for a long time."

"You are staying here long-term, aren't you?" Charlie asks.

"Yeah, I am. I mean I hope," I tell him. "I don't have plans to leave."

"Good," he says.

"So what's your family drama all about?" I ask and with a big sigh, he starts talking about how his parents are divorced but they play nice every holiday. His older brother is a gambler and has lost his house and his younger sister is a stoner who still lives with the mom, and now his mom is juggling both kids while the father gallivants with his hot new wife. Even though Charlie's family drama is a lot different than mine, it just goes to show how no family is perfect. Every family is fucked up in one way or another, it's how you deal with it and how you accept it that makes us different. Denial is the easiest alternative in the short-term but it fucks you up over time.

"And you?" Charlie asks. "You can't take and not give, sweet thing."

I finish the second shot, feeling woozy already. "I'll spare you the boring details. But my mother is the deputy mayor of Chicago, and my father is kind of her bitch, and from the moment we were born, my mother groomed Juliet to be perfect and she groomed me to be just like Juliet. Only I'm not Juliet and never will be. But as far as my mother is concerned, Juliet was the golden child and I was some sort of mistake. Now that Juliet's dead, she's this legend I'll never live up to." I cough and give Charlie an apologetic look. "I'm sorry. I know that sounds callous of me."

"No, no, I get it," he says. "I could see how hard that would be. I mean…not to add to it, but Juliet pretty much was perfect."

"I know," I grumble.

"But I mean, like sometimes it wasn't in a nice way…if that makes sense."

"What do you mean?"

He shrugs. "I don't know…it doesn't seem right to talk about her like this."

"Right or not, we are. If Juliet has something to say about it, she can give us a sign."

Just then a bottle behind the bar crashes to the ground and smashes to smithereens. People in the bar give a hearty cry, "Opa!" and the bartender gives a bow.

Charlie and I look at each other warily.

"Anyway," I say quickly. "Keep going."

"You ever seen that movie the Stepford Wives? With Nicole Kidman?"

"Yeah."

"Like that. A little too perfect. Always smiling, always had the right thing to say. She never raised her voice, never got upset. She was kind of robotic, and sometimes I thought it was a little bit fake. Like a mask. Like she was hiding something underneath that was anything but." He throws up a hand. "I don't know, don't listen to me. These are just things I think of when I get too high."

Juliet the Stepford Wife. I can't help but feel there's some truth in what he's saying. But if we only saw the mask, then who was the real Juliet? Did Logan ever see her? Or was she a mystery to him to?

Maybe that's why he cheated on her, I think. *He never felt he was married to someone real to begin with.*

But of course that's just making excuses for him, and that's the last thing I want to do right now.

"Anyways," Charlie goes on, a bit pink in the cheeks and clearly uncomfortable, "I don't mean any harm by it. She was lovely. And I could see how living up to that would be hard when you're clearly nothing like her."

I frown. "What does that mean?"

He sighs and adjusts himself on top of the tiki stool, slipping his bare feet on the metal rung beneath the bar. "I feel like this conversation has the power to take a horribly wrong turn. For me."

"Charlie," I warn. "Tell me or I'll tell Kate you were with another girl tonight."

"I wasn't!" he exclaims. "She's just a friend." Then his features go aloof. "And there's nothing between me and Kate anyway. So I don't care."

I kick his leg. "Tell me."

"It's not an insult," he says. "You're just…the opposite. Yeah you kinda look the same, the eyes mainly. But you're like…a hurricane. And she was the…"

"Calm before the storm?"

"No. She was the underground bunker. The shelter. Could withstand anything and come out looking clean while everything around her is destroyed. She could hide and avoid damage." He groans. "Fuck, I'm getting intro-spective and I'm not even high. Do you want to go?"

I nod, even though Charlie is making more sense than

he thinks.

When we get back in the truck, he asks. "So what was the drama you were discussing with Logan then?"

"It's a long story."

"Does the story involve unresolved sexual tension?"

"What?" I snap.

He grins at me. "I'm just messing with you."

I watch him carefully for a few beats, making sure he really is "taking the piss" as Logan would say, before I say, "You better be."

Even so, as I go to bed that night my brain is reeling with too many things.

And then I'm dreaming.

About Logan.

About Juliet.

About her swimming during the golden hour, when the sun goes down behind the mountains and the ocean is tinged with gold. Metallic waves crash on the shore, pink and coral clouds float above. It's my favorite time of day in Kauai, maybe because I'm always working at sunset and rarely get to see it.

In my dream Juliet has swum far past the reef and Logan is on shore, yelling for her to come back, that there are sharks and rips and other dangers. That she will die.

But she doesn't listen. She waves, happy as always, and just keeps swimming. Everything is fine with her, everything is perfect. Nothing could ever endanger Juliet.

So Logan takes off his shirt, about to jump in after her. His body gleams in the light, every taut muscle, every slope and ridge.

Then he stops. Pauses.

Turns around and sees me.

"Ronnie," he says, using my nickname. "I didn't see you

there."

Juliet is in danger, I want to say. I can see her now, getting smaller and smaller and smaller.

But I can't talk. I can't do anything but wait for Logan while he strides toward me, scoops me up in his arms and kisses me until I can't breathe.

"You've always been mine," he murmurs and kisses me again as we fall to the sand.

Somewhere in the distance, Juliet is drowning.

CHAPTER THIRTEEN

It's Thanksgiving. It doesn't feel like Thanksgiving, since I'm not battling frigid temperatures and the early start of crazy holiday shoppers, but it's Thanksgiving all the same.

Charlie has been gone for a few days now, so Johnny and I have been working overtime to make-up for it. They said that Thanksgiving is supposed to be the slow time of year but I guess they were wrong, because there seems to be more customers than ever. Johnny says they're coming because of my cooking, but I have yet to confirm that.

I do know that the staff at Moonwater at least appreciates it, because Johnny and I slaved all day making the perfect Thanksgiving meal for everyone, which included a tofurkey for Kate since she's vegan. We were able to shut the restaurant for the night in order to do so, with Logan's permission. Johnny handled that one, since, once again, Logan

192

and I have been avoiding each other this last week.

Now, the turkey carcass has been annihilated and everyone looks sated. It's just Daniel, Jin, Nikki, Kate, Logan, Johnny, and I, but any more people and we would have had to get another bird. Johnny was born on Kauai (not a *haole*) so he's having dinner with his family tomorrow afternoon, but he still ate his fair share of the turkey.

"Pumpkin pie?" Johnny asks, coming out from the kitchen and to the middle of the restaurant where we've pushed a few tables together. "With Kauai spices. It's vegan, just for you Kate."

A few people groan, including myself, rubbing their bellies.

Logan gets up. "Thanks but no thanks, I better head back to reception."

And then he's gone, heading out across the parking lot, the rain this evening coming down steadily. Everyone looks at each other in mild surprise. He had put a sign on the reception telling guests where to find us if there was an emergency, so the real issue is that Logan doesn't want to be here and I have a feeling it's because of me.

"Well now that the boss is gone," Daniel says, getting up and heading to the bar. "How about we graduate from the wine and onto something else?"

Soon everyone has some crazy cocktail in their hand that Dan whipped up on the spot and Jin, of all people, goes over to the stereo and puts Grandmaster Flash on.

"Brother," Johnny exclaims. "All this time and I didn't know you were a Grandmaster Flash fan!"

"Who is Grandmaster Flash?" Jin says, completely sincere.

"Never mind, good choice." And then Johnny moves to the center of the room and starts dancing, making his big belly fly.

I'm not one for dancing, no matter how drunk I am and especially not when I'm still stuffed with turkey, so I stay at the bar with Daniel and watch the scene unfold as everyone gets up to dance, lured by 80's rap and alcohol. Even Jin is doing a boogie that involves shuffling from side to side.

"Too bad Logan is missing this," I comment, taking a sip of a pineapple-ginger concoction and laughing as Johnny starts doing some Michael Jackson-esque moves in front of Kate. She is not impressed.

"Yeah," Daniel says carefully. "But I don't think this holiday is easy on him."

I give him a look. "And you think it's easy on me?"

Daniel doesn't back down. "No. But things are a bit different on Logan's end. He has no one here. Juliet was his family."

"You're all his family," I point out.

He shakes his head. "Nuh-uh. Maybe at one point we were but he shut us out. He got burned and then he lost it all. People seem to blame him but I really can't. I know what he's gone through."

The conversation is confusing me—I'm not sure we're talking about the same thing. "You've lost someone too?"

"No, I mean—I know what happened…" He lowers his voice over this last part, leaning in slightly, as if handling a secret.

"Well I know what happened too," I tell him. "And he's a dick. It's completely his fault if their marriage fell apart."

He straightens up and frowns. "That's a bit harsh. How do you figure?"

I look at him blankly. "Uh, because he cheated on her."

"Juliet?" Daniel asks.

Oh shit. Did he not know that?

"Yeah," I say slowly. "Logan cheated on Juliet. I don't know who with. I already asked him if it was that Charlotte chick but he denied it. He did not deny cheating on her though."

Daniel stares at me for a few moments before tucking a piece of hair behind his ear. "Wow. Okay."

"What?" I lean forward, pressing my hands on the table. "What?!"

Daniel takes a furtive look around and leans in. "Where did you hear that from?"

"From my own sister."

He seems to think for a moment, then he straightens up and shrugs, turning his attention back to the bottles behind him. "She was lying," he says simply.

It takes all of my strength to keep my next words to a whisper. "What the hell are you talking about?"

He exhales loudly and then turns around. "Look. I was there okay? It was my client."

I can only blink at him, my heart pounding in my head. I feel like I'm about to have an out of body experience.

"Listen, I shouldn't be the one to tell you this because it's none of my business, but I thought you knew so you can see I'm in a bit of a predicament." He looks around as if we're being bugged and starts wiping down the bar. "Jared Bellamy. That was my client. A hot-shot lawyer from LA. You know, the type that takes on celebrity and high-profile cases. He was here looking to buy a house on the north shore. Says his buddy Ben Stiller loves it here and he had to do the same." He rolls his eyes. "Anyway, he comes here to the bar and I say I'm also a real estate agent. I give him my card. Juliet comes in and, well, you know what happens when Juliet walks in a room."

I don't say anything, I'm too enthralled. I nod at him to keep going.

"So Bellamy, he's got it hard for her, obviously, and I point out that's the boss. You know, she and her husband own the hotel. And it's like he doesn't care. But whatever, not my problem. The next day, I pick him up and show him around. He hangs out at the bar later. Juliet takes a seat. They're talking most of the evening. Nothing weird about that, right, because Juliet always liked talking to guests and people. Kind of a politician in that way. But then he's here every night. Even on the days when I'm not showing him houses. And she's here too. Like clockwork."

My throat feels thick as I try to speak. "Did anyone else notice?"

"No," he says. "But Logan did eventually. One night. It got kind of awkward. Walked on over and gave Bellamy the look like he was going to murder him. I had to make all the introductions and play it off, but Logan knew there was something wrong. And me, I only suspected." He pauses. "You sure you want to hear the rest?"

"You've gone too far to stop," I whisper.

He takes in a deep breath and leans in closer. "So Bellamy is staying at the Westin Princeville resort. Has his own little hut. I'm supposed to pick him up at four to show him some houses on my day off, but Lucia calls in sick, so I can't. And I can't get a hold of him on the phone either, so I decide to drive up there."

I feel like I'm watching a movie. A terrible movie playing inside my head and the climax is building and building and building. I'm on the edge of my seat, the edge of something that will change everything. If I stop Dan from speaking, I can preserve the world as I know it. If he keeps talking, my world will fall apart. I know this now.

And I let him keep talking.

"The door was open. I still knocked. It's a two-bedroom condo, he would have to hear me. I step inside the front door. I hear the shower going and figure I'll leave him a note. I go into the kitchen and pick up a pen and paper and I write him a note about the change of plans. As I do so I notice a purse on the counter. Normally I would think, hey Bellamy, good for you. But the purse is familiar. Juliet had a designer bag, Kate Spade or something I think, with lots of palm trees. It was the same bag. And then I notice the woman's underwear on the floor, a skirt, a man's polo shirt. A trail of clothes leading to the bedroom. And that's when it hits me…this is Juliet here. He's showering with her." He sighs sharply. "I'm not proud of what I did next but I had to be sure in my mind. I opened the purse, found her wallet. It was her."

I don't know what's wrong with me. The truth is laid out plain and clear and I've been a complete fucking fool but even so, the hero-worshiping illness I have with my sister is too strong. "That doesn't mean anything," I say feebly. "She could have left it there…and been there for another reason. You don't know it was her in the shower."

He nods, a placating smile on his lips. "I got out of there. A few days later, Logan brings me aside. Asks me all about Bellamy. Breaks down and says that Juliet has been cheating on him. I've never seen him cry, Ronnie. But he did. I'm not saying his marriage with Juliet was full of love and roses. They were an odd couple and they had problems. But I know Logan was at least faithful. Juliet was not. She was still seeing Bellamy the day that she died. She was driving back from his place up on the ridge."

I'm stunned. I'm stunned but I don't feel anything at all. I'm just this grey, numb mass, and all the things I should be feeling are bouncing off me, deflected.

Everything had been a lie.

Juliet. Perfect Juliet. She had cheated on her husband and then turned around and made it look like he was the one at fault, not her. And oh my god. I believed it. So did my mother. So did everyone. She made Logan out to be the villain and we were all so blinded by her, we all believed her.

And then the strangest emotion comes crawling to the surface.

Anger.

Not over Juliet. No, I'm too numb to feel anything about her. If she's a bomb shelter, I've taken some of that armor when I swooped overhead as the hurricane.

No. I'm angry at Logan.

"I have to go," I tell Daniel.

"Oh fuck, please don't say anything," he says.

"I won't," I tell him, though I know I probably will. I want to keep Daniel's trust and I don't want him in trouble, but this takes precedence.

I storm out of the restaurant and head over to reception, the rain warm and steady, streams of water forming in the parking lot. I fling the doors to the office open. But it's only Shannon there, the nightshift worker.

"Aloha," she says in her throaty voice. She always looks like she just broke out of women's prison.

"Yeah, aloha, where is Logan?" I ask, trying to keep my voice level as I brush a strand of wet hair out of my face. My red cotton dress is already sticking to me from the walk over.

"He told me to come a couple hours early. Overtime. Double overtime cuz it's a holiday. Like I would say no."

"Do you know where he went?"

"He said he was going home," she says.

As I run out of the office I can hear her call, "Happy Thanksgiving!" after me.

I haven't been inside Logan's house but I know what the interior looks like, thanks to Juliet's Facebook photos. It's a block or two from the hotel, across the road from the beach, and a modest rancher with nice landscaping.

I run down the streets of the small suburban area to the left of the hotel, my flip-flops smacking the wet pavement and echoing down the quiet road. I keep searching the houses as I go past, peering at them in the dark through the rain, until I find Logan's. In some ways I want to keep running, even though I already feel like a drowned rat. It keeps my mind from dwelling on what happened, it keeps me focused on putting one foot in front of the other. There was too much truth to swallow along with those drinks and I'm keeping all of it on the backburner until I talk to Logan, until I finally hear his side of things.

I open the wooden gate and step into their yard, dimly lit in the darkness. There's a narrow stone path of lava rock, the short, stiff grass bordering the sides, Logan's Jeep in the driveway. Plumeria, banana trees, and naupaka bushes line the fence, giving the feel of a tropical oasis. Rain drops hit the thick leaves with a soft *thwack*.

I go up to the door, noticing a worn doormat beneath my feet that has dolphins all over it. Obviously my sister's, she loved dolphins as a kid. Even the diary she used to have had them all over it.

Daniel can't be right, I think to myself, but then I'm making a fist and pounding on the door. Moths fly around, bumping at the light above me.

I won't stop until he answers.

Eventually he does, flinging the door open. He's in grey

sweatpants, no shirt. That's a fucking kryptonite combo for me but I manage to ignore it. My anger and confusion override the eye candy.

"What's wrong?" he says and his eyes are wide with concern. "You're all wet."

"You lied to me!" I yell at him, storming past him and into the foyer, not caring that I'm dragging water into his house. "You lied to me."

He slowly shuts the door behind me and gives me an incredulous look. "You'll have to bring me up to speed here."

"You never cheated on Juliet!" I cry out. "She cheated on you!"

He watches me for a few beats, seeming to think. "Who told you that?"

"Why does it matter? Why did you lie to me?"

He chuckles. "Freckles, I never lied to you."

"It's not funny!" I tell him, marching over to him and poking my finger into his chest. "It's not funny at all. You let me believe a lie. You let me believe that you were a monster that ruined my sister before she died. You made me think you were an asshole."

His brows raise, wrinkling his forehead. "I never made you think anything."

"You did! You had countless times to correct me, to tell me the truth and yet you kept letting me think it. Why? Why did you do that? Why couldn't you just tell me? I deserved to know!"

"Let me get this straight…first you hate me and think I'm an asshole because I supposedly cheated on your sister. Then you find out I didn't cheat on your sister and you still think I'm an asshole?"

I jam my finger into his chest again, my face turning

hot as the anger and frustration pour through me. "I hated you so much and you let me!"

He wraps his hand around my finger and yanks it away from him. "That's all on you, kid. You could have found out the truth if you dared to dig a little deeper, if you questioned who Juliet really was instead of blindly accepting it."

"I didn't know the real her!" I cry softly.

"None of us really did," he says. "I doubt even your mother." He pauses. "Admit it, you just wanted to hate me. It's what I said earlier. Why you never bothered to find out the truth."

I pull away from him, walking across the room, my hands at the sides of my head like I'm keeping it from exploding. "Oh, this fucking shit again."

"Because you wanted me," he goes on, his voice carrying across the room. "You wanted me just as I wanted you. From the moment you first came and stood beside me and let me know that you were my equal, that you were on my side."

That makes me pause in my tracks. "What are you talking about?" I whisper.

"One of the reasons I never told you, or your mother, or anyone in your family the truth about Juliet, the truth of what she did, one of the reasons why I took the blame and let her paint me the villain, was because I already felt guilty."

Don't turn around, I tell myself. He's walking closer to me, I can feel his heat, the power of him, at my back. It's like the sun. "Why were you guilty?" I ask carefully.

"Because I should have been with you, Ronnie. It's always been you."

My heart vaults inside my chest, bouncing in circles. It's everything I've wanted to hear and yet I'm still afraid to hear it.

"I spent part of my marriage wishing I was married to you instead."

I shut my eyes, trying to keep the tears back. I can't help it. Everything I've been led to believe has been a lie, a lie told by both sides. Was anything ever real? Was anyone ever going to share the truth with me, or was the truth something else that I didn't deserve, another thing I was unworthy of?

"Veronica, please," he says. "I never wanted you to hate me. But it was the only way this could work."

"Who are you then?" I scream, whirling around. "Who was she?"

And then he's right in front of me, his massive frame taking up all the space. He grabs my wrists, yanking me toward him. His gaze is all fire. "She was a person, okay? She was just a person."

"She was my sister!" I cry out, tears starting to burn at the corners of my eyes. "She was everything I tried to be!"

"And in the end she was just as flawed as you are," he growls, his grip tightening. "She wasn't perfect. She wasn't even a nice person half the time. You want the ugly truth or do you want to keep putting her on that pedestal?" He takes a breath, closing his eyes briefly. "Veronica, I know you're angry that you wasted so much of your life trying to become a lie, but you don't have to do that anymore. You never did. God, you're so beautiful just as you, you're better than you'll ever think you'll be."

Now my heart is competing for space in my chest, swelling and growing. It's hungry, so fucking hungry for more of his words and only Logan can feed it.

"We…I," I try to say but the sobs are masking my words.

"I told you how I feel," he says, voice so low and gruff it

makes the hair rise on my arms, my body erupt in goose-bumps. "And that still stands. So I'm sorry I'm not the ass-hole you thought I was. I'm sorry if that makes everything that much harder now." He licks his lips, his nostrils flaring as he breathes. I get the distinct feeling that he's trying to control himself, and it's maddening how much I want him to lose control.

"How can this work?" I ask meekly, my eyes drawn to his lips. "How can we do this?"

"It's very. Fucking. Simple."

And then his lips are on mine, crushing and soft. Pure velvet lust that turns sweetly violent.

His hand is at the back of my neck, his other fingers are pressing at my jaw and cheek as his tongue assaults me with such rolling passion I can feel it all the way in my toes. Just like the last two times he kissed me, he's in complete control and I surrender. I surrender completely. I want him to take me, take me over, devour me, annihilate me. I want every single part of him, deep, deep, deep. I want to see how much of him I can take, how he feels from the inside, what it's like to be thoroughly fucked by Logan Shephard.

It's wrong, the thought snakes into my head.

But it's fleeting. For once, the guilt is fleeting. I don't want to listen anymore to what's right and what's wrong. Right and wrong have no more bearing on my life, have no value. Everything has been a lie. I just want him. Right here, right now. I want him to let us out of the cage we'd put ourselves in and turn this world upside down.

And Logan does just that. He's a wild animal, feral to the core as his mouth sinks into the valley between my neck and my shoulder, biting with hunger and lust.

I groan loudly and one of his hands slips low along my hips, hiking up the hem of my dress. Every nerve ending on my body dances with anticipation.

I can't believe this is happening. I can't believe we're doing this.

It can't be stopped. I can't be stopped. His hand skirts over my belly, sliding inside my underwear and down, down to where I'm absolutely soaked.

"Christ," he murmurs against me. "You're too good to be true."

He feels too good to be true. His thick rough finger slides along my clit and my body immediately melts into his hand, needing more, wanting more. I'd never had the need to get off strike me like this before, like a match against the striker. It's almost a ride or die situation.

I grab hold of the back of his neck, his skin hot to touch, my body greedy for him. His fingers play gently along my clit, teasing like fluttery wings, before the they plunge up inside me.

A gasp escapes my mouth.

"Oh god," Logan says thickly, bringing his lips back to mine. "You keep making those noises and I won't last very long."

"You don't have to last long," I tell him, sucking in my breath as his fingers slowly withdraw. "Just fuck the hell out of me."

I can't even believe I said that but I'm so fucking crazed that I don't care.

"A woman after my own heart," he says before he's lowering his head to my breast, pulling the neckline of my dress to the side until my nipple is exposed and hardening in the air. His lips gently suck at the tip before he draws it into his mouth in one long, hard pull.

My back is arching for more and breathless groans are coaxed out of me. We're still standing in the middle of the living room and I'm not sure how much more I can take like this. I'm getting desperate for him in a way I never thought possible, an aching need that's clawing its way up through my core, turning every part of my body into an addict.

He pinches my nipple between his teeth and, as he does so, plunges his fingers back inside me, three of them this time. I expand around him, needing more. Every inch of my skin is on fire for him and only he can put out the flames.

"Fuck," he growls as he withdraws his hand, putting his fingers into his mouth. He doesn't break eye contact as he tastes me, licking the side of his finger with his large tongue.

My eyes widen. In all the sex I've had in my life, I've never had anyone do something like that, and now it's Logan, Logan of all people, in front of me and he's breaking down my barriers and bringing me somewhere completely new.

Somewhere that still scares me.

Somewhere I need to be.

"Taste yourself," he says before his mouth crashes against mine again. I'm salty, musky, slightly sweet as his tongue probes further against mine, whipping up my desire to the boiling point. This is already the hottest thing I've ever experienced.

Before I know what's happening, he's pushing me back, his massive body looming over me. "Get on the floor," he says, his voice husky and rich, screaming of sex.

I drop down to my knees on the rug, staring up at him while he quickly yanks down his sweatpants. His cock bobs free and I'm breathless once again.

There are pretty penises and there are some decent dicks, but Logan has been packing one hell of a python in his pants. I know I've felt it before, its mass crushed against me while we kissed, but now that it's in front of me, it's fucking dangerous-looking.

I can barely tear my eyes away from his cock to look up at him. Of course he looks smug—why shouldn't he—but there's a sense of awe in his eyes, like he can't believe this is happening. That makes two of us.

Since I'm already on my knees and I'm salivating for the taste of him, I grab his ass with one hand, my fingernails digging in as I tug him toward me. With my other hand I grasp his cock at the base, making a ring around it. He's so goddamn hard, it's like velvet steel, and silky to touch. I can feel the hot blood rushing underneath, the way his cock ticks with each beat of his heart.

I close my eyes and tentatively slide my tongue along the sensitive underside before circling his crown, dark and lush, licking at the precum. The salt hits my tongue, revving my desire for him to another level.

His hand goes into my damp hair, pulling lightly, and he groans as I try and take him all into my mouth.

"I told you I wouldn't last long, Freckles," he says breathlessly. "I mean that still." He pulls away from me, his cock wet and bobbing from my mouth and glances down at me with heavy-lidded eyes. "No offense, you can suck me off later if you're so inclined, but if I don't fuck the living hell out of you right now, I might just die." He jerks his chin at me. "Turn around."

My heart is pumping hard in anticipation as I pivot around on the rug so I'm on all fours, my ass raised in the air. He drops to his knees behind me and I hold my breath, waiting for his touch.

Swiftly he lifts up my dress until it's bunched around my waist. I expect him to slide my underwear down over my ass but instead I hear a fucking *rip* as he tears it in half.

"What the fuck?" I cry out and try and turn around.

"I'll buy you new ones," he says gruffly, moments before he grabs my ass, squeezing hard so I stay in place. I flinch, the pressure from his fingertips is firm and yet the moment he yields, I want it even more.

He pulls me toward him as he positions himself and with one swift jerk, pushes into me. The air is expelled from my chest as he fills me, a gasp broken on my lips.

"Are you okay?" he asks, shuddering the words as he pushes himself fully inside.

I can't speak. I can't think. I can only feel, every single inch of his hard cock as I squeeze around him. I try and nod, get my breath.

His grip around my ass tightens. "I can't promise I'll be gentle," he says. "But I can promise you'll come so hard you won't know any name but mine."

Holy hell. His words shock me to the core, dirty enough to make my skin grow even hotter. I'm on fire inside and out.

"Does that sound good?" he asks, his voice thicker now. "Can you handle that?" He pauses, slowly pulling out in such a teasing, languid way that it's torturous. I feel empty, aching for him, I want him to fill me up and up and up, like a balloon ready to burst.

"Give me hell," I tell him and if I feel a flash of embarrassment over talking like this, it's over in a second because his hand cracks across my ass with a loud slap as he hisses, "Yes," and then he's pounding into me, fast and deep and relentless. Over and over and over again, this breakneck pace that has me trying to hang on to the rug for dear life, my breasts jiggling with each quick, hard thrust.

"You feel better than heaven," he says through a husky groan. His pumps become quicker, deeper, and messy, like he's losing control and going over the edge and taking me with him. I've never had a man in so deep like this, not just inside me but inside my head. He's everything I've ever wanted and everything I shouldn't have and he's fucking me like we might lose everything tomorrow.

The same urgency that's running through him is running through me. I drop onto one elbow, and with my other hand reach for my clit, the pressure building to unbearable heights as he fucks that sweet spot inside me.

"Don't cheat," he growls, batting my hand away and grabbing the back of my hair until it's gathered in his hand. He pushes forward until my cheek is pressed into the rug and he's holding me down, grunting hard with each thrust.

Jesus. He's out of control. He's become someone else, an animal, a beast, as relentless as the waves. I'm at his mercy and I don't think I've ever wanted something more than for him to take such control and just fuck the living hell out of me.

Hell, heaven, whatever this is, I know it's something I'll never come back from. I know I'll never want to. In my wildest, kinkiest dreams about him, it's never been *this* good.

While he yanks back at my hair and then holds me down in place, he slips his other hand under my stomach, his fingers finding my clit.

I'm so wet, slick and ready for him, it doesn't take long for him to push me to the edge. I feel just as I did when I was surfing, at that terrifying moment when you know you're going over. But the waves here are completely different. They promise to make me anew.

He is merciless, grunting hard with each thrust, this rough, animalistic noise that gets louder and louder the closer he gets to coming. It's such a fucking beautiful noise that it causes the heat to build in my core, coaxing the last bit of fire I have left.

I don't even have time to tell him I'm coming. It just happens, quick and swift, and I'm swept away, tumbling and turning, over and over as the orgasm churns through me. It's an undertow, it's a rip, it has me in its clutches and I never want it to let me go. My body quakes and shudders from head to toe as I pulse around him. I am light and heavy and my heart has wings. I never want to feel anything but this, never want anyone else but him.

"Veronica," he groans out my name and then I feel him as he comes, the pressure in my hair, the slamming of his hips into my ass. The sounds coming out of his mouth are crude and I'd give anything to watch his face as he empties into me. "Yes. God, yes."

His thrusts slow down, his hand in my hair slowly letting go, releasing the pressure from my head. He's breathing hard, his hulking body hovering over me. Drops of sweat fall onto my back, making me shudder.

Then, as the orgasm starts to slide away into the background, the reality of what we'd just done hits me, like those sneaker waves that get you when you're trying to get back on the beach.

Logan Shephard just fucked me on his rug. From behind. My head pressed—no, *held*—to the ground. He fucked me like I'd never been fucked before and I'm starting to think I need a new word to describe that because "fuck" just isn't enough.

And you didn't use a condom, I remind myself. I'm lucky I'm on the pill, though I should be more careful next time.

Next time. What a crazy thought. Part of me can't assume there will be a next time. The other part of me thinks that's all there is. Next time. There has to be. Sex can't be that good and only happen once. It's an insult to the act of sex itself.

Meanwhile, as my brain starts to come to grips with everything, Logan is still breathing heavily and his hand slowly trails down my head, over my neck and down my spine.

"Veronica," he whispers, grabbing my waist.

"Yeah," I say.

He slowly pulls out, cum dripping onto my thighs, and exhales loudly. "God, you're everything I dreamed you would be."

I can't help but smile. "So you've been dreaming about me?"

"Every day, Freckles. Every bloody day." He sighs and runs his hand back up my spine. "I hope I didn't hurt you." He touches my hair gingerly. "I do love your hair."

More smiling. I'm kind of glad he can't see my face right now because I know I have the look of a teenager with the world's biggest crush. Heart eyes have nothing on me.

"Nah," I tell him. "Maybe a bit of rug burn, but it's worth it." I turn around to look at him, his eyes glazed and sated, cheeks flushed. I've never seen him like this before. He looks vulnerable. He's beautiful.

We stare at each other for a few beats before I try to get to my knees and pull down my dress. He reaches out and stops me, his hand on my wrist.

"Take it off," he says.

I blink at him, give him a crooked smile. "The dress?"

"Off."

For some reason I expected this to be the part of the night where we put our clothes back on. I can see I'm wrong. I quickly oblige, lifting the dress over my head, glad I hadn't worn a bra. If I had, there's a chance it would be lying on the rug ripped in half like my underwear. And a good bra isn't cheap.

Of course my mind is thinking about this because it's having a hard time coming to terms, once again, that I slept with Logan. I know that all those worries, all that guilt I carry in my heart, is waiting to come loose.

Luckily, Logan himself is a brilliant distraction.

"Get on the couch," he says, nodding toward the tan couch in the living room.

I'm not really sure what to expect but I get up and walk, very naked, very awkward, over to the couch. I mean, I've lost a bit of weight since coming here but I still have my cellulite (though a bit more disguised because of my tan), I still have my jiggly thighs and butt and padded hips, and I'm walking completely exposed. Which is something I have never done before, not even for Erik. I can feel Logan's eyes on every inch of my body as I go and it takes a lot of willpower to not cover myself up and run for the hills.

"Get on the couch," he says. "Spread your legs."

I turn around and stare openly at him. "What?"

He gives me a predatory half-smile as he gets to his feet and walks over. My eyes are drawn to his dick, of course, and the holy specimen of man that it's attached to. Good lord, this man needs to have statues erected in his honor. And that's not just a play on words.

I sit on the couch, totally out of my element. I don't spread my legs. Everything is so new and shocking, this side of him, how fast this is all moving.

As if he can read my thoughts, he stops in front of me and says. "I don't know how long I have before you hate me all over again."

There's a gravity to his voice that wasn't there before. The lust is put on the back burner and in his eyes I see a man who's prepared to get hurt over me. A man who thinks tonight might be all he has left to lose.

I shake my head. "Logan…" I lick my lips. "I'm not going to hate you over this. I've…well, like you've been driving at these last few weeks, I've wanted this just as much as you. It's just that—"

"Don't say her name," he says quickly. "Please. Just for the rest of the night. Don't say her name. She doesn't…this is about you and me right now and that's it. That's all there is. You and me. And if it's not forever, then just for tonight."

I nod. "I know."

"So," he goes on. "Spread your legs. Or I'll do it for you."

I raise my brow. This could get interesting.

CHAPTER FOURTEEN

A ND SO HERE I AM, LYING FULLY NAKED ON LOGAN'S couch and he's dropping to his knees in front of me, like I had dropped to my knees earlier. I know he's told me to spread my legs, but that's just a little too far out of my comfort zone—I mean, I just walked across his damn living room naked and totally thought I was going to die of embarrassment—but I can tell the man is up for a challenge.

That's a bit of an understatement, too. The man *wants* a challenge.

He comes to the edge of the couch and leans over, kissing me. After how thoroughly he just fucked me, I didn't think I'd still have that raw need pulsing through my veins, the kind that made me throw nearly all inhibitions to the wind, but clearly I do and all I need for that extra push is to have his warm tongue in my mouth.

Fuck, he tastes amazing. Our kisses are nothing but supernatural, this easy rhythm that we both fall into, kisses that invade my bloodstream and make me burn for him. I could eat him, he's that addicting.

"God, I want to fuck you with my mouth," he whispers against my gaping lips. "Everywhere."

Yes. Yes, please.

He brings his lips and tongue down the length of my body, caressing my collarbone, my breasts, sucking and biting at my nipples until I'm crazed, nearly mad with all the sensation. My fingers are desperate as they dig into the hard muscles of his back as he teasingly moves downward.

I shiver as his tongue skates over my stomach, my hips jerking as his beard brushes against my skin, contradicting the soft sweep of his lips. One of my hands makes a fist in his thick hair, the other grips the edge of the sofa. My body moves independent from me, a mind of its own. My hips rise again and again, desperately needing to feel his tongue between my legs.

Finally, his head settles between my thighs and I part them wider for him, thirsty with dire anticipation. He slowly parts me open with his hands, taking his time as he lets the rough pad of his fingertip brush over my sensitive, swollen flesh.

I'm groaning louder now. I don't care. I have no shame.

Then his tongue snakes out, sliding along my clit and setting off the volcano inside me. My breath is shaking, unstable, my fingers clawing at him, at the couch. My hips lift up, wanting more of him. His tongue, inside me, deep as he can go. I want to know what it feels like for him to lap me up, uninhibited and wild, like I'm the world's most decadent dessert.

Yes, yes, more, more.

More of this, from him.

Always.

He obliges, putting his mouth and lips into it and while I'm watching the beautiful sight of his head between my legs, he looks up. Those intense eyes are watching my every movement as he gives me more and more pleasure, his teeth razing over my clit, his tongue plunging deep inside.

It's too intimate. He's in too deep, into my deepest, darkest, most shameful parts, the ones I keep hidden. But I can't look away. I can't break his heated gaze. He's seeing me, all of me, and I want him to. For once, I want him to see everything.

The wild, determined look in his eyes is enough to make me come. My body is doing everything it can to hold on, to prolong the pleasure, to never let the moment end. Yet at the same time I'm chasing my release, needing it like a drowning woman needs air. I need both and the duality is tearing me apart in the most delicious, torturous way.

Fuck, I've *never* felt like this before.

My head flops back onto the couch as he licks in long, hot lines, from taint to cunt to clit, before swirling around in a frenzy around where my nerves are ready to explode. The noises he's making, wet, lush and unreserved, add to the insanity of the moment.

I can't hang on any longer.

"Let go," he murmurs into me and the vibrations are that extra push over the edge. "Let go for me."

I arch my back and the world becomes warmer, hotter, tighter, as if I'm made of lava and it's fighting its way to the surface. The feeling grows and spreads, this impossible force inside me, as primal as any mother nature has created, that gathers every single nerve and piece of my body until its wound over and over again like the tightest string.

The slide of his tongue makes me snap.

"Logan," I cry out, and he groans into me, vibrating deep inside and kicking me over the edge. I'm going over, falling into a burning ocean and my fingers grab his hair, pulling at him in desperation, trying to hold on even though there's no use. The orgasm never seems to end and I am pummeled over and over again.

I'm boneless, my muscles quivering as the orgasm still rolls through me, lying here with legs spread. My breath is hard to catch, my thoughts are hard to corral. I'm as high as I've ever been and I don't ever want to come down.

Then Logan is on his knees, and grabbing hold of one thigh and lifting it high, positioning himself. His darkened cock is in his hands, the most lustful look in his eyes. He pushes inside me with ease, his dick even harder than he was before. I'm so wet it feels like fucking heaven, even as my body is still tingling with the last orgasm. He fills me like nothing else.

"I need you again," his accent muddled with lust. "I don't think I'll ever stop needing you." He grinds into me, his hips slowly circling, pinning me to the couch as he pistons himself in and out. But unlike earlier, when his thrusts were this relentless, merciless machine, now he's in control and enjoying every teasing push. "I've waited so fucking long to enjoy you from the inside."

I can't think about the implications of his words. I can't think of anything. He's everything right now, the past, the present, the future. Each slow thrust, each decadent push inside me, time slows and the world stops and it's just him and it's just me and it's the wool over our eyes, making us think it's always been this way.

His eyes grab hold of mine, as tight of a grip as his hands on my thighs, and we're locked together. I'm lost in their depths and somehow I'm found. There's a new me, maybe the me he's always seen.

And beneath the gaze, beneath the sex and the desire and the pleasure we're bringing each other, there's something else. Fear. He'd said you couldn't have one without the other and here was our fear. It was alive and it was real and it was something that we both now shared.

I just don't know what fear it is.

I close my eyes as he pushes in deeper, his fingers sliding over my clit until I'm gasping and breathless. He has a way of making me forget everything, a way of losing my thoughts. He's always done this to me, just never in this way.

"I'm coming," he groans out, his voice shaking as his pumps get quicker, the rhythm picking up. And for the third time tonight, I'm coming too. I just manage to hang on long enough to keep my eyes open, to watch him as he comes.

He doesn't disappoint. His head goes back, mouth gaping, eyes pinched shut. The corded muscles of his neck stand out, his biceps taut and sinewy as his grip tightens. Beads of sweat snake down his wide chest.

I have that effect on him. The thought is unreal. He's coming because of his desire for me.

But those thoughts only fuel my own flames. I'm ripped apart again, my bones becoming jelly, my world blooming with fire and heat and stars.

Logan collapses on top of me, just his elbow on the couch to keep his weight from crushing me. He rests his damp forehead against mine, our breaths deep, chests pressing against each other and creating their own heat.

His lips gently brush mine, kiss my chin, kiss the side of my mouth.

"All those things I said I wanted to do to you," he whispers, voice hoarse. He stares at me tenderly as he tucks a strand of my hair behind my ear. "I hope you don't mind… I'm just getting started."

I grin at him, my hand cupping the side of his face, marveling that I can do that, amazed by what we are now, if only for this moment.

"Good," I whisper.

A rooster's crow cuts into my dreams, the fragments of them thick and sticking inside my head. It was a sex dream again, I think, the vague feeling of Logan being inside me, his hands and mouth all over my body, the heady, drugged desire of…

Oh. No wait.

It wasn't a dream. The truth comes sliding in like the sunrise.

I open my eyes to see a warm glow filling the white walls of the room. This unfamiliar room. Without meaning to, I hold my breath, like I'm afraid to breathe, and then turn my head.

Logan is asleep beside me, sprawled half out of the sheets, his muscled thigh and firm ass naked and on display.

Oh hell he's gorgeous. I blink at the sight, taking it all in. This isn't the seductive glow of night - this is the unfiltered reality. And it's beautiful. His body really is a sight to behold, manly perfection in every way, and I'm in bed with him.

I lift up the sheet and look under. I'm completely naked. I think my clothes are somewhere on the living room floor. I think Logan owes me a new pair of underwear.

Did we really do that? The way he took me on the floor, my head pressed against the rug while he fucked me, raw and real, from behind, that moment was the moment I knew I was his, like I always should have been, a moment neither of us can escape from.

And do I want to escape? That's the next question. Here I am, sleeping in Juliet's own bed after I've been thoroughly fucked by her husband. What kind of person am I?

What kind of person was she? my conscious counters. For the first time it seems to be arguing against her. She cheated on him and then lied to me about it, covering her own ass.

"What are you doing?" Logan murmurs into his pillow, causing me to jolt in surprise.

"Um, staring at you?" I tell him. "Wondering what the hell just happened?"

He raises his head and looks at me. His dark hair is all rumpled and falling across his forehead, making him look way younger than he is. "Nothing *just* happened, Freckles. It happened three times. Last night. You've had hours of sleep since."

I bite my lip, feeling bashful and out of my element. He couldn't blame me. This was the last thing I saw coming.

"Hey," he says, easing himself up on his side. He reaches for me, grabbing my hand. "I can't tell you what to do, lord knows I've bloody well tried. But please believe me when I say you have nothing to worry about."

I nod, though I know his words won't reach as deep as he hopes. Because, I mean, how can they reach the reserves of guilt I seem to have an endless store of?

"Veronica," he says and my eyes snap to his. "I mean it. Please don't lose your mind over this."

"What makes you think I'm losing my mind?"

"I know you enough to tell. You're seconds from storming out of here and never looking back." He sighs, frowning. "Look, neither of us planned on last night, but it happened and I'm glad it did. It was overdue."

"You can't…you can't say things like that."

"Why not?"

"Because of she who will not be named."

He scrutinizes me for a moment. "Listen to me carefully. I don't know about you, but last night wasn't a one-off thing for me. It was the prelude to an ongoing thing. Meaning, I don't just want to fuck you, Veronica. I never wanted just that. I want a lot more. So whatever is going on right now with us…I can't have that be the bloody end of it."

I don't know what to say. I don't know how to feel. I know he's saying everything I ever wanted him to say and I know it's doing something to my heart. It's making it warm, it's making it swell, it's making it so it's hard to breathe. But when I take a moment to look beyond the two of us being in bed together…how could this ever work?

"And then what?" I ask him, flipping onto my side, holding the sheet up to my chest and propping my head up with my elbow. "Then what happens?"

He stares at me and sighs. "I don't think it's rocket science."

"Logan," I tell him. "I'm not just some girl that you want to fuck and you're not some guy I want to sleep with; there are layers here."

"I know about the layers."

"Well the layers are what can prevent us from ever… moving forward."

"Tell me what you're afraid of," he says, adjusting

himself against the pillow. "Tell me all your fears and I'll carry them for you."

That's unbelievably sweet but…"Jeez, I don't know, everything?"

His frown deepens, that line showing up between his eyes that I want to press my finger against and smooth. "Are you afraid of me? That I'll hurt you? That I'll leave you?"

I have to take a moment. Until, well, last night, I would have said yes. Once a cheater, always a cheater. That I knew from personal experience. If he cheated on Juliet, he would cheat on me. But after last night, now that I learned the truth…I don't know. Of course the fear of having my heart broken is there but that would be true with anyone you're falling for. Every time you have the chance to climb high, you also have that chance to fall.

But it's not as much now. Because what kept me and Logan apart wasn't just my own fear that he would humiliate me and break my heart. It was the fact that there wasn't a person alive who would understand us and that our path seemed doomed from the start.

Look at it from any angle and this is what you get – a girl who betrayed her family, her dead sister. The man who betrayed his dead wife. Insert all those "keep it in the family jokes." Only it's not funny at all. None of this is.

"Veronica," he says again, reaching out and cupping my face, his eyes searching mine imploringly. "Tell me that's not what you think."

I shake my head, closing my eyes to his touch. "No. It's not. It's everything else."

He sighs and brushes a strand of hair behind my ears. I open my eyes to see him staring at me with such tenderness it makes my heart bleed.

"This isn't going to be easy," he says. "But I want to be

with you and I can't think of any other way. We can hide it from everyone for a while, if you want, but I'm not ashamed and I'm not afraid."

"Really?" I can't help but ask. "You know how bad this looks. For both of us."

"I do. And I don't care. What should it matter what people think? Those that know me, that know you, those that understand…those are the people you hang onto. Everyone else you discard."

"It's not that easy," I blurt out. "Your family would never judge you but mine would. Mine would…they'd disown me. They'd disown you. They own most of your resort, Logan. Don't you think they could and would do some real damage?"

He swallows and looks down at the sheets, his hand dropping away from my face. "I know this isn't how you see me, but I like to see the best in people. Just like you usually do."

"Not when it comes to my parents."

"Maybe so. But I'm not afraid of them."

I shake my head, my heart feeling like it's in a rock tumbler, but instead of coming out smooth and polished, it's stuck in this never-ending turmoil. "You don't know them like I do."

"Be that as it may," he says, leaning forward to kiss me softly. When he pulls back, his eyes are deep and probing. "I know you. And I know you don't want to upset them. So for now, they don't have to know anything. They don't know your life here. You've told me they barely keep in touch, and you know they don't contact me anymore. Except when they want you out of their hair." I roll my eyes at that. "So in the meantime, fuck them. And fuck anyone who cares."

"How can you just throw yourself into this so fast?" I

ask him. "We've been fighting since the day I arrived."

"Maybe I'm tired of fighting. Ironically, now I've found something worth fighting for."

I raise my brow. "I don't know. You know what happened to me before."

"As I said, people here don't have to know," he tells me. "It's up to you. If you think it's better for both of us to keep it a secret, I will keep it a secret. Look…I just want to be with you. That's all."

That's all?

But that's everything.

Logan has been doing nothing but telling me everything I've always wanted, needed, to hear. It's to the point that I'm not even sure I'm awake and not dreaming. It's one thing to have a sex dream, it's another to hear that the man you're in…well, that you're obsessed with, feels the same about you.

"Do you want me to show you?" he asks and before I can answer he's pulling me toward him. I let out a shriek, dissolving into nervous laughter. One hand disappears into my hair, the other hand trails up the inside of my leg, soft and teasing, inch-by-inch over my sensitive skin. Even though my body is still a bit sore from last night and drowsy from sleep, I'm already shivering at his touch, craving him all over again.

I've found something worth fighting for.

He can't know what those words do to me.

How deep and far they reach. The hope they bring.

But he can know just what his body does to mine. *That* I don't mind sharing.

He keeps his eyes on mine, burning with lust and I'm so turned on, that I'm wet to my thighs. "Veronica," he groans as his fingers find my clit, teasing it, his eyes never breaking from mine. "You're soaked."

I give him an anxious smile. Even after last night, I'm still a bit nervous. The day is shining a new light on things, making me feel beautiful and exposed. "What can I say? I've been dreaming of you all night."

"This isn't a dream, Freckles," he says gruffly as he grabs my hips and pulls me closer. I hook my leg up around his waist, keeping him against me, as he continues to tease me. I'm starting to get impatient, the ache inside me increasing with each slick stroke of his finger.

"Easy," he whispers to me as he reaches for his cock and runs the crown of it up and down my clit, pausing to dip it briefly inside before bringing it back up. The sound is so loud in this room, so wet, it's almost obscene.

My eyes close, surrendering myself to this torturous tease. He's not pushing in, it's just a slow slide, back and forth, but I feel myself opening for him anyway, my body hungry for more.

"You like that?" he murmurs, his voice so thick with need that I can't even answer him. I nod, relaxing back into the pillow. I'm both languid and tense, surrendering and spurring him on as he rubs against me, over and over again.

I swallow hard, making a noise that's nothing short of begging. My heart is starting to sound in my head, my skin is hot and tight, my nipples are hardened pebbles in the cool air as the sheet brushes against them.

With a slow exhale, he grips my hip as he pushes himself inside me from the side.

Slowly.

Very slowly.

Inch by inch.

It feels good, then it feels too much, then I don't even know what I feel because all I feel is him. I stretch around him, decadently full. This is nothing like last night, where it was hot and wild and rushed. This is a slow dance between us, taking the time to enjoy and worship each other's bodies, to see how we fit, how good we can make each other feel.

This is nothing but pure indulgence.

"Want me to go faster?' he asks, groaning through the words.

"No," I say, licking my lips. I look at him. "This is good. It's too good."

He nods and watches me intently as he pushes in further. His lips part as he sucks in his breath and his forehead creases in lust and awe, like he can't believe this is happening, can't believe how good it feels.

That makes two of us.

"Ronnie," he moans, his grip tightening on my hips, sliding up to my waist, to my breasts where he pinches my hardened nipples. "Fuck…you're so fucking perfect."

And in this moment, I feel perfect. He's watching me, watching himself, watching *us,* where his cock sinks into me, his shaft wet with my desire. He's entranced by the sight, the slow push in, the slow pull out.

So good. God, this is so, so good.

Each rock of my hips, each thrust of his, pushes him in deeper, makes us connect like puzzle pieces. The way his abs clench as he pushes inside, the tiny beads of sweat that gather in the creases, the dampness of his brow. I reach around and tug his ass toward me, wanting more, and he drives in so deep that the air leaves my lungs.

My head goes back again, my eyes pinching closed in shock before I surrender. He's in me, in so deep, and I don't ever want him to leave. This feels beyond right.

This is us.

It sets something off inside me, a whirlpool in my core that's slowly increasing, spreading, heating up. It's going to take over me, it's going to pull me under, and I've never wanted to come so badly in my life.

"More," I whisper, my voice choked with my sudden hunger for him.

He responds instantly.

With a throaty growl he starts thrusting faster, one hand at my back to hold me in place, the other in my hair, making a fist. Because we're fucking on our sides, he's able to slide in deeper than ever, hitting me where my body is ripe and swollen and dying for him.

He brings my head forward and kisses me, quick and hot, tasting like sweat. My mouth is ravenous against his, the need inside me building and building.

And then we find our rhythm, our bodies coming together in synchronicity. He's pounding and pounding and pounding me, working up into a frenzy because it *is* work to fuck like this. I can't keep my eyes off of him, the muscles in his neck are corded and strained as the sweat rolls off of him, his eyes are lost in a fiery haze. The sounds that come out of his mouth with each thrust are deep, real and raw.

The bed slams back against the wall, the sheets are pulled loose, my breasts are jostling. The whirlpool inside me is now at a roar and I have seconds to hold on.

But why would I want to?

"I'm coming," I cry out, my voice raw and raspy and drowning with desire, trying to hold his gaze. He holds mine back, his eyes burning in victory.

Then I'm twisted, sucked under, as the orgasm washes over me. My body jolts and shudders and I'm high above this world, fading into the stars, into the black. Only warmth and joy remain as I'm washed up on shore.

I never want anything else but this.

Ever.

"Fuck, fuck, fuck," Logan grunts, bringing me out of the haze. His growling, animalistic noises, the slap of his sweat-soaked skin against mine, the creak of the bed, all fill the air, becoming a deliciously lewd symphony.

Then he lets out a long, primal moan, shoulders shaking as he comes.

The pumping slows. His grip loosens.

He collapses against the pillow, his hair damp and dark and sticking to his brow. His eyes take me in, his breath heavy and hard. "Good morning," he manages to say. He's still inside me and I'm still pulsing around him, the torrent inside me slowing.

"Good morning," I tell him, breaking into one stupid, happy grin.

CHAPTER FIFTEEN

B Y THE TIME WE FINALLY GET OUT OF BED IT'S NEARLY eleven a.m., and I need to get going so I can get an early start helping Johnny. With the restaurant closed yesterday and Charlie still gone, we have extra work to make up for.

Unfortunately, this means I'll have to do the walk of shame.

"All right, let's go," Logan says, grabbing his keys as we walk out of his door. He locks it, then grabs my hand, the movement seeming automatic.

It takes me by surprise, even though my first instinct is to pull away, which I do once we get to the street. This is what I want but it's going to take some getting used to.

"I'm going to head back by the beach," I tell him.

He frowns. "Why?"

"Because I'm wearing the same dress I wore last night

228

– sans underwear – and it's going to look pretty obvious if we both show up together like this."

I expect him to be a bit insulted that I won't go back with him but a wry smile tugs at his lips. "You're really going to take this sneaking around thing to another level, aren't you?"

I just give him a levelling gaze.

"All right," he says. Then he grabs me by the waist and pulls me to him, kissing me passionately. "But I'm not letting you walk off without giving you one of these," he says against my mouth.

I'm smiling through the kiss. I can't help it. One moment I think I can keep my head on straight, the next I'm absolutely giddy that this man is kissing me, holding me. That we can do that now, even if just in private.

Which means we probably shouldn't be doing it on the public street where any of his neighbors could see, but he obviously doesn't care about that.

He pulls away slowly, resting his forehead against mine, noses touching, while is hand slips down to my ass. "This isn't going to be easy," he says softly.

"I know."

"Don't forget about me." He kisses me on the forehead.

"Don't stop being an asshole," I remind him. "Or people will think something's up."

He grins at me and smacks my ass. "That can be arranged. I'll see you, Freckles."

I watch as he walks down the road, past the rooster strutting parallel to him in the red dirt between the asphalt of the road and the stiff grass of the bordering properties. Large banana leaves and palm trees sway in the humid breeze, the hazy mountains rising high in front of him. I feel like the moment is going to be ingrained in my head forever, the moment where I realized that Logan has a big, *big* piece of my heart.

And I'm pretty sure he always did.

I literally can't stop smiling. I turn and cut through a narrow path, bright green leaves and blooms in purple, red and yellow, pulling at my hair until I spill out onto the beach. With the golden white sand and the crystal clear waves crashing feet away onto the lava rocks, I throw my hands up into the air and grin at the sky, breathing in deep.

All this time. All this waiting. And now Logan wants to be mine in the way I always wanted to be his.

Almost.

But I shut that thought down. It has no place in today and it shouldn't have any place in the days after this. I've spent too long worrying and caring about what everyone else thinks of me. What we have is worth more than that.

So I do something relatively crazy. Though the waves are strong at the reef, I come to the spot where I had my surfing lesson with Charlie before Logan took over. It feels so long ago and that feeling, that pure joy of riding my first waves, feels like nothing now compared to what Logan and I shared last night.

I can't help but laugh, gleeful and childish, like I'm a little girl again, then I run straight for the water, jumping in with my dress on. The water feels like a bath tub, such a vivid aquamarine that even a painter couldn't duplicate it. I swim out a little bit, enough so that my feet are still touching the bottom, and stare back at the resort, my home, a place I never ever want to leave.

I'm buoyant – in the water, in spirit, in my heart.

But I don't push my luck. You never do with the ocean, I know that by now. As quickly as I splashed in, I trudge out of the water and head over to the hotel, passing Nikki as I do so who gives me the once over, a mug of coffee in her hand.

"Did you go swimming in your dress?" she asks, looking me over.

I shrug. "The ocean called to me, what can I say."

"Did you see the whales this morning?"

"Whales?" Humpback whales arrived this month to the islands and its always been a dream of mine to see them. In fact, it was the one thing that Juliet and I bonded over as children. When she was ten, she was obsessed with becoming a marine biologist. That was the last that I remember her really being a kid – after that she seemed to grow up so quick. And naturally, wanting to be just like her, I started loving whales and other marine mammals too. But by the time I graduated onto sharks, Juliet had moved onto something else, leaving me in the cold.

"Yeah they were just out there," she nods at the shore, "breaching and everything." She adjusts the brim of her bright pink trucker hat and looks at me. "By the way, what happened to you last night? You just disappeared."

I try not to smile. "I went to bed early. Turkey coma."

She seems to buy that and pushes out her belly in a vain effort to be relatable. "I feel you on that. It was awesome though," she adds quickly. "Your mashed yams are a million times better than my grandma's mashed potatoes that's for sure."

I take the compliment with thanks and hurry back to my room to take a proper shower, all the while my eyes going over the grounds, looking to see if I can spot Logan already. Even though we've been apart for, oh, I don't know, twenty-minutes, I already have that itching need to see him again, like a junkie seeking her high. It's ridiculous and I don't even care that it's ridiculous.

Luckily I have work to distract me and I head into the kitchen earlier than I should, an hour before Johnny is supposed to show up.

Since I started working at Moonwater, I've had some creative input in the dishes and a few of them have really taken off. But I haven't had that kind of urge that used to plague me when I was a struggling chef-to-be. There's something to be said about the monotony of being a line cook that really gets your mind and heart wandering, dreaming about what kind of dishes you'd be serving and making if the restaurant was yours.

Here, I have the freedom and yet, until today, I haven't really felt the urge. Maybe because moving here has been such a distraction, maybe because I just haven't felt that creative push. After all, it's taken me nearly two months now to really get into the swing of things and know the job and the food and the people.

But with knowledge comes confidence. And with happiness comes creativity. As I stand in the kitchen, taking a look at all our ingredients, glancing over the menu, I can feel everything come together with one jab of inspiration.

I'm thinking about Logan and how hard he's had to work to get this hotel up and running. I'm thinking about the hardships he's had to face with Juliet gone. I'm thinking about Juliet and the pride she must have taken in Moonwater, even if she took none in her marriage. I'm thinking about the way Logan looked at me last night, the way he looked at me this morning, the way it felt to have him inside me, wanting me in every single way. I'm thinking about my family here, how people have my back for maybe the first time ever.

All of those feelings are boiling to the surface and there's only one way for me to express it. I need to create something that would please everyone, that would bring us all together. I need to make Moonwater's signature dish, something a bit salty, spicy, sweet. Something that tickles all the senses and makes eating the pleasure that it should be.

I get to work. I don't even think, I just run off of this creative juice that's replaced my blood. I think of plumeria flowers and creamy sand beaches and salty-breezes and the freshest fish. I think of eating fruit; fresh mango from the stands in Hanalei, the juices running down my arms and pulling over in Charlie's truck to buy green coconuts that you drink from the shell. I think of humpback whales frolicking off shore, happy to be alive in these warm waters, thriving under the sun.

By the time Johnny comes in for his shift, I'm done and staring at the plate with a discerning eye, not sure if what I created is total garbage or not.

"Aye, Ronnie," Johnny says, grabbing his apron off the wall. "You're here early. What are you doing?"

"Honestly I don't know," I answer absently, still searching the dish for some sign that it's edible.

"Is that Mahi Mahi?" he asks, bending down to sniff it. "My god, that smells amazing. What did you do?" He's practically salivating.

"Try it," I tell him.

He purses his lips together, frowning. "Is it laced with arsenic?"

"Just do it. I haven't tried it yet. I have no idea if any of it works."

He shrugs. "Well if it tastes even a fraction as good as it smells," he says, grabbing a fork. He eats like a tasting judge would, getting a little bit of the fish, a little bit of the rice and a little bit of the sauce and flowers.

I hold my breath as he puts it in his mouth and after one chew, his eyes are shutting and the most orgasmic noise comes out of him. I never thought I'd see Big J's O-face and it's mildly disconcerting.

"What the hell is this?" he asks incredulously and when he opens his eyes, they're dancing.

I try not to get giddy. "I wanted to create Ohana Lounge's signature dish. So this is it, the aptly named, Ohana Mahi Mahi."

"Is that a macadamia nut sauce and…?" His eyes close again as he tries to place it. "Cinnamon? What? Nutmeg."

"I crusted the Mahi Mahi with red salt and a bit of nutmeg-laced panko for the salty, crunchy aspect, then created a macadamia nut sauce spiced with cinnamon for a nice mouthfeel and creaminess, then the mango and lilikoi sauce is the tart component. The flowers are just for show, though perhaps we could use orchids so they're edible. The rice I figured we would leave plain or maybe add some spice for added heat or furikame. Whichever works."

By now I'm not even sure Johnny's listening, he's nodding and has practically cleaned the plate. "This is perfect the way it is. Logan is going to flip out."

"Are you sure?" I ask, beaming at the sound of his name.

"Oh yeah. He's been wanting a signature dish for a long time, a reason for people to come here." Johnny starts licking his fingers. "This will be pricey, the macadamias are going to drive up the food costs and the Mahi Mahi is market price…"

"Then we won't give it a set price, we'll go on the market price of the Mahi, and then raise it a few from there. That way customers are liable to spend a bit more if they know it's not really us raising the price. Plus, we can adjust it that way."

"I like the way you think," Johnny says. "Veronica, I knew you had it in you. Those calzones you made were just the tip of the iceberg. Keep them coming. All the time. You have an idea, don't even ask, just do it. At the very least, I'll be here to eat it."

I've honestly never felt prouder. Now I want, *need*, Logan to come in here and try it. I want him to see just what I can do, not just in general, but for his restaurant. This is nothing compared to whatever I cooked for him at Piccolo.

"Hey where were you last night anyway?" Johnny asks as he switches on the radio. Low and behold, "Purple Rain" comes on, which gets another smile out of me. Logan's favorite song.

"Decided to head in early," I tell him, swaying slightly to the song.

"I saw you at the bar. Looked like you had a pretty heated argument with Daniel," he says innocently.

"We weren't arguing." I'm quick to shoot that down.

"Well you were talking about something that looked very important."

I shrug. "Just discussing Juliet."

"Oh really?"

"Yup," I tell him. I smack him on the shoulder. "Stop being so nosy Johnny and get to work."

He rolls his eyes.

The rest of the shift goes really well. The restaurant is full and everyone seems in a really good mood. I meet Daniel's eyes every now and then as I pass the bar to the toilets, and I can tell that he's afraid I've ratted on him to Logan. I try and tell him otherwise.

At the end of the night, when the last order has gone out, Logan clears his throat from behind us.

Johnny and I turn around to see him standing in front of the swinging doors of the kitchen.

"What's up, Mr. Gruff?" Johnny says with a wave.

"Mr. Gruff?" Logan repeats, coming into the room and walking toward me. It seems my nickname for him has spread.

As always, Logan looks like a breath of fresh air. Even dressed simply, a black t-shirt that shows off his tanned muscles and olive green cargo shorts, he manages to skirt the line of being rugged and playful, manly and elegant. When he looks my way, he starts smiling, small at first, then spreading across his face, his perfect teeth white against his golden skin.

Obviously I can't help but smile back.

And now Johnny is looking between the two of us. "You all right Shephard?" he asks warily. "I can see your teeth. Are you…smiling?"

"Fine, just fine," he says. "Wanted to come in here and see how you guys were doing."

"It was a great night," Johnny says.

"Great night," Jin agrees from the sink where he's been working diligently and quietly, as usual. Then he speaks up. "Ronnie made a new dish. The Ohana Mahi Mahi."

Logan stops right in front of me, raising his brow as his grin spreads. Good lord, his smile can bring me to my knees. Everything inside me feels like it's blooming, warm, hot, fizzy, like champagne. I want nothing more than to just wrap my hands around his neck, feel his skin, kiss his smile. Feel the strength and warmth of his body against mine. I want to ride him to oblivion again. I want all the things that I never thought possible until last night.

"Uh, Ronnie," Johnny speaks up. "You going to tell him or am I?"

I blink, my cheeks going hot as I look over at Johnny. "Huh?"

He's scrutinizing me with a coy wariness, looking between the two of us. "Tell Shephard what you made."

"Oh right," I say, looking back to Logan and meeting his eye. "Um, well, actually I'm not sure if I should tell you or just make it for you."

"I would be honored if you made it for me," he says. "How about tonight?"

"Phhhfff," Johnny says, waving his hand at Logan. "Tonight? Give the little *wahine* a break, aye. Her shift is over and you're not a slave driver."

"No, I honestly don't mind," I quickly say. "I could do it right now."

Johnny makes a noise of disbelief. "Well I'll be, hell is freezing over. Ronnie is volunteering to make the *habut* some food, overtime."

"Not overtime," I tell him. "Just for fun."

"Okay, now you've really lost your mind."

"I think we're all allowed to lose our minds from time to time," Logan says. His eyes are burning into mine, reaching into my core and stoking the flames I've been trying to ignore all night. "Here, let me help you clean up."

"Okay," Jin says, poking his head around the corner. "Who are you and what have you done with Logan Shephard?"

Logan laughs and even that seems to scare everyone. I can try and hide our relationship, or whatever this is, from everyone here, but with Logan acting like a whole new human being, it's not going to be so easy. Thankfully Johnny and Jin aren't the type to jump to conclusions. They'll first assume that Logan's been abducted by aliens and his body has been shuttled back to earth, controlled by a robot.

And though it's an odd proposition, none of us usher Logan out of the kitchen because we can use the extra hand with Charlie being gone, plus I think the guys get a certain thrill of seeing their boss roll up his sleeves and get down to the dirty work.

As it happens, with Logan's help, we're done a bit early. Johnny and Jin leave the kitchen in a hurry, as if they think Logan will pull a 180 and haul them back into work.

It's just him and me here now. Out in the restaurant we can hear Daniel talking in a low murmur to Johnny and I think Kate, serving them drinks.

I turn to Logan, clearing my throat.

"So," I say, keeping my voice low.

"So," he says, taking a step toward me until all the space between us disappears. He runs his fingers underneath my chin and raises it so I'm looking at him in the eye. He smells like my dreams, that musk that runs deep into my veins, a chemical reaction. "Is it that obvious if I go and bar the kitchen door?"

"Afraid so," I tell him.

"You have no idea how long this day has been," he whispers to me. "I can't quite believe that last night even happened. I might need you to prove it did."

I bite my lip, playing up the look of the coquette. "That can be arranged. Anywhere but in here."

"We can go at any time," he murmurs, leaning over until his mouth is at my ear. "I can go at any time."

Jesus. Just his hot breath, his words, and I'm transported back to last night. I don't blame him for thinking that last night – and this morning – was a dream. This man had tasted me, *licked* his fucking fingers. He told me he wanted to fuck me with his mouth and then he fucking *did*. Not only a dirty talker, but a man who follows through.

"I think they would suspect something," I manage to say, "you know, when they walk in here and find us fucking on the floor."

"God," he says, licking up my neck, a slow, languid pace to my ear that makes me shiver. "Don't talk like that." His hand slips down the side of my waist, down to the front of my work pants and starts sliding underneath the waistband.

"I think I'm supposed to make you a famous meal," I manage to say.

"I think you're my meal."

I put my hand at his chest and push him back an inch. "I'm serious. I made something tonight that you're going to be proud of."

He cocks his head, studying me. "I already am proud of you."

"How so?"

He gives me a lopsided grin that makes him look boyish. "You don't realize what you've done here. Or maybe you do. I don't know. I know I've been giving you a hard time since you arrived."

"You can say that again."

Now he's full on beaming. "I've been giving you a hard time," he repeats. "And it's about to get harder."

I laugh. "Okay, you are the worst at innuendo."

"I know. But I am serious. I'm proud of you."

I don't think I've ever heard anyone tell me they were proud of me, not like this. I try and brush it off but the fact is, it hits deep. It hits in a place I never thought possible. Tears are springing to my fucking eyes. All those years, all those years of just needing someone to believe in me and having no one, no one in my corner at all. You grow up thinking that your family will be the ones to believe in you but that's not the case at all. Your family might be the first ones rooting for you to fail.

"Hey," Logan says softly, brushing away the tears from my eyes. "What's wrong?"

I shake my head, looking away.

"Ronnie," he says and the sound of my nickname makes my heart soar. "Please."

I take in a deep breath. "It's nothing. It's stupid."

"Hey," he warns, his eyes turning hard and glinting.

I sigh. "I've never had anyone tell me they were proud of me."

He seems stunned. "Never?"

"Never," I admit. "I mean, I never really thought about it until you told me. It didn't seem to matter what I did, it's just that no one seemed to care. And, contrary to popular belief, I did do things that were worthy. At least I thought so. But…no one noticed."

He doesn't say anything for a moment. "I'm sorry," he says, voice throaty as he runs his thumb over my lips. "I'm sorry that no one has ever seen how special, how beautiful you are. You need to know that the moment I saw you…I couldn't forget you."

I know I should just take the compliment and move on but I can't. I stare up at him. "Then why did you marry her? Why did she steal you away from me that day?"

He closes his eyes briefly, breathing out of his nose. "I was a fool."

"It's that simple?"

He nods, looking me dead in the eye, washed with regret. "Sometimes there isn't some elaborate story why two people end up together. I was…dumb. Thinking with my dick." I grimace. "Sorry. And I bloody hate talking about this, you know. Because…I was blind. I saw your sister and she was beautiful."

"Thanks."

"Veronica," he whispers. "You know more than anyone the ability she had to blind people. You're a million times more beautiful, gorgeous, real and everything, and I knew that. I knew that when I saw you and I knew that you would take me on a ride. I knew that if I had left that bloody party with you our lives would have been turned upside down. In the best possible way. And I wasn't ready for that. I was so business-minded. I could only think about the hotel, about getting it off the ground. I was blind to everything else but my ambition. And I saw Juliet and that way she had, that way she tricks people. She made me believe that I would rise to the top with her. And I fell for it. Somehow she fell for me."

I can't help but look away.

"You know I don't like talking about it," he says. "But it's the truth. By the time we were married, it was too late. I was in too deep. And little by little, day by day, I started realizing the woman I was married to wasn't at all like I thought. It was like she was hiding every aspect of herself until she had me and only then she came out. You have no idea, Ronnie, no idea." He pauses. "I don't think she was trying to trick me. She wasn't…duplicitous, like the plumeria flowers. It wasn't like that. It was just a case of hiding your true colors. She was afraid to be real."

"Well she was hiding from me too, if that helps."

"I think she was hiding from everyone. You, me, your mother, your father. I don't think anyone knew the real Juliet. I don't even think that prick she was with knew either. She died a mystery. And that's a shame. But that was on her. The sad thing is, no one ever knows when we're going to die. So it's best to live life as open as you can. Juliet thought she was invincible, like we all do sometimes. I'm sure if she knew she'd die young…she would have made amends." He runs his hands through my hair. I close my eyes. "You want the truth about me and your sister?"

I nod, closing my eyes.

"I loved her." His words are a fist to my gut. "But I didn't like her. Does that make sense?"

"Perfect sense," I whisper.

"Look," he says to me, leaning in so his nose is brushing against mine. "Sometimes you love someone but you don't actually like them as a person. Like family, right?"

"Right."

"I know this is hard to hear…"

I give him a small smile. "It's not hard to hear. I would just rather not hear it right now."

"Fair enough," he says. "How about we save your dish for tomorrow night?"

"Then what's on the menu tonight?"

He grins. "Do you even have to ask?"

He grabs my hand and hauls me over to the door.

"Wait," I say, taking my hand out of his and untying my apron. "We can't just go out there holding hands. Remember? You're supposed to be an asshole and you're failing at that."

He's still smiling. "I can't help it." He clears his throat and slides his hand over his face, his expression changing to stone. He looks burly and wild and fuck I want this man more than anything.

"Better?" he asks, voice low and rough.

"Yeah. In many ways," I tell him.

"I'm going to head out the door. You do what you need to do. Meet me on the beach." He pushes open the doors and steps out.

A thrill runs through me as I wait a few moments,

hearing him say goodbye to everyone. Who knew sneaking around could be so much fun? I mean, with Erik it was the same idea but it was his idea we keep it a secret, mainly so he could screw other chicks on the side. Thank god I was smart enough to always use a condom with him and then had myself tested a few times after, just to be safe. An STD would have been icing on the cake.

I step out of the doors to see Kate, Johnny and Daniel all staring at me from the bar.

"Hey, get your butt over here," Kate says, waving me over.

I sigh. This isn't going to be easy.

"What's up?" I ask, trying to keep my smiling to a minimum.

"What's up?" she repeats. She's tucked a red hibiscus behind her ear that matches her Moonwater Inn tank top. Which reminds me, I need to get one of those. "First of all, where were you last night?"

I roll my eyes and avoid looking at Daniel. "Why does everyone keep asking me that? I turned in early."

"Did you really?" she asks. Because the light was on in your room all night," she says. "And I called out to you but you never answered."

Shit.

"I passed out. I don't know what Dan was serving but they were just as potent as that fucking luau punch."

"You did look really tired," Daniel says carefully. "Must have been the turkey."

"That's exactly what it was," I say, giving him a grateful smile. "Anyway, I'm zonked right now as it is. Think I'm going to go for a walk on the beach and clear my head."

Then I get out of there before they can grill me anymore.

The rain has moved in again, a light drizzle that makes

the night come alive. Everything smells like the world is being born again, every flower perfumes the air, making it sweet and heady. The earthy loam of the wet grass and soil, the tang of the waves.

I try to inhale it all but my breath is shaking. I'm too nervous, too excited. My heart is dancing, skipping, spinning around inside me.

My feet sink into the damp sand and I walk along the shore, going around the large dark lava rocks that dot the beach. Then I see him, up by the plumeria bushes, his tall silhouette backlit by one of the beach houses.

"Hey," I whisper to him. "Sorry to make you wait in the rain."

"I've been waiting for you for seven years," he says, "a little rain is nothing."

He reaches out and grabs my hand, pulling me to him. I breathe him in deeply, my nose to his chest. I can't help but run my hands down his sides, kissing him, before I drop to my knees and sink into the wet sand.

He stares down at me with hooded lids. "I see."

"The other night I couldn't finish what I got started," I tell him, unbuttoning his pants.

He grins, wicked, devious, and helps me out, unzipping and taking his cock out.

Even in the dim light from the houses in the background, I'm mesmerized by the hardness of his cock as it bobs in front of me, the rain as it falls on us, highlighting his length. I wrap my fingers around the thick base of his shaft, tentative at first. I'm eager for him, to have him come inside my mouth, to feel his desire, but it's been such a long time since I have given someone a blow job, I don't want to rush it.

I take in a deep breath and slowly, carefully slide his

tip through my lips. My eyes fall closed at the sound of his moan. The taste of him hits my tongue and spurs something deep inside of me, making me crave him even more.

"Oh hell," he murmurs as his voice breaks into a groan, grabbing my hair and tugging, which brings a moan out of me, the vibrations spreading outward. I slide my lips to the end then stroke along the underside of his shaft with my tongue, feeling how hot his skin is, smoothing over every vein and rock-hard ridge. Fuck, he feels beautiful.

"Look at me," he says, voice hoarse. "I want you to watch me watching you."

I look up, rain in my eyes, slowly bringing his length out of my mouth, and our eyes meet in a torrent of lust. Slowly, so slowly, I slide him back into my wet lips.

It's too much for him to handle. He pinches his eyes shut, forehead wrinkled, mouth dropping open as he sucks in air, a deep groan rattling through his chest. All because of me.

With my confidence up and this man in my hands, I want to take my time, watch him slowly succumb. The power I feel is incredible and while he may be getting his world rocked, I'm feeling on top of mine.

The moans that come out of his mouth now as I work him steadily with my hands, lips, and tongue, are becoming lower, like they're rising from a deeper, more animalistic side of him. I want his complete surrender, here on this beach, in my mouth, all because of me. I want him to crave me to the point of insanity. The rain continues to fall, adding to the wildness of the moment.

His legs stiffen and his body becomes strained, the tension building inside him. I glance up and our eyes meet briefly and his glazed expression tells me that he's in awe, that at least for now, he's mine and at my mercy.

Then his mouth drops open, panting with lust, as the rain streams down his face and he groans. "I'm coming, oh *fuck*." His voice is hoarse and broken and another rush of power rolls through me. His cock becomes hotter, his skin stretched under my lips, and I keep going as I feel him change in my grasp.

He stills, strained, almost like he's being put on pause, and then he's over the edge, shaking, groaning, wild. His cum is shooting into my mouth, almost to the back of my throat and I swallow almost immediately, wanting every part of him.

"Bloody hell," he rasps, his hands still tangled in my wet hair. "Freckles...I had no idea you had that in you."

I slowly get to my feet, the instability of the sand and the rush I'm feeling cause me to waver off-balance. I grin at him and the sated expression on his face, and work out the kinks in my mouth.

"There's a lot more where that came from," I tell him, wiping the rain from my eyes. "As soon as my mouth gets used to the size of your dick."

He laughs, then shakes his head, droplets falling from his hair, and exhales loudly. "I'm still shaking inside," he says. "Come on. We're just getting started."

He zips up and takes my hand. We giggle as we walk along the beach and to his house.

CHAPTER SIXTEEN

C HARLIE GOT BACK FROM VACATION TODAY AND NOT A moment too soon. I normally don't mind all the hours in the kitchen and working overtime here and there but lately, work is the last place I want to be right now. And who can blame me?

It's been a few days since Logan and I started up our... what's even the right word? Affair? Sounds too shameful. Tryst? Too vulgar. I guess the only way to phrase it that makes sense to me would be love affair. Not that either of us have uttered the L word, I know I'm trying my best to not put a label on my feelings. I'm trying not to think too much and just enjoy it, even when a feeling is burning away inside of you, growing day by day.

Anyway you put it though, what we have has been stealing my thoughts and my heart away from everything else. All I do is think about him, all want is to be with him.

It's like I've finally given myself permission to feel all the things I've tried to ignore and I'm drowning in it. It's a beautiful way to go.

I've been with him every night except last. I think Kate's gotten a bit suspicious with me disappearing and coming back so late. What I really want to do is sleep overnight at Logan's again and wake up in his arms, but I think from now on she'll notice if I don't come home. She's tricky like that, maybe because she and Charlie were sneaking around.

I kind of hope now that Charlie is back the two of them will start up again, if only to keep them from noticing what Logan and I are doing.

I know I shouldn't really be so concerned with what everyone thinks but it's still all so new and so fucking fragile. Logan and I have so much to be wary about, our relationship with each other…it's a sensitive thing and needs to be handled with care. We move in secret because we're afraid that people will look at us differently, at least I am.

By keeping it under wraps, we don't have to explain it to anyone but ourselves. And even then, that's a hard pill to swallow sometimes. When I'm with him everything feels right, like fate, kismet, and destiny have joined forces and moved mountains in order for us to be together. But then I might see a sign of her in the house or he might mention her name or I might be reminded of some time that Logan and Juliet were together and then it all comes crashing down.

I try not to let it crush me, though. We feel right, and how can something this right be so wrong? Logan was never meant to be with Juliet, and Juliet knew it herself. It's only her death that makes things so damn complicated, more for other people than for us. People who wouldn't know the whole truth – and that makes everyone but Dan and Juliet's lover – would see us as cold and callous, and if anyone had believed that Logan had been a cheater, as I had, they would be quick to point fingers.

There's also the fact that working in such close quarters with everyone at Moonwater, knowledge of our relationship would raise more than a few eyebrows. I know they're my *ohana* now, but even then I don't want to test the waters.

And yet, sometimes you need to just get out there and swim.

"Hey," I hear Logan's accent from outside and head out onto my balcony. He's standing below it, staring up at me, wearing just swim trunks and nothing else. Today is a gorgeous day and hot like anything, and he seems to have broken a sweat, his muscles gleaming in the sunshine. If I had no shame I'd offer to lick the sweat right off of him.

"Hey," I say back to him, leaning on the railing and trying to hide the fact that I'm clenching my thighs together to no avail.

"Now that Charlie's back," he says, "did you want another surf lesson before your shift?"

Now, I'm not exactly sure if "surf lesson" is innuendo for something (and by something, I mean wild, hot, sweaty sex), we are in public after all. So I give him a tentative, "yes?"

"All right. Get your bathing suit on and meet me at the Jeep." He turns and heads back across the lawn.

Still not sure if this is innuendo or not. By "bathing suit" does he mean fancy bra and underwear? By Jeep does he mean his house? But to be safe I put on my bikini and a rash guard shirt and grab a towel before I head outside.

"Where are you going?" Kate asks, leaning against the door to reception and fanning her face with a brochure. A gecko climbs up the wall beside her but she pays it no attention.

"Surfing," I tell her.

"With Charlie?"

I jerk my head toward the parking lot where Logan's pulling his Jeep around, a longboard sticking out the back. "No. Don't worry. The *habut*."

She narrows her eyes slightly. "Hmmm. Somehow this isn't surprising."

I shrug and try to play it off. "Hey, he got me riding my first wave, not Charlie. I think the Australian knows a little more than the dude from Colorado."

"Do you know who knows better than both of them?" she asks and sticks her thumb into her chest. "Me."

"Well if our schedules ever match up, then maybe." I start to walk away and throw a saucy look over my shoulder at her. "Or maybe I'll be so good by then, you'll be getting lessons from me?"

I don't have to keep looking to know she's rolling her eyes.

Meanwhile Logan is in the driver's seat of his Jeep, dark aviator sunglasses covering his eyes and a cocky grin on his lips. "Get in, Freckles."

I quickly climb in the passenger seat and we burn out of the parking lot, taking a left at the road and heading to Hanalei.

"Are we really going surfing?" I ask.

"What did you think we were doing?"

"I don't know. Having sex?"

"Woman, you're going to tire me out, you know that?"

I laugh. "I know firsthand that's impossible."

And it's true. I don't care how old Logan is, he has all the control in the world combined with the stamina of a fucking teenager. Meaning, he can go again and again and again. That first night together wasn't a one-off thing, that's the way it is with him every night. It gives new meaning to the word insatiable.

It's still pretty early in the morning so the dirt parking lot at Hanalei Bay isn't too packed and it's easy to find a spot. We walk through the pavilion where a lot of the derelicts hang out and drink their cheap beers, and head out onto the beach.

Hanalei Bay is a gorgeous spot, and, in my opinion, the prettiest beach on the island. At one end there's the historic pier which stretches out into the water where people fish from and outrigger canoes flank the shore. In the middle, where we are, the waves are gentler and a few surf schools dot the swells, while hobby cat sailing boats are lined up on the beach, waiting to be used again in the calmer summer months.

At the far end, the more experienced surfers take the waves and the long stretch of white sand gets wilder, peppered with reef and volcanic rock. And of course the ever-present mountains of the Na Pali Coast preside over all, reminding you at all times that this island is a wondrous, magical force of nature.

Logan takes the board, carrying it with ease on his head, and starts heading down the beach away from the surfing classes and the kids until we've got space and privacy. In a couple of hours the beach should be packed, especially on a day like today.

"Get in," he says, nodding at the water.

Honestly, even though the fact that I'm alone with Logan here is pretty amazing, I'm not sure if I'm sold on the whole surfing thing. I would much rather go back to his place and shove his head between my legs. My memory of surfing to "Kashmir" is a pretty good one, and I don't want to mess that up by bailing.

"I said get in," he says.

"Did anyone ever tell you that you're bossy?"

He raises a brow, crinkling his forehead. "Well I am your boss, aren't I?"

"Not right now," I tell him, hands on my hips.

"Fine," he says. Before I know what's happening, he's striding over and picking me up, carrying me caveman-style over his shoulder. I yelp and he starts running into the water, slicing through like there's no resistance at all.

Then he chucks me over his head like I'm a volleyball, and I fly into the water with an ungraceful splash.

"You jerk!" I cry out as soon as I break the surface, spitting out the water. Luckily the bay here is shallow for a long time and I can easily stand on the bottom.

Logan is laughing, a full-on gorgeous sound that almost makes me forgive him. Almost.

"Well now you're in, Freckles. Who's the boss now?"

I stick my tongue out at him. "Just because you're some superhuman caveman that can throw me around like a rag doll, doesn't mean I don't have a few tricks up my sleeve."

"Oh yeah? Like what?"

"Like…withholding sex."

He laughs. "Right. I'll have you changing your mind pretty soon. Now stay put. You're surfing."

He goes back on the beach and grabs the longboard, hauling it into the water beside us.

"Wait a minute," I tell him, treading water where the bottom slopes into a sandy hole created by the waves. "You still owe me a surf."

"This is about you."

"Yes and you promised me 'Purple Rain.' Now get on the board and show the student who the master really is."

"Master," he muses, eyes twinkling. "I like the sound of that."

I pat the board and swim toward the shore until my feet touch again. "I mean it. Sing."

"You do realize I made that all up, don't you?"

I stare at him in confusion. "What? Made what up?"

He bites his lip, trying to keep his smile in check. "The whole 'sing a song and ride the wave' deal. It was complete horseshit. Made it up on the spot."

I blink. "Are you kidding me?"

He's grinning now. "Nah. I just wanted to hear how bad of a singer you were."

"You asshole!" I smack him on his arm.

"But it worked!" he protests, shrinking away from me. "You caught that wave and rode it."

"While looking like a total idiot!"

"You only *sounded* like a total idiot."

I growl at him and smack him once more. "You know what? You owe me now on principle. Get up on the damn board and sing me some Prince!"

He hesitates until I give him my most venomous look. With a heavy sigh, he concedes. "Fine, fine. I guess it's only fair."

"Fuck yeah it's fair," I tell him.

He climbs onto the board and lies on it, looking over his shoulder at the waves. There's one swell coming that would have been too big for me.

"That one," I tell him.

He cocks his eyebrow. "Now who's the bossy one?"

I swim away from him, heading toward the peak of where the waves are breaking and hang back there for the best vantage point, then turn back to see him start to paddle.

"Sing, bitch!" I yell.

He gives me something like a snarl and then starts. "*I never meant to cause you any sorrow.*" Like his Robert Plant impression, his Prince impression is dead on.

Even so, I yell, "Louder!"

"*I never meant to cause you any pain!*" he sings as he glides past me, getting on the board in such an effortless manner, like it's as second nature to him as breathing, eating, fucking. Every muscle ripples, from his rigid abs, to his shoulders to his arms, and he truly looks one with the board, with the ocean, with the world.

"*Purple rain,*" he belts out, over and over again as he cruises toward the shore, the water shredding behind him. Once he reaches the beach, he hops off, grabs the board and comes back in towards me.

"Well?" he asks, pushing his wet hair off his forehead, a wet Adonis.

"That was something else," I admit. "Color me impressed."

"Color you purple?"

"Color me anything. You're a triple threat. You can sing, surf and…"

"Make you come like crazy."

My cheeks grow hot. I like to think it's the sun. "Well in that case it's countless since you have this habit of making me come over and over again."

"You got a problem with that?" he murmurs, wrapping his arm around my waist and pulling me toward him. His eyes have gone from being light and teasing to half-glazed with arousal.

It's funny how just a look from him can get my body humming and ticking like a finely tuned engine. I wrap my legs around his waist and he slips his fingers to the front of my bathing suit, rubbing them against me.

"Here?" I ask, looking around. We are definitely in public and though the nearest surfers are about halfway down the beach and there are some people sunbathing on shore, I have no doubt it would be pretty obvious if we were to screw right here and now.

Then again, I'm living a world of firsts lately.

"No one will know," he whispers, leaning over and taking my lower lip between his teeth and tugging on it.

A small moan escapes from my lips, the pressure from his fingers growing harder. He reaches down with his other hand to free his cock from his shorts while I grab the board and lean back against it with my arms spread out.

"Can you touch the bottom?'" I ask as his lips go to my neck, sucking the salt water off of me.

"Mmhmm." He pushes aside my bikini bottom and runs the tip of his cock up and down my slit, teasing oh so slowly.

To be honest, I've never had sex in the water before, and I'm grateful that he gets me wet and ready so fast, because when he starts to push in, it's friction city. I suck in my breath, my fingers digging into the surfboard, trying to hold on.

"Just breathe," he tells me, licking my earlobe. "I'll take it slow until you tell me otherwise."

I nod and let out my breath, feeling myself expand around him. The pressure of his fingers on on my clit fill me with an aching hollowness, like I need more of him inside, like I'll never have enough of him.

"That's it," he groans, mouth at my neck. "Fuck yes. You're so tight, Veronica, so fucking tight."

I can't say anything back to that, I can only breathe, my head back and face to the blue blue sky above. He starts pumping into me faster, deeper, controlled jabs of his hips against mine. The friction of the water seems to slow down time, making me feel every single inch of him as he thrusts in and out.

Someone has to be watching us, someone has to know that we aren't just two people hanging out in the water. They have to know I'm getting royally fucked in public.

We're so bad. But so, so good.

Each spot he hits brings me to a new level. I don't know if it's the shimmering water that envelopes us or the stark sunshine that illuminates everything, but I've never felt so alive and exposed at the same time. The darkness and the doubt and the guilt are banished for this sweet moment. It's just us, all of our flaws and imperfections exposed. It's us and we're in this together, stronger for it.

I'm starting to think this man is my world. I'm starting to think he'll never not be.

Logan looks up from my neck, staring right into my eyes. His breath is ragged and rough as he moves in and out of me, picking up the pace. But his eyes never break from mine and I watch as the fire inside them builds, just as it builds inside me.

I can't hang on anymore. "Oh, oh," I cry out softly. "I'm coming."

"Fuck," he swears, his eyes snapping shut as he thrusts in harder, deeper, his fingers on my clit rubbing me to completion. My legs convulse, trying to hold on as I let go and he pumps into me until he's grunting and cursing into my shoulder, finding his own release.

"Don't drown," he manages to say, his voice thick and sated.

I grip the board harder, aware that I'm floating in the ocean while I'm floating in the stars. Just when I think he can't make me come harder, when I think he can't make me feel more, he does.

When I've finally caught my breath, I raise my head and give him a lopsided smile. "If this is included in every surfing session, you're going to have a hard time keeping me out of the water."

He kisses me softly on the lips before he slowly pulls out of me. "Freckles, you have no idea how hard it is to stay away from you in general." He brushes a strand of hair from my face, eyes searching me for something. He almost looks pained.

"What?" I ask.

He gives his head a slight shake. "Nothing. I just…can't believe I have you."

My heart warms from those words. I don't think I'll ever get used to knowing that I'm his. "Of course you have me."

"But I don't want you just for now," his voice grows softer, deeper, just as his gaze does. "I want you forever. Just like this. Under this sun, in these waves. With me."

Something inside me is starting to break. Little cracks, here and there, in the hardened plaster that used to keep me together. If Logan keeps this up, I'll be shattered in no time. There will be nowhere to hide and I'll have no chance to rebuild.

I don't know how to answer him. I'm feeling too much, my body still aching from where he was inside me. He clears his throat and looks up at the sun, squinting. "Well, since we've got a beauty of a day, we might as well take advantage of it. Your turn. Don't worry, I won't make you sing this time."

"You better not," I tell him. "Though I wouldn't mind if you sang 'Purple Rain' to me again."

"We'll see," he says.

So, I get on the board and he coaxes me to stand up on yet another wave, all while he is singing "Purple Rain." Even if he made that shit up and I'm not the one singing, it still works.

Well, at least the first time it did. I bailed on the last two waves, getting pummeled both times. Guess I was picking waves a bit out of my league and getting over-confident.

Funny what love can do to you, I think as I drag myself out of the surf.

The thought nearly stops me dead in my tracks.

Love.

It's nearly as terrifying as the wipeout. Hell, love is the wipeout. It pummels you, turns your world upside down until you don't know what way is up. The only difference between the two, is when you're underwater, there's always the surface. When you're in love, there's no way out.

I'm not quite sure where I am in this emotion but the longer I'm with Logan, the more I'm tumbling, turning, and lost.

"You all right there, Freckles?" Logan asks as he comes out of the waves and onto the shore. "That last wave got you pretty good."

I think you've got me pretty good, I want to say.

After that we head to Tahiti Nui to catch some lunch, sitting out front and having their Mai Tais and poke bowls, watching the world of Hanalei go by – when we aren't watching each other, of course. Logan is probably the only person more stunning than the scenery.

We're careful with each other since everyone in town knows Logan (as demonstrated by every person that passes our table stopping to chat with him), but even though we're not touching each other or whispering sweet nothings, we're one-hundred-percent invested. We spend hours there, just talking about everything under the sun, and the more we talk, the more I want him to talk. You know those people you could just listen to for hours, that always have something interesting to say? That's Logan. Whether it's his thoughts on local politics or growing up in Australia or whether traveling the world should be as mandatory as a high school education, the man makes me *think*, as well as feel.

And let's face it, listening to that accent over and over again gets me as drunk as the Mai Tais do.

But our fun has to come to an end – for now. He has to take over for Kate at reception and I have to start my shift, though he asks me to drop by his house when I'm done.

I get through work with a smile on my face and even Johnny is wondering what kind of crack I'm smoking, and as soon as I'm done, I'm hanging up my apron and heading out into the night. Charlie asks where I'm going – I think he's a bit insulted that I haven't been boozing it up with him at the bar since he got back – but I just tell him I'm going for a walk.

Light rain is starting again as I hurry down the street and right to Logan's. He doesn't even have to answer the door, he's waiting for me on the porch with a glass of wine in hand. I take it from him, take him in with my eyes, and then we disappear inside, making a futile attempt to watch something on Netflix before I'm riding him on his couch like a damn cowgirl.

I can't stay the night though, and when it looks like it's getting late, I have to go. I make a joke about becoming Cinderella and I'm halfway out his front door before he hauls me back to him, kissing me hard, kissing me so I'll never forget him.

I walk, crooked, half-drunk on lust and wine, back out into the cooling rain and start walking down the road back to the hotel. I'm smiling into the night.

Then…

"Veronica," a hushed voice comes from the darkness behind me.

Startled I whirl around to see Kate emerge out from underneath a dimly-lit streetlight.

"What are you doing here?" I ask her, my hand to my chest, trying to calm my heart. Oh my god. Did she see? *Did she see?*

"What am I doing here?" she exclaims in a hiss. "Charlie told me you went for a walk. Hours ago. In this fucking rain. I was worried so I went to see if Logan knew where you were and, well…what the hell, Ron?" She gestures wildly to Logan's house, where the lights are going off, Logan inside and having no clue what's going on. "When were you going to tell me that you're fucking the boss?"

Shit. Shit. Shit.

I give her a shaky smile. "Um, right about now?"

This is going to be a long night.

CHAPTER SEVENTEEN

"I CAN'T BELIEVE THIS," KATE SAYS, CLAPPING HER hands together as she stands there in the middle of the road. I can't tell if this is a good thing or a bad thing, she's still so hard to read, and even when she's happy sometimes she looks like she wants to murder someone – and vice versa.

"It's not a big deal," I say meekly, trying to play it off. "We really should head back, I'm getting wet."

"I fucking bet you are," she comments as we start walking down the road away from Logan's house. Talk about awkward. "How long has this been going on for?"

"Um…since Thanksgiving."

"I knew it!" she says, jabbing me on the shoulder with her finger.

"Well we kissed before. After the luau."

"Oh my god," she says. "I mean, I told you, didn't I? I

told you the way he looked at you, I just didn't know if you'd feel the same. You seemed to hate him so much but I guess that was all an act."

"Oh hell no," I tell her. "That wasn't an act...I just. It's complicated."

"No shit it's complicated! He's your sister's husband."

"Was my sister's husband."

"Well they'd still be married if she wasn't dead." She pauses, her hand flying to her mouth. "Ah, I'm so sorry. I'm being a bitch."

"No. Well yes. It doesn't matter though."

"That I'm being a bitch or that you're hooking up with your sister's widower? Who is, also, by the way, your boss?"

I sigh. "Look, Logan and I started off...when we first met...Juliet isn't who you..." I have no idea how to explain any of this without exposing Juliet and throwing her under a bus, even if she may deserve it. See, this is exactly why we needed to keep this a secret! I take in a deep breath. "Logan and Juliet didn't have a happy marriage."

Kate wipes the rain away from her face. "Right. I guess I could see that."

"And Logan and I have a history..."

"I thought you barely knew him before you came here."

We turn the corner to the hotel and I lower my voice. "I don't expect you to understand, which is why we're trying to keep this a secret. But haven't you ever...met someone and you knew that, without a doubt, he was supposed to be with you?"

"No," she says flatly.

"Well then you aren't going to get it." I sigh as we climb up the stairs to our place. "Look, can we just keep it between us. You trust me with all your Charlie stuff."

"That is so not the same," she says, opening the door.

I walk in after her. "It is. You keep going back to Charlie for reasons I don't know and I don't pretend to know. Maybe he's awesome in bed. Maybe you like guys who don't wear shoes. Scratch that – you *definitely* like guys who don't wear shoes. But the point is there is something between you guys that's hard to ignore."

"His dick is hard to ignore. That's it."

I give her a dry look. "Fine. Blame his dick. I blame Logan's then."

"Oh my god," she says, throwing her hands up and going over to the couch, sitting down in a huff. "There's no way I want to think of Logan that way."

"You don't think he's hot?"

She scrunches up her nose. "He's hot in an older, burly, Hugh Jackman kind of way, yes. Hot like maybe one of my dad's younger friends."

"Kate, he's still in his thirties, he's not that old!"

She shrugs. "You're not thirty yet, so what, you have a ten-year age difference? More? It doesn't matter. He's old. A few more years and he's in silver fox territory."

"So you admit he's a fox."

"I admit nothing."

"Well he is and I have to ask who the hell your dad's friends are if they look like Logan."

She actually seems to think that over, tapping her fingers on her chin. "Well there's this guy who used to work with my dad…"

"Kate," I warn her. "Back on track here. I need you to promise not to say anything to anyone."

"Why, are you ashamed?"

"Me? No. Hell no. But you just proved why people wouldn't understand."

She exhales loudly and flops down on her side. "You've

turned my world upside down, dude."

"And he's turned my world upside down," I say quietly, taking a seat beside her, lifting one of her legs out of the way.

She lifts her head, studying me for a moment before letting it fall back on the pillow. "Damn. You're serious."

"I am serious. I think I'm in love with him."

I'm in love with him.

Nope, it's not getting any less terrifying.

Kate groans, covering her face with her hands. "This keeps getting worse. You love him?"

Yes.

I shrug. "No. I don't know. It's complicated."

"You keep saying that."

"Because it is."

"Look, Ron, we have a judgement free zone right, so I'm not going to break that. I just want you to think long and hard about this and, nope, don't laugh at that, it's not a pun. If you're actually in love with Logan and this isn't about hot sex or whatever the old man gets up to, good for you. But no matter what, this isn't going to be easy. I mean, you know what it looks like. That Logan is a heartless bastard…and he kind of is a heartless bastard sometimes, so that doesn't help."

I nod, my heart flinching at those words. "I know."

"I mean it. What good can come of this?"

I glare at her. "Ouch."

She sighs and sits up straight. "I'm sorry. I'm just worried about you. I care. Believe it or not, I do have that capacity in me and I don't want to see you get hurt."

"Logan wouldn't hurt me."

"I agree. I think the man is head over heels for you and has been for a long time. Kind of like the kid that used to pull your hair and tease you in grade school because he had a crush on you and didn't know how to show it." She pauses. "But where can this relationship go? Either you're just fucking around or it's going to lead to more and if it leads to more…will it be strong enough to survive what's going to come?"

I don't even want to ask what's going to come. It will be a lot like this but with people being even less understanding. Maybe something worse.

"You couldn't possibly marry him," she adds quietly. "Do you know how bad that would look?"

Fuck. Obviously I know this, it's just been something I've tried really hard not to think about. For one, I don't want to jinx things and assume this relationship is going somewhere, even after what Logan said to me today. For two, I don't want to think about how people would take it. How do we even explain what's going on without painting Juliet in a bad light? There's no way we'll come out of it looking like decent people. Talk about a fucking scandal.

I look down at my hands. "I know it would look bad. That's why we're keeping it a secret and why you have to too."

"And you're just going to hide this forever? That won't work. Believe me. People are already talking about how weird Logan has gotten lately, being all nice and smiling and shit like that. He wasn't even like that with Juliet, and people are going to start putting two and two together."

I get up, needing a shower badly and a good night's sleep. "Well until they start adding things up, this is under wraps. Promise you won't say a word."

"I promise," she says.

I hope for our sake she keeps it.

Despite Kate knowing our lurid secret, Logan and I grow closer. Or maybe it's because of it, I don't know. After Kate found out, I told Logan right away. He didn't seem as concerned about the whole thing, not like I was, maybe because she's on his payroll and because of that, he knows she's not going to sell us out in the name of hot gossip.

It's also made it a bit easier for us to sneak around. The last week or so has reminded me of that episode of *Friends* when Joey finds out about Chandler and Monica, and though we're not quite that terrible, it is nice to have her cover our asses from time to time.

Like tonight. It's my day off and Logan has officially asked me on a proper date. He wants to take me to a beach-front restaurant down in Kapa'a where no one will know our names. I have a hard time believing that, but at least it's away from the prying eyes of the north shore.

And it's a date. Frankly, I'm fucking giddy. I get to dress up for once. No more uniform or apron, no flip-flops and cut off shorts and trucker hats.

I take my time selecting my most elegant and sexiest dress – a strapless maxi in jade green – and pull my hair back so it's high on my head, borrowing Kate's curling iron to add some oomf to a few strands I've left loose in an artful way. I do a dusting of golden highlighter over my cheekbones and some peachy blush and enough mascara to let my eyes do the flirting. And, naturally, I'm not wearing any underwear. I've discovered I have an aversion to them whenever Logan is around (and his tendency to rip them off is leaving me with less and less).

Of course the trickiest part of any of this is getting to

Logan's since he can't pick me up from the parking lot at work (that would be a huge tip-off), so I sneak around the complex, heading down the beach and toward Tunnels before I cut inland toward Logan's house.

The moment I reach his driveway he steps out of the house.

Holy moly.

I mean, hell does he ever look fine. Black pants, a grey polo shirt that shows off just how hard he works those muscles. He looks like sex on a stick.

"How did I get so lucky?" I ask loudly as I open the gate and start down the path toward him.

He watches me in silence, running his hand over his beard, his eyes trailing up and down my body in amazement as I stop in front of him.

"Well?" I ask. "What do you think?"

He gives a slight shake of his head, licks his lips. "Are you sure you don't want to skip the dinner and just eat in instead? Because, Freckles, I could eat you all night long. Every god damn inch of your body."

It's tempting, I have to admit it. But it was only a few nights ago that I made the signature Ohana Mahi Mahi in his kitchen, and even though another night of sex is always worth it, I really want to go out and be with the rest of the world.

"I would rather show you off," I tell him as I run my hands down the front of his chest and kiss him softly on the lips.

"Can't say I feel the same way," he says against my mouth. "You're for my eyes only, especially when you look like that." His hand drifts down over my backside, giving my ass a firm squeeze. He groans. "Commando, too." He pulls away, gives me a pleading look. "I promise I'll be five minutes."

"Let's go," I tell him with a smirk. "You said the reservation was for six, right? I want to catch the sunset."

With a whimper, he grabs my hand and leads me to the Jeep. As we drive past Moonwater, I keep low and ducked over in my seat, just in case, and Logan laughs. "Believe it or not, I just saw Charlie in the parking lot. He would have the gums flapping if he'd seen you." He pats my hand. "You're safe now."

I lift my head and look around warily. "I feel like I'm being smuggled."

"People only smuggle what's valuable. There isn't much more precious than you."

I give him a shy look. "Why, you're spouting poetry already. So far this date is living up to its expectations."

"I'm afraid that's all I got," he says, slipping on his shades and flashing me a wicked grin. Even though the sun will be going down in an hour, there's still enough light to make everything soft and bright. It's my favorite time of day, the lazy winding down toward dusk, and I put down the window to catch the smells of the taro fields and Hanalei River as we pass by, stand-up paddle boarders cruising down it and getting in one last jaunt before night.

The restaurant we go to is down on the east side, the coconut coast as they call it, just south of Kapa'a with the most gorgeous view of the beach and ocean. It puts the Ohana Lounge to shame.

We're seated at a private table, located closest to the shore, framed by wavering tiki torches. Even though it's the east coast, the sunset here doesn't fail to be spectacular, the sky slowly turning cotton candy pink and lush coral, the waves reflecting the metallic pastels.

And then, just after we place our order with the waiter,

it happens.

"Look," Logan cries out softly, grabbing my hand. I follow his gaze to the horizon where the water looks foamy, just in time to see a massive humpback whale breech clear out of the water.

Oh my god.

The whale lands with a heavy splash, so close we can hear it from where we are. The water explodes around it like someone dropped a bomb and sprays for what seems like ever, just as two other whales appear, spouting as they get breath from the surface.

Now everyone in the restaurant is noticing, some of them clapping, others taking pictures.

But for me, it's just Logan's hand in mine as we watch one of the most spectacular sights I've ever seen. We barely notice the drinks as they arrive, or our poke chips appetizer, and for the next twenty-minutes as the sky darkens from rose gold to purple to navy blue and the last splashes of the whales disappear, I'm enthralled, so much so that my heart feels like it's being stirred until my chest is heavy with a million different emotions.

"Ron," Logan whispers to me, squeezing my hand. "What's wrong?"

I look at him and try to smile and it's only then that I realize that I'm crying. I quickly wipe away the tear, trying to wrestle with everything inside.

"It's okay," he says softly, raising my hand up to kiss the back of it, his eyes never leaving mine. "I've got you."

And I know he does. That's why it's all so much to handle.

I take in a deep, shaking breath, and try to explain. "One of my best memories of Juliet was when she was ten years old and wanted to be a marine biologist. She was so obsessed with the whales, especially the humpbacks, and I became obsessed too. Because I wanted to be like her. And for a short time, she liked that. We finally had something in common." My throat is thick as I try to swallow. "She of course moved on and forgot about it and went onto something else and we never had that connection again. But then I see the dolphin doormat at your house and the pictures of whales in the bathroom, and the wood carvings of them in the backyard and I know that was all her doing… she still loved them."

He nods slowly, his own eyes looking wet. "She did. She loved to collect them. And she would get just as excited about them as you did right now."

"So I just…we saw these whales, like they were meant for us, you know? And I wonder in some ways if that's… her? I know it sounds dumb but…I feel like maybe she knows about us. About this. And maybe this is her way of saying she's okay." Another tear falls from my eyes, darkening the top of my dress. "Maybe she even approves."

Logan squeezes my hand harder. "*Aumakua*," he says quietly. I sniff and give him a curious look. "Hawaiians believe that when someone passes on, their spirit can live on as an *aumakua*, or guardian. Johnny would be the first to tell you that what you felt was Juliet in the form of that whale."

"And you? Did you feel anything?"

He gives me a kind smile. "I feel Juliet all the time around me. It's neither good or bad. She's just there, maybe in that dolphin doormat or the curtains she picked out for the hotel rooms or when a certain song comes on. She's never going anywhere, Ron, and that's a good thing. If you felt that was her in those whales out there, then I'm sure it was her. This island is a magical place and I've seen some pretty special things happen here. You feel it in the air, in the ocean, in every sunset and sunrise. But more than that…I think this is a sign for us to stop being afraid."

I rub my lips together, taking in a deep breath. "I'm not afraid," I tell him.

"You are," he says. "And that's okay. I'm afraid too. Deep down. About what the world will say. But in the end, it's not going to matter. The only thing that matters is us. I don't want to hide us anymore. Veronica, I want you. I want all of you. All the time, every day, until the end. I want to tell the world just how much you mean to me because you are my world."

I'm melting from the inside out. I always though Logan would be the one to make me shatter, but that's not the case at all. It's less violent than that. I'm liquefied, I'm reduced, I'm shedding every ounce of hardness I have, that plaster cast, the hard shell, it's sloughing off until there's nothing left but my heart, beating and exposed and all for him.

"Veronica," he says, adding a nervous smile, "Ronnie. Freckles. I am one-hundred-percent, madly, endlessly, hopelessly in love with you."

And there I go.

Veronica Locke has lost her heart.

Last seen in a puddle on the floor.

Now suspected in this man's hands.

I can barely fucking breathe.

He loves me.

He loves me.

I try and speak. I try and get the words out. I know that the tears are coming to my eyes again, that I'm smiling so broadly I think my face is cracking open. I know this world is stop motion, slow motion, that the planet might actually be spinning backward. I wouldn't notice.

And Logan, this beautiful, amazing man, has my heart. He has all of me.

"I love you," I whisper, choking on my words. "I love you."

His smile lights up the darkness, fuels my spirit. He leans across the table, grabbing my face in his hands and kisses me until I'm reeling, breathless, wild.

"Ahem."

We break apart, grinning like fools, to see the waiter standing by us with our main courses.

"Sorry to interrupt," he says.

I barely hear him, and even though our food, grilled mahi mahi and wahoo, looks amazing, I've lost my appetite. I can't think of anything right now but Logan, I don't want to have anything else but him and his beautiful words.

He loves me, he loves me, he loves me.

To be honest, I've never had those words spoken to me before. I never knew what it would feel like to hear them, and only imagined how good it could be. But now that Logan's told me he loves me, now that I've told him, I know my imagination never even came close to this gorgeous reality.

I'm flying.

Logan has a dashing smile on his face, one of awe and wonder, and pushes the food around on his plate. "Honestly, and I'm not just saying this because you're here, but food never tastes good unless you're cooking it. Did you want to get these to go and get out of here? I don't think I can eat right now. Not this, anyway."

"Yes," I say emphatically. I want go back to his place and fall into bed with him and never leave. I want him inside me while he says those words, I want to feel what it's like to make love while being in love.

The waiter doesn't seem all that surprised. I down the rest of my lychee martini and soon we're in his Jeep, heading up the highway, until Logan quickly stops by the Foodland grocery store and picks up two floral leis.

"The plumeria is for you," he says. "The hibiscus is for Juliet."

"Juliet?" I think to her marker on the side of the road. "You're the one who leaves the flowers for her?" My heart pinches at the thought, both for him being so thoughtful and for him being so invested still.

"I try to," he says. "But other people do too. I think someone at Moonwater does, maybe Johnny. And I think that prick she was sleeping with does too."

"I guess that makes him less of a prick though," I point out.

"Yeah, I know," he says, adjusting his hands on the steering wheel. "Believe me, it doesn't hurt to think about the two of them together, more a blow to the pride than anything, and I'm used to that." He glances at me, his eyes glinting in the passing streetlights. "Did I tell you I went to his house once."

"What?"

"Yeah. A few months after Juliet's accident. I went over there looking to kill him and…well, it didn't turn out that way. I told him what happened and he was wrecked. Not quite in the same way I was wrecked, but at least I realized it wasn't just a fling between the two of them. He had feelings for her and he was sorry. His apology didn't change anything but he was sorry."

"Wow," I say. "I can't imagine how hard that must have been."

He sighs heavily. "It wasn't easy. But it had to be done. And it made me realize some things. Though the guy was sorry, he was still a dickhead. I mean, an absolute wanker. Not so much in the sense that he was a vile homewrecker, which he was, but just in his personality. And, to be honest, he was better suited to Juliet than I was. He was a lawyer. He was ambitious. He had all the makings of someone who wanted to climb to the top and would do anything to stay there, and Juliet was like that too."

"Tell me about it."

"What I mean is, I finally saw why she and I never worked out. And now I see why you and I do. We're far more alike than you would guess. That's what I first saw in you." He glances at me, frowning. "I know I told you that my mother couldn't come to our wedding because of her illnesses. Well that's not exactly true. My mother does have some problems but the reality is…she's a horrible human being."

My eyes widen.

He goes on. "I know it sounds bloody awful for me to say that but it's the truth. And I only had her growing up. My dad left us when I was young, I barely have memories of him, though the memories I do have aren't bad. At least there was some love there, but my dad got caught up with gambling and that did him in. And I'm sure my own mother didn't help either."

"What did she do?" I ask quietly.

"It's more like what she didn't do. Which, to put it bluntly, was to fucking love us. But compared to you and Juliet, it was different. Both Kit and I got the shit end of the stick. My mother would sit around all day in her bloody chair, smoking packs of cigarettes until her ashtray was piled high, and she'd make us cook and clean and do everything for her. If we did it, we didn't get harassed. If we didn't do it, she would go out of her way to make sure our lives were a living hell. My brother and I got nothing. Of course back then, we were growing up rural and this seemed to be the norm. Emotional abuse was never talked about and lack of love was something that was swept under the rug. My mom worked her job at the bank and when she wasn't there, she was terrorizing us and we thought that's how life was supposed to be. Loveless and full of fear."

I had no idea at all it was like this for Logan. I knew he was reluctant to talk about his mother, but I thought it was because he had nothing to say about her or just didn't want to seem like a dick when I had my own mother to complain about. Instead, his mom sounds worse than mine.

"I'm so sorry," I whisper. "I wish you told me this sooner.

"I should have. I don't know why I didn't. " He shrugs. "And the crazy thing is, I grew up still wanting her approval. It's no wonder that Kit ended up in the outback up north, far away from where we grew up, and I ended up all the way over here." He looks at me, a softness coming over his eyes. "And so when I met you, I knew. I knew you'd come from a similar place. Your mother can be pretty awful, I'll give you that much, but thankfully you never had to do what we had to do. Even so, I recognized them as the same. Sometimes I think I fell for Juliet because I saw it as another way to prove myself, even though it was to your mother and not mine. How fucked up is that?"

He exhales heavily through his nose, staring out at the headlights on the road. "Anyway, seeing that wanker that Juliet was with made me realize that we've all got our own people. Somewhere out there there's someone who is part of your tribe, who belongs to you, who should be with you. You have always been my people, Veronica. From the moment we first met till now, through all of those years where we were both lost and stolen. You're mine as much as I'm yours. And I swear nothing, nothing, is ever going to change that for us. You will always belong in my heart. It's your home."

My chest is expanding with a joy so acute, I'm not sure how to handle it, where the feeling should go. I'm just drowning in it, taking in his words instead of air, until it's everything I am and all that I'll need.

"If you'll belong to my heart," I tell him breathlessly, reaching across and tracing my fingers along his ear, his cheekbones, down the length of his beard to his chin. "I know you always have."

What a bunch of fucking saps we are. But I wouldn't trade it for anything in the world.

On the way back to Moonwater we stop by Juliet's marker, the scene of the crash, taking great care as we park on the side of the road. We don't have time for a vigil or even a few words – it's a narrow, dangerous spot and you have to make it quick. But the two of us get out, hand in hand, and run over, laying down the lei, the headlights from the Jeep illuminating us. A soft rain is starting to fall.

Even though we don't say anything out loud, I tell Juliet that I liked seeing her today, that I hope I'll see her again, whale or not, and that I love her. Maybe just as family, in that deep-rooted way you can't escape, but I love her all the same.

Then we head back to Moonwater, the place she helped create, and I vow to keep it going in her honor, and to one day make her proud.

CHAPTER EIGHTEEN

"**R**ON, HELP! HELP! I'M STUCK."

I'm already smiling at the sound of Kate's panicked voice and look up from my bed to see her trying to walk across the apartment, in her underwear, a dress all bundled around her head, her arms caught inside at an uncomfortable angle.

"What did you do?" I ask, coming over to her and trying to yank it up over her head.

"I told you I don't wear dresses," she says, trying to twist her body away from me. I keep thinking I'm going to pull her arms out of her sockets.

"Just because you don't wear dresses doesn't mean you should be trapped in them every time." I grunt, holding the sleeves and trying to yank it off. "It's not rocket science. You put your head and arms where the holes are."

"That's what she said," she mumbles and then suddenly

she's free and nearly falling backwards.

I avert my eyes politely because she's topless, and shove the dress in her hands. "Anyway, I told you to borrow one of my dresses. They're much bigger and you won't get stuck."

"Fine," she says, waving her hand in my face. "Give me something."

"Go put on a bra and we'll talk."

She grumbles as she turns around and heads back to her room.

It's New Year's Eve and we're having the party of the century at the Ohana Lounge. Well, maybe not the century, or even the year, but definitely the month. It's not just for staff either, there are guests here too. I'm just lucky I don't have to cook – I convinced Logan to let me have the night off and to hire catering instead. Pupus for everyone.

Of course it didn't take much convincing for Logan since he's in love with me, which makes him a pretty shit boss these days. It's been almost a month since we told each other how we felt and a month where we've managed to keep our relationship on the lowdown.

Even Kate is getting used to it. I think. At any rate, it's brought us closer together since I'm in full-on "in love" mode and every single thing revolves around Logan, which means all I want to do is talk about him all day long and there's no one else to confide in.

Actually that's not true. Daniel for sure knows something is up, but he's not saying a word and we don't discuss it with each other either. But even when it comes to my friend Claire back at home, I'm still keeping Logan a secret.

To be honest, the sneaking around is getting a bit tiring. When we're around each other at Moonwater we have to pretend to be on a strictly professional level, and when you're constantly screwing and you're in love, that gets really hard to hide. We've messed up on a few occasions but luckily no one has seemed to notice. The only time we can really be together, be ourselves, is at his house or in here if Kate isn't around. She doesn't mind that much that he sometimes comes over but I know she finds the whole thing weird, and so far we've been able to not act like a couple around her, just for her sake.

When Kate comes back in my room, she's wearing a bra, so I give her a blue and white cocktail dress I picked up at Anthropologie before I moved here. It's not exactly formal, but since Kate lives in board shorts and tank-tops, any dress will make her look like she's going to the goddamn Oscars or something.

She slips it on – with ease this time – and sighs, hands on her hips. "Do I look dumb?"

"You look cute," I tell her. "Charlie won't know what hit him."

"For the last time, I'm not kissing him at midnight," she growls.

"Oh, then who are you kissing, because it ain't Logan."

"Phhhf, please, you couldn't pay me to kiss that old man. His teeth would probably fall out in my mouth or something."

I roll my eyes. "Okay, then Daniel."

"Nah, he's kissing Nikki. If you're wondering why no one has caught onto you and Logan, it's because the coupling of Nikki and Danny Boy is going on. You'll see tonight. It's so obvious."

"As obvious as you and Charlie?"

"Dude, shut it. Now put on your dress and finish getting all pretty so we can start drinking."

Despite having a pineapple mimosa already while getting ready, I put on a simple black low-back maxi and the finishing touches on my makeup and some fresh plumeria flowers in my hair and then we're off to the restaurant on this humid night.

Me, Nikki, and Kate spent the morning getting Ohana Lounge ready for the party, gold and black streamers all over the place, a silver countdown ball, plastic NYE hats, glasses and tiaras, plus the prerequisite noisemakers.

Our sound system still sucks and we're going off a playlist, but that doesn't matter because Dan is making his famous punch again, as well as a champagne based one, and the caterers have already set up their pupu platters everywhere.

We're still some of the earliest people to arrive though. Johnny is over in the corner already inspecting the food.

And he's wearing a fucking tuxedo.

"Oh my god, Johnny Cakes!" Kate squeals, hunching over and clapping her hands together. "Look at you!"

Johnny looks up from the tray of food and gives us a discerning look. "What? Can't a brother dress up like James Bond every now and then?"

"Damn right he can," I tell him. "Did you rent that or what?"

He smiles. "Nah, I had this for my brother's wedding a few years ago. Luckily I've stayed fat this whole time so it still fits."

"So how is the food?" I ask, nodding at it.

"Nowhere as good as our stuff. I told you we should have been the ones to make it."

I pat him on the back. "Look, we're allowed to have time off every now and then."

He grumbles something and shoves some kind of miniature Spam roll in his mouth. "At least the Spam still tastes like Spam."

Hawaiians and their Spam, I'll never quite understand it.

"Aloha, ladies," Dan says, coming over to us with two drinks in his hands. His hair is loose tonight, to his shoulders which is a change, and his Hawaiian shirt is more understated than usual, peach and grey tones. On his head is one of the plastic top hats. "Brought you some drinks."

"Aye," Johnny says while we take the drinks from Dan, "where's my drink?"

"Let me guess, you wanted a martini, shaken not stirred."

"Who the fuck stirs a martini?"

He follows Daniel back to the bar grumbling all the way.

It's not long before the rest of the staff enters the room, followed by some of the guests. Everyone looks great, happy to be here and dressed up for the occasion. But I'm still waiting for Logan, briefly wondering if he'd come in a tuxedo too and if he did, what exactly would he look like and where the hell could we escape to for a quick screw because that shit would be like kryptonite to me.

And then he appears. Not in a tuxedo, but in black pants and a black dress shirt, a loose grey tie around his neck. I should have figured he wouldn't be going for a suit. One of my first thoughts about the man was how uncomfortable he looked in one.

He sees me from across the room and our eyes lock in a wordless gaze. The corner of his mouth quirks up into a smile and he nods. I do the same, watching as he enters the restaurant and starts greeting the guests one by one, offering them his gorgeous smile.

I love watching him work like this. For all his broodiness and quiet mannerisms and, well, inclination to be grumpy, he's actually really good at what he does. He cares about the guests here, more now than when I first started, and is personally invested in how they are doing. It's no longer just to make money, to stay afloat. It's because he actually is concerned and wants them to be happy.

And when they're happy, he's happy. So many nights I've stayed up with him at his house going over the budget and reports and the feedback from the guests, and he's giving everything he has to not only keep the business alive but to keep it moving forward. He wants to take what he had with Juliet and he wants to improve upon it, bit by bit.

And he wants to improve upon it with me. Not in so many words, but he's hinted at my career long-term here. Becoming partners in the place. In having it more than just my job.

I honestly don't know what to think. I don't want to get ahead of myself and I don't want to jinx anything, because running Moonwater with him would be a beautiful dream. But we've been good about not talking too much about the future. We've just been enjoying being in love and that alone is a lot to handle (in the best way) before we start making those kind of plans.

But that doesn't mean I don't think about it. I do. And every single thought I have of the future always comes back to him. He's my people, my heart, my home. He's my world and reason for everything and I don't ever want anything different.

"He's really changed," Kate says in a low voice. I'd forgotten she was standing next to me to be honest, lost in my Logan-induced daze.

"Yeah," I agree quietly.

"I mean it," she says. "The place has never been better. I'd like to thank you for that. Love has fueled him well.

He's connected to this place, to this island again. The aloha spirit. For a while there he was lost from all of this." She nudges me in the side. "If you wouldn't mind telling him to pass that aloha spirit onto me though, that would be great. I could use a raise."

I give her a wry look. "I'll see what I can do."

Soon the restaurant is pretty much packed, a few more guests showing up than we had planned but everyone is having a great time. The catered food is just fine – sorry, Johnny – and Dan's drinks are keeping us all loose and lubricated.

"How are you doing?" Logan asks, coming over to me and Charlie while we mow down on coconut shrimp.

"Great party," Charlie says, munching away. Even he's managed to dress up – a white and red Hawaiian shirt and dark pants, his normally spiky hair smoothed into a mini pompadour. "Though I'm waiting for someone to get wild."

"It's still early," Logan says, checking his watch. "Another two hours, then we'll see." He raises his glass at me. "Aren't you drinking, Freckles?"

I look around. "I put my glass down somewhere, not sure what happened to it."

"What are you having?"

"The champagne punch."

He nods, a small smile on his lips. "Coming right up."

As he turns and walks over to the drinks, I take a moment to admire his firm ass as it disappears into the crowd.

I can feel Charlie's eyes on me. He clears his throat.

I glance at him, raising my brows. "What?"

"Remember when I thought you and Logan hated each other?"

"No."

"Well, I couldn't have been more wrong. I'm pretty sure

you*'re his favor*ite."

You're right, I think but I can only hide my smile by shoving another shrimp in my mouth. I shrug. "I have no idea what you're talking about."

"Right," he says slowly. "You're not a very good liar, you know that Ron?"

I roll my eyes. "Well if I'm Logan's favorite, it's because I show up to work on time."

Logan comes back with the glass of champagne, his eyes not leaving mine as he hands it to me. "Cheers," he says, clinking his glass against mine, giving me a sly smile, a moment for just us.

Suddenly Charlie's drink appears between us, trying to clink against ours. "Yes, hello, hi," he says, glancing between the two of us and pouting. "I'm here too, you know."

"Yes, of course you are," Logan comments dryly.

Charlie frowns. "Fine, I know when I'm not wanted," he says and then stalks off toward Johnny and Kate, who are dancing.

"Touchy, touchy," Logan says, watching him go off.

"He said he thinks I'm your favorite," I tell him.

He grins and takes a step toward me. "Because you are my favorite," he says, lowering his voice to those irresistibly sexy levels. "Let him be jealous."

I laugh. "Oh, I'm not sure he'd want to be your favorite after all. There's a lot of inappropriateness and work harassment."

"Yes, I'm quite the scoundrel when it comes to that," he says, leaning in even closer. I have to still myself, afraid that he might kiss me here in front of everyone. That's what this is starting to look like. "Though I'm pretty sure Charlie doesn't want what I want from you right now."

"If you're going to say something dirty, please don't

bring Charlie's name into it."

"I would never," he says, cocking his head as he looks me over, like I'm a dessert tray and he doesn't know which treat to try first. "But," he whispers, leaning into my ear. "I wouldn't mind hauling you off to the bathroom right now and fucking you up against the wall. I bet you're already wet and ready under this dress."

"You're awfully optimistic," I manage to say, closing my eyes. Thing is, he's right. He just has to look at me a certain way and I might spontaneously combust.

"Optimistic because I have a great track record with you," he murmurs, lips still to my ear. "Perfect, even. If only your dress were shorter, I could have my fingers inside you right now and no one would know." I automatically clench at the thought. "Finger fuck you right here, among all these people, until your knees gives out."

"Logan," someone's voice breaks the spell. I'm not even sure whose, I'm too turned on to function and he hasn't even laid a finger on me.

Slowly he pulls away from me and I open my eyes to see Daniel staring at us.

Logan clears his throat. "Yes?"

"Uh, sorry to interrupt. We're running out of champagne for the punch. Should I dip into the stash you got for midnight?"

"Nah," he says, taking a sip of his. "We'll just move onto the Mai Tais. You do a good job with those."

"Thanks," Daniel says, tipping his plastic hat at him before he looks to me, giving me a mild smirk. "Guess I won't be *pl*anning to kiss you at midnight," he says before he walks off to the bar.

Logan raises his brows. "If he kissed you, I would have punched him the bloody face."

I smack his shoulder. "Oh come on, caveman. Besides, he and Nikki are apparently an item now. Or again. I can't keep up with the dating antics around here."

"It's like bloody summer camp," he comments with a sigh. But instead of looking put-off by it, he looks pleased. I know he takes a lot of pride in how close-knit everyone is here.

The two of us part ways for the rest of the evening while he does the rounds, making sure everyone is having a good time, and somehow Kate convinces me to dance. The Mai Tais help, as do the feather boas, shiny hats and tiaras, and noise makers, and soon nearly all of us are cutting loose on the dance floor, ready to bring in the New Year.

Then the slow music comes on as we near the countdown. "Purple Rain" starts to play and while I'm looking to the computer with amazement, I see Logan stepping away from the playlist and heading right for me.

"I would have played 'Kashmir,'" he says, taking my hand in his. "But that's a great song to fuck to, not to dance too. Will you have this dance with me?"

I blink at him as he pulls me close, wrapping his arms around me. What he just said is the kind of thing he normally says in private, not in the middle of a crowded dance floor.

"Oh relax," he murmurs, his head against mine as he starts to lead me around the floor, swaying slowly back and forth. I can't remember the last time I slow-danced with someone.

Actually I can. I think it was with my father at Logan and Juliet's wedding.

I swallow hard at that thought, but for once it's not the punch to the gut it used to be. Our days together have brought a peace about her that I hadn't had before.

Soon other people start dancing alongside us. Johnny and Lucia, Charlie and Kate, Daniel and Nikki. Even Jin is dancing with an elderly lady and showing off some pretty impressive moves, making her laugh.

"I never wanted to be your weekend lover," Logan sings into my ear, his voice deep, rich, washing over me like tropical rain. I hold him closer and rest my head on his chest, hearing his heart beat underneath. Strong, just as he is, and getting louder, faster, as we dance into the night, dance into a world that's just our own.

And when the song is over, we don't break apart. We keep dancing. We keep dancing as Charlie stands on one of the tables, shirtless, a party hat on his head and starts counting down loudly.

"Ten! Nine! Eight!" he shouts, pumping his fist.

"It was a hell of a year," Logan says to me. There's a gravity in his voice as his eyes search mine.

"It was."

"Seven! Six! Five!"

"I could never have believed it would end like this," he says.

"Neither." My voice is small as he places his fingers on my jaw, a light, delicate touch.

"Four! Three! Two!"

"I love you," he whispers. "So bloody much."

"I love you, too." My words are breathless.

"One! Happy fucking new year!" Charlie yells, stomping his feet on the table and throwing his hat into the crowd.

Everyone erupts into hollering and cheering and laughing, punctuated by a ton of loud noisemakers. Logan and I, we smile knowingly, feeling that love run deep, deeper than I could have ever thought possible. Soul to soul, what we share is fathomless.

And then he kisses me. Not the timid, shy kiss usually reserved for New Year's Eve. But the kind of kiss that tells the world that I am his.

And he is mine. I kiss him back with just as much passion, my hands in his hair, at his back, one of his hands at my waist, the other cupping my face. Our mouths are lost to each other, warm and wet and bigger than my wildest dreams. This man is all I need.

I know we are getting carried away and I don't care. Time doesn't seem to matter at all, it has no place in our world where the beautiful moments seem to last forever.

So when we break apart, we're slightly surprised to see the staff at Moonwater Inn all crowded together at the edge of the dance floor and staring at us with open mouths.

Well. Not Kate and Daniel. They're actually smiling, looking relieved. But Johnny, Charlie, Lucia, Nikki, and Jin? Well you could shoot golf balls into their gaping maws. I've never seen a group of people look so shocked before.

To be honest, it's a good feeling, to have it all out in the open like this. This is who we are, judge us if you're going to judge us, but we love each other and that's all that really matters.

"Looks like we've been caught," Logan comments with good humor. He takes my hand. "Come on Lucy, we have some splainin' to do," he says in his best Desi Arnez impression.

I take in a deep breath for courage and he leads me over to them.

No one says anything for a moment.

Then Kate blurts out, "Finally!"

"What, uh," Johnny says pointing at us. His bow-tie is undone and he has red lipstick on his cheek from where Lucia must have kissed him. "What was that?" He points at my hand in Logan's. "W*hat i*s this!? The hab*ut and* the little wahine?"

"We have something we would like to announce," Logan says smoothly.

"Uh, pretty sure you announced it with your tongues down each other's throats," Charlie says flatly.

"N' Sync, go put on a shirt," Logan says, then looks to everyone else. "It's not anyone's business and I know you're unlikely to understand. But all we can ask for is for a bit of respect. You don't have to approve, but as it stands…this is the reality. This is who we are." He clears his throat.

"Dude," Johnny breathes out. "Wow. This explains so much."

"Yeah," speaks up Jin, who is grinning. "Why you've been so happy lately. You've been getting lucky."

I laugh at that, high, girlish giggles. My stomach is churning with nerves and yet I feel happy, happy and free that this is actually happening. It's scary but so worth it.

Logan gives him a calm smile. "Believe me, none of this was taken lightly. We all know what Juliet was to both of us and who she was to all of you. But life has a funny way of working out. You can't always choose who you fall in love with and only sometimes are you lucky enough to have a second chance at love. What I have with Veronica, though, goes far beyond a second chance." He squeezes my hand and gives me a tender look, one that makes me nearly buckle at the knees. "She makes me want to be a better man. She makes me get up each morning and live without fear. She's everything I could have dreamed life *could be.*"

Oh god.

Don't cr*y, I tell myself. Don*'t cry, don't cry.

"Freckles, you're my love, you're my home, and you're my light," he says, turning to face me, taking both my hands in his.

And that's when I realize it. That's when I realize that this confession, the announcement of our love and coupling or whatever you want to call it, is more than I thought. That this wasn't something spur of the moment and it wasn't because we were caught kissing and enjoying it. This was thought-over, this was planned.

Logan is nervous. There's a bead of sweat at his forehead, his eyes are wavering. *It's not over their* approval.

It's over mine.

"I know this is fast," he says to me. "I know we have obstacles. I know that the path will get rough for a while. But I would rather walk over coals with you than stay safe and alone. I would rather face the misgivings and the judgement and be by your side, than go the safe route without you. You're worth it all, so worth it, and in the end, that's all that matters to me. You are all that matters."

He clears his throat, glancing anxiously at the crowd who are standing in shock and awe.

Then he drops to one knee.

Nikki and Kate gasp dramatically in unison.

I can't. Fucking. Breathe.

He holds my hand while he reaches into his pocket. My mouth is clamped together, fighting back tears, my other hand at my chest.

Is this real? IS THIS REAL?

What is happening?

Logan stares up at me and in his eyes I see it all – he's afraid but it won't keep him from me. Nothing will.

"Veronica Locke," he says, voice choking up. He brings a shiny ring out of his pocket, holding it out in front of me. "Will you marry me?"

My world is spinning, a warm gentle cycle, but I'm

spinning all the same.

Logan is asking me to marry him.

There are a million thoughts and worries and layers of doom swirling around me, wanting in, to take this moment and ruin it with doubt, with guilt, with shame.

But I don't let them in. I push them out, where they belong.

I'm going with my heart now.

Logan is asking me to marry him.

To become his wife.

There's only been one answer.

"Yes," I gasp, tears spilling down my cheeks. "Yes."

Everything becomes a blur. He slips the ring on my finger – through my tears it shines like a new star – and then I'm dropping to my knees beside him, grabbing his face in disbelief.

"Is this really happening?" I ask.

"Yes," he whispers. "It really is. I love you. I made mistakes and it should have been you, it always should have been you, and now it is. It's happening. And if it's a dream, I don't want to wake up."

"Me neither," I sob and then I'm kissing him, my lips on his mouth, his cheeks, his forehead and he's embracing me and people around us are erupting into applause.

I look around, smiling, crying, embarrassed, overjoyed. And I look at everyone, all my friends, my *ohana*, and I know things are going to be okay. Some of them are smiling, some of them are still in shock, some of them look suspicious. But in the end I know they stand by me, and stand by us, and if it's weird right now, they'll allow it to get better.

Eventually we get up, Logan hauling me to my feet, brushing my hair from my face, kissing me with tears in his eyes.

"It's you and me, Freckles. Me and you."

And then, then, the party *really* starts. The champagne is flowing, guests are congratulating us, the music is blaring. Johnny comes up to us, pulling us both into a hug, and says, "This is weird but you both know that. You're good people and you both deserve to be happy. Even you, *habut*. No, especially you. God. Give the rest of us a break, man."

Soon after, Kate and Nikki come up to see the ring, which I can fully appreciate now that my eyes have dried. It looks almost vintage, an asymmetrical pearl offset by diamonds that sparkle like the Hawaiian sky under these lights. Then they bombard me with questions about being bridesmaids and where the wedding will be held and all the things that I never dared to dream about but now is a total reality. The only person who is a bit stand-offish is Charlie, but I figure he's drunk (still shirtless, too) and just needs some time to come around.

When it gets late and things start to wind down, the new day seeping into the night, Logan takes my hand and leads me home to his house.

There's so much to discuss, so many things we're going to have to face.

But we're doing it together.

And for tonight, we're the only people that matter.

CHAPTER NINETEEN

WAKE UP IN LOGAN'S ARMS. I WAKE UP WITH A GORGEOUS diamond and pearl ring on my finger. I wake up with this man's love. A pledge for endless love.

And I wake up afraid.

I take in a deep breath, turning my head to see Logan sleeping soundly beside me, snoring lightly. He's so beautiful, the perfect face at first glance, but the closer you look, the more you see the imperfections. The acne scars on his cheek, the way his nose twists in the middle, a surfing injury from back in the day. When he smiles you can see a few crooked bottom teeth, and his grin itself isn't fully even.

But all these little flaws only make him more gorgeous. They make him more mine. In our flaws, outside and in, we see each other and understand each other.

And yet I'm afraid. Afraid of what's about to come. I love Logan with all my heart but I know there's a world out there that won't see that love and won't understand. And while I'm prepared to fight them, I'm prepared to turn my back on those who will judge us, I'm worried that they can fight back harder.

I'm going to be Logan's wife. It's everything I've wanted and then some.

But this isn't going to be easy.

I have to tell my parents.

"Are you watching me sleep again?" Logan mumbles, keeping his eyes closed.

"Yes," I say, voice creaky from sleep. "Can't get quite enough of you."

"You're going to get a lot more of me," he says, slowly opening his eyes, fixing them on me. "I can't believe I get to wake up next to you like this for the rest of our lives."

His love is intoxicating, banishing the dark clouds I have threatening my heart. I kiss him softly as he runs his hands through my hair and we are lost to each other.

Eventually we get out of bed. A new year, a new life. The restaurant is closed for the holiday but Logan does have to go relieve Kate from reception later. She's getting paid triple overtime out of the goodness of Logan's heart, but I'm sure she's raring to go back to bed and sleep. Everyone has to be a bit hungover.

It's weird not to hide it anymore, but it feels good. And with everyone being so happy for us, it puts an extra bit of pep in my step. In fact, as we walk back to the hotel together, I'm practically skipping, swinging on his arm like a schoolgirl.

While he heads off to do some work, I head back to my place. We have plans to meet later for dinner, which either means a spot in Hanalei if any are open, or I'll just cook for him again. There's no one else I'd rather slave over the stove for, and how much he enjoys what I make is just icing on the literal cake (coconut is his favorite).

But the minute the door closes behind me, the rays of happiness start to fade. The fear is back, lurking behind the dark clouds, threatening the happy little life we've built with each other.

I have to call my parents. I know their opinion doesn't matter but this is different. I don't care if my mother and father don't approve – I know one-hundred-percent that they won't. But my mother is in politics and she's not just a bitch in a way that makes her strong, in the way she gets things done. She can be downright horrible and I can't trust *her for anything.*

Don't tell them.

I should list*en to t*hat voice.

Elope.

I should listen to that voice.

I should, I should, I should.

But what if they could just see it from my point of view?

What if they could understand?

I stick my phone underneath my pillow in my room, out of sight out of mind, and take a long shower, but my brain is being torn in half. There's a moment of utter happiness that Logan and I are together, no more secrets, that I'm going to marry him.

Then there's one of utter rage and despair. When I think there's no way it will ever happen. That there's no way I can feel this happy without having the rug pulled out from under me. Nothing has ever been this easy before – why should this be?

And it hasn't been easy. It's been a battle to fight the shame. But the love is the easy part. It's free-flowing and never-ending and I feel it from him just as much as I give and that truly makes ev*erything worth it.*

*Get married. Don't tell them. Don't let them ruin your one cha*nce at happiness.

The thoughts again. Louder this time.

Would it be cowardly not to say anything?

Or is it smart to protect the one true thing I have?

Because I know the risk…it's not just that my parents could disown me.

They could take away Moonwater.

And I wish I lived in some other timeline, some other life, where that wasn't a possibility, but it is. I can't underestimate her. I can't ever do that.

The only solution is to live a lie once more. It's a small price to pay to keep what's ours.

I take my phone out from under my pillow, about to plug it into the wall since the battery is low, and move on, forget about it. Talk to Logan, see what we should do, if I should say anything at all.

It rings in my hand.

I gasp, staring at it blankly.

It's my mother. On my new phone I haven't had time to program in her number, but it's her all the same.

Holy fuck.

I hesitate before answering it. Thank god my battery is dying and I can use that as an excuse. She's probably just calling to wish me a happy new year, anyway. This should be a short call.

I answer the phone. "Hello?"

"Hello Veronica." Her voice is like ice. "Happy new year."

"Thanks," I say as cheerfully and casually as possible. "Did you guys have a good night?"

"We did," she says. "You know, had the usual party

down at the Palmer House."

An eerie silence fills the line. I'm about to say some-thing benign when she sighs. But it's not drawn-out or overdramatic. It's sharp. It's a *war*ning. "I heard you had a great time," she says. Her words are a loaded gun, hinting at damage.

"Last night?" I ask cautiously.

"Yes. There was a party at Moonwater, wasn't there? For you, the staff, the guests…"

My breath freezes in the top of my lungs, refusing to move onward. "How did you know that?"

"Veronica, Moonwater is more our hotel than it is Logan's. Not by a lot, but it's enough. Do you seriously think I wouldn't know what's going on in our own hotel?"

Oh no. Oh no. This can't be going where I think it's going.

The doom settling over me is insurmountable.

I can't even speak.

"I know what happened last night," she adds and now her voice is cracking, brittle with anger, acidic to the core. "I know what people saw."

"What happened?" I whisper. I can't hide the fear in my voice.

There's a sharp intake of breath, like I've struck her.

"What happened?" she repeats. "I know what's going on with you two. What you've done. Tell me right now that you and Logan are not…together. Tell me right now that you aren't and I'll believe you."

Oh my god. I nearly drop the phone. I can't even stand up, I stumble to the couch, sitting down. My heart is shrinking.

This can't be happening.

How could she know?

"Who told you we were together?" I ask, my face going hot with fear and blistering anger.

"It doesn't matter."

"Who told you!" I yell. "It matters!"

"Oh, fine. It was Charlie. And he's been honest so far, he wouldn't start lying now."

I am stunned. Slapped in the face, kicked in the stomach.

Charlie?

"What?" I'm gasping.

"Yes, there's nothing unusual about that. I have to know what exactly is going on with our investment, we don't trust Logan to report the truth. Your father and I check in with Charlie every now and then. We checked in with him this morning and he told us something that couldn't possibly be true."

I'm going to kill him.

Logan's going to murder him.

"Don't get all concerned about Charlie," my mother goes on. "He assumed we knew. But I'm glad he told us at any rate, even if he's mistaken. Is he mistaken, Veronica?"

My mouth flaps open, closed, like a fish out of water.

"Answer me!" she yells, the malevolence coming to life.

I nearly bite my tongue off, my mouth snaps shut so fast.

"Your silence is speaking volumes," she sneers, her voice going low, to the vile levels. "You have no idea what you've done, no idea what you're doing. You think you're going to marry Logan? Is that it? You think you're going to be the next Juliet? Is that what this is about?"

"No," I tell her, trying to find my voice, my strength. "No. I love him and he loves me."

My mother erupts into laughter, the kind that comes

from hate.

"Love? Oh cut the crap, you don't know what love is. What you're doing is because you're tired of being second best, of never measuring up. You're trying to take what was rightfully Juliet's, you won't even let her rest in peace."

I'm so temped to tell her the truth about her, about who she really was. It takes everything I have in me to protect Juliet.

"Mom, please, I knew you wouldn't understand so I didn't tell you but…it's the truth. We're in love and it has nothing to do with Juliet, only that we had to make sure that we were being respectful and –"

"Bullshit!" she yells. "Respectful? You're only showing how pathetic you are. I expected more from you Veronica, I really did. I never expected you to be Juliet, no one could be, she was one of a kind. But I did think you'd at least grow up to a be a woman with class and honor and dignity and you have none of those values. None. You're an opportunist. You take what's not even yours."

"You're calling *me* an opportunist?" I sneer. I feel like I'm about to lose my fucking mind. "You, of all, people are the biggest opportunist of them all. You're a fucking politician! You based your whole life on lies, starting with how you pretended to love us. You never loved me, admit it! You just pretended to because it's what you were told."

"You don't know anything about love, Veronica. If you did, you wouldn't be doing this to her, to us. To me. How do you think it will look for you to marry your sister's widower? We'll be the laughing-stock of Chicago. I'll lose more than you will, is that what you want for me? Is it?"

I can only shake my head. I can't believe it and yet I can.

"Their marriage was over when she died," I tell her. Everything inside me is seconds from breaking. "And far before that."

"Because he's a liar and cheat. I can see now why the two of you would start up together, he had no respect for Juliet either."

"Well then fuck you, mom," I tell her. I am all rage and I am rising. "You know what? I don't give a shit what you think. I don't care if Chicago has a problem with it, or if you lose power, or whatever the fuck you think will happen, which probably won't because no one cares about you as much as you think they do. This is my life and I am choosing him and he is choosing me and that's all I can say about it. I'm going to marry him regardless, without your blessing or your permission, and there's not a goddamn thing you can do or say to stop me. So tell me that I'm weak and he's a liar and that we're both horrible people, I really don't care. He has my back and that's more than I can say for my own damn family."

I'm breathing hard from that, the blood is pounding in my head, pressing on my temples. The line goes black with silence.

"I will not be made a fool of Veronica," she says. "I have worked too long and too hard in this industry to be the laughing stock. I will not lose people's respect for me and my family just because you've lost respect for your family and yourself."

"Then I'm sorry. It is what it is."

She exhales loudly. "I'm sorry too. Because I liked that place and it's going to be a shame that we're forced to sell it."

"What are you talking about?"

"Well I no longer want a man like Logan deciding how our investments go. It's obvious now his judgement can't be trusted. We can't always make the best investment decisions, but if we sell now, I'm sure we'll make some money on it."

"You can't…you can't just sell. Logan is a shareholder."

"He doesn't own the majority of the hotel, dear. If he did, I wouldn't be keeping tabs, now would I? When he first met Juliet, he was getting the hotel off the ground. We swooped in and came up with the remaining funds, money he used to purchase Moonwater. That's never been a secret."

"But…it's his! It's all his! It's his flesh and blood. It's his passion. It's his job. Maybe you gave some money, but without Logan, you would have nothing at all."

"That was his decision. It kept him and Juliet busy, but now that's over."

I'm starting to shake. This has to be a bad dream, a nightmare, and I can't wake up.

"Mom," I whisper. "You can't do that. There has to be some legal way about it. It's still his company, his business, his hotel. You can't just decide to sell. He has to approve."

She gives off a small, merciless laugh. "Oh, you're so naïve. I thought I raised you better than that. Let me make this clear, Veronica Locke." Her tone becomes as hard as flint. "If you don't call off this marriage, call of this silly relationship, your father and I will sell what's rightfully ours. Logan will get a small chunk of change, plus whatever he invested. Which, by the way, wasn't much. And that's that. Frankly, this has gone on for too long anyway – we should have done this as soon as Juliet died."

No. No. There has to be some way out of here.

There's so much to say. I want to scream. Cry. Protest. Swear. I want to revel in my anger, I want her to feel what I'm feeling. I want to beg for forgiveness. I want to plead for approval. I want to be given a chance.

But the only thing I can manage to ask is, "Why do you hate me so much, mom?" My voice is broken, ruined, weak.

"What did I ever do to you?"

The silence says everything and nothing at all.

"Give him back his ring, Veronica. Do the right thing. Even if you don't care about Juliet's honor or my reputation or your self-respect, even if you don't give a shit about any of that, think about Logan. Do you really want to be the one to ruin all that he's worked for? Do you want to be the one to crush his legacy? The man has been through so much. Do you want to make him lose it all?"

"Fuck you, mom," I tell her and hang up the phone.

But the act seems worthless. Because she's already won. She's right.

My fingers go to the ring, the beautiful ring, and twirl it around, trying to gather strength from it, trying not to cry. Could I be the one to call it off? Do I tell Logan what just happened? Do we try and find a solution together?

Or would that ruin everything anyway? I know Logan. He loves me. He's stubborn. And he's not going to let me go without a fight. If I tell him what we're faced with, he'll give up the hotel. He'll let my parents take back Moonwater and he'll lose all that he's worked for in order to keep me.

Can I live with myself if that happens? Can I marry him knowing I ruined his life, that I made him lose it all?

Or do I get up and walk away to save him.

Do I tell Logan the biggest lie I've ever told and break his heart in order to keep this piece of paradise for him?

I sit down on the couch, numb.

This is going to hurt beyond belief.

CHAPTER TWENTY

THEY SAY THAT LIFE ISN'T MEASURED BY THE BREATHS we take, but by the moments that take our breath away.

I have to agree with that.

When I first laid my eyes on Logan, I was breathless. I knew he would have a significant impact in my life, even though I had no *idea* he would become my life. He was Juliet's for so long, and I accepted that as much as I could. Everything else was a shameful, hopeless dream.

And I am breathless now.

Because I am breaking.

Breaking inside, fragments, jagged and sharp.

Breaking in slow motion.

I am paralyzed by this decision, a decision that can only be mine, one that will destroy everything I love no matter what I do.

I don't know how long I stand in the middle of the

living room. I don't know where to go, what to do. I'm a robot, I'm on autopilot, I'm a zombie.

This can't be happening; this can't *be happening.*

But you knew it, *I tell myself. You knew it would be this way. You knew you would never ge*t away with it.

And yet I still had hope. Sometimes you tell yourself to expect the worst, sometimes you let yourself become jaded and realistic, because you know the chances of getting burned are high. And yet, no matter how much you try and harden your soul, shackle your heart, hope has a way of getting in. As the late Leonard Cohen said, the cracks are where the light gets in. And with that light comes hope.

I knew this was coming, I knew it wouldn't be easy. But I still had hope, foolish hope, that refused to be buried. Hope that Logan and I would be allowed to live out our happily ever after under the sun, stars, and moon.

It's that persistent sliver of hope that's killing me right now.

I have to break up with Logan.

I have to return the ring.

I have to leave him.

I know my mother's threats weren't made in vain. I know what it's like to damage her pride and reputation. I know she will fight back with everything she has, and in order to preserve what she is and what she's fought for, she will take this away from Logan.

I can't be the cause of that. I can't. I couldn't live with myself if Logan ended up stripped of everything he fought so hard to get. As much as I love him, as much as he loves me, I can't be worth more than this place, and I won't let myself be.

Logan.

Losing Logan.

The thought makes me double over, my knees hitting the tile floor with a sickly thud. I cry out in pain but it's not my knees, it's my heart, seeping open and bleeding. The pain is physical, deep, a fish hook that I can't reach.

I cry out but there is no sound. My mouth is open, gaping and I can't scream, I can't breathe. Low, guttural noises rip through me as my lungs strain and strain.

I can't make this choice.

I can't throw all of this away.

I crawl to the couch and pull myself up, fingers digging into the cushions like an injured animal. I can't imagine life without him, without being here. There has to be another way, there has to be.

Taking in a deep breath, I turn my phone over in my hands.

With what strength I have I call my father's cell phone.

He answers right away, not even giving me enough time to process what I was going to say, let alone how to figure out how to speak.

"Veronica," he says, his tone is hushed. I already know that my mother must be somewhere near him and that thought causes a dark, thick rage to boil inside my throat. "Is that you?"

"Daddy," I say, my voice is so low and broken it doesn't even sound human. "How could you?"

He sighs unsteadily. "Listen, dear, you know we love you."

That was always my dad's thing, to tell me "you know we love you" without having to tell me that they love me. If I knew they loved me, this wouldn't be happening. I wouldn't be who I am and I wouldn't be begging my father.

"I love him," I whisper.

"Whether you do or you don't doesn't have any bearing

Veronica, and you know this. Your mother and I…she has a lot to lose. What will it look like to the world to have you marry your dead sister's widower? It's beyond reproach and you know it."

"What will it look like?" I repeat. "You keep saying that, what will it look like, because you're so fucking scared of what people think and see of you, that you have no regard for your own daughter and her feelings."

"Oh hush now," he says, "don't be absurd. We have total regard for you and your feelings, that's why we know this won't work."

"What?"

"We're your parents, Veronica. We've watched you your whole life, your fascination with Juliet, trying to be like her. It's normal, completely normal, for the youngest to try and emulate the oldest. But this is going too far. You know, if you reach deep inside yourself, you'll see that whatever you think you have with Logan, whatever your feelings are for him, they aren't real. It's manufactured by your brain to make up for losing Juliet. By keeping Logan, you keep her alive. Maybe it's the same for him, I don't know, but either way it isn't what you think it is." He sighs. "Your mother and I are trying to prevent you from making a big mistake and costing our reputation. Can't you think logically for one moment and see that?"

I swallow painfully, shaking my head. My tongue is pressed against the roof of my mouth. No words come out.

"I have to go, your mother is waiting," he says. "We're going out for dinner, you know, our usual New Year's celebration with Aunt June. But listen, we can talk later. We can talk about all of this."

"There's nothing to talk about," I whisper.

Another loud sigh. "If that's what you think, then I

guess that means you're not changing your mind. You know dear, if it were up to me, I would give Logan time to buy us out and own it outright. But we can't let this happen. Your mother…it's her career that made us all who we are."

"And I hate who I am."

"Sometimes I do too. But this is life. And you have to make sacrifices sometimes. I'm sorry that this is yours but you have a choice. Come back home and start again. Or stay with him, and he'll lose the hotel. There is no other way here and you know it. I know you do. Do the right thing for us all. For you, for Logan, for Juliet, for us. Do the right thing Veronica."

I shake my head, dead tears falling from my eyes. "Juliet would have understood."

"No, dear. Juliet is the reason we are doing this. To honor her, even if you won't. I'll book you a flight home so you don't have to spend your money, you have enough experience now on your resume anyway and can start again. We all will. Together, as a family. See, this might even be a great thing. It might be the reason for everything."

I don't know what happens next. I'm caught in some kind of vortex, alternating between going numb and pulsing with rage. I'm at once a child, helpless and afraid, and then I am me, I am now, and I am the same. Angry, lost, and so fucking desperate.

When Kate comes in from reception, hours later, I'm sitting in the armchair and staring blankly at the wall, the wicker creating grooves into my sweating skin.

"Ron?" she says, appearing in front of me, hands on hips. "What are you doing?"

I can't even look at her. I'll have to say goodbye to her too. There's no way I can do this to Logan and then stick around to watch our love collapse.

"Ron?" she says again and now her voice is higher, concerned. She comes closer and crouches down at my level. "Hey," she says, putting her hand on mine and then recoiling. My hand is covered in sweat. "What's wrong with you?"

I slowly bring my eyes over to meet hers, but I can't do anything but blink.

I've never seen her look so worried.

"Are you having a seizure?"

"I need your help," I whisper. That wasn't at all what I was going to say. I was planning on saying nothing, on leaving her in the dark. But now I'm not so sure. I can't do this alone.

"What is it?"

I lick my lips. My mouth feels like sandpaper. "Can you keep a secret? I mean a big secret."

She cocks her head, unamused. "What do you think I've been doing this last month?"

She's right. She kept me and Logan secret this whole time. No one knew.

I burst into tears.

Big, sobbing tears that spill from my eyes, tears that torment my body.

"Oh my god," she whispers. "What's happened? Are you dying?"

It feels like it. Fuck, help me, it feels like it.

"I have to leave," I say between sobs. "I have to go."

"What, why?"

Somehow I manage to explain it, I explain everything my parents told me and everything that I know they're capable of.

When I'm done, Kate is stunned. "I don't get it. You sure they aren't bluffing?"

I shake my head. "No. They don't bluff. My mother is a

politician."

"A born bluffer."

"Not when it threatens her career."

"But I don't get it. I mean, yeah okay I can see how bad it would look, but people get used to things, and really it's not a big deal."

"Kate. Believe me. This is a big deal. And this, what they're doing, is nothing to them. It's minor. But it will ruin everything we have. Kate, you'll lose your job. We'll all lose."

"Fucking Charlie," she swears. "I'm going to chop his perfect dick off."

"Don't get me started on Charlie," I tell her. "Right now, he's not important. What's important is…"

I take in a deep shaking breath. I can't say it again. I can't do it.

"Just stay," Kate whispers to me, taking my hand. "Stay and fight it. Maybe Logan has the money." I shake my head, closing my eyes. More tears spill. "Maybe he's ready for a change."

"That's why I can't tell him what's happening," I tell her. "Because no matter what happens, he'll give it up for me. I know him. He's good. He's too good for me. I have to do this or he'll lose it all and I can't be the one to make that happen."

"So what are you going to say to him?"

"I can't say anything," I tell her. "About any of this. And neither can you."

"So you're just going to give him back his ring and leave?"

I nod, though my chest is aching from the sobs. "Yes. I have to tell him I don't love him anymore and I'm not ready and I'll have to leave a note and leave."

She stands up. "A note?" she exclaims. "You can't leave

him a fucking note. You owe him way more than that. You owe him the truth. You owe him what's going on. You're going to destroy him *inside*, Ron. He loves you." She puts her hand to her forehead and stares at me with a pained expression. "Please, please, don't do this to him."

I have no choice. Can't she see this? "I have to!" I cry out. "If I try and lie to his face, he'll see right through me. He'll know. I can't keep that lie up with him in front of me. It's this or it's nothing."

"Then choose nothing, Ron, please, stay!"

I get up and hold out my pink finger. "You promised you wouldn't tell, now swear on it."

She stares at me with wild eyes. "Please, Ron."

"Do it! Promise me. Let me be the bad guy here, let him blame me for leaving. It's better than the alternative."

She clamps her lips together until they are pressed into a thin, hard line and for a moment I think she's not going to do it. She's that stubborn. But then her finger wraps around mine and I know, pray, hope, her word is still good.

"I hate this," she says, looking sick. "I hate that you're leaving, I hate that you're leaving him broken hearted. Don't you think he's gone through a lot with Juliet? Now you're going to tell him you never loved him? Do you know what that's going to do to him?"

"I can't live with the guilt—"

"Did you ever think that maybe you should?" she questions. "That it's a better sacrifice if he loses the hotel and you live with the guilt over that than it is for him to keep it and lose you?"

Maybe it is selfish. But I still think it's the only way he'll come out of it.

"What would you do?" I say to her. "If you were in my position. Forget Charlie, he's a piece of shit. But think if you were in love. What would you do?"

"People don't like having their life decided for them," she says after mulling it over.

"You didn't answer my question."

"Because I don't know." She sighs. "I just want you both to be happy. And this way neither of you will be."

"Yeah well, maybe it was a mistake that I came here to begin with."

"Ron…"

I push past her. "I have to pack."

"You can't be going now."

"My father sent me an email. I'm on the eleven-p.m. red-eye to Seattle."

"What the actual fuck?" she practically explodes, following me into my bedroom. "You are fucking joking!"

"I need a ride to the airport soon," I tell her. "Not Charlie."

"Dude, no, no, no. You can't just up and leave."

"I have to! I told you I can't face him, he'll know and he'll make me stay and he'll give everything up for me when he shouldn't. What the fuck am I supposed to do, just keep this a secret until the time is right? There is no right time, this is all horrible, it's so horrible!"

"But…what about me? And Johnny? Daniel? Jin? Nikki? Your ohana? What about this place? What about everything you've worked so hard for here?"

I swallow hard, my nose clogged, my eyes hazy with tears. "You, Johnny, Jin, Nikki, and Daniel will no longer be here if I stay. We will all lose everything. Logan will lose the most. Unless you have extra money lying around to buy out my parents, nothing will change. Maybe you'll keep your jobs when someone else buys it, maybe you won't. But your life, our lives here, as we know it, won't be the same if I don't go. So you can see, I have to. It's not just Logan, it's all of you. And everything will go back to the way it was before I ever showed up."

"But it won't be the same," Kate says, wiping away a tear. "Because you brought us all even closer together. Your effect on Logan is the same on us all. We're all *closer*, a better ohana. Without you here, we won't have that. We'll be in mourning all over again."

I stare at her for a few moments until I pull her into a hug. "I'm so sorry. So sorry. This is the only thing I know to do."

And then I start packing. Kate watches me for a bit, then walks into the kitchen to crack open some rum, then comes back and sits on my bed, drinking and watching me until she finally joins in.

"You know he'll come for you," she says to me. "You know he won't let you escape."

My heart pangs. "There's a lot of ocean and a lot of land between here and Chicago."

"He'll come," she says. "I won't say a word because I promised, but he'll come. And then you better be ready."

She's trying to plant hope inside me. I have learned from the last time that the hope that gets in the cracks is the one driving the knife at the end.

So I don't listen. Instead I take out the Moonwater Inn stationary and pen and I write a note. The hardest note I've ever had to write because every single line of it is an absolute lie.

I have to break Logan's heart into pieces in order to get out of here. I have to have him hate me in order for him to believe it. The letter is what will decide whether Logan will come back *for me or not.*

Dear Logan,

I write this because I know if I say it to your face, I will feel sorry for you and change my mind. I know it makes me seem like a coward to do it like this and maybe I am. But this is the only way.

You've been a great boss to me and a great friend during my months here at Moonwater, but I'm afraid it's time for us to part ways. I am returning your ring, as beautiful as it is. I know it was given to me with the best intentions, and the manner of your proposal made it so hard to say no. I didn't want to embarrass you or hurt you in front of your staff.

But the truth is, last night made me realize that I have to stop what we have now, that it's gone too far. I have played you and for that I am sorry.

I don't love you Logan, and that's the hard truth of it. I wish I did. It would make things so much easier. But while I care about you, I don't love you. Whatever we have shared was purely physical, and more than that, I was with you for all the wrong reasons.

I have always been in Juliet's shadow, from the very start. When she died, I felt like I would never get a chance for closure and I would never measure up to her. This you know about me.

I'm ashamed and afraid to admit this but here it goes: I was only with you because I wanted what Juliet had. I wanted to feel what it felt to be Juliet for a moment.

That moment went on for too long. I got carried away.

And now that moment must end.

Please know that this isn't easy since I think you're a nice guy. But what we had was never real and I was never the person you thought I was. I never meant to hurt you though I know I am now.

Take care Logan and remember that there is someone else out there for you. Someone you deserve. You love hard and you need to be with someone who can give it back to you.

I cannot.

I'm sorry.

Mahalo,

Veronica

Tears are streaming down my cheeks, I have to hold the paper away so they don't stain the ink. A single tear stain on the paper and Logan would know the truth. He would know how much I care, how hard this is to do.

Kate tries to take it from my hand but I snatch it away.

"You can't read it," I manage to say through sobs. "It's for him."

She frowns. "How mean is it?" she asks softly.

"One hundred-percent believable," I tell her. "At least I know it's exactly what my parents think happened between us."

Kate shakes her head, her mouth grim. "This is so wrong and so fucked up. You have no idea."

I have some.

I put the note on my bamboo dresser and then…then I slip off my ring.

It feels wrong.

So, so wrong.

It belongs on my finger, this symbol of us, this symbol of our love.

Don't do it. It's not too late. Change your mind.

But I can't.

I place the ring on the note and turn away, hauling my bags over to the door.

Kate is standing there, barricading it.

314

"I don't know if I can let you do this," she says. "As your friend, I should stop you."

"As my friend," I plead, "you need to let me go."

Our eyes are locked in a match, seeing who will look away first.

Kate does, looking utterly defeated. I feel a million times worse. I feel like I've crawled out of a swamp, a dark, damp place I belong in.

Because Logan is at reception, Kate heads over to her car in the parking lot and I go around past the pool to the service entrance.

I try not to think about what I'm doing.

I try not to take it all in.

I try to deflect everything.

It's working.

Until I see Charlie coming out of his place.

Sees me with my luggage.

"What the hell?" he asks. "Where are you going?"

I'm so angry. I thought I could get through it, past it, but I can't. Every single ounce of rage and hate I have burning away in the pit of my stomach is rising, rising, rising.

Charlie stops in front of me, a brown tank-top, backward cap. Looking like he always does.

I don't even think.

I punch him square in the nose.

He yelps, doubling over, covering his nose with his hands. "What the fuck?" he squeaks.

"You know exactly what that's for," I sneer at him as he looks up at me. "You fucking snitch."

"Wait, what?' he cries out, whimpering. His eyes are watering from the pain. "I don't…wait, is this about your mother?"

I laugh. It feels like acid. "Oh and the truth comes

out. Whether you meant to or not, you ruined everything, Charlie. And if you dare speak of this to Logan, you know he'll destroy you."

"Ron," he says, examining his fingers as he pulls them away from his nose. No blood. "I'm sorry, I didn't know…"

"You knew enough," I tell him, looking him dead in the eye with as much venom as I can spare. "You knew about my family and me and our relationship. You knew I was at the bottom of the barrel with them. You knew it all and you talked to her and you kept it from all of us and now you've gone too far. You may have thought you were doing the right thing, you may have thought you were important by being the one person my mother had to talk to. But the fact that you kept it a secret from us all says something else entirely." My throat feels thick with jabbing pains as I try to swallow. "Goodbye Charlie."

"Goodbye?" He reaches for my arm as I rip out of it. "Where are you going?"

"Home." I tell him, pressing my hands to his chest and pushing him away. "Where I can't embarrass my family anymore."

I hear Kate honk her horn from the street. I quickly open the gate and bring my bags through. Charlie looks over my shoulder, eyes widening at the sight of Kate in her car.

"You're actually going?" he squawks.

"And it's all your fault," I tell him, not caring that I'm being overly harsh. "When you see Logan later, you can fess up to what you did and lose it all. Or you can keep your mouth shut and keep your job. Your choice."

"Ron," he says again. "Kate!"

But Kate is out of the car and quick to get my bags in the backseat and the trunk.

"Kate," Charlie says again, coming forward.

Kate narrows her eyes at him and jumps back in the driver's seat before peeling out of the lane with both of us in it.

I'm silent the rest of the ride. I'm heading to the airport way too early, I don't know how I'm going to handle it. I don't know what I'm doing.

"I know you don't want to hear it right now," Kate says to me later as we pull over at Lydgate Park to watch the ocean, a way to kill time since we are so early for my flight. "But I really do think Charlie will be hurting. I'm not saying this because I like him. I know him and I honestly think he didn't think. He loves you both, he would have never said anything if he knew this would be the end result."

"It doesn't matter," I say with a heavy sigh. My hand still hurts. "He said it and whether it was an accident or not, we can't change it. My parents know. And it's just as well. I would have told them one day. I was under the very naïve impression that they would understand."

"Ron, there's nothing naïve in thinking your parents would be happy for you if you were in love."

"It's naïve when I should have known what they'd do. I thought it too. In the back of my mind, I knew this was all too good to be true."

"What? Love? Love is never too good to be true. Love is true."

I give her a look.

She shrugs. "What? People fall in love, people fall out of love. But in the end, almost everyone in the world gets to feel it, live it, taste it. Love is never too good to be true because it is the original truth. And everyone deserves it. Everyone."

It's the most poignant thing I've ever heard Kate say,

which of course doesn't help.

The tears start flowing again and they don't stop. Not when we're pulling up to the airport, not when I'm saying goodbye to my roommate and my best friend here. Not when I'm hauling my luggage through the agriculture inspection and security. There's no space inside the actual Lihue terminal to hang out without getting on a plane, so I have to say goodbye to Kate right away.

And then the unthinkable happens.

Just as I step through the detector, grabbing my items and carry-on from the x-rays, I hear my name.

Loud, rough, broken.

The voice is a hand reaching over my heart and yanking me into submission.

I look up.

Logan is on the other side of the security gate, Kate hovering behind him.

I meet Logan's eyes and the world goes still.

This man, this beautiful, loving, loyal man is here for me, fighting for me.

And yet I have to convince him I'm not worth fighting for. After the ring and the note, he's still here, he's still not believing it.

I didn't think my heart could break anymore.

"Veronica, please," he cries out, loud enough that everyone turns to look at him.

"Sir, you need to step out of the way," a TSA agent says.

Logan ignores him, staring at me in such pain and disbelief that it knocks the wind out of me.

"Do you know him?" a TSA agent on this side asks me.

Shaking my head is the easiest thing for all of us.

"Please, Ron, we need to talk, come out here, please!"

But I can't.

"Sir, please," the agent says, putting his hands on Logan. Logan immediately shrugs him off, beyond agitated, as another guard comes over.

"Just go!" I yell at him before he gets in any more trouble. "Please, go back to your home. I'm going back to mine."

The lies slice me open. They do the same to him. Kate is covering her mouth with her hands, knowing the pain we're both in, both of us diced in front of her eyes. Meanwhile, everyone around airport security is watching, waiting for what Logan will do next. They can't figure if this is a tragic love story or a fucked-up apology. It doesn't happen like this in the movies.

Logan can only shake his head. Utter disbelief. Fear. Hate. Hurt. I see it all running through his head, projected through his eyes. He doesn't understand, he doesn't believe. No matter what I've said, he doesn't believe.

There's warmth to that thought, even though there's fear. That he doesn't believe the note, won't believe any of it.

But at the heart of it he knows that I have to go. That I wouldn't do this lightly or otherwise. That I have my reasons.

Maybe on his darkest days he'll reflect and wonder if the note was truth and that he was wrong. Maybe he won't.

All I can do is stare into his eyes, past the TSA agents and the passengers and the screening equipment, and tell him to please, please let me go.

Let me go.

I mouth the words.

And then, then, I think he gets it.

He nods. He is living pain.

I am dying, trying to memorize this face and hold it in my heart.

He turns around.

319

Defeated.

Broken.

Ruined.

And he walks away.

Come back, I want to say. *I've made a mistake.*

I want to run through the screener, push the people out of the way, jump into his arms and have him hold me. That strength, that heat, that love that always has my back. But I remember why I have to do this. That too much will be ruined because of us being together.

I give Kate a small wave but she can't even return it. In the distance, a chicken struts past them. And that's when I realize how much I'm giving up. I thought that Logan and my *ohana* were everything. I'm giving up this island, too.

I'm leaving my home behind and trading it in for a place that never understood me, where I never thrived.

Oh, Kauai. Another love lost.

I don't even know how I make it through the airport. I can't look at the gift shops, can't eat. There's no internet and even if there was, there's nothing to see or do. None of my music appeals to me, I won't read.

I just find a spot, alone, and stare at the wall and I sink into a cold, numb state. After a while my heart feels like it has frostbite, where it's so damaged that you can't even feel the cracks.

And every now and then, Logan, Logan, Logan, I'll see him, feel him, hear him and it all seems like such a dream. Such a dream.

Even when I board the plane.

Even when I take my seat, packed in the back of a full flight.

Even when the plane takes off and we soar over the coconut coast before heading northeast for home.

Such a dream. A nightmare.
It doesn't end.
Hawaii is left behind and this pain doesn't end.
What have I done?
What have I done?
What have I done?

CHAPTER TWENTY-ONE

Six Months Later

"SO, TELL US ARCH, WHERE DID YOU GO TO SCHOOL?" my mother asks, before she slices a bit of prime rib, spearing it with her fork.

I look over at Arch, knowing he's been waiting for this question all evening.

"Harvard," he says proudly, in that way that all Harvard graduates have. Like they're a bit embarrassed even though they totally aren't *and have to show this false humility*.

And why am I dating this guy again?

I think I've asked myself that a million times tonight, especially as it was his idea to meet my parents and take them out for dinner. He can't pretend he doesn't have some sort of agenda that doesn't involve me.

But it's the first time I've started seeing a guy since I

left Kauai and I know I would never, ever get over Logan again if I didn't go out there and try and put him past me. You can't move on without moving on, and so Arch was it.

And yes. His real name is Archie. Archie and Veronica. I know. Thankfully he goes by Arch instead, which suits him a little bit better. He's a good-looking guy, tall with a strong jaw and sandy hair that flops to the side. I met him through Claire, whom I'm living with now, and she kept on trying to sell him on me, knowing how badly I needed to just get laid.

I haven't gotten laid, yet, by the way. Arch hasn't really broached the subject, and despite the fact that we've gone out five times in the last two weeks, he's done nothing but kiss me goodnight. Yet another reason why I think he's dating me to get close to my mom.

Hell, if it weren't for him, I would have only seen my mother twice since I moved back to Chicago. I know she thinks that everything can go back to normal, the way it was before, but our relationship before was a real piece of work and strained to the max. Now, I don't want anything to do with her. She fucking blackmailed me to get rid of the love of my life and I'll never, ever forgive her for that.

I know I haven't forgiven myself. I know what I did to Logan broke him in two just as much as it broke me. That may be one reason why I can't move on, can't forget about him, why my heart won't stop aching every single night as I clutch my pillow pretending that it's him. Because I wonder if I did the right thing. I wonder if destroying what we had and making it all out to be a lie was the only way out of it.

But I also know Logan. And I know that he would have risked everything for me. That man had already lost so much, and he wasn't going to lose me without a fight. So I created something he couldn't fight against. Had I not handed back his ring and told him I didn't love him, had I not told the biggest lie of my life, he would have lost everything he worked so hard to get. I couldn't do that to him. I couldn't have him risk it all in order to have me. I was never worth it.

And so I'm back in Chicago and trying to come to terms with everything. It's not easy. I've been too afraid to include Moonwater on my resume, and I'm still not using Piccolo, so I'm starting over again and working as a line cook in a seafood restaurant part-time.

Claire has been a big help though. Not only is she letting me live in her spare bedroom rent free, but I'm working for the wine store she now manages, doing wine tastings on some evenings. It's a lot of fun but I miss being back in the kitchen and using my creativity.

I miss a lot of things.

But this is the bed I made and now I have to lie in it, as cold and lonely as it is.

"Harvard," my mother drones on, eyeing my father with one gleefully raised brow. "Finally Veronica has found a smart one."

Arch seems to have missed the whole insult and instead grins proudly at me. I don't give them anything. Since I'm battling my mother, she's battling me more than ever, doling out passive aggression like it's going out of style. Luckily I've had a lifetime to grow an immunity to it.

"You know Veronica's sister, Juliet," my mother goes on. Oh boy, here we go. "She was going to go to Harvard. She certainly had the grades. She was top of the class, valedictorian. Life got in the way, of course, but it was our dream for her."

"I'm very sorry for your loss," Arch says, like he's rehearsed it. "I saw a picture of her at Veronica's, she was very beautiful."

I do have a picture of me and Juliet together at her wedding on my bedside table. For the longest time I had kept it in a drawer. I hadn't even packed it when I moved out to Kauai. I think I was pretending that she hadn't died and if she hadn't died, I didn't have to wrestle with my feelings about her.

Logan was the one who put it all in perspective. It was him that taught me how to grieve for someone you loved but didn't like. How to come to terms with my relationship with Juliet even though I was the one left to put it all back together. No one ever wants to speak ill of the dead, and people treat death like it erases all of one's sins. But it doesn't. And that's okay.

Of course I figured all this out a little too late. I know that Juliet is gone and our relationship won't ever be anything but flawed, full of missed chances. But I don't have any regrets. I wish she was still alive today so I could try to get to know her for who she really was, the person she hid from everyone, but I'll have to live with what we had. It wasn't much, but it was something.

Naturally my mother still puts her on that pedestal. I tried to tell her the truth. The first time I saw her after coming back from Kauai, she showed up at Claire's door wanting to check-in with me. We had an all-out screaming match (luckily Claire wasn't home to witness it) and I let everything fly. I told her the truth about Juliet, that it wasn't Logan who cheated, that Juliet had the affair. And, like I thought she would, my mother turned a blind eye to it all. I know it makes me out to be a terrible daughter to bring it all up like that, but I just wanted her to see the truth for once.

Now I know that nothing I ever say will change my

mother's mind. I have to let her be and believe all that she wants to believe. Despite our differences, I know my mother will forever be grieving over her. I know she truly loved Juliet and only wants to believe the best.

Times like this though, it's hard for me to keep my mouth shut.

"Juliet could have been a movie star," my mother says, taking a sip of wine. "Sadly, she was too beautiful for this lifetime." She looks to me. "And Veronica, what have you been up to lately?"

Arch gives me a strange look, probably because it's a sign that my mother and I don't talk anymore.

"Living the dream," I tell her and the phrase makes me think of Charlie when he first picked me up from the airport in Lihue. I miss my friends there so much that it hurts, my chest feels like it's being squeezed and drained of every last drop.

Even though it's hard, I still keep in touch with everyone. I talk to Kate, Johnny, and Nikki on the regular, usually through email since I try and stay off of Facebook. The idea of seeing Logan's photo pop up in a tagged pic or something scares me too much.

I talk to Charlie sometimes. We've had a few emails back and forth over what happened, and honestly I can't go on blaming him. He knows he fucked up and he feels forever guilty (Kate says he's really taken it to heart). Charlie has always meant well, it's just a shame it had to come to this.

I ask about Logan sometimes, usually via Johnny since he's a guy and doesn't try and tiptoe around the subject. Usually they tell me he's doing fine, working harder than ever. I haven't spoken to him though. I want to. I think about it every night. Just texting him. Sending an email. Mailing a letter even. I want to hear his voice, I want to know how he's doing. If he misses me. If he hates me. If he forgives me for what I did. I want to tell him the truth, and even though nothing will come of it, I want to tell him I always loved him and that everything I'd said in my note was a lie.

He reached out to talk to me after I left. A lot. Phone, email, Facebook, whatever he could. He even called my parents on a few occasions, though I would hear about it from my father a few months later. But every time he tried to talk to me, I couldn't bring myself to answer. What was there to say. Nothing I could say would ever make him believe me and it wouldn't make it better.

After a while, the calls stopped. No more texts, no more emails. It meant that Logan was over it, moving on. Done with me, and who could ever fucking blame him.

The thought hurts. It hurts like my heart is breaking all over again and I have to double over from the pain. The idea that I'm alone and reeling from my decision, that he doesn't think of me the same way. I know I have little right to complain but I can't help it.

You reap what you sow. I chose what I thought was the lesser of two evils and not a moment goes by that I'm not reaping it.

When dinner is over, the four of us step out of the steakhouse and into the hot Chicago night. It's nothing like Hawaii. You can't see the stars. You can't hear the crickets. There are no chickens. There's just this smoggy orange glow above you, the dirty smells and grating sounds of the city.

My mother wants us to go to a cocktail bar down the street, though I can tell my dad has had enough, just as I have had. That's the last thing I want to do. Arch turns to me and tells me he'll pay for my cab back to my place and I honestly couldn't be happier about that, even though it's a slap in the face that he doesn't even want to come.

So here comes the awkward goodbyes. I give Arch a quick hug and then am soullessly engulfed by my mother who smells like lavender soap and expensive perfume. I have a feeling she just had her hair done before this dinner, though being the deputy mayor she never really needs an excuse to look her best. Growing up, I used to envy the amount of time my mother put into her appearance, like it was magic. Now I know it's just a mask, hiding everything ugly underneath.

"You can call sometimes, you know," she says to me stiffly, her chin raised. I know she doesn't mean it, she just wants to keep up appearances.

I hug my dad next whose embrace is surprisingly strong.

"Sweetie," he says to me, whispering in my ear. "I need you to call me tomorrow. On my cell. There's something I have to talk to you about."

I pull away slightly and stare into my father's eyes. He's alert for once, not drunk, and his expression is stark. He just gives a little knowing nod and then slaps me on the back.

I spend the cab ride back to the apartment wondering what the hell he wants to talk to me about. I get along better with my father than my mother, especially after coming back, but he still treats me like someone he's not supposed to be seen with.

"How was dinner?" Claire asks as I step inside the door. Our apartment—well, her apartment—is really tiny and my bedroom isn't much bigger than a closet, but it's a million times more preferable than living on my own right now. For one, I couldn't afford it, and I obviously wouldn't move back home with my parents. And for two, after spending so much time with Kate as a roommate, I think I'd be lonely without someone there to talk to every night.

I groan loudly and throw my clutch on the couch beside her and shuffle over to the kitchen to bring a bottle of wine out of the fridge. A bonus of working at the wine store, endless bottles all the time.

"That bad, huh?" she asks, munching on a bag of salt and vinegar chips. I take my glass of wine and sit next to her, putting my feet up on the coffee table.

"Well it was more my mother than Arch, obviously," I tell her.

"But I can tell it's not really working out," she says.

I shrug and she goes on. "Hey, it's okay if it doesn't. The point is that you're trying. I never thought that Arch would be the one for you, but he seems like an okay guy. He buys really expensive bottles of wine, so there's that."

"But he's a lawyer who went to Harvard," I remind her. "And I'm pretty sure the only reason he said yes to me was because he found out my mother was deputy mayor. I think he thinks she can get him a new job or something like that."

"Maybe. But don't sell yourself short."

"I'm not selling myself at all, Claire," I say with a laugh. "I mean look at me. This was our sixth date and I'm here. He had a cab drop me off. Alone. The dude doesn't even want to get laid."

She mulls that over, chewing thoughtfully. "Maybe he's gay."

"Way to set me up with a gay man, Claire Bear." I elbow her in the stomach.

She nearly spits out her chip. "Hey, how am I supposed to know? He agreed, didn't he? Anyway, my whole point was to get you distracted and it worked. Besides, you're a turbo-babe, you'll have men lining up around the block once you put yourself out there, and this is the first step."

"Turbo-babe?" I repeat, rolling my eyes. "Please. And what about you?"

"What about me?"

"You're also a turbo-babe, yet here you are still single."

She gives me a haughty look, that on her baby face looks totally adorable. "I'm not denying my babeness, but I am picky and that's okay. Maybe I'll have better luck if I move to Hawaii."

I know she's joking but even the mention of the word Hawaii still burns deep inside.

"I don't know," I muse, trying to get over the feeling, "if you're picky, you're not going to have a lot of luck where most men don't wear shoes."

She wrinkles her nose. "Seriously?"

I shrug. By the end of it, I wasn't wearing shoes around the compound either. In fact, I miss that, the feel of the spongey grass beneath my feet, the sun-warmed dirt and grains of sand.

She clears her throat. "So, how was your mom?" her tone is softer now. "On a scale of awkwardness."

"A seven," I tell her, taking an even larger gulp of my wine. "It was only awkward when Arch realized how fucked up we were. Other than that, I was able to ignore her."

"And her touches of motherly love?"

That's code for insults and passive aggression.

"Oh that was at an eight," I tell her. "She brought up Juliet and the whole dinner went sideways."

"Man," she says, crumpling up the rest of the chip bag, "I honestly don't know how you deal with all that."

"Well you know," I tell her. "A lot of tears and early morning jogs through the city, dodging muggers."

She adjusts herself on the couch to face me, fold*ing her*

leg under her. She pauses her Better Call Saul marathon on Netflix. "You know I never told you this, but I'm proud of you."

I raise my brow and side-eye her. "Why?"

"Because, stupid, I don't know how I'd handle being in the situation you're in."

Well it helped when I had someone who understood. I know sexual attraction is what ignited Logan and I to begin with, that and a sense of not belonging. But it was Juliet herself and who we were to her that furthered it on. We both understood each other like no one else could.

I sigh and finish the rest of my glass, placing it on the coffee table with a clink. "Family is complicated. You love them because they're blood, but that's only because you're told you have to. What I had on Kauai…they were my family. Don't get me wrong, you're my family too. But at Moonwater, that's where I felt I really belonged. I had everything. And it was all by choice. By people who chose to accept me as family and because they wanted to, not because they had to."

"Then why did you leave again? Was it because you couldn't handle anymore Jack Johnson?"

I swallow hard and give her an acidic look. "You know why. My mother would have destroyed everything he worked so hard for."

"But don't you think that should have been Logan's decision?"

I close my eyes and lean back into the couch. "Yes. No. I don't know. There's not a day that goes by that I don't think about the choice I made. That maybe it should have been his choice. But I couldn't live with myself if he lost that hotel on my account."

"I don't know the man," she says, putting her hand on

my shoulder. "But I would be willing to bet that he would have gladly given that place up for you."

"I could never have asked him to do that."

"And you wouldn't have had to ask. He would have done it because that's what you're worth to him."

I shake my head, pretending my fingernails are utterly interesting. "He would have resented me."

"Ron," she says, her tone sharp enough to make me look at her. "That isn't how love works. You don't resent each other. You gladly give up whatever you have to in order to keep the other. It's a compromise and if you love someone, the compromise is always worth it. You don't think about it, you just do it."

I don't want to argue with her. I don't have the strength. The fact is, I would have lived with a lot of guilt if I had stayed with Logan and he lost the hotel. There's no way I could have believed I was worth it, and I was already juggling my guilt over Juliet. If I stayed, it would have torn us apart. Even if Logan would have been okay with it, I wouldn't have.

"It is what it is," I tell her. "Somethings just aren't meant to be."

And at that, I get another glass of wine and watch a bit of Netflix with her before I drag myself off to bed. I'm not exactly tired, but I need to be alone to gather my thoughts and put them away in their compartments. It's the only way I get through this.

My room looks like a transplant of Moonwater. I packed in such a hurry when I left that I didn't have time to grab the souvenirs that I would have, and even though I had time in the airport, shopping for memories seemed like the last thing I wanted to do. I just wanted to forget.

But now, now I'm trying to live in the memory. I have a

trucker hat that says "Hanalei is my Bae" up on my wall and Java Kai stickers on my computer. I've printed out photos and created a collage inside a large tiki frame. I have little things too that I had randomly squirreled away during my time there. On my bookshelf I have a mini shrine, coasters that say Ohana Lounge, that Pupus t-shirt Charlie finally got us to order in, Moonwater Inn stationary I would often smuggle from Kate, along with the hotel's plumeria-scented toiletries, and a few bags of Kauai coffee that they served in the hotel rooms. I haven't had the heart to make it yet, figuring once the coffee is gone, it's gone. Hanging on my dresser is a fabric lei that was left over from the luau, a few drink umbrellas I stole from Daniel, the party hat from New Year's Eve.

I take the party hat off my dresser and hold it in my hands, turning it over.

This was the moment he kissed me in front of every-one. The moment that he told the world he wasn't ashamed, that he was no longer going to hide who he was and what I was to him. This was the moment when I knew without a doubt that this was going to be the man I'd spend the rest of my life with. The moment that our first meeting all those years ago was building towards.

When I had first laid my eyes on Logan, staring across Lake Michigan, I knew he wanted to be somewhere else. Now I knew where he had been—already on Kauai. In mind, in heart, in spirit. And somehow I looked at him and I knew that's where I needed to be too. Wherever he was, anywhere at all, as long as it was with him. I knew he was a man who could take me far away, to the future, to better versions of ourselves.

How different life would have been if Juliet hadn't walked in at that moment. But then again, maybe we needed those years apart in order to learn what we really wanted. Logan and I were both blinded by her in our own ways, and in the end it was Juliet that kept us united.

So for that, I owe my sister the world.

A tear falls from my eyes, splashing on the hat. I take in a deep breath, trying to keep calm and steady. It's nights like this that are the worst. When I come home and I'm alone and there is a world out there that I'm no longer a part of. My heart aches to belong again. It aches to belong to the island, to the spirit of aloha. It aches to belong to my friends, my *ohana*, and it aches to belong to him.

I close my eyes as the feeling rushes through me, trying to stay strong. I don't want to cry over this anymore, I don't want to want anymore. I just want to move on, I just want to be happy in the way I was happy before.

Tomorrow, I tell myself. *Tomorrow see about a raise at your job. Tomorrow look for other positions. Go out and meet someone. Start anew.*

It's easier said than done, but I know it's the only way I can move forward here. Going back to Kauai and Moonwater and Logan isn't an option. I have to stop pretending it is.

I put the hat away and get changed into my tank top and shorts, turning up the small air conditioning unit in my room. It's overly cold and I wake up with a stuffy nose, but it's the only way to survive the summer here. It isn't like Hawaii where a wooden overhead fan would suffice.

I'm just about to crawl into bed when I hear a faint knock at the front door. I eye the clock. It's ten at night. I briefly wonder if it's Arch having a change of heart, or perhaps one of the guys that Claire shuts down on a regular basis. Either way, we don't normally get visitors at this hour, or really any hour. Claire and I aren't exactly welcoming to people who randomly drop by. We don't work that way and anyhow, that's what the god damn buzzer is for and why we usually ignore it. Unfortunately, in our building, the main door is open half the time.

I'm about to go open my bedroom door and spy when suddenly there's a knock at it and I jump back nervously.

"Ron," Claire says quickly from the other side. "Ron open up, please."

Oh god. What the fuck is happening?

I open the door an inch to see her peering at me wide-eyed.

"What's wrong?" I ask.

"Someone is here to see you," she says in a hush.

"Who? Arch?"

She just stares at me, her eyes going wider and takes a step away from the door, looking away toward the front door. She doesn't say anything.

I frown and step out into the apartment. "What's wrong with you?" I hiss before I follow her gaze. The front door is open and there's a shadow in the hallway beyond it. I can't see who it is. Everything about this is ominous.

"Claire," I say to her. "Who is that?"

She just shakes her head and says, "I'm sorry. I didn't know what to do."

I push past her and head for the door, my heart thudding against my rib cage like an animal trying to escape.

I feel like I'm teetering on the edge of a wave, moments before the fall.

And then it happens.

I look out into the hallway.

Standing there, like he's always been there, is Logan Shephard.

CHAPTER TWENTY-TWO

I CAN'T BELIEVE WHAT I'M SEEING.

My heart is lodged in my throat, my lungs have turned to stone. The only part of me that's working are my eyes, blinking rapidly, trying to take him all in.

Because this can't be what I'm seeing.

This can't be him.

"Veronica," he says and the sound of his voice, that beautiful, rich, accented voice, causes the rest of me to slowly come unglued.

He looks like he does in my dreams, the Logan I imagine whispering to me at night as I fall asleep, the Logan I cried over, wishing I could see him one more time in case my memories weren't enough.

And they weren't enough. Seeing him in the flesh makes me realize that my memories could never compare. Hair that remains dark and strong, thick, with the lightest amber highlights peppered through, no doubt from the sun, with just a hint of grey. His eyes that aren't just brown, but mahogany and teak and the koa wood that the Hawaiians use, shiny and dark and rich. His mouth isn't just full and wide, it twists crookedly even when he's not smiling.

And he's not smiling now. He's staring at me with the same sort of pained awe that must be on my own face.

"What are you doing here?" I ask. My words feel so small, muffled by shock.

He stares at me, eyes searching, his chest rising as he breathes heavily. The hallway seems so stark and cold, too big for the both of us. I have to lean against the doorframe to stay upright, centered.

"I've come back for you," he says, and I'm struck. By the strength in his voice, in the boldness of his statement. Struck by what this means. None of it makes any sense. To see him here in Chicago again feels like he's been sucked into the wrong timeline. He should be strolling on the beach with a surfboard under his arm, driving around Hanalei with the top of his Jeep down, wind in his hair, coconut palms reflected in sunglasses.

"Do you want to invite him inside or what?" Claire says from behind me, her eyes shining as she looks between the two of us. "I'm going to bed. Just…if you don't invite him in and sort your piles of shit out, you're going to have one angry roommate on your hands come the morning."

Then she turns and heads over to her room, closing the door behind her.

"Can I come in?" he asks quietly.

I nod, not finding the words, and head back inside.

It's even stranger to have him in my place. It was small before, it's smaller now, his large frame taking up all the space. But that's nothing new. He's always been larger than life, not just in muscle and height, but in energy. I can feel him burning like the sun, drawn to him like the moon. He's a force of nature.

I can't sit down. I can't do anything but stand in the middle of the room and fidget, my arms at my sides, fists opening and closing.

I can't take my eyes off of him. I'm afraid if I do, he'll disappear, back into my dream.

Because I have to be dreaming, right?

"Freckles…," he says.

And it doesn't matter what else comes out of his mouth. My nickname. I haven't heard it in so long. It brings me back, hard and fast, to the life that was, the life where I was really me, the life I thrived in. Just hearing that, having Logan in my apartment, makes me realize that I was doing a piss-poor job of pretending to be happy, trying to move on. Who I am with him is who I am. Who I am in Kauai is who I am. I'll never be able to pretend otherwise.

The pressure builds behind my eyes, warmth in my nose. Before I can stop it, the tears are spilling over and I'm gasping for breath.

And unlike every time I've cried over the last six months, wishing he was here to take it all away, he is here.

He comes right to me and envelopes me in his arm, holding me tight, my head pressed against his chest. He smells like love. He feels like a soul. He holds me tighter, even though I can barely breathe through my sobs, because he knows it makes me feel safe, that he'll never let me go.

"It's okay," he whispers, running his palm over my hair, kissing the top of my head. "It's okay. We're going to fix this."

I cry for a long time like this, letting everything out and he takes it in. He doesn't say anything other than that he's here and we'll fix this and he's not going anywhere. His words only make me break down more, the beauty in them, their truth.

But eventually I have to ask, I have to know.

I pull back and stare at him through raw eyes. "How can you still want me? How can you not hate me?"

The corner of his mouth quirks up into a smile, even though it doesn't reach his eyes. "Because I never believed a word you'd said."

"The note…"

"The note meant nothing. Giving the ring back meant nothing. I knew those weren't actions. I know you Veronica, and I know your heart. I know what you're about and none of that was true. You're not that good of a liar and I can always see your truth. That's why I came after you, to the airport. I wasn't about to let you fly away."

"But you did," I say quietly.

"I did," he says, nodding. He sighs. "I had to. Not just the security, though fuck them. Because I saw in your eyes what I needed to see. It wasn't confirmation of the note. It was confirmation that you still loved me. That this was tearing you apart like it was tearing me. And that I had to trust you."

"That's it? You just…trusted me?"

"I've always trusted you. I knew that whatever you were doing, there was a reason for it. That you still loved me and you wouldn't do something that drastic, that crazy, unless you had to. Unless it was against your will."

"It was my parents."

"I know. I knew it b*efor*e Charlie told me."

"Charlie told you?" I exclaim. Again, something he never mentioned when I was emailing him.

"Right away," he says. "He was the one who told me you'd left. It was only later that I noticed you'd broken his nose. He confessed pretty quickly. If it weren't for you, I would have done some damage to him myself. But you know Charlie didn't really know what he was doing. And he's not really the point of any of this. But I knew."

"Why didn't…" I begin, then stop myself.

"Why didn't I come after you? Talk to you? I tried, you wouldn't have any of it. I wasn't calling to try and change your mind, I wanted you to know that I understood."

I shut my eyes. "Why are you so good to me?"

"Because I love you," he says, running his thumb over my lip, my cheek. "I love you more than ever."

"But I was horrible. I ran away. I should have known you'd understand."

"Yeah, you should have known. And it was horrible. And you left me a broken man, Ron. That wasn't easy to get around." He breathes in deeply. "But it was a bit easier because I knew the truth. I knew it wasn't because you didn't love me that you left, but because you loved me that much. I knew your reasons. I could never fault you for them. If you had told me what was happening, we would have put the marriage on hold while we figured stuff out. We would have done it together."

"I didn't know…"

"You should have known," he says quickly. "But like I said, I understand. I know what your parents are like. They were my bloody in-laws for long enough, I'm adept at dealing with them. I knew that you felt guilt over Juliet still, that you wanted to do the right thing by me and that leaving was the best option for everyone. I know that's what I believed. But it doesn't matter anymore." He pauses, eyes searching and searching and searching me. "Freckles, I'm taking you home."

Oh, my heart. Blooming, growing, perfumed like a

flower.

So fucking fragile.

"I can't go," I say and I can't even believe those words are leaving my mouth. "I can't go. My life is here now. I have a job. Two of them. Claire needs me. I…" The thought of Arch flashes through my head. He doesn't even fucking count.

"Your life was never here," he says gruffly, hand at my jaw. "Ever. Your life belongs with me." He kisses me and if I didn't get a shock before, I'm getting it now. These lips, his lips flush on mine, the warmth of his mouth, brings me back to life. It's a meteor slamming deep inside me, a shake-up, a change.

I don't ever want him to stop.

Ever.

His fingers lost in my hair, making me whimper against his mouth, his arm around my waist, holding me in place, the same feeling as if he's about to fly off somewhere, like a superhero, bring me with him.

But I can't. He's right, what I have here in Chicago is false, like the façade of an old-west town. It isn't a real life and it was never really mine. It was something I put on to protect myself from a cold, new land. Claire will understand.

It doesn't change why I left in the first place though, it doesn't change any of that.

"I can't," I tell him, breaking our kiss, our mouths wet and breath heavy as we stare at each other. "They'll never change their minds."

"I don't give a bloody fuck if they don't change their minds," he says, voice booming. It makes my nerves stand on end. "I love you. You're going to be my wife, I don't care what happens to me, what the world says is right or wrong,

341

what other people think. You are my world and that's the only world that matters."

"I can't watch them destroy what you've worked so hard for!" I cry out.

"They won't," he says. "They won't."

"Did you not hear me? They will! They'll never go for this, they'll never understand."

He raises his chin, staring down at me. "Veronica. I'm old. I know a thing or two about how to deal with people and make a bad situation better. Some things take time and planning."

"What are you talking about?"

"What did you think I've been doing for the last six months," he asks, "sitting around on my ass, surfing with Charlie, picking my nose?"

"Well, no, but—"

"I've been saving money, I've been switching things around in my portfolio, talking to banks, I've been working with a goal in mind. A goal that should have always been on my mind, but I got lazy and complacent with Juliet. That isn't the case now."

I stare at him blankly.

"As of last week, I own one-hundred-percent of Moonwater."

Still staring at him blankly. None of this computes. Wires in my brain are fried.

"What?"

"I contacted your father. I bought him out."

"My father?" I repeat. "He just…"

"He's more reasonable, as you know. And technically all of your parents' money in the hotel was his money, from his offshore account, unrelated to your mother."

"Why would my father have an offshore account for

himself and not her?"

Logan shrugs, frowning with annoyance. "Who knows. Maybe for tax purposes, maybe as a contingency fund if shit hits the fan. Maybe he's smartening up and leaving her. Who knows, but it doesn't really matter because have you heard a bloody thing I've just said?"

"I have I just…" I can't believe it. That's what it is.

Logan grabs my hand, squeezing it. "It's a lot to take in, but while you've been thinking I'm over in Kauai and forgetting about you, I've been working my ass off in order to bring you back. And I have. There is nothing to fear anymore, not for you, not for me. There isn't a single tie between your parents and I anymore. There's nothing but ocean." He sighs and tilts his head, studying me with warm eyes. "It's going to be okay, Ron. From this moment on, it's going to be okay."

It still takes time for it all to sink in.

Freedom.

So much freedom.

Logan owns Moonwater. He owns his pride and joy. He did it to save himself, to save me. There's no one that can stop us, no one to hold anything over our heads.

Except my parents. But their threats have no meaning anymore.

I wonder if that was what my dad wanted to talk to me in private about. It has to be. He was going to tell me that Moonwater now belonged to Logan.

And then what?

"Did my dad know you were coming here?" I ask.

He shakes his head. "No. I didn't say anything about that. But I think he knows. Maybe not right away, but he knew why I bought them out. He knew I did it for you. And I think he knew that there wasn't anything that would stand in my way until you were standing by my side."

God. As if my heart couldn't grow any bigger, it's pressing against my chest, warm and glowing.

He did it for me.

"And it was worth it and then some," Logan says. "As long as you come back with me." He reaches into the pocket of his dark jeans and pulls out my ring. The sight of it floors me. "As long as you wear this again." He pauses. "Do you want me to propose again? Because I thought the first time was pretty hard to beat."

I laugh. Small at first, then a big belly laugh that rolls out of me. He's laughing too, eyes crinkling in joy as he slides the ring on my left hand.

"Please, Veronica Locke," he says, clearing his throat, the graveness coming back into his features. "Agree to… agree to marry me. Again." He sighs, shaking his head. "See, that was bloody awful. Ruined it."

I grab his hand, his face, stare up at him. "Yes, Logan Shephard, I agree to agree to marry you. Again."

We kiss, smiling against each other's mouth, feeling the joy course through my body like bubbles in fine champagne. If it weren't for Logan's strong arms around me, I swear my feet would be lifting off the ground.

But it isn't as easy as the moment is leading me to believe. The joy of our love, our reunion, is overshadowing one more harsh reality.

This isn't over.

We aren't home free.

Not yet.

I break away, my heart picking up the pace. "We have to tell my parents. Together. In person."

He nods. "I know. I wasn't sure if you would be up for that. As you know, sometimes it's easier to leave."

I punch him in the shoulder. "Hey."

He takes my punching hand, opens my palm, kisses it. "But if you're ready, I'm more than ready. They won't understand, you know this. And when your mother finds out she has nothing to hold over us, if she *does*n't already know, then she's going to get ugly. I don't want to put you in that situation if I don't have to."

I square my shoulders. "I'm ready. I've been waiting for this."

Indeed, it feels like I've been waiting for it my whole life.

"Okay," he says. "Look, I should get back to my hotel."

I raise my brows. "Are you kidding me right now?"

He shrugs, a small smile on his lips. "Well, I don't want to go back to my hotel."

"You're insane," I tell him. "Insane and I love you for it." I grab his hand and lead him toward my bedroom. "You're staying here, with me, and we won't be sleeping."

I hope Claire has her earplugs in, because the moment I shut the door, we both fall into each other's arms, fall into the bed, fall back into a love that never went away.

We spend time kissing each other, our mouths exploring each other's bodies like we're seeing them for the first time. Our fingers caress and tease, our eyes linger and stare. After being apart for so long, after thinking I might never see him again, I'm amazed at the restraint. Maybe because we know now why you need to hold onto every single second you're with someone.

Eventually he climbs on top of me, his heavy weight pressed against my chest, my legs open for him, waiting, yearning. He pushes in, slow at first, a long, deliberate thrust that fills me up, filling the hollow places, making me feel like I'm finally whole.

We move in an easy, rocking rhythm, slow, sensual, his finger in my mouth, another hand at my breast. I suck, I moan, I lean back as his lips and teeth trail from my ear, down my neck, to my nipples. I'm being feasted on, slowly, beautifully.

When we come, we come together, gentle cries that fill the room, gripping each other like we'll never let go. And I know I'll never let go.

Not this time.

Not ever.

The next morning Logan raids our kitchen and cooks Claire and I a huge breakfast. This is actually a first for us, I've never seen Logan cook and though it's just bacon, eggs, and hash browns, it tastes like the best damn thing on earth. I warn him that when I come back to Kauai, he's going to be cooking a lot more often. I may just go on strike.

Kauai. Home. I still can't believe it and I'm sure it will take a few days to really realize what's happening. But I'm doing it, and it feels right.

We didn't even have to tell Claire, she knew the moment she saw Logan in the hallway that I was leaving and not coming back. I know she's sad to see me go, but she also wants me to be happy, and I have not been a fun roommate this year, moping every single day.

My line cook job is easy to quit. I do it over the phone and though I feel bad leaving them hanging, I was completely expendable and replaceable there. They'll be fine. Besides, my job at Moonwater doesn't require references. Apparently it never has.

Logan books us both plane tickets back to Lihue tomorrow. Since it's so last minute, it's going to be a real journey with infinite layovers but as long as he's by my side, I don't care. I'll sit on a million planes with him, be stuck in a million airports, and it won't make a difference.

Together we spend the rest of the day packing up my stuff. I never thought of Claire's as a permanent home, so some of my stuff isn't even properly put away and I haven't purchased anything new since my return. It's easy to throw everything in the suitcases and be done with it.

Even so, I take my time, mainly because I know I'm putting off the inevitable. The longer I linger in the apartment with Claire and Logan, the more that I don't have to face my parents.

But when we're finished and it looks like I'm leaving no trace of me behind, we know there's only one thing left to do.

"Time to say goodbye," Logan says, bringing my two suitcases to the door. And it's not just to Claire, whom I just spent five minutes hugging tearfully. It's to my parents. We know how this is going to go.

We get in a cab and head to their house.

I'm a barrel of nerves. I jump when Logan puts his hand on mine.

"It's going to be okay," he says. "All we have is the truth, and if they don't like it, then that's the end of it. We turn around, we go home. Got it?"

I got it. Doesn't mean I like it. And contrary to what I said last night, it doesn't mean I'm ready.

But before I know it, before I can prepare, the cab is pulling up in front of their house in Lincoln Park. I say their house, because it doesn't feel like mine anymore. It doesn't seem possible that it was ever my home. The Veronica from then is a different person than me, a twin, long lost and never to be found again. I'll never search for her.

"Here it is," Logan says, taking in a deep breath. He slips the cabbie a twenty and asks him to wait for ten minutes.

"Ten minutes?" I ask as we get out.

"Do you think your parents are going to invite us in for tea?"

Good point. I guess knowing there's a cab waiting to sweep us away makes it easier.

Logan grabs my hand, holds it up between us as a sign of solidarity. We are a team. Team Gruff.

We go through the gate and walk up the long stone path to the house, stopping in front of the door.

Logan rings the bell.

I figure that Mary, the housekeeper, will answer but instead it's my father.

He doesn't look surprised to see us at all.

"I figured you would be here. Maybe not today, but some day soon." His voice is burdened.

"Hi dad," I tell him, giving him a shy smile. I don't want to hurt my father, but it's something I'm prepared to do. "We need to talk to you and mom."

He nods with a heavy sigh. "Yes. Well I just had a talk with your mother myself. It's good timing. She's still in shock about it all."

"Who are you talking to?" I hear her voice boom from inside the house.

Logan squeezes my hand tighter and shoots me a hopeful smile. He's got me. We've got this.

When my mother sees us, she gasps loudly, hand at her mouth, then her chest. Talk about a pearl-clutcher.

"What the hell is he doing here?" she says, looking between the two of us. Her lip curls up with disgust when she notices our hands entwined with one another.

"Mrs. Locke," Logan says. "Always a pleasure to see you."

Her eyes narrow, her cheeks turning red. My mother is a beautiful woman for her age, but it's moments like this that make her ugly as sin. Her true self can't help but show.

"Are you here to make a fool of me?" she sneers. "Is that what this is?"

"No one is making a fool of anyone," Logan says. "We came to tell you…"

"That I'm leaving," I speak up, finding my voice. I clear the uncertainty from it. "We've decided to be together. To get married. We're heading back to Kauai tomorrow, staying in a hotel tonight. I just wanted to say goodbye."

She's speechless. My father tries to put his hand on her shoulder but she shrugs him off. "This is all your fault," she says to him, her tone pure acid and vinegar.

My dad takes his hand away but doesn't back down. "I did what was right. We had no business in that hotel, Rose, and you know it. It was to help Juliet and Logan. Juliet's gone. Our interests are too."

I'm glad my father is speaking up. He's going to pay for it later, but since it seems like he's already paying for it, I have faith this might make him stronger in the end.

But it's none of my business. I can only worry about me and Logan, just as they will only worry about themselves.

"I know you don't want Logan and I together, I know you think this will create a scandal, make people talk. But let them talk. Let them think what they want. I'm sorry if you have to suffer in any way but I'm not going to give up the love of my life over that. And if you can't be happy for me, if you can't see my heart and see the good this man brings me, then I'm sorry. But I choose him. I choose love.

And I choose this life, the one I'm leaving for."

For a moment I think I see softness in her eyes, maybe a glimmer of understanding, maybe I've let her feel, for one moment, what it's like to be me, what I truly deserve. But then it's gone. Her gaze hardens, her posture stiffens. Whatever empathy, sympathy, she might have felt is buried deep down. I'm not sure she'll ever see this for what it is.

But that's on her now. I've done my part.

"I love Veronica," Logan says, his voice low and strong. "And you can choose not to believe it. But she believes it. And so do I. We'll be out of your hair now and you know you can always reach out to us and we'll be there for you. As a family. But you aren't family unless you want to be and that means accepting all that we are. In Hawaiian you would be ohana. And it will always be an option."

My mother stares at us with all her fury, and I can see how ruined she is by all of this. That she thinks that I am choosing Logan over her, just as Juliet chose Logan over her. She hates to lose, even though she thinks what she's losing is replaceable.

It's not.

I'm not replaceable. And maybe one day, one day, she'll recognize this.

But I'm not holding out hope.

I have Logan.

I have my hope already.

"Get out," my mother says, her voice low, close to breaking. "Get out and never come back."

Don't cry, I tell myself.

And I don't.

I look over her shoulder at my father and give him a nod.

"I love you, dad." I look at my mother, who can't even

look me in the eye now. She's staring at the ground, her jaw grinding. "I love you, mom. That will never change, even if we do."

I swear my dad is shedding a tear. I can't stare at him for too long either or I'll break down. I turn around, Logan putting his arm around my waist and leading me down the stairs.

"If you ever need us, you're always welcome in paradise," Logan says over his shoulder.

The door slams behind us. I don't look back.

We go through the gate and I feel like I'm in a daze. I'm not happy, I'm not smug or vindicated. I'm not destroyed either. I'm just…sad.

Sad that it had to be this way.

Sad that I couldn't have the family I wanted.

But then I remember I have a family back at Moonwater.

And I have Logan.

And now we're free.

I swallow the lump in my throat and just before we get in the cab, Logan pulls me to him, holding me tight.

"You always make me proud," he murmurs. "And I know that was the hardest thing you've ever had to do. But I've got you. I've got you." He pulls away, brushing my hair behind my ear. "Now, how about we go home?"

We get into the cab and it speeds away.

Kauai is waiting for me.

EPILOGUE

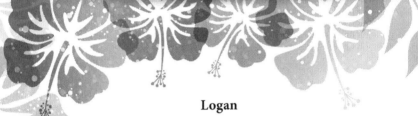

Logan
Four Months Later

I RISE AT DAWN.

Grab my board.

Head out the door.

Cut through the bushes, quickest way to the beach.

It must have rained last night. The leaves are wet, brushing against me as I go. The roosters are crowing from all directions. The beach is damp and hazy, the light at the horizon muddled a navy and purple, slowly draining with the sun.

From this vantage point I can see down to Tunnels Beach and the beach in front of the hotel. The way the swells are coming in, it's better to head toward Moonwater.

There's no one out here. It's just me, the ocean, the sand.

Some of the guests will be rising soon. With the time change from the mainland, everyone is up with the sun.

But I still have time.

A few waves to myself.

They wouldn't dare head out into the water right now, and other surfers will be at Haena Beach, down the road. Here the breaks are more complicated as is the access to them. But I never back down from a challenge.

I get in the water, the reef cutting into the bottoms of my feet, but years of walking around barefoot will leave you pretty protected. It's not just here in Hawaii, growing up in Australian surf culture you forget the need for shoes. Here, I do it for the guests. It's amazing how appalled they get.

A system passed through here a few days ago, high surf warning signs litter the beach. Someone was swept out at Lumihai, just around the bend, but they survived somehow. Now the waves have calmed, from twenty-five feet, down to seven. Still big and bad.

I swim out past the break, getting a feel for the sets coming in, the wind, the air. I watch as the sun slowly turns the clouds over the Na Pali Coast candy colors before the orange glow comes from the east.

I'm not a religious man, but I believe in god. And on that same note, I believe in moments. Not just the things that happen to you but the things you make happen. You can make anything a moment. Anything at all. I'm sure this is the key to getting through life. If you make everything memorable, you hold onto each second. You live a thousand times.

Surfing makes you hold onto moments. It's my church, the place to ground you into the present. It cements you in your place in the world and it makes you pay attention to that world.

You never feel so small as you do with mother nature. She is control and you do your best to control the ride. You pay attention to the moments because you are one with everything. Plugged into the spinning world.

When I first saw Veronica, she was inspecting a shitty appetizer at her mother's party, glass of champagne in one hand, her face scrunched up. At that moment, I felt I knew her. That moment became ingrained before it was even a memory.

When you know, you know.

She was the only one who looked like she didn't belong there. This wasn't because of how she looked—she was as prim and polished as the rest of them, though maybe decades younger. In some ways, probably too young for me.

But it didn't matter. It was her mannerisms, the way she looked like she was telling stories in her head, the way she made the rounds of all the food, sizing it up. She drank with relish, she had a gorgeous smile that lit up the room, and the one time someone made her laugh, it was like pure joy. Not fake, not forced, not like anyone there. She was her own thing.

I wanted to be part of it.

But I was also a fool. There were no times for distractions. I was there for a reason.

I had dreams. Big ones. Foolish ones. Ones that were over my head.

And my dreams were based on something very bloody silly.

Growing up, my favorite TV show was Fawlty Towers, the much-loved 70's British sitcom starring John Cleese. My brother and I would watch that and a handful of other shows since we only had a few stations on our shitty little TV.

Unfortunately, we had to watch it with our mother but she loved the show too, the only time she wouldn't call us little shits and berate us for just breathing.

And every time Basil Fawlty did something stupid and made me laugh, I felt happy. It made me think that despite Basil's bat-shit crazy behavior (of which I can now relate), he surrounded himself with people who were like family.

Since then, the idea of running a hotel was always in the back of my mind, until I decided to take the plunge and make it my reality.

Reality was a bitch. It wouldn't bend with ease. I had to work hard for it, saving with everything I had. My ambitions were through the roof, I had too much to lose.

I thought I knew what I needed.

I was wrong.

Veronica struck a chord in me but Juliet was the one who promised a brighter future.

Veronica was young, on the brink of her career and life, the type to buck the trends and go against the status quo.

Juliet was the status quo.

Stable.

Safe.

Promising.

Everyone always said how easy it was to be dazzled by her, that I was so lucky to have her. She was stunning, there was no denying that. But I didn't fall for Juliet because of her looks. I fell for the life she hinted at, the promises she never had to make.

I thought Juliet would make me a better man.

She only made me worse.

I made the wrong decision that day, and later, as our marriage began to fall apart, I would look back on that moment and wonder what the hell was wrong with me. Why did I pick what was safe when I should have chosen what was real?

It was something I lived with and was prepared to live with. I viewed Veronica through a distorted lens as her brother-in-law, keeping my distance and any thoughts at bay. I admired her from afar and did my best to never think of her in any way but innocent.

And it worked for the most part. I didn't want to live out my marriage being attracted to someone else, let alone be in love with them. I didn't want to give up on Juliet.

She gave up on me.

And then she died.

And I was broken. Yes, there was grief. Pure grief and loss. And there was regret, that things went this way, that she died with our marriage upside down, that we never addressed the elephant in the room, that things were left unsaid.

But more than any of that, I was drowning in hatred in the years after. Because of guilt. Because of thoughts of being free, thoughts that shamed me. I hated myself for it and I became a bitter, bitter man.

Then Veronica showed up at my door, at the place Juliet and I created, and I knew that everything was going to change. I can't say I wanted it to—I was comfortable in my rage and bitterness. It fit me like a worn glove. I thought I was going to die with a thorn in my side.

But Veronica removed that thorn. Slowly at first. She jabbed me with the bloody thing a few times, kept me on my toes. She still does. But it was only through her that the light got in. She became more than I ever thought she would.

Today, I'm going to marry her.

With that thought in mind, I get up on the wave. I surf

it into shore, feeling unstoppable. The sun rises above the palms, the rays hitting me on the back, and this is the start of the rest of my life.

I spend the next hour catching a few more waves, then it's time to head back in. I've got a lot to do and I still haven't prepared my speech. I'm going to wing it, which is probably a terrible idea, but I feel like I don't have to worry about what I'll say. Staring at Veronica will make the words flow straight from the heart.

She stayed the night at the St. Regis hotel in Princeville with her maid-of-honor Claire, as well as Kate and Nikki, her bridesmaids. I have no idea what they got up to, though Ron texted me late last night telling me she loved me and hated tequila and that we should get a chicken called HeiHei and let it be the ringbearer.

My best man is my brother Kit, who I flew out here from Darwin for the ceremony. I hadn't seen him in seven years, so it was long overdue. My groomsmen are Warren, who was one of the hotel's original investors, Johnny, Daniel, Jin, and yes, Charlie. It took a long time to come to terms with Charlie being a snitch of sorts, but in the end it was clear that he really didn't know what he was doing.

It doesn't matter now. What's past is past and Veronica *did* get to punch him in the face anyway, saving me from obliterating him. We're all a united front with the hotel, and the Lockes are no longer in the picture.

Which I know bothers Ron. She's got a soft heart even when she tries to hide it. The moment we told them that we were getting married and that there was nothing they could say or do, was the moment they cut us out of their lives. I said that life is made of moments, and that was one in which Ron knew who her family was. It was me. It was everyone at Moonwater. Her real *ohana*.

Her father does reach out to her every now and then, trying to keep the peace. He's not a bad man, he's just a weak man, and as long as his wife has complete control, he'll never be fully on Veronica's side. But at least he tries.

Naturally, he's not here. None of her family came. Not uncles or aunts or cousins. No one approves. The fact that I'm marrying Juliet's sister is too much for them to take. Some families are built on appearances and politics, and we're better off without that in our lives.

It sounds tired and cliché to say but honestly all we need is each other.

The wedding is held at Moonwater, in the same spot where we have the luau, so when I get out of the surf and cut through the hotel grounds, it's already alive with people bustling about and getting things ready.

"Shephard," Johnny says, stepping out of his room. "You went surfing? You're getting married soon, you know."

"You don't have to tell me twice. How are you feeling?"

While the girls were at their fancy hotel, we just drank at the bar. I managed to keep myself in line but Kit, Johnny, and Charlie got blitzed. I don't give a damn, so as long as they show up and don't get sick anywhere, we're golden.

Johnny grins at me. "Happy as a clam, bro."

I spend the rest of the day moving from moment to moment.

- Getting dressed (black pants, white shirt, no tie)
- Checking on the guys
- Coordinating with the DJ and caterers
- Hiding from Veronica (she believes in the whole "don't you dare fucking see the bride in her dress" nonsense)
- Pacing my living room

- Greeting the guests
- Nearly shitting myself

I'm not nervous, per se. I think it's more excitement, a restlessness. It's not my first wedding, I know what to expect and I just want it over with. I want to get started on our marriage right now, sweep her off her feet far away (although our honeymoon is just to Oahu for some fun and games in Waikiki) and be the husband I can't wait to be.

"How are we feeling?" the minister asks me as I take my place up at the front, grinning nervously at the guests. Her name is Betty, Hawaiian to the core, and also a talented musician who plays guitar and sings at Trees Lounge in Kapa'a.

"Great," I tell her.

She nods with a gentle smile. She has such a joyous, calm way about her that when I proposed to Ron, I already knew Betty was going to be the one presiding over the wedding. "Good. Hang on to each moment today, so they will live on and they will last."

It's like she can read my bloody mind.

So I commit myself to more moments. Kit by my side, in a Hawaiian shirt and knee-length shorts, just like the rest of the groomsman. He's the spitting image of me, if you take away half my beard, all my greys, and maybe a few wrinkles. Okay, a lot of them.

I look at Johnny who is laughing at something that Charlie has said, the two of them nearly busting over, their faces growing red. I have no doubt in my mind that whatever they're saying is taking a shot at me. But that's to be expected.

Daniel is looking more nervous than anyone. I think it's because he's proposing to Nikki tonight. He asked me a few days ago if it would take away from the event, and I said go for it. He's worried about stealing my thunder, so he said he's going to do it late and outside of the reception, but he's doing it all the same. Seems Moonwater is making more than a few love matches.

Even for Jin. He's looking proud, standing with his hands behind his back, looking over the crowd and nodding at everyone he knows. Which is, pretty much everyone. He looks like a bobble-head figure.

But the apple of his eye is Carla, an elderly lady who lives in Hanalei. Ever since New Year's Eve, they've been an item, and what I hear from Johnny, Ron, and Charlie, he won't shut up about her. They've started bringing earplugs to their shifts.

When I brought Ron back to Kauai, I wasn't sure how she was going to adapt. Being with me, a part of this, would she want to keep her role in the Ohana Lounge? Would she want to concentrate on hotel management, was she burned out?

But she loves it more than ever. She's head cook alongside Johnny, a title they share, and while she's helping out with Moonwater as a whole—after all, this is her hotel now—I don't think her passion for cooking will ever change. When I brought up the idea of her taking the position of chef and running the restaurant and having Johnny and Charlie officially under her, she balked at it. I think once upon a time she just wanted to have the title and respect. Now she has the respect and doesn't need the title.

But we'll see. The woman is ambitious. If she runs with it one day, I wouldn't be surprised if a few Ohana Lounges open up across the islands.

Speaking of, where the bloody hell is she?

"Now you must be nervous," Kit says, nudging me in the side.

"Nah, mate," I tell him. "Just want to get this over with. You know I don't like being the center of attention."

"Never too late to run for the hills."

I cock my brow at him. "One day, Kit. One day you'll know."

"You knew it twice," he says with a smirk. "I think I balance you out."

I ignore that. When I told Veronica once that Kit was a bit of a Croc Dundee character, I wasn't stretching the truth. He does have this overt machoism about him, the kind who will hike into the jungle to wrestle snakes and crocodiles. I know the tour he leads is borderline illegal because of the shit he puts his customers through but he's charming and all that bullshit, so he gets away with it. He may be scared of the ladies but I'm telling you, no lady wants to cuddle up to a bloke who spends his days looking for reptiles.

"Here they are," Johnny says, the bridesmaids turn the corner and head toward us, flowers in their hands. Because we had an uneven number of girls and guys, and no parents on either side, we decided that the girls should just all arrive together, like a "squad," as Kate described it.

Kate and Nikki, dressed in strapless Hawaiian dresses that match the guy's shirts, take their place on the other side of me. I give them a wink.

And then a hush comes over the crowd, a nervous tittering.

The ukuleles and guitars from the band start to play, strumming the Hawaiian version of "Somewhere Over the Rainbow."

I can't bloody believe it. What a funny, lovely, bitch life can be, that this is happening at all.

And then Veronica appears, rounding the corner of the restaurant, coming across the grass with her friend Claire on her arm.

She's beyond beautiful.

She's the sunrise, the moonrise, all four points of my compass.

She's every gorgeous moment in my life all rolled into one.

And she's mine.

"Hi Freckles," I say to her softly, trying to keep my emotions in check. The tears keep wanting to creep up there but I'll be damned if I cry in front of my brother.

"Hi old man," she teases. She grins, her cheeks glowing with the sun and blush, her actual freckles making her look fresh as a morning wave. Her caramel-colored hair is pinned back with plumeria, her white dress long and gauzy, like she's a Grecian goddess, on earth for just one day.

But I know she's here for more than that.

She's here for now and forever.

Betty clears her throat and starts the ceremony as I grab onto Veronica's hands, holding her tight.

This is it.

This moment is the beginning.

Later that night, after the food and the cake (which Veronica baked herself—coconut, macadamias, and chocolate), while the guests are still dancing and the music is blaring and the drinks are flowing, I take Veronica's hand and lead her to the beach where we had our first surf lesson.

We settle down in the sand, the bottle of champagne between us, watching as the moon rises up over Moonwater Inn. The ocean is bathed in silver, our bodies glimmer in the dark. We look like immortals. I feel immortal.

"Look," Veronica whispers, bringing my attention back to the horizon.

A humpback whale is surfacing, its breath shooting high into the air like a feathery plume. We watch in awe as it dives, its back illuminated by the moonlight, gleaming.

Its massive fluke disappears into the waves and then it's gone.

We wait with bated breath, expecting it to come back, for others to be with it.

But that's it.

And it was enough.

THE END

Before you go…if you want future updates on my books and all the crazy and zany adventures I get up to, please:

- Join my exclusive readers group on Facebook where I have awesome giveaways, sneak peeks, fun trivia, great people and lot's more. Seriously. We're the best group of readers on the internet: Karina Halle's Anti-Heroes (www.facebook.com/groups/912577838806567)

- Sign-up for my newsletter (www.authorkarinahalle.com/newsletter-sign-up) to get alerts when new books come out, plus exclusives such as FREE books, excerpts and cover reveals!

- Follow me on Twitter (@metalblonde)

- Watch my daily adventures on Instagram, www.instagram.com/authorhalle. (I practically live here, plus you can see a bunch of snaps of Kauai, especially if you're reading this around release week)

Also, I have written over thirty novels in a range of different genres, from contemporary romance, to romantic comedy, to romantic suspense, to paranormal romance. Want a list of them all? Visit my Amazon author page and give me a "follow" while you're at it so you can stay up to date with new releases!

Read on for the acknowledgements (am I the only one who loves reading the acknowledgements section?)

ACKNOWLEDGMENTS

After so many books, it gets hard to think of something original to write in the acknowledgements and I usually just end up thanking the same people over and over again. But that's okay because, hey, without them, my books wouldn't be here. As much as I like to think that I am an island (like Kauai), I am not and it takes a village to make a book.

I'll make this short and snappy…thank you to Kelly and Alex St-Laurent for all your advice with regards to being a chef. Alex is the best chef there is and I had to learn a bit about the whole thing before I made Veronica one. But if I messed up in anyway regarding the way kitchens are run, that's completely on me.

Thank you to Laura Helseth for her proofing and edits, to Dani for her promotion, for Hang Le for the stunning cover. Thanks to Ali and Jay for keeping me from jumping off a cliff and being such a good sounding board. Thank you to my readers for being so understanding, caring and supportive, even when I'm saying crazy shit, and especially my ARC readers who were left hanging with this one.

To my parents and my husband…sorry. Here's the thing. I was supposed to finish this book before we went to our annual trip to Kauai. This trip was going to be a real special one too because this time I got to take my parents and let them experience the Kauai we've fallen in love with. Nothing like being in paradise with your *ohana*.

Well, it turns out I was writing Heat Wave well into our vacation, so I haven't been as "available" as I normally am. But hey, I'm still here, the book is done, and I've got a few days to relax. I have to say, it's been funny actually being in Kauai while writing about it. I went to visit the hotel Moonwater Inn is based on (the Hanalei Colony, if you're wondering – worth a stay! But don't go swimming in the ocean, it will kill you!) and I could have sworn I saw Logan and Veronica, Johnny, Kate, Charlie…the thing about Heat Wave is that so many of the characters can be found on this island. Including Daniel, Betty and others.

Kauai is a special place to me and to many people and I hope I was able to convey that in this book. The aloha spirit is prevalent here and it truly is a place where you feel connected to man, to nature, to yourself. Even the mythology of Hawaii is fascinating to me and I see myself dabbling into that subject one day. If you ever have a chance to visit Kauai, please take it. Bring this book with you. And if you can't visit, I hope this book provides the same kind of escape.

Last but not least, I'd like to thank the Anti-Heroes, for always having my back. You guys are the best.

Mahalo, mahalo, mahalo.

Made in the USA
Middletown, DE
14 April 2022